W9-BLD-673

Praise for *The Brothers of Auschwitz*

'An emotional gut-punch . . . It clawed my heart but made me count my blessings' Glynis Peters, *USA Today* bestselling author of *The Secret Orphan*

'Great courage is needed to write as Adler does – without softening, without beautifying' Yehudit Rotem, *Haaretz-International New York Times*

'This is a book we are not allowed not to read' Leah Roditi, *At Magazine*

The Brothers of Auschwitz

Malka Adler

OneMoreChapter

One More Chapter
a division of HarperCollins*Publishers*
The News Building
1 London Bridge Street
London SE1 9GF

www.harpercollins.co.uk

This paperback edition 2020

First published in Great Britain in ebook format by
HarperCollins*Publishers* 2020

Copyright © Malka Adler 2020

Malka Adler asserts the moral right to
be identified as the author of this work

A catalogue record for this book
is available from the British Library

Ebook ISBN: 978-0-00-838611-5
Paperback ISBN: 978-0-00-839843-9
Audiobook ISBN: 978-0-00-839293-2

This is a work of fiction based on personal memories. Every reasonable
attempt to verify the facts against available documentation has been made.

Set in Birka by Palimpsest Book Production Limited,
Falkirk, Stirlingshire

Printed and bound in the United States of America

20 21 22 LSC 10 9 8 7 6 5 4 3 2 1

All rights reserved. No part of this publication may be
reproduced, stored in a retrieval system, or transmitted,
in any form or by any means, electronic, mechanical,
photocopying, recording or otherwise, without the prior
permission of the publishers.

Content notices: graphic depictions of violence,
child abuse, anti-Semitism, and genocide.

This book is dedicated to
Israel, Leora and Avi
Ravit, Yonit and Hadar

Prologue

Israel, 2001

7:30 in the morning and it's frrrreezing.

I'm huddled in a heavy black coat on the Beit Yehoshua railway platform. I have a meeting with Dov and Yitzhak in Nahariya.

There was a time when Yitzhak was known as Icho and Dov as Bernard. Yitzhak is seventy-five and can still lift a whole calf. Still strong. Dov at seventy-six is bigger than Yitzhak and loves cocoa cookies, television, and peace and quiet.

They have wives. Yitzhak has Hannah, a goodhearted woman. Dov has Shosh, who is also goodhearted.

The rain stops falling like a scratch. Like pain. At first it falls hard, abundantly, then trickles down. Branches drop to the ground indifferently. *Shhhh.* The tops of the eucalyptus trees travel from side to side in the wind and already I need to pee again. The loudspeaker announces the next train. The lamp flickers.

In two hours' time I'll meet with Yitzhak and Dov. Yitzhak no longer pushes forward. And Dov never pushes, not even before. But Dov will bring good coffee and cookies with cocoa and raisins.

Pew. Pew. Pew.

A man in a long coat fires at the approaching train. *Pew. Pew. Pew.* Wearing a beret pulled to one side, he holds a black umbrella and fires. His face is divided in dark lines, forehead, cheeks, chin, even his nose. His face is taut, as if someone slipped underwear elastic beneath his skin and pulled and pulled, almost tearing it, but no. He takes short, hurried steps, flapping his arms hither and thither as if brushing away a swarm of flies or insects, or stinging thoughts, and firing. Raising his umbrella high in the air. Aiming at the eucalyptus trees or the train and shouting, *pew-pew. Pew-pew. Pew.*

I look the man straight in the eye as he shouts, *pew. Pew. Pew. Pew. Pew.*

I'm beside him now and he says, stop. *Stop.* Aims and fires, *pew-pew. Pew. Pew. Pew.* All dead, he says, and wipes his hand on old pants.

I cough and he frowns, thrusting out his chin and biting his lips as if to say, I told you, didn't I tell you? You had it coming, sickos. And then he breathes three times on the end of the umbrella, *phoo, phoo, phoo,* brushes imaginary crumbs from his coat, straightens the beret, and returns to the middle of the platform. To and fro. Back and forth and back again, his hands in fighting mode all the time.

The soldiers have grown used to Friday shootings, the great rage that explodes on the platform from seven in the morning. Everyone knows he comes from Even Yehuda on his bicycle. Winter, summer, he comes on a Friday. A constant presence. The trains pull out and he remains until noon. Firing, without resting for a moment. In summer he uses a cane. People say, eat, drink, rest, why tire yourself? Go home.

Too bad, he's in his own world.

Seven in the morning, Friday – he must be seventy, maybe less – shooting on the platform in dirty clothes with wild, white hair.

Every Friday he leaves on his bicycle at twelve-thirty on the dot. The cashier tells everyone about him. Eager cashier. Fat cashier with blond bangs and black hair. The man has no watch. There's a clock on the station wall but he stands with his back to it. It isn't important for him to see the time. He knows. He prepares the Sabbath for his dead.

Ah. The Beit Yehoshua platform is the closest thing to the platforms at Auschwitz. This is what the cashier tells us, and we fall silent.

At Auschwitz he touched his family for the last time. That's what Yitzhak would say, and he'd raise his hat and shout, why should Jews stand on platforms at all? Are there no buses?

Sometimes you have to stand on a bus.

Well, a taxi then.

Taxis are expensive.

So what? He refuses to stand on the platforms.

Dov would cough if he heard Yitzhak getting mad about something. Then Dov would be silent. I'd pay no attention. I'd look first at Yitzhak, then at Dov, and turn on the tape. Yitzhak would say loudly, why do you stand on the platforms, why don't you take a taxi too?

Yes.

Now the eucalyptus trees are still. And the cashier is telling someone about Yajec. She has to talk fast before the new person shouts at Yajec. Every Friday the cashier protects him. Every Friday there are people who don't know about him, haven't heard him despair.

But the cashier has heard him, and she tells the older folk so they won't bother him. Leave him alone to kill with his umbrella, *pew. Pew. Pew. Pew-pew*.

Once she told some new people, leave him alone, leave him be. Yajec was a little boy when he grabbed his mother's dress, crying, yes. He wept incessantly, screamed, don't leave me, but poor woman, she pushed him towards the group of men, and he ran to her, Mama, take me, but poor woman, she didn't. Looking at her child, her face white, she screamed in his ear, Yajec, you aren't staying with me, go over there, you hear? And she slapped him and pushed him fiercely. You heard me. Yes. She went with the women and he stayed with strangers who didn't see him because he was seven or eight, yes.

The train enters the station and stops.

Quiet.

Three minutes of quiet. Even the cashier doesn't speak when the train stops. She doesn't want people to get confused. Whoever has to boards the train, whoever has to gets off. The train leaves, and the cashier says that Yajec's father disappeared too. And his grandfather, grandmother, four sisters, and Aunt Serena, and Uncle Abraham.

The face of an Ethiopian woman tugs at my belly. A gentle, fragile face, her mouth stretched outward as if she is about to weep, her eyes dark with sadness, a sadness from another place, distant, a sadness arranged in layers according to height, on her forehead a fresh upper layer, her face strong. If Yitzhak and Dov were here, that face would probably make them weep. But Yitzhak never visits anyone and no one visits him. If Dov came, he'd probably give her a cookie and juice, tell her to sit down, sit down on a bench and rest a while.

Another train pulls in. The platform empties, only the man in the long coat and the beret is left.

The Ethiopian woman boards the train. She knows there'll be pushing, but she gets on. The cashier says she is also a regular on the platform. She's on her way to get a telling-off from the head teacher of the boarding school. That daughter of hers has behavior issues morning and night. She makes the teachers mad, wants to go back to Ethiopia, wants to live among her people, run off to town on a Friday night, fool around at a Reggae Club. All she wants is to sing. She's always running off in a long skirt and a long-sleeved blouse, and in her bag she hides a small pair of shorts and a colorful top that shows her belly. She doesn't want to be in boarding school, doesn't want to! Her mother shouts, you are not coming back with me, you're staying, understand?

Yitzhak would say, she'll get used to it, in the end she'll get used to it, and why does her mother get on the train every Friday? Once every two or three months is enough, and she can go by taxi, didn't they tell her?

Dov would say, why insist with kids? It never works, best take her home. That's all, right?

A white sun pushes through a narrow crack. It peeps out from behind the backs of the eucalyptus trees creating a huge, shining kaleidoscope. The loudspeaker announces: Attention, attention. The sun disappears. The train leaves the station.

I'm on my way to Nahariya.

Yitzhak won't receive me.

He might. But on the telephone he said – we'll see. Yitzhak has no patience.

Dov will sit with me. Dov keeps his word. Yitzhak too. But Yitzhak makes no promises. Yitzhak says – call on Thursday and we'll see.

I call every Thursday, and he says, we'll see. Finally, he says, yes, you can come.

Dov waits at the station with the car. Dov takes me to Yitzhak. I'm not certain of anything. Will they agree to talk to me?

Come again once or twice and we'll see. That's how they talk on the phone.

No "we'll see". They must.

Right.

Will you let me tell your story?

We will. We will.

We'll take it slowly, slowly.

Maybe quickly, in case we regret it, ha. Ha. Ha.

Separately or together?

However it works out, but I have a cow farm to deal with.

So more often with Dov.

Sure. I'm willing to talk to you whenever you want.

Only on rainy days, come when it rains.

Okay, Yitzhak.

I can't leave the cow farm in the middle of the day.

No need.

I have to feed all the calves, and I also go away sometimes.

I'll come when it rains.

That would be best, I'm only home when it rains.

So when it rains.

All right.

But call first, and we'll see.

Chapter 1

I am Yitzhak: The State of Israel gave me the name Yitzhak.
The Nazis gave me the number 55484.
The goyim gave me the name Ichco.
My Jewish people gave me the name Icho.

In Yitzhak's Living Room

The hardest thing of all was being evicted from our home.
We woke as usual. I got up first and wanted to go with Father to the market.

I forgot it was a holiday. Father came back from the synagogue. He was black-haired, medium height. Even with his coat on, he looked thin. Father sat down on a chair. Called us. Leah, come here. Sarah. Avrum. Dov, call Icho as well.

We gathered around Father.

Father's face was the color of tin in the sun. Sickly. Our eyes looked for Mother.

Father said, we have to pack. We're leaving the village. We jumped, what? Where are we going, where, don't know, the Hungarians are sending us away from here. Where, Father, where. They didn't say, we have to be quick, pack some clothes and blankets, he coughed. Leah, a glass of water please, take some cutlery, a few plates, socks, don't forget socks, Father, where are they sending us, where, asked Avrum.

To die! said Dov. Enough, Dov, enough, they're sending all the Jews in the village somewhere else, to the east, to work in the east. Why are they only sending Jews, asked Sarah. So we'll die and they'll finally be rid of us, get us out of their lives once and for all, don't you understand?

Father covered his face with thick, dark, strong fingers.

I heard the sound of choked weeping. We looked for Mother. Mother was tiny with brown hair and a gentle face, like a flower wary of the sun. Mother was chewing on the fingers of both hands. I told her, tell Father to explain to us, I don't understand, tell him, tell him. Mother sat down on a chair. At a distance from Father. She was silent. Father rubbed his face as if wanting to peel off his skin and ordered: Enough! And then he got up, stretched, held onto the chair, his fingers white, almost bloodless. He looked at Mother, saying hoarsely: Hungarian soldiers came to the synagogue with rifles. They told us to prepare for eviction from the house. They said within the hour. They said only to pack a suitcase with what we need. They said to go to the synagogue. To wait. Orders will come.

We shouted in unison, but Father, the war is over, we can hear the Russian cannons in the distance, tell them the war is over. Father said faintly: They know. Avrum shouted, so why are they taking us, Father, what do they want to do to us, what?

They want to burn Jews. I heard it on the radio. We'll all die, said Sarah, almost crying.

That's exactly what Hitler planned, said Dov, putting an apple in his pocket.

Father stamped his foot, enough. Go to your room, go on, go, we have an hour to pack. Mother said, but we don't have any suitcases or bags, how can we pack?

Father said, put everything in sheets, or even tablecloths, we'll make bundles and tie them with rope, Avrum, run and fetch ropes from the storeroom, help the children tie the ropes, Leah, you're in our room, I'm in the kitchen. Mother fell silent. Motionless, she folded her arms very tightly.

Sarah wept.

She said, I have to wash the dishes left from Passover night, I have to put them away in the cupboard, Father shouted, never mind the dishes, they're not important now.

Mother rose from her chair, stood at the sink, opened the tap full force, grabbed a dirty plate and quickly began to soap it. Father beat his hands against the sides of his pants, as if drawing strength, stood next to Mother, turned off the tap. Mother turned round, threw the plate on the floor, drying her hands on her apron, straightened up and said, we'll go and pack. Sarah bent down and picked the pieces off the floor, crying harder, but the plates will smell by the time we return, they'll have to be thrown out. Dov said, don't worry, they'll make us all smell. Mother lifted Sarah, hugged her, brushing her hair away from her forehead, stroking her head and said, we're going. Mother and Sarah went into the rooms. Avrum returned with rope. Followed Mother. Dov stood at the window. Father collected cutlery in the kitchen.

I put on a woolen hat and went to the door. I grabbed the handle. My legs felt weak.

Father called, Icho, where are you off to?

The cowshed, I have to feed the cows, I'll get them ready to leave.

Father was alarmed, no, no, that's impossible, we're going

without the cows, just clothing and blankets, put your clothes in a bundle. Father stood opposite me.

I asked, what about the cows? Who will take care of the cows?

Father gave me a long hard look, said, don't argue.

I couldn't leave our cows. The cows lived in our yard.

The cowshed was behind the house. I enjoyed milking cows. We'd talk sometimes, as if we spoke the same language. The calves were born into my hands. I looked at Dov. The curls on his head seemed small. He looked as if he'd just had a shower.

Dov signaled me, drop it, drop it. I said to Father, and who will milk our cows, the cows will die without food. Father didn't know anything, believed the neighbors would take care of them, maybe one of the soldiers with a rifle, he wasn't sure of anything.

I remembered my cat. I wanted to know what to do with my cat that had caught cold on Passover night. I had a large cat with black and white fur. I went back to Father. He stood with his back to me, opening cupboards and he looked like a grandfather. I begged, at least the cat.

I'll take my cat, it won't bother us, all right?

Father spoke from inside the cupboard, leave the cat, Icho, don't go outside. And then he straightened up, gripping his back, went over to the window opposite the road and said, come here. Look out of the window. Do you see the soldiers? They will come in soon and throw us into the street without our bundles, now do you understand?

I felt as if a sickness was spreading through my body and taking away my life. I wanted my cat. The cat that came into my bed with its purrrr purrrring. It loved having its belly tickled and a spray of milk straight from the teat on its fur. Loved licking itself, for hours. Avrum, my older brother stood in the doorway. Avrum was tall, thin, and gentle like Mother.

He said, come on, I'll help you, Dov is also waiting for you. Just a minute. I wanted to hug my sick cat. Sarah stood beside me. Took me by the hand. We heard a noise outside. Sarah rushed to the window.

Her bony body leaned out and she called Father: Father, Father, the neighbors are in our yard, they're calling you. Sarah was also thin. Father didn't turn round, said, not now Sarah. Sarah called more urgently, the neighbors are coming to the door, Father, go out to them. Dov came into the room, put an apple in his other pocket and then some matzos inside his shirt. He had brown eyes and muscles like a ball in each arm. He'd tossed a sweater on his back.

A knock at the door made me jump.

Father went to the door. I heard our neighbor asking, where are you off to, Strullu? It was Stanku. He always wore a peaked cap; he had a red-tipped wart on his cheek.

Father said, you tell me, maybe they said something to you.

They said nothing to me. It was you they spoke to.

Father fell silent. Stanku straightened up. And the children?

Father said, they're leaving with us. The old people too.

Stanku took off his cap, you need bread. Father didn't. He said, we've got matzos.

No, Strullu, you need bread and water for the journey.

I don't.

Take cakes, we have large cakes we made for Easter. We'll give you the cakes. Hide them in your clothing. Who knows what will happen.

Dov said to himself, a tragedy is what will happen. A terrible tragedy.

Father smiled sadly at Stanku. He said quietly, that child is always thinking about tragedies. Don't know what's wrong with him. Stanku grabbed Father's hand. His hand trembled. His blue eyes were moist.

Stanku said, we'll take care of the house, Strullu, we'll look after the cows, and you'll be back, you have to come back.

Father and Stanku hugged. I heard thumps on backs. I heard Father say brokenly, I don't think we'll be back, Stanku, forgive me, I must go in. Father left.

I turned to Stanku, so you'll look after the house, the cows too, and the cat, and you'll feed it, yes, and if people come by and want to take it, what will you tell them?

Stanku cleared his throat. And again, holding his throat. I whispered, I have a small sum saved, I'll give it to you, Stanku.

Stanku threw up his hands, stamped his foot on the path, said, no, no, no, and don't worry, Icho, I'm here to take care of everything until you come safely home. We shook hands. I went inside.

Dov jumped out through the window.

I was sure Dov was escaping into the forest. I was glad he'd run away. Glad no one saw. Glad that at least one of our family would stay to take care of the house. Father, Mother, Sarah, Avrum and I went to the synagogue with our bundles on our backs. Hungarian soldiers counted us. Someone snitched, said a boy from our family was missing.

Soldiers threatened Father, shaking a finger at him: By nightfall. The boy must return by nightfall. Or we'll stand all of you against the wall, *boom boom boom*. Understand? Father called Vassily from Dov's class.

Vassily was Dov's best friend. Vassily liked going without socks and hat. Winter or summer, the same. Vassily came at a run. He had a coat with one short sleeve and one long one.

Father hugged Vassily's shoulder, saying, Vassily, bring Dov to us. He's in the forest. Only you can do this. Vassily looked at Father and was sorry, Dov, Dov. Father bent down and whispered to Vassily, tell Dov, remember Shorkodi, the young man from Budapest, he'll understand.

Dov came back swollen from a beating.

That night he returned with Hungarian soldiers. His face stayed swollen for two days. He had a deep cut from forehead to ear. He had a crust of blood under his hair. He didn't say a word. I was sorry, pity you came back, Dov, a pity.

Two days later, they took us by train to Ungvár, now Uzhhorod.

In the town of Ungvár they put us in a huge pit like an open mine. There were thousands of Jews there from that area without an outhouse or shower. Just a small tap and pipe. Rain kept falling. The rain washed out the mine. We were drowning in mud and a strong smell. First came the strong smell of people who were going to die. Then came the smell of human excrement. I couldn't get used to the bad smells. I wanted to vomit even after I finished vomiting.

Our family was given a space the size of a living-room sofa. We slept on planks and wet blankets. We ate a bowl of potato soup after waiting in line for hours. One bowl a day. We were still hungry. We saw peddlers walking around the pit. They made signs at us with their hands. Signs of the cross, signs of slitting throats as if they held a knife in their hands. They grinned toothlessly, *hee hee hee*. I could have pummeled them with my fists. Mother spoke to me wordlessly. I pummeled myself with my fists until my leg was numb. People with important faces and wet jackets walked among us. They were known as the *Judenräte*.

They promised, just a matter of days and you'll be in the east. They spoke of many work places.

We waited for the train that would take us east to many work places. The train didn't come. People became impatient, at first a little, then increasingly so. After three days they yelled at one another for no reason. If they unintentionally touched an elbow in the line for soup or the tap, they yelled. They argued about where to place their head or feet when going to sleep. Or why they farted right into a baby's face.

Poor little thing, he choked, a little consideration, Grandpa. They argued about rumors. Yelled, yelled, yelled, a day later, they repeated the rumors and reported new ones. There were no rumors about death, no words about death; about liberation, yes. Many words about imminent or distant liberation. We were ignorant about the news they reported, we just heard and waited. Waited almost a month.

Finally, a special cattle train arrived on the track.

We were sure it was a mistake. Soldiers pushed us into the cars. They forcefully pushed entire families. Entire villages. Towns. Cities. I understood. The Hungarians wanted to cleanse the world of Jews. Didn't want to breathe in a world a Jew had passed through. Wanted to look far into the future, ah, no Jews. None. Clean sky, sun and moon, too.

The journey by train was a nightmare.

We traveled three days without food or water. We traveled in a car with a tin bucket for the needs of a small town. The infant in the arms of the woman with cracked glasses cried ceaselessly. A yellow thread oozed from his ear. My mother cut a strip of fabric from a sheet and tied it around his head. Like mumps. The infant's crying increased. The woman tried to give him her nipple, but he didn't want it. He only wanted to cry. After two days the crying stopped and the woman began. At first she wept alone, then another five or six people alongside her began to weep, like a choir. Finally, she covered the infant's face with a sheet. Refused to give him to the tall man standing beside her. She had a brown spatter on her glasses. I dug my nails into my leg, dug and dug, until there was a small hole.

Dov said, he was saved, the baby died in his mother's arms. We will die alone.

We stood in line on the platforms at Auschwitz.

Trains were standing the length of the track. Like an enormous, long-tailed serpent.

Babies flew into the air like birds. Pregnant women were thrown onto a truck. One woman's belly exploded mid-air, everything scattering as if there was a watermelon there, not a baby. Old people who couldn't walk were smeared on the floor. Whole villages stood on the platform without room to move.

In the air, a column of smoke and the sharp smell of burned chickens.

That's what I remember.

First they separated the women from the men.

I never saw Mother or Sarah again.

We passed by an officer with a pleasant face, as if he liked us, felt concern. As if he cared about us. With his finger, he signaled, right, left, right, left. We didn't know his finger was long enough to reach the sky.

Then they asked about professions. Dov jumped first. We didn't have time to part from each other.

The soldiers shouted, *builders*, are there any builders?

Avrum and I walked forward together. Father remained to choose another profession.

I never saw Father again.

They took us to a building where we were to strip. A long, never-ending line. As if they were handing out candies there. And then they told us quickly, strip quickly. Naked women ran in the direction of a large iron door. The door constantly opened. Naked women were swallowed up into the black opening of the door. Like the large mouth of the sea. Men and boys ran the other side. Bearded rabbis screamed Shema Israel, Shema Israel.

Avrum and I stood trembling opposite the building that had swallowed the most people.

The building had a black door and another one just the same. My brother and I didn't know where we should run. Naked and confused we ran from one side to the other, treading on legs, pushing with our hands. Around me I saw people spinning with their hands above their heads, beating their chests, pulling their hair from their heads, their genitals. I saw people weeping to their God, telling him, God, hear me, give me a sign, where is the Messiah, Master of the Universe?

The was a sound there like a low hummmm, heavy as a snowstorm. *Hummm. Hummm.*

I called to my brother until my throat was hoarse.

I called, Avrum, Avrum, which door should we run to? Avrum, *answer me.*

Avrum caught my hand. He sobbed, here, no, *there*, no, no.

Avrum, what do we do, where, where?

The first door, no, *no*, the second. Icho, what are you doing? Icho, listen to me, wait, *liiiiisten.*

We were inside.

We were inside a huge hall with benches. A huge hall with barbers who shaved our hair. Tirelessly, they shaved and shaved. Then they took us to the showers. And then, *phishhh*. Water.

I called, Avrum, it's water, water, we're alive, Avrum, we're still together, Avrum, we've been lucky. Avrum?

I sobbed during the entire shower.

Chapter 2

I am Dov: The State of Israel gave me the name Arieh-Dov,
Dov for short.
The Nazis gave me the number A-4092.
The goyim gave me the name Bernard.
My Jewish people gave me the name Leiber.

In Dov's Living Room

I was sure they were taking us to die.

Father thought they were sending us to work in distant factories. I thought about death. My death had a shiny red color. Red like the blood oozing from the ear of the man standing beside me on the train to Auschwitz.

This man had refused to board the train and the blood refused to stop streaming for three days, perhaps because of the crowdedness and the pressure, everyone was pressed against everyone else. We were like fish in a barrel stinking of fresh death, a new smell that came into my life and didn't leave me for a long time.

The train to Auschwitz stopped.

The car door opened quite suddenly. Torches like projectors exploded in our eyes. The loudspeaker announced, quickly, quickly, *schnell, schnell.* Leave your belongings on the train. We heard irritability in a voice that was sharp and loud, as if there was nothing but a voice there, no human being, just a voice, *schnell, schnell.*

On the platforms were soldiers with guns and voices like loudspeakers. Get down, quickly, quickly. They yelled as if they had a loudspeaker installed in their throats.

To the side stood piles of striped pajamas, a head and arms sticking out of them. I saw nothing else of them. They stood to one side with bowed and shaven heads. They were more frightening than the orderly soldiers. They looked ill, as though they were suffering.

The soldiers didn't.

The orchestra was also healthy. They played cheerful marches suitable for a victory parade.

Dogs on leashes barked wildly. Dogs with sharp teeth and runny noses, their hackles up like nails.

Soldiers pushed an old bearded grandfather who didn't understand, who said, excuse me, sir, to the commander, what should . . . *Thwack.*

The old man fell. Soldiers beat up other frail old people. Smashed shoulders, bellies, backs. They didn't let them die on the spot, they left them to sob. And they sobbed with pain. Others wept in worry or because of the orchestra. There was a good orchestra at Auschwitz. I could immediately hear it was good. I almost wept for the beauty of it, but the large pile of striped pajamas stayed in my mind, and I didn't cry.

On the other side, soldiers were kicking a small child about like a ball; he was maybe three years old. The child hadn't heard, move, quickly, quickly. The little boy had black curls, a short coat, and a heavy diaper in his trousers. A diaper full of poop from the journey. The child had lost his mother and father and all he had left was a brown teddy bear that he held under his arm. The teddy bear was first to fall. The child followed. Another kick. Again he didn't hear, *move quickly*. It was a little hard to hear because of the music. The child's head opened slightly. Another kick, and that was it.

He remained on the platform beside his teddy bear like a black stain on the road.

The place grew very quiet. For a moment nobody spoke, not a word, just cheerful music.

I was dragged forward and the noise increased. It was a great weeping. The greatest weeping I had ever heard. The weeping of a large ocean, a stormy ocean. Weeping like waves breaking against rocks on the shore, *whoosh*, *whoosh*.

Soldiers screamed, stand in line, quickly.

Soldiers divided, women to the left, men to the right. Men hugged young children. Children sobbed Mama, Mama, Grandma, where's my mama? A grandmother with a scarf hid her mouth behind her hand. She had no teeth. Grandmother made strange sounds, like a life-saver at the beach. A life-saver who shouts into a megaphone, not a big one, in the wind. *Waaah, waaah, waaah, waaaaaah*.

A grandfather with a cane took the hand of a crying child. Held him firmly, saying, *sha, sha, sha*, don't cry, boy, and collapsed to the ground. *Thwack*. The child fell silent.

A soldier seized a baby wrapped in a blanket from a mother's arms. The soldier ripped the woolen hat from the baby's head and smashed the bald head against the car door. I heard a scream like a calf being slaughtered in the village, before the knife.

Mother and Sarah grew steadily more distant.

Mother threw her hands up in the air. As if she wanted to chase off spirits and devils. She pulled the scarf from her head, pulled at her hair, shrieked: Children take care of yourselves.

Mother shouted more loudly: My children, take care of yourselves. Do you hear me? Mother's cry made a wound in my heart. As if someone had put a nail on a nerve and hammered it in.

To this day, I ache when I remember Mother's tears and her last words.

Mother and Sarah were among the first four. They walked and walked until they vanished in the middle of the platforms.

Soldiers yelled to stand four to a line, quickly, and the orchestra played.

The loudspeaker continued to issue orders. The torches hurt less. People were running about like cockroaches in the dark. They forgot there was light. They were looking for relatives with whom to make a foursome. The noise was immense. An order from the loudspeaker momentarily stopped everyone on the platforms, then everyone began to run, call, Tibor, come closer, Solomon, Yaakov, come, come, we'll make up a foursome.

Shimon, who sold meat with them, came up without his glasses, tried to push in. You aren't with us, Shandor-with-the-limp was alarmed, move *back*.

Cross-eyed Yaakov from our village said, that's enough, we're four, and you'll stand behind us. Cross-eyed Yaakov began to walk.

Shandor-with-the-limp grabbed his hand, where are you going, stand next to me, here, one, two, three, four, five? No, no, move, no room. Yaakov, wait, what's wrong with him? He's throwing down his hat and pulling down his trousers, Shimon, come here, come back quickly, stand here, here, don't move, no more room, you will all stand in front of us, so what if you're cousins, nu, start another foursome.

The platform's loudspeaker changed station. Moved to dance music. We stood there, three boys and Father, thin and beardless.

Father raised his head, Avrum caught Father's arm, Yitzhak took two steps towards SSman.

Avrum forcefully pulled Yitzhak into the line. Whispered, what d'you think you're doing?

I stood like a heavy stone thrown into an abyss. Spin, spin, spin, *thump*.

Like a stone that had crashed on a rock.

Father was silent, pressing my arm like hot pliers.

A calm German officer signaled with his finger, right, left, left, left, left, and right again.

The orchestra changed the dance. The officer had eyes like the crack of a window.

He wore white gloves. He had shiny buttons and a wine-drinking face.

We went right. Whoever went right went to work. Whoever went left, went.

I saw smoke traveling not far from a cloud. I remember it, a black cloud, *special*. The smoke came out of the chimney of a large building, a huge building. The smoke drew a mushroom.

I asked Father, what's that?

A steel factory, Dov.

Father, answer me.

It's a factory, Dov. A steel factory for the war.

This is where they burn Jews, Father, that's the smoke of Jewish flesh.

Father jumped as if he'd trodden on a snake, no. No, of course it isn't, it's a factory, that smoke is from machines, Dov.

Soldiers called out, mechanics, any mechanics here?

I shouted, I'm a mechanic, me, me. I jumped out of the line. Jumped alone.

I wanted to run as far away as I could. I wanted to escape the piles of flesh in the smoke to come. Father, Avrum, and Yitzhak remained behind me.

I didn't look back, I wanted forward, far away.

Soldiers in polished shoes and leggings like tarpaulins took me to a two-storey building. They put me on a storey with German political prisoners. German prisoners with blond hair, and one with a mustache. The prisoners had received food packages from home. They sat eating in a group. They had a wooden box at the end of the bed. A box with a lid and a medium-sized lock.

I sat on the last bed and observed the mouths of the people in the room. I watched them take a bite with their teeth, gurgle, chew, swallow, chatting, offering to each other, saying thank you, sucking, wiping, burping, scratching, laughing, wrapping left-overs in a napkin, putting them back in the box, locking it and going to sleep. The German prisoners didn't notice that I'd come, they were oblivious. For them, I was a bit of dirt on the wall.

The smell of food drove me mad. My mouth filled with saliva. I could smell sausage and cakes. Bread and smoked fish. And peanuts and chocolate.

I heard sounds in my belly. I smacked my belly. But the sound didn't stop.

I took off my shoes and lay down on my back. A Jew from Budapest came in to sleep next to me. A fat, older Jew, about sixty. He had drops of sweat on his cheek. He breathed heavily, like an old train engine. He told me about the enormous farm he'd left behind in Hungary. I was shocked. A Jew with lands?

Yes, boy, lands the size of three villages.

Really?

Yes, boy, and what use is it to me now that I'm dying, dying of hunger. What's your name, boy?

Bernard, that's my Christian name. At home my name is Leiber.

How old are you, boy?

Sixteen and a bit.

The man caught hold of my shoulders, shook me firmly, staring at me, one eye healthy, the other made of glass, and said: Bernard, look at me, I don't stand a chance, you do. Steal, kill, live, do you hear me? You're young, Bernard, you're a boy with a good chance of coming out of this war, understand?

I made a small movement with my head: I understand.

The fat man collapsed back on his bed. We fell asleep in a second.

The next day he was gone, in the way of Auschwitz, as I understood in time. One moment you're talking to someone, the next moment he's gone.

Chapter 3

Yitzhak

At Auschwitz, in the year 1944, I received a new name.
55484 was sewn onto the side of my trousers and this was my new name. I was given striped clothing. A shirt and trousers from the same fabric, like the pictures we see today. I was given a striped hat and plastic shoes with wooden soles.

We stood in the dark, rows and rows of prisoners, everyone the same. Like a convoy of ants with numbers on the chest and side.

We were put in Bloc 12. In the bloc were three-tier beds. Not really beds, more like sleeping benches. We were ordered to stand in a line next to the beds. Avrum and I stood next to each other. Avrum was eighteen and asked where Dov was. I was fifteen and a bit, a year younger than Dov and didn't know where he was.

Avrum was at least a head taller than me. He had broad shoulders and the bristles of a beard. I had room in my shirt at the shoulders and a smooth face with no sign of a beard. In the bloc were other children my age. They stood among the older prisoners, looking down at the floor. I glanced at my brother, fiercely rubbing the thumb of my left hand. I couldn't stop rubbing.

An SSman entered the bloc. He stood straight with legs apart and a hat on his head. He stood with one hand on his hip and the other playing on his thigh. He pursed his lips as if whistling and slowly passed from one prisoner to another. Advanced. Stopped. Went back. Stopped at a boy of maybe thirteen, maybe less.

The thirteen-year-old puffed out his chest and belly, made himself taller and taller and taller.

SSman beckoned with his finger.

Boy stepped out of the line. Boy cried quietly. Boy trembled. SSman hit him on his thigh. *Thwack*. Boy fell silent.

SSman scratched his neck with the long nail of his little finger. Slowly scratched his bristles. I heard the scratch of sandpaper on a board. He scratched, scratched, scratched, stopped.

I stopped breathing.

SSman pursed his lips. Began to scan us again.

A boy opposite me pinched himself on the arms. I saw him stand on tiptoe. Fall. Stand. Fall. A boy beside me pulled his shirt away from his trousers, as if he'd grown fatter since standing in the line. Someone at the end of the line fell. They dragged him to the boy standing on the side.

SSman took three children and the one who'd fallen, and they left.

I didn't know the crematorium. But I did know I mustn't go outside with SSman. I understood everything through the crack in his eyelids. I was fifteen and a bit, thin as a match, and it was my great good luck not to go out with them. That was my first stroke of luck. And there was a second stroke of luck. Two brothers from my village saved me.

They were in the bloc, two beds away from me. Two large brothers, with swollen muscles in their arms, and bull-like necks.

The brothers lifted me onto the third tier of the bed, covered me with a straw mattress, saying, when there's *appel*—counting— you don't come down. Understand, Icho?

I stayed on the third tier for four days. SSman came to our bloc every day or two, took small thin prisoners. Avrum gave me bread and whispered the situation to me from below.

After a week they announced over the loudspeaker: Go to work. Not counting.

The two brothers from my village didn't believe the loud- speaker. They told the group, they're taking us to the crematorium.

The two brothers climbed onto the bed and helped me get down.

I got down from the third tier and felt my legs fold by them- selves. As if they'd been filled with margarine. I held onto the wall and looked at my brother. Avrum grabbed me by the hips and stuck out his tongue. Dragged me to the door. We were the last to leave and I glanced at the fence. An electric, barbed-wire fence at least four meters high. I saw a sign with the drawing of a skull and several words.

Someone behind me whispered, careful, death hazard. I thought, a long time ago, ordinary people walked to and fro behind the fence. What happened to them, are they alive or dead?

I had no answer.

SSman shouted, left, right, left, right, in the direction of the train tracks.

Again the crowding in the car. I calculated, if I kill the one in front of me, and the one behind me, and if I kill those to the side, how much room will I have? Maybe the length of a ruler on each side, no more.

I looked for my brother. I saw there was no point in calling him. He was pressed between two tall people. Pale. I saw his eyelids jumping like a broken automaton.

We traveled for several days. A quarter of bread per day, no water. People around me died without a murmur. They died a purple color, their mouths closed. They had purple under their fingernails. Like iodine poured on a wound. Someone died and we immediately searched him for food. Then we laid him down, while he was still warm, and took turns sitting on him.

There wasn't enough air in the car for everyone.

Sour sweat dampened our clothing. We stood pressed against one another with our mouths open, we shouted, air, air. We beat on the door. Screamed for an hour. I lost my voice. Finally they opened a narrow strip above. We climbed over the dead and the frail in order to breathe. We climbed on them as if they were our staircase to life.

Through the window I saw we had reached Weimar. There was a prominent sign there. From Weimar they took us to Camp Buchenwald. I knew it from the sign.

We arrived at Bloc 55. The first thing a prisoner with a wounded hand said to me was: Careful, they're looking for children, and in a moment I threw myself onto the third tier of the bunks. The barracks door would open, and I was on top, just as I did at Auschwitz. My brother Avrum told me when to come down. After two days the loudspeaker called my brother Avrum to report. We knew by the number they called.

Avrum came to say goodbye, but in the end, he said nothing. He looked at me and trembled. His face was white as a sheet. I fell upon him, oy, oy, oy, it's a mistake, they mistook the number, don't go, Avrum, don't leave me alone.

Tears wet Avrum's shirt. The trembling of his chin worsened. His mouth stretched up and to the sides as if he was telling me many important things. He was breathing very fast, and his nose ran like a tap.

The loudspeaker called Avrum's number again. I was afraid.

Avrum jumped and hugged me hard. I wept into his ear, I want to stay with you, what do we do, Avrum, let's go together. Avrum refused.

I felt as if both our ribs were breaking, and then he pushed me, breathing in and out, dried my face so I'd see him more clearly, left. I ran after him to the door. The guard at the entrance wouldn't allow me to leave. He gestured, go back to your place or you'll get it. He had a baton in his hands. A baton with an iron knob at the end. I wanted to shout, Avrum, Avrum, wait for me. I opened my mouth wide. Closed it. Went back to my place on the third tier.

I felt myself falling, falling, as if into a bottomless pit. As if they'd tied me to a heavy weight and thrown me into a dark place among strangers. I lay on my bunk and cried for an hour, until they brought a new prisoner to Avrum's bunk. I immediately turned my back. Couldn't bear to see someone else beside me. I got down. I knew I was angry enough to kill that prisoner. Two hours had passed and I still couldn't calm down. A German from another bloc came into the barracks. I didn't have time to climb up.

We were ordered: Line up, don't move.

The German half-closed his eyes and scanned us slowly. Back and forth. Back and forth. He had a crooked smile and puffiness under his chin. Like a pocket full of food. His eyebrows were joined like a fence and he had a pointed belly under his belt. He held white gloves in one hand, tapping them against his other hand. As if the gloves were helping him to think. Back and forth, back and forth. I stopped breathing. The German put on his gloves and took me and four other children. I followed him, oblivious to anything.

Outside, the late-afternoon sun was warm, the beginning of summer. Bright light filled the spaces between the blocs. I searched for Avrum in that bright light. Examined the parade grounds. I saw trucks with tarpaulins. I didn't know if there were prisoners inside or if they were empty. I never saw Avrum again, never saw him again.

The German with the white gloves took us to Bloc 8. Things were good for us in Bloc 8. Food on time. Lights out. A shower every day. Beds with blankets, clean sheets. A place with discipline and the color white. Fifty or sixty children with Baba – Uncle Volodya in charge. A fat man with a fat nose and a fat voice, and a large handkerchief in his hand. He liked to travel with his handkerchief on his bald head, *pat-pat-pat-pat*, but also to wipe children's tears with it. It was mainly at night that he wiped and fondled everywhere. I was quiet, almost unmoving, when he wiped and fondled. I barely breathed and my mouth was closed.

A doctor came into the bloc every morning.

Doctor had alert ears like an antenna. Doctor said hello, how are you, children. Doctor laughed with white teeth, and I saw the slight tremor of the antenna. Doctor would choose a child and leave.

In the meantime, Baba Volodya fondled children. Baba Volodya pinched cheeks and sent kisses to the ceiling. Children jumped on Baba. Children hugged Baba. Children said thank you, Baba, thank you. Thank you for the good food. The clean sheets. The shower and hot water.

And I saw method: Children who went with doctor didn't return to the bloc. Their beds remained empty. I didn't understand. Healthy children leave with doctor. Plump children leave the bloc. Children with color in their cheeks don't come back to sleep in the bloc.

I hung onto Baba Volodya's shoulder, asking him, where do the children go, Baba, and why don't they come back to the bloc to sleep, what's going on here, Baba, huh? Baba didn't respond. I felt knives in my belly. I felt I had no air left at the open window. Every time the doctor came in I would catch Baba Volodya's eye. Catch his eye and hold it. As if I were hanging onto his shoulder from a distance, as if telling him, you're my father, you're my father, and you won't leave me alone like my first father, d'you hear me? Only when the doctor left did I leave Baba Volodya and breathe in from the deepest place possible.

I started wandering around, asking questions.

I walked the length of the bloc. And back again. I walked back and forth, counting. I asked, where do the children go, where, and got no answer. I went over to stand near the older prisoners. I knew they were old-timers by the numbers on their clothing and their silence. They neither asked nor answered, just stood there staring nowhere. I said, tell me, where do the doctor and the children go, where is that building?

One said, there's a special place for experiments on young ones and a place for experiments on grownups. Doctor and child go to a place for experiments on young ones.

I said, experiments, what are experiments, what do you mean, tell me, I don't understand. He had an eye infection that leaked like a slug.

He looked at me without seeing me, as if thinking about me, then, finally, he said, go away, boy. My blood pounded fast in my veins, *tam-tam*, *tam-tam*. Someone else with a swollen belly who had heard me stuck to me. My blood pounded even faster.

My new friend said, be careful. I don't go anywhere near that place. Every child goes into a pot with gas, they close the lid on his head, like with soup. There are other cases. They examine some children according to a clock: How long can they live without air. Some last for a long time, others not at all. They die the minute the clock is set.

I stamped my foot and ran back to the bloc. I grabbed a freckled boy by the neck, calling agitatedly, boy, wait. What does it mean when the doctor leaves with a boy and returns without. Tell me, is it true they cook him in a pot? Cut him?

The boy said, don't know, and ran away as if I were holding a butcher's knife. I didn't give up. I ran outside. I caught a short prisoner with saliva on his chin.

Asked, what are experiments, and why do healthy children leave beds empty, huh?

He asked, where.

I muttered, in Bloc 8.

He sat down, are you in that bloc?

I hit him on the shoulder. Shouted, tell me, now, what's going on in my bloc.

He rolled his tongue and said, they inject a needle with a substance into the boy's vein, but first they talk to him nicely. Then they measure how long it takes for the substance to reach the heart. For some it takes three minutes. For others one minute. For some even less. But you should know it doesn't hurt to die like that. They die well there, without a nasty smell.

I asked who talks such nonsense, the one who dies?

The man said, no. Not the one who dies, and he wanted to go.

I tugged at his shirt, the doctor says so?

No.

So who says it doesn't hurt, who? The prisoner turned and walked off.

I decided to escape from Bloc 8.

I heard they were looking for a cook for the women's camp. I told Baba Volodya I'm a very good cook. Get me out of here into the women's camp. Get me out, Baba, please. As if I were your boy now. Baba Volodya stuck a match between his teeth and pressed hard. I didn't move from him. Volodya wrote down my name.

Volodya said, wait. I waited. I watched him from wherever I stood. I pursued him and waited.

Achtung. Achtung. 55484, report.

My heart stopped. I didn't know where they were sending me, to the gas chamber of the Jews, the experiments' pot, or to cook in the women's camp. Gas. Kitchen. Pot. Gas. Kitchen. Pot. Kitchen. Kitchen. My tongue went dry in a moment. I felt a strong pain in my backside. I went out.

Soldiers took me to a petrol station. Soldiers put me on a train car. I moved from Buchenwald to Camp Zeiss. An entire day on a cattle train.

Chapter 4

Dov: Do you remember when they took us from home to Ungvár,
we sat in open cattle cars and heard train whistles?
Yitzhak: Remember.
Dov: Do you remember our rabbi saying, when the Messiah comes, you'll hear a shofar?
Yitzhak: Nu?
Dov: When I heard the whistle, I thought,
maybe our rabbi was right, maybe the Messiah did come.
Yitzhak: Nobody came to save us. Nobody.

Dov

At Auschwitz, in 1944, a number was tattooed on my arm, A-4092.

"A" signified a transport from Hungary. The next day they made us stand to attention for eight hours on the parade ground. The rain didn't stop falling. I was cold. Cold. Cold. I had goose-flesh like pinheads on my skin. I felt as if they'd stuck a board in my back. In my shoulders. My legs trembled rapidly, rapidly, slowly. Rapidly, rapidly, *snap*. The muscle jumped. I was sure everyone could see.

SSman yelled, Do Not Move. Do Not Sit. I grabbed my trousers and pushed the fabric forward.

Anyone who fell did not get up.

Prisoners usually fell quietly. Sometimes they'd cheep like chicks in a nest. Sometimes I'd hear a blow, *thwack*, and that was that. Prisoners with a function had stripes and a ribbon on the arm and they'd drag the fallen out of the row. I focused my gaze on the nearest wall. I saw black circles running along the parade ground. The circles brought prickles to the temples and shoulders, two-three minutes and the prickles settled in the legs. Suddenly, hot. Hotter. And that was that. I couldn't feel my legs. Like paralysis. In my shoulders and neck as well.

They announced numbers over the loudspeaker. The voice over the loudspeaker was cheerful. As if he had a few chores to finish before going home, *la-la-la*. A prisoner next to me, an older man, began to cry quietly.

I heard him say *Sh'ma Yisra-el Adonai Eloheinu Adonai Echad – Hear, O Israel, the Lord is our God, the Lord is One* and immediately fall. He had white foam on his lips. He made the mewling sound of a cat kicked by a boot. Within seconds he was dragged out. Vanished. Poor man, poor man, God didn't hear him. I wanted to scream, where are you. God didn't answer. He cut me off too. I gave myself an order, stand straight, Dov, don't move, huh. I heard my number over the loudspeaker. I went with other prisoners. They sent us to work at Camp "Canada," named for the belongings left on the platforms by prisoners from the trains. They called us "Canada" Commando. They put me in a huge storeroom and told me to sort out clothes. There was a huge pile in the storeroom. Like a colorful hill of sand. There were suitcases. Many many suitcases with a number, or a name, or a label tied on with string. Sometimes, just a small ribbon on a handle, a red or green ribbon, like the ones used to arrange little girls' hair.

I divided the clothes into piles. Men's suits to the right. Dresses, skirts, and women's blouses, to the left. Coats, apart on the right. Children's clothing, behind me. Best of all was touching children's clothing. They were stained and worn at the edges. Sometimes a patch or a tiny pocket, and another pocket stretched out of shape, sometimes embroidery with bright thread, a flower. Butterfly. Clown. Ah. The clothes had the smell of a regular home. The smell of soap and moth balls. Among the clothes I found some mama's apron. A blue apron with a large pocket. I thrust trembling fingers into the pocket. I don't know what I was looking for, but I found nothing. The apron smelled of fried pancakes and sausage. My mouth watered. I wanted to take the apron, hide it under my shirt. I didn't dare because of the tall SSman who stood behind me, keeping an eye on my pace.

For hours, I ran among the piles, without stopping to rest. My legs ached but I didn't even stop for a second. The SSman stuck to my back. Out of the corner of my eye I could see a hand and a gun. I knew he'd put a bullet in me where it prickled. In the hollow of my neck. Ever since I've felt a prickling in that hollow whenever autumn comes. Once I saw his face and there were nails there instead of pupils.

Daily routine at Auschwitz was consistent.

We got up early, in the dark. We straightened blankets, ran to the holes in the latrines to clean up, ten minutes to pee or shit, crowded together in a suffocating stink, then splash the face with a little water, the line for thin, tasteless coffee, parade – and then we were divided up for work. Groups upon groups of prisoners with dry faces, shaved heads, dirty and quiet.

We worked for twelve hours a day on a shrieking belly with pains in our muscles. Again the line for a bowl of soup. Again roll call in the bloc, and the evening parade, on the parade ground. Count. Mistakes. From the beginning. They hit a prisoner on the head with a baton. *Thwack. Thwack.* Scream into the loudspeakers for hours. I wanted to sleep. I so badly wanted to get to my bunk in the bloc, fall onto the board, sleep. I'd fall asleep in a second.

After three weeks they sent us on foot from Auschwitz to Birkenau, a distance of three or more kilometers. I dragged my feet in a convoy of uniform stripes. I could barely walk. I raised my head and saw a yellowish-brown color, like the moment before a storm. Smoke coming out of a chimney. Dense, thick smoke without holes. Without spaces. There was a sweet smell outside. The smell of good meat cooked over a fire. I wanted to vomit. Thick saliva rose in me, disgusting. In the distance I saw a row of barracks with walls built of rough logs. I couldn't see any windows.

Again I sorted through the piles of belongings emptied out of the suitcases. Shoes to shoes. Coats to coats. Bags to bags. Piles as high as a mountain inside the huge storerooms. I knew. The hands that had packed the suitcases were now pressed into a black smudge rising upward.

At Birkenau I lived in a barracks.

The barracks that finished off the most people. Between five and eight hundred people. The barracks had cubicles of three tiers. I slept on the third tier. Six prisoners to a cubicle. Every morning new prisoners would arrive and there was always space for them to sleep instead of the dead they'd dragged outside. Prisoners would take hold of the thin legs of the dead and pull them down from the cubicle to the floor. Sometimes I'd hear *thump. Thump. Thump.* The head would knock on the board, as if coming down steps. *Thump. Thump. Thump-thump.* Sometimes they stripped off their clothes there in the passageway, sometimes not. It depended on the smell of the dead from the night. Dead that smelled were left in their clothes.

Every morning I saw different faces beside me. Faces with hunger and certain death in them. Every morning I heard questions, as if I had answers. The cubicle stank like Father's cowshed. I hadn't seen a shower in two months. The lice were in rows on my skin, as if SSman had given the order. I scratched until I drew blood. A lot of blood. I wanted to bite myself.

The head of the bloc, a giant with a triangular head, wore a striped vest. On his chest was a green triangle. The head of the bloc screamed, struck with a baton he always held in his hand like a long finger with a knob. The prisoners in the bloc whispered, they barely spoke. They reminisced about people they'd known back home. Reminisced about food. Asked one another how to erase spots that grew on the skin. Rashes, small sores, odd singes, signs of burns, scaly skin, infections here and there. They were alarmed by skin problems and by the doctor who'd examine naked prisoners and send them to *Selektion*. Between *Selektion* they'd argue about the chances of winning the war, or about a door that was left open to the cold. I didn't interfere in anything. Whispers didn't interest me. I'd put my head down on the wood and fall asleep.

* * *

One morning the loudspeaker played my number: *Achtung, Achtung*, A-4092 report outside. I was sure they'd throw me into the oven, that it was my turn for the Garden of Eden. I told myself, say goodbye to the world, Dov. Say goodbye to the sun. Say goodbye to the blue number on the arm. Say goodbye to the rags you're wearing. Goodbye to the stinking cubicle. Goodbye to the lice smeared all over you, damn them. You and the lice into the fire together, but first the gas, because there is order.

I came out of the barracks like a boy with dignity.

I looked for the sun. I couldn't find it and trembled as if they'd put ice in my trousers. Three more left the bloc with me. The large prisoner beside me didn't stop crying. I walked upright, didn't interfere. What could I say to him? I knew the Germans took strong guys for labor and it didn't always help. What determined it was what they needed: If they did or didn't need laborers for work. If things were held up at the crematorium or not. There were cases when whole transports were sent to the chimney, they didn't even look at them on the platforms. And there were strong young men among them, each shoulder a shoulder, not just any hands, but hands that could carry a heavy calf without a problem. And there were cases they took so-so young men to the crematorium and then, right at the crematorium they told them to return to the barracks, why? The *Sonderkommando* hadn't finished emptying out the previous transport. I was a boy and I knew I didn't stand a chance.

On the side was an open truck of prisoners in striped pajamas. SSman, baton in hand, signaled us to climb into the truck on the double, to move in close. Beside him stood two guards with guns. We ran to the truck. Another SSman was waiting for us with a leg in the air. A strong kick in the backside and we were off. I didn't know where they were taking us, and I didn't ask. I thought, maybe to the forest to meet with a machine gun, a mass grave in a field, maybe to work? I didn't dare ask the guards, didn't want to talk with prisoners.

The truck stopped at a labor camp: Jaworzno.

Israel, 2001

14:18 boarding a suburban train on the Nahariya platform.

Because of the sea I stick to a window, wait for it to bring a few waves to Nahariya. Blue sea and cellphone ringtones. A cheerful Turkish march fails to wake the phone's soldier. Stops. A message. On the left, Khachaturian's Sabres attack and at the end of the carriage another tune and a message. *Blah. Blah. Blah.* A slight, pin-like pain digs sharply into my head, releases. Yitzhak would say, what do you want with a headache in a carriage, better you take a taxi. Dov would say, best to use headphones, you wouldn't even hear the Auschwitz orchestra, would you?

I'd look at Dov, swallow saliva, and remain silent. Finally I'd say, I just can't wear headphones, can't wear them, Dov, I have so much noise in my head, I need an opening. And then Yitzhak would ask, what noise do you have, huh? And I'd tell him, never mind.

If I told Yitzhak and Dov the truth, if I told them that between May 15th 1944 and July 8th 1944, they transported 501,507 Jews from Hungary, most of them to Auschwitz, Dov would say, I'm no good at math. They took us away before we learned such big numbers. And Yitzhak would say, what do you mean, immediately pouring vodka into a glass of grapefruit juice, and his wife, Hannah, would say, what do you need that for, and he'd say, for life, Hannah, and then I'd focus on Dov, and he wouldn't believe a single word for five minutes. Then he'd clap his hands loudly, how did they manage that, wanting me to say: How did they manage it in two months, transport five hundred and one thousand and another five hundred and seven Jews out of Hungary, huh?

Less than two months, Yitzhak would correct. Less than two months, Dov.

Are you sure, Dov would ask me. Yes, yes, I'd say, I saw it on television, and then Dov would ask, what program, I know all the programs, and I'd say, Channel 8, maybe, or maybe Channel 23, and then Dov would say, boring, with a gesture as if brushing away a fly. Is there a crematorium on your channel? We can't describe a crematorium standing there without smoke and smell. We can't imagine the smell of flesh not coming out of the television.

The train stopped just as the nausea from the smell of flesh began. The end of the track. Impossible, Dov would say, possible, possible, Yitzhak would say, the Germans were good with large numbers, and then Dov would say, break. Bring juice for everyone, and I'd throw off my shoes, roll up my sleeves as high as possible, and look for a shutter to open, and Yitzhak would say, what's the matter with you, and I'd say, hot flashes, it's the age, pay no attention.

Chapter 5

Yitzhak: How come I only studied up to third grade?
Dov: You didn't want to study after third grade.
Only I studied all the time.
Yitzhak: Do you want to know the month of my birth in 1929?
When they took compost out to the field and planted cabbage.
The month of November.
11.11.1929. Dov was also born in November. One year before.
Dov: I was a year old when they sent me away from home.

Dov

We were born Czechoslovakians. Sent to die as Hungarians. In 1944, my family was taken to a concentration camp. My father, Israel, was forty-nine. My mother, Leah, was forty-two. The children were between fifteen and twenty.

We lived in the village of Tur'i Remety in the Carpathian Mountains, near the town of Perechyn. A small place, maybe six hundred families. Maybe thirty Jewish families. Our village was known for horse racing.

People from the area would come to us with their beautiful racehorses. I didn't buy a ticket to the races. I had no money. I sat on a platform near the mountain. Ate an apple, played my harmonica with a *phoo phoo phoo. Phoooo. Phoo. Phoo. Phoo. Phoooo. Phooah.* That's what came out and in the meantime, I speculated on the horses' chances. The races were in the time of the Czechs. The Hungarians put a stop to the races. War was already raging in Europe but they didn't talk about it in the village, we were far away in the mountains.

The goyim – Jews – in our village were farmers. The Jews were merchants. Butchers, grocery, bakery, a flour mill, things like that. Jews always had money in their pockets.

In the village we'd gather in the evenings to peel corn with the goyim. Let's say the corn in the Korol family's corn field was ripe. The Korol family cuts the corn. The Korol family brings the corn to the storeroom. The village youngsters gather together in the evening to peel the corn.

The youngsters work, sing, eat hot corn. Sometimes two youngsters, a boy and a girl, yes, would peel the corn with a scrap of shirt, or trousers; and, unintentionally, yes, we'd soon start throwing peels at them, lots and lots of peels with hairs at the end, like a blanket, so they shouldn't get cold, God forbid. By morning we were in *vecherkas*, as we called the gatherings with the goyim. The next day we'd go to another farmer and start the *vecherkas* and the fun all over again. Everything ended when soldiers came to the mountains and forced us to wear yellow patches.

Father Israel was a butcher.

We had a butcher shop next to our house. Father was also an animal trader and away from home three nights a week. We had a cowshed in the yard and we had geese and chickens. Mother raised the children. Mother milked the cows, helped in the store, ran the home, Mother was an expert baker, her cakes tasted like the Garden of Eden. Mother worked and worked, didn't rest for a moment. When we were hungry we took food for ourselves. We only sat down to eat a meal together on the Sabbath. When I was a year old my brother Yitzhak was born and I was sent away from home. My sister Sarah was five. My brother Avrum was three. Mother couldn't take care of everyone at once. I was sent to Grandmother and Grandfather. They lived in another village, maybe thirty kilometers from my village. When I was three they brought me back home. My sister Sarah said I didn't stop crying.

Our village was near a huge forest in the Carpathian Mountains.

What I loved most was walking in the forest. Always with a stick, because of the wolves. I loved swinging from branches and climbing trees. I would climb almost to the top of the tree and look out over fields, over houses. I only ever felt safe in trees. I knew no one would find me up there. I had my own private hiding place in the forest. I hung up a hammock made from a blanket I took from home and I ate fruit from a hoard I collected, all according to season. In the forest I knew where to find pears, mushrooms, berries and nuts. I was the first to know when the fruit was ready to eat.

In winter I suffered.

In winter I waited for the snow to melt so I could throw off my shoes and run barefoot to my forest. Mother embarrassed me. She'd run after me, shoes in hand. She'd call my name aloud in front of the neighbors, worried that I'd catch cold, shouting Avrum, Avrum, Avrum, to help her with me, but he'd go off with Father. I'd hear, Sarah, Sarah, leave your book for a moment, nu, and go and look for your brother, put his shoes on and bring him home.

Sometimes I'd come back with Yitzhak, shoes in hand. Sometimes with Sarah. I liked feeling the cold earth. It was a nice tickling feeling in my back, right up to the hollow in my neck. Maybe that's why my feet didn't hurt when I walked in the camp with paper-thin soles.

Yitzhak and I went together to *cheder* – a traditional elementary school teaching Judaism and the Hebrew language. We started there at the age of four. We left home every day at five-thirty in the morning. In winter the temperature was twenty-five below zero. We'd hold hands and walk in the dark. We wore a coat, a hat, a scarf and gloves and woolen socks with shoes. Despite this my face hurt, like an iron stuck fast to my skin. I couldn't feel my feet in that frost. Our legs were like planks bent in the middle. Our ear-locks were like barbed wire. We didn't talk so our tongues wouldn't fall out and stick to the snow.

We'd study for two hours in *cheder* and then go home. At the age of six, after *cheder*, we went to the Czech elementary school. We studied until 13:00 and went back to *cheder* in the afternoon. For at least another two or three hours.

A city rabbi would come to bless the village on two fixed occasions twice a year. The city rabbi was an important and respected man. He had a black coat, a hat, and a thick beard like steel wool. The rabbi would comb his beard with two fingers, stopping only to spit into a handkerchief. The rabbi didn't say they're throwing Jews into the Dnieper. The rabbi didn't say they're throwing Jews into the Dniester. The rabbi didn't say they're shooting Jews in forests. People in the village asked him as they had always done over the years, rabbi, what should we do. What should we do, rabbi, on the radio they speak against Jews, there are rumors, rabbi. They send families far away, where is far away, rabbi, what do they do to us there, does it hurt? And there have been whispers, rabbi, passing by word of mouth, whispers about mass graves of hundreds, thousands, danger is coming, rabbi, what is waiting for us, rabbi, tell us what is waiting for us, is this the end?

The rabbi would think and think, and in the meantime, a woman with an enormous belly pushed two Jews with beards and hats who stood in the aisle, and approached the rabbi from the side, punching him, *boom*! in the middle of his back and the rabbi jumped and the two Jews with beards and hats fell on the woman and she rolled about like a full barrel, shouting, hooligans, leave me alone, and they wouldn't leave her alone, but rolled her out of the synagogue, and three old women with covered heads would call out in unison, she's crazy, she's from a goy family and she's crazy, and the rabbi would arrange his hat, pull his coat and bend down to us with raised eyebrows, asking the nearest man, tell me, Jew, do you light candles at home?

Yes, we light candles, and you, tell me, have you checked your *Mezuzahs?*

I've checked them, and you, Jew, do you remember to put on *tefillin*, we remember rabbi, we don't forget a single day.

And then the rabbi would say, nu, good. There's a God in the heavens, open the *Siddur*, say *Shema Israel* and the Messiah will come.

The village people said, very well, and looked down at the ground. The rabbi requested a chair. The rabbi took off his hat and wiped his forehead with a handkerchief. The rabbi put his hand in his pocket and played with coins. *Chink. Chink. Chink.* People stole glances at one another but refused to buy the rabbi's medications. A few minutes later they continued to badger, what should we do, rabbi. Should we run away, answer us, rabbi. They had the voice of a hungry chick. Many chicks that weep and weep.

The rabbi would frown, saying: Certainly not, Jews. Forbidden! Forbidden to leave the village!

People said, very well, but immediately longed for Eretz-Israel, rabbi, Palestine, you know, the Jews are studying Torah there, maybe we'll escape to Palestine?

The rabbi shouted: Forbidden! A boycott on anyone who goes to Palestine. Boycott! Boycott! Boycott! We must wait for the Messiah!

The people said very well, but until he comes, rabbi, what must we do?

We have a strong God, He will help, shouted the rabbi banging his hand on the Ark.

The people said very well. Men and heavy coats, and women with head coverings and handkerchiefs in their hands, crowded in front of the synagogue Ark, weeping and shouting in unison, help us, our Lord. Save us from Hitler, damn him, bring the Messiah, and then they went home. On the way, if they saw a priest or a white horse, or a chimney cleaner in black clothes and a black hat, they'd grab a button on their clothing, against the evil eye, not letting go until they reached home, believing that this would help them get through Hitler. Some kissed the *Torah* morning, noon and night, some wept. Small children rushed around the synagogue yard with sticks in their hands. They cursed Hitler and beat the ground.

The rabbi wanted to go back to his city. They lined up the children to say goodbye and shake his hand.

I didn't like the rabbi and didn't want him to ask me a question about the Torah or about Jews. I didn't want him to speak to me about anything. I was ashamed when people laughed because I didn't understand a thing about what I studied in *cheder*. I was most ashamed at farting in my trousers from the stress, because in *cheder* we read Hebrew letters that looked to me like sticks with a lot of mosquitoes, the rabbi translated the sticks with mosquitoes into Yiddish, and I knew Yiddish from home, but I couldn't remember the Hebrew letters, not even one. I had no head for letters. My brother Yitzhak had even less of a head for letters. Yitzhak escaped from life in *cheder*. I suffered more. Every day I farted on the way to *cheder*. I squeezed tight but they got out, *phut. Phut. Phut.* I'd often whistle so my friends wouldn't hear and, hopefully, wouldn't smell before I had time to reach the hole in the shithouse. I'd sit above the hole in the plank to pass the time, I'd whistle melodies quietly. I'd play my harmonica in my mind, or draw on the wall with a piece of chalky stone I had in my pocket. I was an expert on butterflies with huge wings. I made enough room on the wings for me and my brother Yitzhak in case we decided to fly far away.

One day I was sitting in the shithouse and saw one of our boys approaching. I think it was Menachem, the shoemaker's son. The boy pulled down his pants and sat down next to my ass. He and I begin to shove asses. Shove, shove, bursting with laughter. In the meantime, the rabbi the *melamed* – teacher – arrived with a scarf around his neck and a smell of cigarettes. The rabbi, the *melamed* had a belt in his hand. The belt was five centimeters wide and at the tips of his fingers was orange colored fire. And then he threw back his hand and *thwack*, he brought the strap down on us. And *thwack. Thwack. Thwack.* The boy and I race away from the shithouse with our trousers down. On the way we step on our trousers and *boom*, we fall to the floor. The rabbi didn't stop yelling and each time *thwack* on the ass. On the back. On the head. Left us in pain for a week with red stripes on the skin, each stripe five centimeters wide.

Our rabbi the *melamed* had another arrangement.

He would start the week with a game. He'd stand in front of us, one hand on his hip, the other scratching his head. Soon I'd see a shower of dandruff falling to his shoulders. He'd frown and ask, who knows which tree we can break on the Sabbath, eh? And I was an expert on trees. I was a professor on trees. There wasn't a boy in the village who knew the forest like I did. I said to myself, I'll find him a tree and impress him. I forgot it's forbidden to break trees on the Sabbath. Nu! He broke my bones and I ran away from the *cheder* and sat in a ditch by the road. For two weeks I lived in the ditch. I brought planks to the ditch and I made myself a room without a roof. I brought a large stone and a blanket and water to drink, and cookies, and a catapult and I was content. I saw boys and girls walking along the road together, arms around each other's waists, whispering into each other's ears, laughing. As if they had no Hitler on the radio.

I frequently counted wagons of hay returning from the field. Wagons with humps of hay. Sitting on top were the farmers. They were usually tired and sleepy. Sometimes I'd flick a stone at them with my catapult. They'd jump in fright, raising their whip and looking behind. Then they'd fall asleep. I saw women on the road, dragging heavy baskets of apples. At noon, they'd return with baskets, cursing the bad day and bad luck brought by black cats.

One day my rabbi the *melamed* came to my room in the ditch. The rabbi held a hat in his hand. He stood above me, calling me. I didn't answer.

What are you doing here?

Looking.

Aren't you bored?

Interested, actually.

Children in *cheder* are asking about you.

What do they care?

They don't understand where you disappeared to.

I like living next to the road.

I want you to return to *cheder*.

Not coming back.

Your parents want you to return.

I caught sand falling from the wall of the ditch.

Come back to *cheder* and you can have this hat as a gift, want it?

I went back, did I have a choice?

I put on a woolen hat with a small peak, a new hat.

Are you coming?

Coming.

I go into the room. See three children turn to the wall making a sound like *chah. Chah.* Quietly. As if they had a pile of mucus to throw up. The rabbi puts his handkerchief into his pocket and sticks his thumb under the belt of his trousers. He towers over me, tells me, read a verse from the book, and my throat constricts.

The children all look at me. At least two make faces at me from behind the book. I look down. The book is open in front of me, a salad of letters on the page. Silence in the room. I keep half an eye on the rabbi. His cheeks flush pinkish blue up to his neck, most of all at the ends of his ears. His hand rises and I go cold. *Smack.* He hits me with his belt. *Smack. Smack. Smack.* Tired, he left the room to smoke a cigarette. The children in the room jump on their chairs, call, na. Na. Na. Na. Na. Na. Some make vomiting noises, only one sits quietly, sticks his finger in his nose and then in his mouth, one slaps two next to him on the head, as if they were drums, they grab him by the trousers and pull hard, he shouts, stop, stop, bending forward, the two pay him back with a fast drumming on his back, he grabs their legs and bang. A heap of children rolling on the floor, the boy with his finger in his nose at the bottom.

I sat in the corner swallowing tears of shame and prayed to God that my rabbi the *melamed* would go blind. That my rabbi the *melamed* would limp and have a permanent stutter. No, no, may his tongue fall into the snow and stick there for eternity, I wish, I wish, that he'd come into the room, open his mouth wide, want to say Leiber, read from the book, and all that would come out would be *mmmm. Mmmm.* I wish, I wish. I know the rabbi decided I'd rebel against him. That I deliberately didn't want to read, to make him mad. But I didn't. I couldn't remember the Hebrew letters.

I also got it from rabbi the *melamed* because of the Sabbath.

My brother Yitzhak and I agreed to bathe in the Tur'i Remety River on the Sabbath for a few candies. Older children said, if you go in the river on the Sabbath, we'll give you all the candies we have in our pockets, want to? They showed us the nice candies in their pockets. We stripped quickly and waded into the river. We got no candies. One of them immediately ran to call our rabbi. The rabbi arrived in his Sabbath clothes and large hat. My brother and I decided to dive. We held hands, took a deep breath, and *hop*. Down we sank. One, two, three, four, five, we ran out of air. We raised our heads. Ah, the rabbi was waiting for us at the river. He shook his head, and I saw a belt hovering over me.

At home I complained about the rabbi.

I said, the rabbi hits me with his belt. Father, it hurts.

Father said, Leiber, you study hard, d'you hear, and off he went.

I went to Mother, Mother, help me, it hurts. Mother was silent.

My sister, Sarah, put her book aside and said, Leiber is right, Father needs to do something, Mother, you tell him.

Mother took a candy from the drawer, gave it to me and said, the rabbi knows what's good for you. The rabbi decides, Leiber, and you have to listen to him, understand? I was silent. Throwing off my shoes, I jumped outside and ran barefoot to the forest. I heard Mother shouting, Leiber, Leiber, come back. I didn't go back. I only went back when it got dark and I was hungry.

A few days later, the Czechs recruited the rabbi. Soldiers on horses were dragging a cannon. The rabbi sat on one of the horses. I sat in the ditch and he rode past me. His face was a whitish gray color, his body had shrunk, and under my woolen hat I felt happy, I called out, there is a God, there is. Because I didn't want him to speak to me. I never saw him again.

Then the Hungarians came and life in the village was turned upside down. The Hungarians sacked the Czech teachers. Replacement teachers arrived from Hungary. Anti-Semitic teachers. They immediately separated Jewish and Christian children. Mainly for sports lessons. Christian children were given wooden weapons to train with before being recruited to the army. The children trained in the yard, right-turn, left-turn. They were known as Levente. They turned us Jews into servants. We had to cut firewood. In the meantime, the village was full of rumors.

The shoemaker whispered in the synagogue that they were taking Jews and burning them. Shooting them at enormous pits, spreading lime, firing, then another layer. The grocer said the Germans were putting Jews in cars, closing the door tightly and pouring poison inside. Then they throw them to the dogs. At home, around the table with a glass of tea, Mother said God would help and Hitler would burn like a candle. Father said, Hitler will burn up like a feeble tree. The bald neighbor came in and said first they should pull out his teeth, one by one, with rusty pliers. Then the childless neighbor came in and said, the British will come soon, they'll hang Hitler on a rope, damn him. They always killed Hitler at the table. Rabbis even came from the city, two I didn't know, one plump, one short and not so fat, they said, Jews, there is nothing to worry about. The plump one said, we have a powerful God. He will take care of us. The short one wiped away the white crumbs at the corners of his mouth and said, very true, trust in God alone. But I was very worried and stuck to Shorkodi.

A handsome young man, he was from the Jewish Forced Labor Battalion. The Hungarians brought them from Budapest to cut wood for the Germans. Shorkodi ate supper with us on the Sabbath. Shorkodi said, listen Leiber, I have a large perfume store. When the war is over you'll come with me to Budapest. I'll teach you to work in the store. I didn't know what perfume was but I waited for the day. Every day I waited. Even when they killed my best friend, Shorkodi, because he took the train to Budapest without permission. He wanted to visit his parents and return. I waited even after the men from Budapest disappeared. I waited even when I knew the end was coming for the Jews.

And we had a chance.

In 1943, a *shaliach* – messenger – came from Israel to our village. A young Betar man with velvety hair and shoulders a meter wide. He had a low thick voice, and he spoke as if Hitler was standing behind the door. He said he'd come to save Jewish youth from Hungary. He came into the synagogue and begged to take at least the youngsters to Israel.

Give me the children, the children. I approached the Betar *shaliach*, don't know why, but I wanted to hang onto his hand and not let go. He smiled at me and put out a large, sunburned, scratched hand. I wanted to shake his hand.

Father stood between us. Father said, Leiber, go home. I ran home. I didn't know what Israel was but I thought, first of all, we're getting out of here. I banged the door and fell upon Mother.

Mother, Mother, I want to go to Israel. I want to go with the *shaliach*.

Mother pulled at her apron and pinched my cheek. Hard.

Mother said, is that what the rabbi taught you, huh? We go to Israel only when the Messiah comes.

I stayed. I knew we'd missed our chance.

I waited for the Messiah. First I sat with my left leg crossed over my right, an hour later I changed legs, crossing my right over my left, for twice as long, and changed. I sat on the steps behind the house. I opened my shirt, showed him my entire chest, I wanted to open my heart to him, I put my palm, fingers stretched, over my heart, I heard it beat, *tuk-tuk. Tuk-tuk.* I seized the beats in my fist, threw my hand forcefully over my head, then I opened my mouth and called him, come Messiah, come, come to me.

In the meantime, I listened to the radio.

I heard Hitler on the radio. His voice was like the barking of the big dog in the neighbor's yard. I heard *heil, heil*. I heard *Juden*, and *Juden* like cursing. I heard incredible singing from thousands of throats. I felt as if the enthusiastic singing on the radio wanted to fix me to the wall and squash me like a mosquito.

I was certain the story would end badly for Jews. As bad as it could be. Even though I didn't understand the reason and I wasn't yet fifteen.

Chapter 6

Yitzhak: *Maybe we deserved it, we were cheats and liars.*
Dov: *Don't say that.*
Yitzhak: *Man-eaters. The Jew in the diaspora wasn't honest.*
Dov: *Not true, don't say that, it's how traders are, it's impossible to buy for a lira and sell for half a lira.*
Yitzhak: *An ordinary goy was honest. A Jew looked for ways to earn, make a living.*

Yitzhak

I liked wandering round the market.

The noisiest place in town. I didn't want to study. Didn't want to sit on my ass the entire day in front of my teacher's mouth. I liked wandering about the market, traveling to places I didn't know with my father. I liked meeting the man with the vegetable stall. He'd say to me, Yitzhak, you've grown, grown, want an apple? I liked meeting the man with a general store. He had burners, lamps, a nut-grinder, a small saw with a special handle, a bird-cage, and work tools. He had an interesting story for me. Sometimes I'd sit apart on the stairs and learn how to buy and sell goods.

I'd see and couldn't believe my eyes. Goy soldiers would come to buy a horse from a Jew. The horse is lame. The Jew hits the horse on the second leg and hammers a nail into the hoof of the healthy leg, the horse looks healthy. The soldiers pay good money for the horse, the Jew spins around them like a happy top, offering cookies and tea, chatting away as if to friends. The goy soldiers say goodbye, goodbye, set off on their way, and then, *boom*. The horse falls. The goy soldiers curse the Jew. The goy soldiers kick a stone, seize a stick and break it on the back of the poor horse. The soldiers say, we'll kill you, dirty Jew, we'll hang you from the highest tree, filth. Ah. Holding my head, I ran away. That evening I told Father and he nodded his head and said nothing.

Goy comes to a Jew in our village. Goy asks, lend me ten agorot – cents – for a bit of tobacco. A Jew lends it to him. How many bits does he return? He returns a lot. Or, instead, a Jew says to a goy, give me some beans, potatoes, cabbage. Goy brings more and more and the Jew isn't satisfied. Sometimes Goy went to market, wanted to buy a nanny goat. He has no money. He came to a Jew and asked for money. How would he give it back? He'd return two nanny goats. That's how a Jew exploited the goy. Goy didn't understand trading. Jew ran the market. Goy looked after the goods. Jew paid Goy at the end of the day. But the goy waited for evening. Yes, yes. He waited for the Jew on his way home. With friends. Five. They hid behind a hill with sticks, knives and an iron rod in their hands. Yaakov approaches in his cart. He has small, red ears and ginger hair. There are two other Jews on the cart. One an uncle, the other a neighbor. One snores loudly, another farts. Yaakov is happy. His bag is filled with money. He hid it under the hay. On the hay he placed a sack of flour, over the sack a blanket. In his pocket he has a little money. Suddenly, a fire in the middle of the road. A small fire, just a small one. The horse stops. Three goys jump on Yaakov, one catches the horse's bridle. The fifth jumps on the uncle and the neighbor. They had no time to wake up. The money was gone.

Then there was lame Friedman. He brought a mill to thresh goy farmers' wheat in the village. He'd make a noise throughout the entire village, *turrrr turrr turrr*. Half the village worked around Friedman's mill. Farmers would bring their wheat, thresh it, and how would they pay Friedman? It was divided up – one third to him, two thirds to the farmer. Friedman wasn't a cheat. Friedman had bought the machine, prepared it for the month of May, fixed it, threshed the wheat, he justifiably took percentages. But Jews also had a mill. The goy would bring a ton of wheat to the mill. The goy would go home with two hundred kilos of flour. Isn't that thieving? A little.

The Jew was smart. The Jew lived at the goy's expense. Jews always had money in their pockets, they bought a hat, boots, a good coat, fresh fruit, like this, as open as my hand. Maybe that's why the goys hated Jews. They always called us, dirty Jew, go to Palestine, there's nothing for you in our country.

We were an ordinary family. We weren't rich. Father was a trader and a butcher. There was no scarcity of food, but life was hard. They didn't always buy Father's goods. Sometimes Father would go to market with a cow and return two days later with the same cow. And if he did manage to sell it, he didn't return home alone because of the robbers. Father always walked around town with a brother, an uncle, or a friend. He traveled in a group. Sometimes he traveled in an old taxi with five or six people. The taxi barely went thirty kilometers an hour, they'd crank up the car more and more, sometimes they'd spend half a day cranking it. In the meantime, they'd drink coffee, play some cards, and they stuck together. Because of the robbers. Jews were uneasy everywhere. A Jew either existed or not, depending on the desire of the goys.

Chapter 7

Dov

The goys always said: It's the nature of the Jew to cheat the Christian.

And I tell you: The Jew had no choice. He had no land. He had to be a trader. The goy had land. The goy always had food in his hands. The goy grew pigs in the yard, cows, geese, he had vegetables in the garden, trees full of apples, a field of wheat and cabbage and corn. The Jew had no land, how was he supposed to live? The goy needed sugar, flour, oil, kerosene, clothing, so the Jew opened a grocery, a bakery, and a clothing store. Sometimes, in order to buy at the store, the goy sold a cow to the Jew. They'd negotiate, but not for business. The goy sold the cow to take products home.

The goys needed the Jews to advance in life. Without the Jews' money they couldn't have bought a cow or a horse, they couldn't have bought a plow to plow the field, or wheat seed for bread. The Jews' money rolled business forward, so what, did it help us? The Germans also needed the Jews for their business, before they decided to throw them into the oven.

* * *

Israel, 2001

14:18 at Nahariya Train Station.

I'm on the interurban to Binyamina. On the seaside. The change to the suburban train is in an hour and seven minutes. I look at the window and see a round face in the glass, a silly smile. Maybe because of the Arak in the grapefruit juice. Arak and grapefruit juice goes well with meatballs said Yitzhak and filled my glass for the second time. Dov smiled, saying, very true, drink, drink, let's make a toast. To the life of the State of Israel. *L'chaim. L'chaim.* To life. To life.

Beyond the window high risers pass, country homes, a date avenue, a fierce green in tiny plots, diagonal furrows, and sea, sea, sea, sea. The froth on the waves is the color of mud. The Mosque and wall are a soft cream color. And again housing units, again the sea. The air conditioning on the train is pleasant.

Opposite me sits an old man covered in age spots. One across half his cheek. He's wearing an Australian cap with the design of a duck. Beside him is a curly-headed little girl with a pony-tail tied with a blue band. She's licking a record-sized candy on a stick with her red tongue. The old man points to a picture in the book and says, kangaroo, that's an Australian kangaroo, and he swallows a yawn. The little girl puts the book aside. The old man pulls his cap down to the end of his nose, falls asleep.

I need the toilet. Don't want to get up. I stand. My bladder is bothering me. Taking my bag, I look for the toilet. The cubicle is at the end of the carriage, near the steps. I peep in, it's like a plane toilet, a large roll of paper under a plastic lid, a tiny sink, a box of hand wipes, it looks clean.

I don't move.

Well, get a move on, go in. Wait. I check the door. Mentally take the lock to pieces, turn it to the left, turn it to the right, an ordinary lock. I go into the cubicle and am afraid to close the door in case I get stuck going out. And if I shout for help, will they hear me? No one will. If Yitzhak was on the train, he'd say, worst case scenario, you could jump, with a little luck you'd get to a hospital, most important of all, no one dies from that, and in any case, I've already said, taxi, taxi. Dov would say, you only die once, best to hold it in.

The nightmare doesn't end: The toilet door doesn't open. In a cinema, for instance. The movie ends. The audience leaves the hall, the lights are switched off, I'm inside. A faded, peeling door, behind a gas station. No one around. An office block, top floor, middle floor, the worst is a basement floor, never happened to me? It's happened, it's happened. The walls were like a sealed room. Two minutes and your shirt is wet.

If Yitzhak was there, he'd say, at least you've got paper to wipe yourself, we had no paper. And there was nothing to wipe. Dov would say, what paper, we had nothing, we'd cut small pieces from the stripes on the trousers and shirt to wipe. In secret. Sometimes we didn't even have that. We'd walk in a line, with a stinking, sticky drip down our trousers, don't even want to think about it. Do you have any idea of what it's like to walk along a road and feel a disgusting drip into your shoes, better you never know. And now, coffee.

Chapter 8

Dov: Remember Mermelstein? Tall, with a beard,
recruited by the Czechs in 1939? He was a
gunner, rode a horse, six horses pulled a cannon.
Yitzhak: One of the boys from that family was with you.
Dov: Yes, but we lost each other along the way.
Yitzhak: We lost ourselves along the way, Dov, look what
happened to us. We lost everything.

Dov

I went by truck from Auschwitz to Camp Jaworzno.

It was the middle of summer. Hot. We traveled standing up. Crowded and stinking. I was finished. Two adults fell on me simultaneously. One died close to my eye, one on my shoulder. I carried them both until Jaworzno. The old pain in my groin came back. The place that would swell up and turn blue when I dragged heavy logs to the train track in the village. At night, I'd drag them with Father and my brothers.

We got down from the train. Even hotter. Saw rows and rows of brown wooden barracks with thick, white smoke above them, like sand. SSman, two meters tall with a cap and a loudspeaker in his hand yelled, strip, you're going to shower. I didn't believe him. I was certain they were taking us to the gas. In my pocket I had a piece of bread. I hid it in my shoe. I thought, if I get out of the shower alive, a piece of bread will be waiting for me. Naked and thin we went into the shower. Tall men, short men. All ugly, disgusting, just like the goys always said about us. Everyone had white skin, sores and a smell. They'd press on their skin and there'd be a hole in the flesh, as if their skin was old. Their bald heads were brown like mud. A thin layer of bristles. Their nails were bitten to the quick. I thought, maybe it's easier to kill people who look like this. I was sure I looked like that, too, maybe I was also disgusting, ugh, stinking. I started looking for a mirror, didn't find one. I smelled my skin, it smelled like spoiled cheese.

We stood stinking and crowded under the taps and I didn't know if they'd give us water and then gas, maybe gas and water together, maybe they didn't have enough water in that camp and we'd have to wait like we did in the train car, and maybe we'd just stand there until we died.

The air became smellier. Someone near me pooped standing up. Two others in front of me did the same. Maybe out of fear. Silently I asked myself, if they'd put naked Christians in here instead of Jews, no, no, if they'd put naked Germans in here, say, the tall, blond men I saw in the newspaper, the ones who always looked as if they'd just had a good shave. Would they also be as ugly as us after two months in Auschwitz? I had an answer. Yes. It would be easy to kill them, because of the sores and the smell.

Some of them began to call *Shema Israel, Shema Israel* and to weep. The weeping spread like fire in cotton wool. I also wept. We all wept to someone about someone. They began to move back and forth, as if they had a beard and were in a synagogue, moving in shoes and coat and hat. And suddenly water.

A flow of boiling water hit us on the head. Water without a smell. We couldn't escape the burning. Nonetheless we screamed water, water, and in a flash, the tap was turned off. We were saved. The men's weeping turned to roars of laughter. The tears remained. For the first time since leaving home I saw Jewish men laughing. I knew a piece of bread was waiting for me in my shoe. I started to hug someone next to me. We wept together. In the meantime, they opened the door. At once we shut up so the Germans wouldn't change their minds. They gave us clean clothes that didn't smell. The black stripes looked darker. They put us in a dark bloc with three-tiered bunks. I couldn't see any windows. The walls were brown. The light bulbs were faint. I managed to get a place farthest away from the floor. I ate my bread lying down; I was happy that day in Camp Jaworzno, higher up than Auschwitz.

The next day we returned to the morning and evening parades. We stood for hours on our feet, sometimes just because of a mistake in the numbers. Those who fell on parade fell and that was that. Didn't get up. A disgusting smell grew in the camp that increasingly consumed our minds and clogged up our asses.

At Jaworzno I worked in construction. Dangerous work. Because I was small. We helped build a factory for supplying electricity. The professionals were Germans.

We worked in excavation and construction. I was lowered in a basket into a six-meter-deep pit. I descended slowly into the darkness. I dug with a spade at the bottom of the pit. I sent the sand up in the basket. It was dark in there, suffocating. The earth was cold and my body full of water. I dug for about six hours straight. After a food break, another six hours, down in the pit. The Germans didn't reinforce the sides of the pit. Grains fell into my eyes all the time. I put my fingers in my eyes, it didn't help. I tried to wipe them with the striped pajamas, that was worse. I remembered that someone had died from an eye infection, but not only from that, he had other diseases. I tortured myself with thoughts of the coming collapse. I knew there was a big chance of a collapse. I knew that only the depth of the pits interested the Germans, I didn't count. I knew I could be replaced by a whole transport. It was clear that I could be buried alive in a heap and that the sand would cover me and get into my ears, nose and mouth, and that I'd have to breathe sand in through my nose until death. I dug as slowly as I could. For months. Other small prisoners like me were digging in the pits next to me. Many died in the sand that fell on them. Don't know how I stayed alive.

And then came winter.

All we had was the same striped clothing. No coat. No socks, vest or underwear. The frost was terrible. I couldn't feel my palms. The same for the soles of my feet, and it was only a matter of time before my fingers fell off. I was certain that tomorrow, the next week, following month, I'd find three fingers on each hand, or three toes on a foot, or I'd come out of the pit in the basket without a thumb. I dreamed of fire. One day, on the lunch-break, I found a few planks. In my pocket I had paper and matches. I went behind a wall, and I lit a fire.

The work manager came up to me.

The work manager was a young Pole of twenty-five. He had huge hands. He had a neck as thick as a bull. He stood the prisoners in a line, dragged me in front of them and ordered: Bend down. I bent down. Waited for a bullet in the head. The work manager took a large plank in both hands and struck me with the plank in the middle of my backside. *Thwack*. I felt I was falling to pieces. *Thwack*. Jew lights a little fire, warms his hands and the Pole, damn him, crushes. Yes. *Thwack*. I counted five blows. There was no flesh on me. I was skin and bone. I felt as if even my bones couldn't hold up under the skin. They were like nuts knocking about inside a towel. *Thwack thwack thwack thwack thwack*. I didn't open my mouth so my bones wouldn't spill out.

For a month I couldn't sit down. During breaks I stayed on my feet. Leaning first on my right leg and then on my left. At night I couldn't sleep. I lay on my belly and didn't know if my ass was open or leaking. I felt a tingling in my backside and was sure worms had got into the wound and were now eating me alive. Every few minutes I carefully felt the place around the wound. It was wet there. Then it was wet and smelled. Then it began to get hard there with a scab. Finally it was dry but really hurt. It hurt for two months.

The bombing of Jaworzno by the Russians almost killed us all. Noon. It was a food break. I was waiting in line for a bowl of hot soup.

I knew I had no chance of getting anything from the bottom of the pot because I was small. Every time I'd stay away from tall prisoners who approached me, an elbow ready. I already knew those elbows. They were like a snake. *Thwack*. And quiet. The guards saw nothing.

Suddenly a rising-falling siren. Bombs fell close to us. The distance of my house from the road. I ran zigzag to the bunker. A concrete structure dug deep underground. At the opening to the bunker were sacks of sand. Prisoners were stepping on one another because of the narrow opening. I fell on the prisoner in front of me. We both fell on the floor. His pants were wet. I managed to get by him and crawl into the bunker. Frightening darkness. I advanced along the ditch with small steps. Prisoners' shouts in the distance behind me grew fainter. And the whining of airplanes. A few minutes went by, and then a short siren. I knew, they were calling us to come out.

I wanted to get out quickly.

I couldn't see anything. I felt the walls and they were rough and cold. I dragged my feet, I felt as if I were walking through mud. I turned left, I passed another wall, a strange silence, I didn't understand where all the prisoners were, where they'd gone. My heart began to beat frantically, I went back, pressing my hands on the concrete wall and changed direction again. I walked on, straight I think, and couldn't find the way out. After a few steps I stood still. The same. Darkness, silent as a graveyard. I realized I was stuck alone in that shitty bunker. A hot needle pricked my ribs, entered the heart, dropped to the belly, settling in my backside. I felt my backside getting warm, swelling. My legs began to tremble. I grabbed the walls, shouting help, help me get out, I can't get out on my own, where are you, help.

I began to run through the ditches like a blind man with an open ass.

I held fast to my ass so my wound wouldn't open up anymore. I ran from side to side, to no avail. I hit walls, got a blow to the head, got up, continued running. My clothes were wet with sweat. My mind screamed, you're lost, lost, this will be your grave. You will crumble in the darkness, and no one will know. I stopped. My breaths sounded like a running herd, lost. I closed my mouth, pressed my nose. Stretched my neck. I heard the sound of sirens. Without people. I didn't understand what had changed. Had the bombs maybe killed the prisoners and guards and I was the only one left? No. I stuck to the wall. Slid down until I was sitting. My forehead was burning. I covered my face with the palms of my hands and waited to die.

I felt a tickling warmth in my fingers.

I opened my fingers a crack. A large blotch of light hit my brain. Right in front of me stood my mother. She had on a scarf and a dress with an apron. Mother smiled at me as if from out of a picture. I wept, Mama, Mama, I'm going to die. The weeping increased, I called louder, Mama, help me to get out, Mama. Mother smiled and then German voices disturbed us. Irritated voices that weren't far away from me.

The light disappeared. I jumped to my feet. I heard Germans running, shouting. And then I saw light. The way out was right in front of me. I hid my face under my arm and left the bunker. Prisoners were standing in two rows opposite the opening to the bunker. My place in the row was empty. I approached them with bent knees.

A Kapo thug fell on me.

A large, fat Kapo hit me in the face with his fists, kicked my leaking ass. I fell. I ate earth mixed with blood. The Kapo didn't stop. He kicked me in the belly, ribs, head and back. I lay there without moving. I stopped breathing. The Kapo stopped. Kicked me again in the pelvis, turned and walked off. The Kapo's kicks paralyzed the right side of my body. I got up slowly, couldn't straighten up. I saw through a mist of blood. I ran crookedly to my place in the line. Don't know how I survived. I was young, I was strong. Stronger than Hitler.

Chapter 9

Yitzhak

The transition from Camp Buchenwald to Camp Zeiss was difficult.

Winter. Rain. Lightning. Storms. When I was in Buchenwald in Bloc 8, I ate well. I slept in a bed with sheets, I showered, there was light at the window.

At Zeiss I lived the life of a rat. There was darkness and damp. I wrapped pipes with steel wire for twelve-hour shifts, at least three or four meters deep. Every day. I had no gloves. My hands were full of cracks. Every crack broad as a ditch. After a few weeks my skin was as hard as the sole of a shoe.

For the first few weeks I ran the distance from the camp to the factory. I still had strength in my body from Bloc 8. Then I stopped running. Barely managed to walk. Hard work didn't scare me, it was the hunger that was scary. In the morning they gave us hot water that tasted like coffee. At noon soup with bits in it I didn't know, but I still ate it. In the evening a piece of bread with cheese or margarine. That's it. I was sixteen and I could easily have finished off a calf for lunch, but I finished off a little water with a few tough bits from the top. I felt the hunger was devouring me from inside. My hunger was full of eyes like the angel of death. Sometimes when my body ached I could see it in the darkness of the factory.

At Zeiss there were aerial bombings, mainly when they were handing out water with tough bits.

We just got out of the earth and the planes came, *boom. Boom. Boom-boom*. They made a terrible noise. They poured down on us everything they carried in the belly and disappeared. The Germans made us go into a huge, open pit. In this way we lost even the little water with the few bits and ran to a pit full of pipes and steel. The guards entered after us. The bombs hit six-inch pipes. Pieces of steel flew up, circled above our heads and *boom* landed on the ground. Like an enormous cannon shooting spears. Steel pieces split open a prisoner's head next to me. He fell without a sound. Jets of blood mixed with mud and soot sprayed us black. The SSmen also got sprayed. I saw SSman collapse with a huge hole in his belly.

There was nowhere to run.

I contracted my body to the size of a pin and lowered my head as much as I could. I heard the terrible weeping of wounded prisoners.

There was no one to save them.

The planes threw more and more bombs at us. I saw my end coming. I refused to die with a piece of steel in my head. Beside me was a young prisoner, maybe twenty years old. His ears stuck out and there was a bulge in the middle of his nose. I shouted into his ear, I'm getting out of here, want to come?

We ran into the open field.

The field was colored white. My face burned from the cold and the wind. My nose dripped and dripped. I stuck a striped sleeve to my nose so it wouldn't fall. I beat on my legs. The earth was as hard as asphalt and I couldn't hear a sound, just waves coming and going in my ears. I was hungry. I got on my knees and scraped at a layer of ice. I prayed, maybe something was growing there, maybe. I dug with my hand. I found cabbage roots deep in the earth. The boy who came with me also got down on his knees. We began to dig like madmen. We found more roots. We collected a large pile. They were frozen. I began to shout, you want to kill us with hunger, but we will live, we will live.

I wiped my face. We found a tin. The boy had matches in his pocket. We looked at each other and together pulled down our trousers. Peed into the tin. We put the roots inside and warmed them with matches from below. We ate roots in hot urine. We ate the entire pile. It tasted as good as Mother's food. I felt full and whispered thank you to the sky. It was black, evil. The planes disappeared. My eyelids were heavy. I wanted to sleep standing up. As if I was resting in my village after a meal. As if I was fixing something in the yard and in a minute I'd be going inside. I see my family. Father Israel would talk about the market, about a rather good deal. Mother would ask, did you bring my buttons? And she'd take a heavy pot from the fire. Avrum would want to know a little more about the business. Sarah would be writing in her book. Dov would help Mother with the dishes, and I? I don't remember anything about me. As if there were no war in the world and no trains to the crematorium, as if the world were alive without Hitler.

After a while we went back to wrapping pipes in the ground.

The next morning began with bad signs. A prisoner two bunks from me ran to the fence and *tzzzzt*, finished.

Burned in a second. Looked like a striped shirt that fell off the washing line, it all happened even before we stood in line, even before the dawn. I took a good look at the dead man and then two prisoners next to me left us and ran to the same place. Together, the two of them, like a couple, one tall, one with a bent back, they both ran fast and *tzzzzt tzzzzt*. As if they'd fallen off the washing line. I couldn't separate myself from the little heap of the dead. I'd also had enough, but then the scream of the SSman reached my ears, stand in a row, quickly, forward march. We filed off. Men as thin and dirty as stained paper. Paper connected to shoes dragging along the asphalt.

I was almost last and didn't move on the asphalt. SSman gave me a blow on my back with the butt of a rifle. *Thwack*. I shut my mouth and he screamed into my ear, forward, in line, dirty Jew.

Walk, quickly. Quickly, *thwack*. Another one, on the pelvis. I paid no attention, let him hit me, kill me, didn't matter. I already knew that soon they'd take all of us to die in the crematorium. We all knew the method at Zeiss. The method: No food, no water, no place to breathe, no shower, no coat, no medication, just work, work fast, until death comes. It takes about three months to come. In the meantime, they bring a fresh, healthy consignment and the old-timers get on a train to the nearest available crematorium. Yes. Three months was enough for the Germans to turn healthy young men into a pile of disgusting rags. Rags should be burned, I thought.

Tomorrow I'm on the fence. Yes, tomorrow. Another moonless night, enough. Was there a moon?

The thought of the fence gave me some strength. Maybe the three gave me the strength to think about the fence. I strode forward and made up the space in the file. And, oops, I unintentionally stepped on the shoe of the prisoner in front of me. He made a cheeping sound and fell. SSman approached us. I grabbed the prisoner's shirt and pulled him up. He pushed with his hands and rose. I saw he was missing a finger and a half on his right hand. He rocked, rocked, stood. I passed him and began to walk with great strides, like the beginning, when I had the strength of Bloc 8. I passed at least eight prisoners and got back in line.

The first morning light began to cover the fields. We approached a German village. Regular houses with chimneys. A low fence and a yard. A few trees, more flowers, and thin ice on the water, but mainly cold that could bury you standing up. Heavy clouds stood on the roofs of distant houses. Mingled with normal smoke, white smoke, a little gray. I knew German farmers were warm in their houses with their stove and chimney, and their woolen socks.

I jeered at them because of the fence I was planning on, *tzzzzt*. And that was that. Silver drops spread over the grass at the side of the road. A rotting bird lay with its feet in the air. Tomorrow I'll be dead. Yes, tomorrow.

Two figures stood by the side of the road just as the morning sun pushed a cloud. One was tall. The other shorter. I remember women's scarves. The tall one wore a dress. The little one wore trousers. As we approached I saw a woman and a girl looking at us. Holding hands. What do the two of them want, what. Want a show, about wretched people, people who weep without tears, well, here we are. Until that morning I'd barely seen any people, I barely remembered there were any in the world. I knew they were hiding in their houses, I knew. I sensed their glances from behind a curtain, behind a sheet on the line. The children were as far away as possible, maybe they hid them under a bed, so their sweet children would sleep well at night. If I had a mirror to see myself, I knew I'd scream with shock. I didn't need a mirror, I looked at other prisoners. I understood the village people. By chance the road near the village led to Zeiss. Twice a day a huge file of wretched, stinking, disintegrating people passed by.

The two women at the side of the road looked only at me.

They looked like mother and daughter. The little girl wanted to stick her head in my face. She pointed at me. Whispered in her mother's ear. The mother nodded, yes, yes. The mother turned to a tall, particularly good-looking SSman. The SSman signaled, halt! We halted. Everyone's heads were looking down. The mother spoke in SSman's ear. She whispered in German and pointed at me. The SSman agreed and she gave him a package.

The SSman approached me.

The SSman gave me a package. Ordered: Open it. The whole line was on top of me. My whole body shivered, my hands trembled, I didn't understand what they all wanted from me, why especially me. I wanted one of the adults to tell me what I should do now and if it was all right to open the package. The adults were breathing heavily with faces like a predatory animal about to jump. Slowly I opened the paper. There was a cooked potato inside. Hot. SSman signaled to me: Eat. I swallowed the potato in a flash. The mother and daughter went towards the village.

The SSman called, march. March.

I strode, fell. Got up. From excitement. My legs tripped over each other. In my head there was a flood. What was this, what.

The prisoners almost killed me with their eyes, and he? He said eat, and didn't move away from me. I felt I was going mad, that's it. I was pulling off the stripes on the pajamas, the tracks of the trains and life. In the meantime, I scraped my nail against my tongue and found a few crumbs. My belly started making strange sounds, I didn't know what to do with myself, and why are they confusing me with good deeds.

That night I felt so good and full I couldn't sleep.

It drove me mad, all that goodness. My heart understood that maybe the little girl saw something the Germans didn't have time to see. Maybe she saw that I was also a child, that all the men had black bristles on their cheeks and I didn't. I'd pass my hand over my face, and it was smooth. And maybe she thought they were big and I was little.

Those two stuck in my mind like a silent movie. I saw them waiting in the distance, I approach, closer, closer, the two are looking at me, looking, looking, looking, and *hop*, I have a package in my hands. I eat. And back again. Closer, closer, closer, they give me a package, and *hop*, I'm eating, and eating, and eating. I couldn't stop crying. I missed Mother. I missed Father. I missed my brothers and sister. Particularly Dov. I wanted to tell him what had happened to me. I wanted to give him half my potato. I barely slept that night.

Morning. I'm the first outside.

From the corner of my eye I see someone running towards the fence. I know him. He slept in my bunk. His brother had watched him for two days. I saw his brother running after him. Talking. I even heard, Nathan, stop, stop, Nathan. Wait. What are you doing, *stop*. Caught hold of his garment. Wanted to pull him away from the electricity in the fence. Nathan was the first to fall on the fence. His brother who tried to fall back was caught in the fence and was finished. He didn't really want to die.

In a second, I turned my back on the fence. Didn't want to see, not that morning. I wanted to go out to work, quickly.

Wanted to get to the road in front of the village. Maybe, maybe, again, and maybe not.

Pains started in my belly. I remember as if it was happening now. Pains started in my pelvis, my head. I wanted to run. The file progressed slowly, slowly. A cold wind cut into the flesh. A prisoner with a swollen foot halted. His body rocked in the wind. He slightly widened his bent knees, stuck his heels into the road. Prisoners behind him halted, waiting for him without moving. SSman picked up a stone and threw it at him. It hit him on the leg. The prisoner sighed and continued to walk. The gap remained. We passed a bend in the road, another one, the village was in front of us, aaah. The two were standing there. The tall one and the little one. The little one in a fire-red coat. They stood there, like yesterday. Aligned with a water tower on which hung a rope ladder.

It took all my strength not to step out of the line, not to make any sign. I made an effort to walk slowly like everyone else but inside, my body was jumping, *bloomp, bloomp*. As I approach them my heart beats like a sledge-hammer. I cough. Want to scratch myself and don't move my hand. Another small step and the little girl points at me. Aaah. We stop. I hear myself crying like a baby, Mama, Mama. Aaah. The mother approaches the SSman from yesterday, smiles at him. He responds with a smile. She speaks to him in German. She says, the girl wants to give, ja. She speaks long and fast. I understand a bit. I understand she's a widow, the wife of Officer Michael Schroder, yes. She was alone, waiting for the train to the city, ja. The SSman pinches the little girl's cheek; the little girl wipes her cheek afterwards. The mother and the SSman laugh, ja. Ja. Ja. Mother gives SSman a package. SSman approaches me. God, God, God. SSman signals to me, open it. I glance at the prisoners. They have huge eyes and ears and they have a large mouth, a black mouth. Four prisoners close in on me. I am paralyzed. SSman raises his rifle. SSman signals the prisoners, back off, immediately. Prisoners take a step back. I hear them breathing fast. I feel as if my hands are on fire. I open the package and can't believe my eyes. I am holding a sausage sandwich. A whole sandwich with sausage, for me. Two thick pieces of bread, and a fat slice of sausage. Two prisoners jump at me. They have yellow saliva on the chin. SSman fires a single bullet into the air. They halt. I swallow the sandwich all at once and feel as if there is a bone stuck in my throat, I swallow saliva, more saliva, and more, and the sandwich goes down slowly, slowly, hurting my esophagus. I am overjoyed. SSman shouts, march, march.

I stride on, my head turning backwards.

She has blue eyes that are looking at me. She has two light braids. One shorter. Her face is full of brown freckles and she smiles at me, and blushes. It took all I had to hold back a scream. Queen, my queen, beautiful queen. I pinch my leg, my ear too. I have a sharp prickling in my ear. Impossible, I'm dreaming. I'm asleep in the barracks and there's a movie in my mind. I bite my tongue, it's hot and it hurts. Another bite and I see the SSman bowing to the two. They nod and say thank you. Mother winks at the SSman. She comes to stand with the girl who has no scarf on her head. Her long hair swells like a gold ball. The SSman laughs, his cheeks reddening. The blue in his eyes glitters.

The file progresses. The wind increases, the cold even more. The trees bend to one side, the prisoners pull their shirts over their ears, it doesn't help. I glance back. The distance between me and the red coat increases. The prisoner behind me hits me with a sharp elbow. He is tall. I am small. Don't care. I want to call out to the girl, wave to her, throw my hat off, kick an imaginary, explosive goal between posts, doesn't matter what posts, even the gate posts of the camp, I want to call to the sun to chase off the wind and clouds and warm the girl's path to the house, I want to find a field of flowers, make her a huge bunch of flowers, want to run hand in hand with her through the fields, her braids flying from side to side, one shorter, one longer, find a white horse in the meadow, toss her up on the horse, sit behind her, hold her hips, reach the forest, scream, gallop, horse, gallop, laugh wildly, I'm alive, I'm alive, Mama, where am I, Mamaaa.

The Kapo's screams made me jump. Two days had gone by and it was morning. The Kapo screams, get up, get up, outside, get in line. I don't get up. Stay with the picture from the dream. I am kicked to my feet. And c-c-c-cold, so cold.

On the path, near the village, there she was again. A girl with braids, her mother beside her. I choked. The little girl pointed to me. Mother approached the regular SSman. They smile and play in German. SSman bends to hear the mother more clearly. The mother catches him by the arm, turns towards the village and shows him a house. He doesn't see well. She gives him a package, he says, a moment please, gives me the package and walks off with the mother to see better. The girl looks at the mother and the SSman. Eight prisoners jump on me. I hold tightly to the package and feel fingers sticking in my ears, nose, neck, belly, I can't see a thing, and then came the burst of fire, *Ra-ta-ta-ta-ta*. Am I dead? No, I was completely alive. In front of me stood SSman with a rifle in his hands and beside me, smeared on the asphalt were three prisoners in pools of blood. I looked down at myself and saw that I was alive. Looked at them – and they were dead.

I got up with the package in my hands. The tall SSman approached at a run, the mother after him. The SSman shooter pointed at us irritably. That is, at me and the newly dead. The SSman shooter walked away shouting, kicking at nothing. The regular SSman glared at me with an evil face. The girl came up, and he immediately signaled to her to halt. He was ashamed in front of the mother. As if saying to her, what can I do, they're animals. Then he said to me, eat now. Eat. He had a low and hateful voice. And I didn't want the mother to agree to marry him. I was mainly worried about the girl with the braids.

Inside the damp paper was a cooked carrot. I swallowed it, heard march. March.

They waited for me with food every day or two until the first snows fell. I ate sandwiches, cooked vegetables, fruit, and cake, sometimes they gave me an uncooked potato. I'd hide it in my pocket and wait for the moment they'd send me to fix things for the work manager. I had a tin box there. I would pour steam on the gas and cook a potato for myself. For long weeks they waited for me, the mother and the girl, and there was also the regular SSman who laughed with the mother. He didn't kill me in the evenings at the camp. He didn't throw me into another group. The regular SSman guarded me from other prisoners with the rifle and it turned out that a German girl saved my life.

I didn't stop thinking about her for many years. I wanted to meet her after the war. I wanted to pull stars down from the sky for her. Make her a queen. I wanted, wanted. But I didn't ask her name. I didn't know that one day, one more day, I'd walk through the snow and no one would be standing there.

Three months went by. We were willing to die in the gas, body and soul.

* * *

Israel, 2001

7:35 at the Beit Yehoshua Train Station.

The muzzle of a rifle aimed at me. Yes, aimed at the pelvis. The rifle of a sergeant in the armored corps, by the color and design of the cap on the shoulder. The sergeant's face is sunburned and he sleeps with his back to a pole, a distance of about four to five meters from me. He looks like coffee on the stove. I miss hot chocolate. Sunburn fattens his lips, a broad jaw, impressive, looks like Kirk Douglas without the dimple in his chin. His hair is cut short, short, and the rifle is pointing straight at me, the magazine inside, ugh. I don't have the energy for a rifle so early in the morning. Because of the rifles in the morning news I want to change my newspaper. I'm tired of reading it with the first coffee.

No rain, just the smell and fat clouds that hadn't thinned for an hour. The eucalyptus trees stand tall as if on parade.

I take a small step back.

My ass is cold and I'm on my way to Nahariya. Yitzhak would say, what are you worried about, people have to walk around today with a rifle, hard times in Israel, and he'd laugh, say he was sorry, and get up to make a call about work. Dov would say, trust the soldier, he knows what a rifle is, he's had training, he can sleep with an automatic in his hand, don't worry and, in the meantime, why didn't you go in for a drink. A small espresso?

If he'd asked, I'd have said, there isn't even a kiosk, and I can't stop worrying, each day and its own tragedy, and Dov would jump up, not even a tiny kiosk? No, Dov. Yitzhak would say, Beit Yehoshua isn't important, come and see ours in Nahariya. There we've an organized buffet with wafer cookies and juice and sandwiches freshly prepared by the woman every morning, yes. But Yitzhak, how come you know what a train buffet has, you don't travel by train.

If Yitzhak had heard Dov he'd scratch his neck and say, right. Can't bear ramps, can't bear them.

Ramps are a bad place for Jews.

A fast train cuts the wind in the opposite direction. A brief *whoosh*, and it's gone. On the opposite platform is a young man in a good suit with a laptop on his knees. His eyes are alerted by a young woman who appears to be successful, judging by her jacket, small mini, nylon stockings and high heels. A cute woman. She notices him, straightens up, sticks out. He stares at her and immediately returns to his computer. Idiot. The cute woman with the mini drops her purse, waits. The laptop closes. The young man gets up, bends down to pick it up and points to the bench. They both sit down. He's silent. She thinks. He opens the laptop and explains something to her. She has no patience. She pulls a mobile phone out of her bag and taps in a number. He blushes. A female soldier arrives with her rifle and stands to one side. Glances at the computer. She has a question. He's glad. The soldier peers at the computer, and he explains. The cute woman with the mini closes her phone, glances briefly at the soldier, crosses her legs with an expansive gesture, and then the laptop falls. The young man jumps first and then the soldier. They pick up the computer together, not noticing how pretty the cute woman is when she's smiling into nowhere.

The train enters the station opposite and the sunburned soldier's rifle muzzle is still pointing at people in the station. I get up quickly, straighten dark glasses and check the clock. Eight. Where is the train to Nahariya, why should I wait for the sergeant to come in my direction. I just hope he doesn't fire by mistake like the report in this morning's newspaper. No reason. Someone was walking along and unintentionally shot someone else.

The train crawled into the station. Everyone pushes forward, I'm dragged forward and smell a sharp after-shave mixed with sweat. His gun presses into my arm, I feel its pressure against my coat. I move my arm, trying to push the gun away, but people are pushing from behind. He sticks to me like Velcro. The door to the carriage is closed. That's it, I can no longer bear the press. I pull back forcibly, and the sergeant is pressed to a young girl who was standing beside me in a sheep wool coat, and the rifle disappears in the wool.

The door to the carriage opens with a sigh and I wait for people to enter before me. Enter last. The seats are taken. I quickly pass through a second carriage, a third, fourth, fifth, stop. An elderly man snores, beside him is an empty seat. About to sit down, I notice a revolver stuck in the belt under his gray battledress.

Lady, sit down.

Lady, sit down please. Nu, sit down. Tickets please.

Don't want to sit down. A state like a weapon depot. Yitzhak would say, better that way, if I'd had a rifle during the war, I'd have killed a few Germans, and maybe I'd have killed myself. Dov would say, you don't know what it's like being small in a camp of adults. I wish I'd had a gun, I wish I had.

Chapter 10

Yitzhak

At Camp Zeiss they prepared us for death by gas. Three months of hard labor. In the middle, snow fell and everything was covered in white. The girl and the mother no longer stood anywhere. I'd walk to the factory feeling as if I was sinking into bottomless mud. My skin itched and bled and I had sores on my legs. The sores stuck to the shoe didn't hurt. My mind was empty. I was like an automaton. They said walk, I walked. They said stop. I stopped. They said ten minutes for your needs, I sat over the hole and nothing came out. I felt my body was as thin as dirty glass. I looked at other prisoners and knew how I looked. Yellow and thin like a disease, the mouth falling inward, the chin without flesh. Everyone's pajamas were all a uniform color, mustard brown like baby's poop. We were on the ramp, waiting to be replaced, standing crowded in the fresh snow. We waited for the train to Auschwitz.

There were rumors of a change. The dogs of the SSmen barked halfheartedly. The SSmen irritably tapped their boots on the snow. For hours we stood on our feet and there was no pity and no chariots of angels.

A cattle train with large lights and a face like a hyena slowly,

slowly approached us, I heard wheezing and whistles like suffering, *choo. Choo. Choo. Choo-oo.* I remember thinking, the train doesn't have any strength either. Prisoners saw the train and slowly began to move back, slowly, like a dark oily stain that doesn't spread out. A prisoner near me began to tremble where he stood, said, the Germans have gone mad, they don't know what to do with the stuff for the fire. Another prisoner with one eye closed, said, who knows if the train can take the whole ramp to Auschwitz. I knew that the fresh transport had already taken over our barracks, and I said, don't worry, they don't lack a thing, trains either, damn them.

Prisoners began to call out to God, to Mama, Papa, three fainted together, *hop, hop, hop*, they fell like dominoes. After them, two more intentionally fell to the floor. I heard whimpers, don't want to die, don't want to go to the cattle car, Mamaaa, Mamaaa. Rifle blows brought us quiet. Some tried to escape, jumping from the ramp, skipping over the track, running in a zigzag, I heard shouts, and a series of shots then silence and immediately God. Oy-vey God. God save us, save us, and *Shema Israel*, and weeping like a stormy sea, *hummm hummm*. And curses, a lot of curses in German.

The car door opened with a loud boom. I couldn't climb up. Prisoners pushed me from behind. The Germans' blows helped us advance, fast, fast. Prisoners grabbed one another's clothing, grabbed the door, rifle butts beating their fingers, I heard terrible weeping, don't want to, leave me alone, don't want to, I fell on the floor of the car. I barely managed to crawl to the wall and stand up. The eyelids of a nearby prisoner were trembling, his head fell forward, dragging his shoulders, and he vanished. At the door they continued to force people in. I felt a trembling below. The door to the car slammed shut. The train didn't move.

I couldn't breathe. A large broad prisoner stood with his back to me. I saw his hand going into the pocket of another prisoner. He waited a moment, removed his hand, put it in his mouth. Swallowed potato peels. Then he pulled down the prisoner's trousers, grabbed his ass, and rubbed and rubbed, rubbed, more and more. The prisoner in front of him didn't move. I wanted to die.

We stood shut up in the car for maybe two hours. The train didn't move. It was suffocating. People were screaming. Vomiting. Shitting in their pants. I heard the whine of airplanes above us. Planes dropped bombs and disappeared. I prayed that a bomb would reach the roof of my car, and that would be that. I prayed for machine gun bullets right to the middle of my face. Leave this life of garbage with one blow, but it didn't happen.

The door to the car opened. The loudspeaker called, get down. Fast. Get down. Fast. We saw that the track to Auschwitz had been broken in the bombing and I realized we weren't going to Auschwitz. We stood on the ramp for an hour or two. We stood stuck together, shivering. We breathed the stink that passed from mouth to mouth. We didn't warm up. Snow fell as if they hadn't bombed the place. I was sure my teeth were breaking in my mouth, I felt with my tongue, didn't find any spaces. Meanwhile the Germans were running about, shouting, and I was afraid, maybe they'd take us to Auschwitz in motor cars, and maybe they'd take us on foot to some forest and we'd have to dig a deep pit with plenty of space for this whole ramp.

Finally they put us on a side train with open cars. I realized that the Germans were looking for an alternative crematorium. We were good for nothing but gas and burning.

The ice consumed us in the open car, sticking us to the floor.

We lay on one another like a pile of wet rags. The clothes I was wearing disintegrated at the seams. The shoes too. I pulled some string out of my pocket and tied the sole to my foot, even though I knew the shoe wouldn't fall off because it was stuck to my foot by the scabs of my sores. Snow fell and fell, mixing with snot, vomit, and blood, it was colorful and shiny, like decorations in the sukkah our neighbor made every year for her and her husband because the children had gone to America and they were left alone and wretched. Those neighbors from the farm had also been on the ramp for a long time, also on the floor of the cars, yes, yes.

We traveled from Zeiss as if in a clean, white sheet, it was only disgusting and stank inside.

The train slowly slowly entered Schwandorf.

Again came the whining of planes and boom, a bombing. The Germans jumped down to find shelter. Some of the prisoners jumped after them, me among them. We rushed about like hungry mice in a burning house. We looked for food. We ran from door to door. Building to building. We didn't find anything. We came to the window of a rather dark cellar the size of a largish room. The cellar floor was filled with closed suitcases. The window was narrow and barred. I stood next to the window with a group as finished as I was, but of all of them I was the smallest and thinnest. Prisoners standing next to me looked at me. At the suitcases. At me. At the suitcases. I understood. I was most afraid of death by gas, least afraid of dying from bullets or bombs. I grasped the bars and put my leg inside. Slid my body in. Passed in my other leg and hung in the air. One two, boom, I jumped. I landed on a full, brown suitcase. I opened it quickly. Shook out clothes, threw aside silver dishes, books, pictures, dolls, sweaters, glasses, slippers, shoe-laces, toiletries, didn't find any food. I opened another suitcase. Looked in coat pockets, dug into the sides, found nothing. Tossed everything out of a third suitcase. Fourth. Fifth. The prisoners guarded me from above. Didn't make a sound. I turned out tens of suitcases, nothing.

I wanted to get out.

The distance from the cellar floor to the window looked scary. A prisoner above called to me, put one suitcase on another and climb up. The prisoner's voice was like my father's. The voice of someone who knows things. I threw clothes into several suitcases, shut them quickly and stood one on top the other like a tower. I climbed up onto the pile. The suitcases sank under my feet. I fell down. The prisoner yelled to me, the bombing is over, hurry, hurry. I felt a dryness in my throat. I felt my legs melting like butter in the sun. I looked for solid objects among the belongings. I shoved books and silver objects on top of the clothes. I made a taller pile. Climbed up carefully. My body rocked, my legs trembled, I straightened up very slowly, raised my head. I heard my father's voice, Yitzhak, jump, jump. Thin pale hands slid in through the bars. Skinny fingers signaled to me to come, to jump. Slowly, slowly, I raised my hands. I was far from them. The prisoner called in alarm, jump, jump. I jumped. Fell to the floor.

The sharp siren of a train paralyzed my entire body. I wanted to get up. My body was as heavy as a sack of flour. I knew, if I couldn't get up, I'd die like a miserable rat in that cellar. I raised my head and screamed to the prisoners above me, I can't die here like this, *noooo*! Help me to get out, I have to get out of here. The prisoners above knocked on the bars. I saw white fingers pressing on the bars. I leaned against a suitcase and pulled myself up. The cellar door was in front of me at the top of stairs. I ran to the door and pressed the handle. Locked. I'd forgotten, we'd tried to open it from above. I banged on my head like a madman, shouted, Yitzhak, think, think, otherwise you'll rot here among the suitcases of the dead. Father's voice called to me: Go back to the suitcases. Try, quickly, SSman coming. I'm waiting for you.

I felt stronger.

I took a deep breath. Wiped my wet hands on my shirt. Looked for the largest suitcases in the pile. Stood one on top of the other in a straight line. Climbed carefully, slowly straightening up, slowly. I barely moved. From above I heard, Yitzhak, jump, jump. I bent my knees slightly. Gathered momentum and jumped in the direction of the bars. Two hands held me fast, God, where did he get the strength, I heard Father's voice breathing heavily from above, hold fast, hold, I'm pulling you out, hold, several more hands grasped me, and pulled, and pulled, I pushed my feet against the wall, I felt my arms were ripping from my body, my head fell back and I didn't have a chance.

The prisoners didn't let go. I reached the bars, got out and heard another siren and heavy wheezing from the direction of the train engine. SSman with a rifle approached the window and found nothing. The prisoners dispersed like hay in the wind.

I ran to the nearest car.

I managed to climb up. The open train left the station as the snow stopped falling. A cold wind whistled in my ears, I was hot. I gathered a fistful of snow from the floor and wiped my face. Until Buchenwald I vomited stomach juices. Until Buchenwald my knees shook and I heard my father's voice, Yitzhak, jump. During all the days in the camps I'd hear, Yitzhak, jump. To this day I still hear it in my ears, Yitzhak, jump, jump.

Chapter 11

Dov: Many people wanted me to tell them
what happened but I didn't want to.
I only want to tell good things.
No one will believe the bad things
I went through; no one will believe me
because it isn't normal.
Itzhak: I don't even want to remember.

Dov

The hunger at Camp Jaworzno ate me up from inside. I felt the end coming.

The food they gave us didn't help. In the morning we were given coffee and nothing else. At noon, soup with worms. In the evening, a piece of bread, with a bit of margarine or cheese. That's it. I felt like a creased sack with all the air punched out of it, *pachchch*. I saw prisoners scratching the wall and eating filth. I saw people eating dust. They opened and closed their mouths as if they were chewing something. I did the same and thick saliva began to leak, like snot. One prisoner ran to the end of the bloc, stuck to the door and began to devour the wood. A blow to his head saved the door.

There were prisoners who didn't get up for morning parade. They were gone before evening. There were prisoners who jumped on the fence. Some laid their bodies on the fence as if it were a bed, their faces to the stars. There were those who tied a rope around their necks and hanged themselves like clean washing from a beam. Not one prisoner in the bloc attempted to stop them. I didn't know where they got the strength to commit suicide. I continued to stand on parade because I couldn't think of another plan. I was a boy. I was a head shorter than most of the prisoners. I had sores on my hands, knee, and neck. The bones of my ass hurt, the lice were relentless, settled in a red mark full of scratches, and I continued to walk in the convoys.

One day we were standing in line before darkness fell. I was the last in the line to go back to the camp. A white sun disappeared behind clouds with swollen bumps like pointed stones in cotton wool. It was cold and stinking. Everyone dragged their feet from the trenches to the convoy. They left blurred, crooked tracks under their feet. Their shoulders slumped forward, almost falling apart at the arms. Everyone was silent, their faces on the ground. We'd barely started out in the direction of the camp when three were left on the road. Those who were leaking from behind were finished off first.

My back hurt, mostly in the hollow of the hip and behind the thigh. I felt a thick bulge in the thigh and a muscle pulling down to the ankle. I stamped my foot on the ground. The pain didn't go away. I felt my stomach dehydrating, disappearing. I was certain, in the end my stomach would come out of my ass. I don't know what reminded me of my friend Vassily. I felt the urge to say aloud, Vassily, Vassily. I opened my mouth wide, let the air out, and no voice came out. And then I felt the urge to laugh. I stretched my lips sideways, laughed in my mind, a sour smell came out of my mouth. I was certain, this is it, this is how people go mad.

The distance between me and the prisoner in front lengthened. I wanted to close the distance, I bent forward, dragging myself, I was like a log stuck in the ground. I could barely take a step, another step, and another. I felt as if my legs were separating from me and walking on by themselves.

Raising my head, I saw a bent old woman.

She came out of the forest in the direction of the convoy. She had a purple kerchief on her head, a black dress and a small basket in her hand. I didn't understand where'd she'd come from. I approached her. She looked in my direction and craned her neck as if waiting for an opportunity. I saw she had one very large nostril and the other was small. An ugly scar ran down from the edge of her nose, raising one nostril and part of the upper lip. She looked as if she was smiling crookedly even when she was sad.

The distance between me and the prisoner in front of me grew by at least ten steps, and I reached her. She gave me a piercing look as if to say, stay with me, stay. She took a package from her basket, lifted her arm and *hop*, she threw it. I was sure she was throwing a stone at me. I bent down, and managed to catch the package. She gestured to me to eat, turned round and vanished into the forest.

I felt as if my heart was falling into my stomach.

The nearest SSman was about twenty meters from me and I prayed he wouldn't turn round and rage at me. I hid the package in my shirt and began to run in my mind. Somehow I managed to catch up.

I put a hand inside my shirt and felt the paper. It was oily and rough. Carefully I opened it. A sharp smell of sausage tickled my nose. I thrust my trembling fingers inside the paper, bread. God, under my shirt I have two thick slices of bread and a slice of sausage. My entire body trembled. My knees buckled, I shouted in my heart, don't fall, walk carefully and look for birds in the sky. I pursed my lips, tried to whistle but only something faint came out, *fff. Fff. Fff. Ffff.* Meanwhile, it got darker. I put my hand under my shirt and tore off a bit of the sandwich. I swallowed it without chewing. Another bit, and another. I only chewed the last bit slowly, slowly. I was so sorry the sandwich was finished. I licked my fingers, looked for crumbs in the paper, I wanted to take a bite of the paper because of the smell. I licked the paper from top to bottom then, *hop*, swallowed it as well.

I felt good.

My stomach immediately became alert. There were sounds like hiccups with a closed mouth. I almost started to laugh because of those sounds but I didn't want trouble from my neighbor, so I increased my stride and patted my belly. I felt like shitting. Put a hand on my ass and pressed hard.

From that day on I tried to come back last in line. I looked for the woman with the basket. I didn't see her again. That sandwich gave me strength. A little. I often think about the old woman. A woman throws away a sandwich once and I remember her for the rest of my life.

Israel, 2001

14:26 stopping at Acre. I'm on the train from Nahariya to Binyamina.

I dig around in my bag and find a chocolate bar in a crumpled wrapper. Three squares of chocolate restore me to life. Four squares. I lean my head against the window of the train and see that according to the headlines on the first page of the newspaper, any hope for a bit of quiet is at risk.

If we were sitting in Dov's living room, he'd say, what will be with us, will we always be afraid? Then Yitzhak would tug at his nose and say, that's how it is with Jews, even if we do have a state and our children have a father and a mother, and our grandchildren have a grandmother and a grandfather, we're not in a normal situation. And then Dov would say, I'd never have believed we'd ever be in such a situation, what will be? Yitzhak would put up a hand and push his chin towards the ceiling, without knowing what would be. This is why we'd stay silent without coffee and sandwiches and cocoa cookies. We'd just sit there, and then Dov would grab the TV remote and turn on Channel Two, yawn at the talk, on Channel One, they're arguing, only on National Geographic would he calm down and say, see how simple it is with animals. They don't just kill, they kill to live.

I wouldn't leave the armchair opposite Dov and Yitzhak, I'd look directly at them, and Dov would say, I see you're not in a good mood, can't have that, and then he'd pull a bottle of Slivovitz out of his sideboard so that every few minutes he could make a toast. After the third or fourth glass I'd feel a pleasant warmth in my feet and say, wait, slow down, I'm dizzy.

But Yitzhak would hurry to ask for a fifth and sixth round of toasts, so we'd never get thirsty, and Dov would say, to the State of Israel.

Instead of dessert, we'd drink strong coffee with cookies, and I wouldn't open my notebook or the tape because in some situations there's no strength for other people's troubles.

Maybe, I'd say, sometimes we have to drop everything and just look at each other and smile with our eyes like a good hug and that's enough.

Chapter 12

Dov

For three months they dragged us along on foot.

I think it was the end of 1944 or, by the height of the snow at the side of the road, the beginning of 1945. I left Jaworzno after six months labor underground, where they lowered me in a basket to dig with my hands and put the soil in the basket. The Germans removed us from Jaworzno because a good transport had arrived and we were no longer useful for work. We walked, just walked. We were like match sticks walking and breaking in the middle. Don't know why they took us on foot. Maybe because they couldn't find an available crematorium. At Auschwitz the crematorium had already been dismantled. They cleaned the pits, filling them with the ash of Jews and they prepared grass so their eyes would fill with the color green. Other crematoriums were working and there was no room for more prisoners. They said there were long lines and people waited on the side for a long time, even days, just to get in. There were a few thousands of us and, in the meantime, they walked us around in the snow so we'd die on our own because there was chaos at the end of the war and we were like surplus that had no room.

We left Camp Jaworzno early in the morning. Black clouds were falling from above onto the barracks. A wind that stung like a razor blade traveled across our faces, as if looking for something conspicuous to cut. We left, several thousand silent men. When the first arrived at the forest, the last was just leaving the camp gate. With us were SSmen and dogs. Don't remember how many, I think there were quite a lot. We wore the striped *häftling* – prisoner clothing, a striped hat, with a folded blanket on our backs. No coat. The shoes were torn – a worn wooden sole with bits of plastic on top. Jewish men wore a sign on the chest. A small Magen David with *Jude* written on it. We walked about the distance from Tel Aviv to Eilat and back, but we didn't know where we were. Sometimes they put us on a train. A closed cattle train, or an open train. Without seats. Among us were Polish prisoners. Some tried to run away when we reached Poland. The Germans ran after them with rifles and whistles like a hunt. I heard shots, heard cursing and firing, but we didn't stop walking.

On the first days we walked without stopping.

People fell like flies. And then, *boom*. They got a bullet. *Boom-boom*. Splayed on the road with their bones sticking out. The bullets didn't kill. Only sometimes, if they were lucky. I heard the screams of the wounded day and night. Every minute. The sound of shrieking and sobbing settled in my ears, didn't leave. Even today I have sounds in my ears. We went to sleep, got up, and the sound remained. The words were the same, oy, Mamaleh, oy, Papa, Grandpa, Grandma. Sometimes they said names, oy my Elizabeta, oy Ilona'leh, oy Yuda'leh, Yudah'leh. I tried to walk at the side of the road, closest to the field. I didn't want to walk beside tall prisoners who would dig their elbows into me, I'd have shattered like glass. Especially when they handed out bread every two or three days. I always sat on the side. We saw no water.

We weren't thirsty when it snowed. We sucked snow. When it rained, we walked with mouths open to the rain, the neck hurt. I don't remember secretions. At night we slept in prison camps along the way, don't know the names. In the morning the prisoners left the camp with us and their SSmen and the dogs. Sometimes we slept in the snow, the forest, or at the side of the road, or in the blanket we carried on our backs. The blanket was wet, dirty. I was afraid of catching some brain sickness that would give me worms. Not all the time, but they did sometimes come for a visit and then disappear.

The tall ones also behaved as if they had a visit from worms. Prisoners peeled the bark from trees and put it in their mouths, scratched a frozen plank with their nails and licked, ate a piece of their trousers, a piece of a sleeve. One prisoner began to eat himself. He bit his arm, ripped the skin, and chewed and chewed. He had blood on his chin. At the second bite he got a bullet. The dogs in the convoy were given an order, and *hop*, they were all on top of him. The dogs pushed, whined, tore at one another because the prisoner was small and thin, not enough for all of them. The SSmen approached the dogs, signaling with their fingers. I understood the signs, they were betting on the dogs. Like the goys in my village who would bet on a winning race-horse. The noise of the dogs is stuck in my ears to this day.

Our SSmen ate well. By the length of time they sat, the tins they opened, the paper packages they threw away, they ate well.

We received bread and nothing else. Beside me walked two young, rather good-looking prisoners. At night I saw them going to the SSmen. In the morning they returned with red cheeks and socks. Their pockets were bulging. The tallest prisoners didn't come near them. The tallest prisoners only dug their elbows into the small ones with pale cheeks, like me.

Boom. Boom. Boom-boom. Piles of thin stripes without spaces but with excrement smeared on the road. We were a long convoy like the dense carriages of a hundred trains, a thousand trains, a million trains, and a hundred million screams of prisoners about to die. The noise in my ears came back, *bvoooom Bvoooom.* Rosy'leh, Meide'leh, *bvoooom.* In the meantime, worms and ants came to me. They traveled from one ear to the other, finally making a home in my forehead. I realized I was going mad, but what I feared most was that the SSman would look at me.

They had slits for eyes. SSman narrowed his eyes in front of me and I felt like a fly, a mosquito, that must be crushed, dirt on the sole of boots. *Du Arschloch* – you asshole, they said to us. You asshole, get in line.

Mann, beiße den Hund – man, bite the dog, said SSman to his dog, pointing at someone. The dog understood every word, and bit. Even when we were frozen and without flesh. Even when we had lice on our skin, it bit.

We reached Weimar by train, the station before Buchenwald. I lay in an open car and waited for the angel of death. I counted fingers up to a hundred and then counted backwards to zero. I remembered home less and less. Forgot which village I came from. Who was there and how many siblings I had. I forgot where my brother was, the name of my best friend. I jerked my head upwards to jog my brain. Jogged it several times. Made motions with my lips, Mama was called Leah, Papa was called Israel, I have one brother Yitzhak that's all. My mind got stuck. I shook my head with both hands and Sarah came in, and that was that.

Airplanes approached the train. Maybe six planes, but there could have been sixty. I counted one, two, three, didn't kill me. Didn't count anymore.

The planes threw bombs. Above me I saw black and an explosion of bright light and smoke. I heard whines like an alarm, ah, a siren. I sat up and glanced out at the platform. The Germans were jumping from the train to find shelter. I realized, here, this is a chance to look for food. I jumped after the Germans.

I ran along the track as if I had a battery up my ass. I had no fear in my heart. I wanted to find food. If I had to die, at least I'd die full.

The whistles all around hurt my ears. Train tracks flew into the air. Bits of iron stuck in the cars, in a wall opposite me, in the floor. Everything was full of thick, stinking smoke. I barely saw the roof of a house burning opposite me like a torch. A jet of water flew to the other side. I heard windows breaking, tossing out glass rain. I heard the screams of the wounded who wanted a savior or a Messiah. I heard a dog howling but continued to run, my ears half-closed.

On a side-track stood closed cars. I heard a terrible whistling, and *boom*! A bomb fell on one of the carriages. A rain of cabbages flew above the car. I looked for shelter but was too late. A cabbage hit me right on the head. I got a hard blow and fell into great darkness.

I woke up, don't know how long it was.

I got up from the track. My head swam, I wanted to throw

up. I straightened up and continued running into the suffocating smoke, ah. Avrum. I had a good older brother who was called Avrum and I want to eat as we did in the village. I looked for houses. On the platform in front of me stood a two-story house with windows covered in dark fabric. I approached the house, checked behind me and knew I was alone. I grabbed the door handle, it opened. I didn't know if there was anyone in the house, I went in.

I saw a sofa, armchairs, a closet. I opened the closet, clothes. To one side were stairs with a rail. I ran upstairs. The strong smell of food almost dropped me to the stairs. I found a warm, steaming kitchen with a large pot on the fire. My nose began to run like a tap. I wiped it with my sleeve. I lifted the lid of the pot. Boiling soup. I thrust my frozen hands into the soup. Fire. I grabbed what I could and threw it into my mouth. Couldn't taste anything. Just a terrible burning on my tongue. I thrust my hands back into the soup. I swallowed boiling vegetables without chewing. I felt as if huge scissors were ripping me open from throat to belly. The pain continued to my groin but I put my hands back in the soup. I found a large carrot at the bottom of the pot. I put the carrot under my armpit and walked around the kitchen. I found no bread. Suddenly I saw a small harmonica on the table. I remembered having one like it. I thrust the harmonica into my pocket and went downstairs.

SSman was coming up the stairs towards me.

I saw hatred in his eyes. I saw holes with trembling walls in his nose. I saw a purple mark on each cheek. He held a gun. I didn't stop. Passed him and continued down. He didn't bother me and I didn't bother him. I heard him coming down behind me. The muzzle of a gun stuck in my back. I raised my hands. The carrot fell to the floor. I thought, this is the end for me.

Pray. My mouth burned, the skin peeled into flakes, and more flakes, and I was mainly sorry about the carrot. I thought, at least I will die full. I almost smiled.

I continued onward. The SSman's gun pressed hard into my ribs. My legs began to tremble. I felt a strong tingling like a cold needle from the hollow in my neck along my spine. I could feel the hot breath of the SSman on my neck. It had the sharp smell of cigarettes. I couldn't understand why the SSman didn't shoot me. I finished going downstairs, passed through the living room, walked out through the door with him behind me. A second SSman waited on the platform, turning his rifle in his hands. He had a large mouth like a wolf waiting to devour. I went on walking. Reached the second SSman, he raised his gun and *thwack*. The blow exploded on my back. I fell to the floor. I saw a part of the rifle's butt falling next to me and everything went dark. I got up in the dark seeing sparks and began to run. I fell. Got up. Continued to run in the direction of the screams. I grabbed the door and climbed into a car that had been bombed. There were between twenty and thirty dead prisoners. I arranged some of the dead like a bed and lay on them to rest. I felt as if I was at a holiday resort with a smell of sewage.

The train set out and only then did I understand it all.

The SSman didn't shoot me because of the mess. He took pity on the Germans who lived in that house. He didn't want to leave the blood of a dirty Jew on the staircase. I wanted to tell my brother Yitzhak that Jewish blood can sometimes save you from certain death. I fell asleep. I slept for an hour, two hours. Slept with a good full stomach. I even had to shit. I pushed two of the dead aside, making a space between them. A hole formed in the space. I shat into my own private hole. Then I wiped my ass with the clothes of the dead. Finally I rolled another of the dead from the side like a lid on top and I felt good.

Israel, 2001

08:25 stopping in Binyamina.

I'm on the way to Nahariya.

To Haifa? Is this the platform to Nahariya?

Here. Here. The journey northward on an interurban. The platforms always confuse me.

People pour from the carriages like sunflower seeds from a packet. They stream towards an underground passage, the platform is being renovated and it's crowded. I look around me. Don't like crowds. Even less this past year. I'm terrified of bombs. I look at ordinary people to see if there's a bulge in their coats, check the faces of people next to me, do they hate or are they killers? They hate. They're killers. Play head-games, kill or hate, in the end it's kill and the nightmare begins.

Dov would say, don't worry, they have security checks at the entrance to the station, and there are cameras, and soldiers, calm down. I can't calm down on the platform. Can't change trains at Binyamina and stay calm. I love trains, only the crowdedness at Binyamina makes me angry, I'm afraid to be ripped apart on the platform with birds singing *pooeey-pooeey-pooeey*, with the good smell of eucalyptus leaves and the loudspeaker calling, attention, attention, and *booooom*! Terror *attaaaaack*.

Don't want to be put into a huge black plastic bag, don't want life and death in a random hand, no.

"She came in by chance. Stood there by chance. By chance she sat in the coffee shop at a side table, lingered by chance, got a call on her phone, and then her bag was caught on the chair, and that saved her life."

If Dov was beside me he'd say, just like the ramp at Auschwitz. By chance they needed laborers for a developing factory that day. By chance that day there was no room in the barracks. By chance the SSman in the white gloves was talking to someone on the side, forgot to point a finger to the left, the line advanced alone.

But I wouldn't tell Dov or Yitzhak about the platform at Binyamina, better to stay silent. I'd say, you know what, it's actually fun on the train, I pray I'll be alone in the carriage, I like being alone. And then Yitzhak would say, what's the problem. I get up before the stars disappear, drink my coffee alone, don't make a sound, then I sit alone next to my son who is holding the steering wheel of the truck. My son has his mobile phone and his errands and I sit quietly and the road stretches out by itself. And then Dov would say I also sit alone on the bench at the infirmary and wait half an hour to get a doctor's prescription for my brother Yitzhak, good health to him.

And I'd say, but there is no being alone on a train, it's always full, and I can't bear the talking. And Yitzhak would say, me too, can't listen to people for a long time, I get mad quickly, as if I had a rifle muzzle up my ass. And Dov would say, I don't have the energy to listen to other people's troubles, even if they're close to me, suppose I was sitting on a bench, and someone comes to me with his crying, and he starts talking, and my ears are bursting. I feel as if hot blood was leaking out of my ears, it's the ears that can't bear to hear any more crying. At the infirmary they gave me pills, gave me drops, and in the end they said, you have to get used to it. And Yitzhak would say, me too, I don't have the energy for people to touch me with their talking and say, listen to this, and listen to that, and that. What we saw in the camps and what we heard in the camps was enough for a lifetime.

For me too.

What about you?

The same, I'm adult and I've heard enough.

09:35 Nahariya train station.

I arrived safely. Thank God.

Dov, how are you?

They're killing Jews.

What?

They're killing Jews. Don't you listen to television? They're blowing up Jews in the middle of a street in the State of Israel. Haven't you heard?

Chapter 13

Dov

We were three months on the journey from Jaworzno in Poland to Buchenwald in Germany.

They dragged us on foot who knows how many kilometers, we were loaded onto open trains, that way they managed to kill almost everyone on the roads. We were about two thousand when we set out from Jaworzno and we reached Buchenwald with only a hundred and eighty prisoners. At the gate to Camp Buchenwald I heard the number. SSman pointed to me, saying a hundred and seventy. I remember turning around. Ten prisoners were behind me, no more. I was among the few who remained alive because of miracles.

One miracle happened at the beginning of the march. We walked for three days without drinking water. I thought I'd die of thirst. Suddenly I heard a familiar sound, a sound I remembered from my village, like from a hundred years ago, a happy, strong sound, like a choir: I heard the *kwaaa-kwaaa* of frogs. *Kwaa-kwaa. Kwaaaaaa-kwaaaaaa. Kwaaaaaa.* And a sharp whistle burst from my mouth. I forgot I was with the Germans. I pressed my hand to my mouth, jumped to the side and saw a small puddle at the edge of the road. I threw myself on the puddle and put my face into the water. I managed to take one sip, and then *boom*! And a burning heat near my ear. A rifle bullet had scratched the edge of my ear. Raising my head I saw the black muzzle of a rifle aimed at me. The rifle was in the hands of a fat SSman with folds of fat at his neck. He stood five meters away from me. Maybe less. He cursed in German and I ran to the convoy.

At the end of that day we were fewer than five hundred prisoners. Some fell without a bullet. Some got it after they fell. Most of them got a bullet right before the first bread. I saw Germans emptying entire magazines on our convoy, just like that. Maybe they didn't have enough bread for the whole convoy that had walked for three days without water or bread.

Another miracle happened in the open car.

Airplanes descended on us with machine guns. The train stopped. The SSmen jumped out to take shelter, I jumped out after them and hid under the car. The noise of the machine guns burst in my ears. The screams of prisoners who didn't have time to jump hurt me more than the noise, even more than the hunger. I pressed my hands over my ears and made myself scream, *aaaah. Aaaah*. I wanted to look for food and I couldn't get out because the place was on fire. I sat crouching on the track and asked for a miracle. A meter away from me was a green lump. I didn't understand what it was. I lifted up the dirty lump with my hands, blew *phoo, phoo, phoo*. A cloud of green smoke went up. I couldn't breathe. I started coughing as if I was sick. I moved back, in the meantime, the dust dispersed. Aha! A whole loaf of bread was in my hand. A large loaf of bread with mold on the outer crust. I checked out the situation and saw I was alone with my treasure. As if I'd been given two weeks' worth of bread. I swallowed all the bread and new life came to my poor belly.

The bombing ended. I went back to the car and the train set off. According to counts there were fewer than three hundred prisoners left after one bombing. I sat among the dead, almost faceless old-timers and the newly dead with blood and torn flesh. The old-timers and the new ones were mixed up. Because of the smell I looked for two newly dead without blood, I took out the harmonica I'd found in the German kitchen and began to play a sad tune, like the one I heard in the synagogue on Yom Kippur. Well, it didn't really come out right. A prisoner not far from me began to tremble. He looked old. He had furrows in his face and his head was full of scales like a fish. He raised his head very very slowly and began to sing. His mouth was large and toothless and his head moved to the tune, back and forth, back and forth, and then he began to quicken the tune, faster, faster, I couldn't keep up. I stopped playing.

His head fell and a red stain spread on the straw beside him. Only then did I see that his legs were strangely crooked. They turned outward as if they had no bones. I leaned towards him, and began to play. Slowly. He opened soft, child-like, brown eyes in my direction. He had pink tears on his cheeks. He moved his fists in time on the straw, opened his mouth wide, stretching it to the sides. He strained his throat muscles, no voice came out. And then he smiled at me and died.

Before Buchenwald, we reached the concentration camp of Blechhammer.

By now, we were seven hundred prisoners less. On that day, the Germans wasted about five hundred bullets, I saw them using prisoners for target practice until they began to get bored and stopped. According to my count two hundred died without their bullets. That evening brought another miracle. The darkness was thick as a blanket and there was a cold wind. I was weak. I took a step, swayed, another step, swayed like a shriveled dry stalk. In front of me, three prisoners fell. *Thump*. They disappeared. *Boom. Boom. Boom.* Large lights lit up the square near the gate. I saw dark posts, barbed wire, a guard tower. A German with a helmet guarded us from above, a rifle in his hand. In the distance I heard the sounds of large pots and the squirting of water. Not far from the entrance I saw four prisoners carrying a box. I craned my neck. The box was full of bread loaves.

My heart stopped for a second and then began to race like a madman. I couldn't leave the bread. Thick, paste-like saliva began to collect in my mouth. My mind screamed, Dov, without bread you are dead, dead. The SSmen stood thirty meters from me, their backs to me. They were talking to the guards just as they always did when entering a new camp. SSmen were busy with absorption and paid less attention to us. By their gestures I realized they had a surplus of people, even a large surplus. One of the guards, a huge irritable man, cut the air with one hand, like a knife. Our SSman removed his hat and scratched his head, thinking, ah. I fixed my eyes on the guard at the tower. Waited for him to turn towards the camp. He turned. Leaving the line, I walked towards the bread. The SSmen were close to resolving the surplus. Leaning, I took a breath and *hop*, I jumped on the bread in the box.

The prisoners were alarmed, they dropped the box on the ground. I snatched a loaf of bread and began to run. I ran in a zigzag, I ran bent in the fire directed at me by the German in the tower. I ran towards the blocs. I glanced back. About twenty prisoners were chasing after me. I knew, if they caught me I'd be left ripped to pieces on the stinking ground. I ran through the blocs, changing direction every second. I glanced to the sides, saw more and more prisoners joining in the great chase. There were prisoners who fell, trampled on by those who joined in and continued to run after me. I moved away from the blocs. I had a terrible stitch. Don't know where I got the strength. Maybe from the bread in my hand.

And in a moment I was on my own. I stopped at the first place I felt safe.

The miracle happened behind a large garbage bin. I stopped, my heart leaping up and down, but I could swallow the bread all at once. I choked, continued to swallow without chewing. I knew, if I left a small piece in my pocket, I'd be in danger. Prisoners killed for crumbs, or potato peels. Once I saw a tall prisoner attack a short one, sticking a finger in his eye, choking him. Only when the prisoner let go of the piece of bread in his hand did the tall prisoner leave him alone. The short prisoner remained behind us, spread out on the cold road.

I wanted to vomit up the fresh bread. I pressed hard on my mouth, I'd die before I vomited. After about an hour I wanted to leave the garbage bin but at that moment I got diarrhea. I sat near the bin and emptied my stomach. I felt good. I did what the fat Jew in Auschwitz had told me to do. Steal, murder, you have a chance.

Only the next day did I understand why the prisoners had stopped chasing me. I'd run with bread to the living quarters of the Germans. The garbage bin belonged to the Germans. I understood this because a day later they hanged all the cleaning staff who'd cleaned up my diarrhea in the German area. Prisoners whispered, they hanged those poor chaps. They hanged them because they found fresh poop near the bins.

It was a miracle I didn't catch some disease.

At least three hundred prisoners who left Jaworzno with me died of dysentery, diphtheria, typhus, fever, diarrhea, vomiting, or rot in the nails or knees. For a prisoner disease was a death sentence. There were no doctors on the march from Jaworzno to Buchenwald and no medication. I wasn't infected by those who passed by me or slept beside me and I don't understand how this miracle happened.

We reached Camp Buchenwald a hundred and eighty prisoners out of the two thousand who set out with striped clothing, a blanket, and shoes if they were lucky. I had shoes and this was very lucky. I was put in Bloc 56. Dark. Bunks, bunks, bunks, all of them filled with skeletons wrapped in striped pajamas and filth. I hate striped pajamas most of all, even more than dogs. Some skeletons made sounds like half-dead birds, most didn't move. I saw a thin stream of urine and excrement dripping from the upper bunks. Prisoners had no time to get down from the bunks to relieve themselves. The filth dripped like smelly chewing gum.

A few minutes later, we had to stand in a line next to the bunks. The head of the bloc came in and immediately began to scream and scream, waving his stick about as if there were flies in the bloc, and made a hole in the forehead of a prisoner standing next to me because he was standing with one leg in the air. His knee was swollen and purple and he couldn't stand. I heard him crying and saw how he stuck a nail in his knee, crying and pressing, and pressing, and he couldn't put his foot on the floor. Poor chap, poor chap, he wanted to live but he died because of the hole in his forehead.

On the topmost bunk three other youngsters lay next to me. One was short and had no eyelashes or eyebrows. A thin, yellow thread connected his eye and nose. The other two were brothers. One had a large head and a small body. The other was the opposite. They all looked under eighteen. Maybe this was why we stuck together in the line for bread that first day at Buchenwald. They were in front of me in the line when two older prisoners pushed in. One of them stood on the foot of the brother with the small head. The older prisoner crushed the poor boy's foot with his heel while whistling a tune. Small-head cheeped and escaped to the end of the line. His brother ran after him. And then the adults came to me. My body shivered. I also ran to the end of the line. There I found three small ones like me. We looked at one another and arranged to sleep together.

That night, in the bunk, they whispered to one another next to me. Said Hitler had fallen. Said Russian cannon were burning Germany. Said the Americans were strong, that they had the biggest planes in the world, the scariest tanks, America would show the Germans, they'd slaughter them one by one, a matter of days, maybe weeks, it's the end of the Germans and it's freedom for us, best to rely on America now.

I was faint with hunger, and I waited for death while they dreamed about great liberty for all the Jews. I made up a play about certain death for myself. Darkness. I go downstairs. A door opens. A slippery floor. I'm inside a hall. A door closes. I hear an order, strip. Pack clothing in a parcel. Tie shoes with laces. Proceed. Another strong door opens. The door of disaster. I proceed naked and barefooted. I'm cold. The door closes. I'm crying, in the dark. I hear a tap open and then, *tshhhh tshhhh*. There's a smell of dust and acid. I run to the door. Knock hard, open, open, I'm dying. The *tshhhh tshhhh* continues. I lie inside a white sheath, closed. It's a rubber sheath. I push my arms to the sides, try my legs, the rubber stretches a bit, and sticks to my nose like chewing gum. I have no air, and I die. A jet of cold water cleans after me. I'm thrown into a full wagon, and I fall. They tie my foot to the handle. I travel to a wet pit. Again powder on the body and the dead below me and the dead above me, and earth in the mouth and nose and the sound of a tractor. The tractor presses from above. They plant a grass lawn on top of me and a tree without my name.

I opened my eyes with strength only the dead have. Gray marks jumped on the wall in front of me and the tingling in my forehead came back and the knocking in my ears. I wanted to sink my teeth into the bunk plank. I wanted to eat a plank for lunch. My head understood, that's it, I'm going mad. I raised my hand upwards. I whispered, that's a hand. On the hand there are fingers. I began to count, I found five. I don't remember how many fingers I had in the beginning, five or six, maybe four? I glanced at the prisoner lying next to me. He was lying on his hand. Carefully I pulled his hand out. He murmured something and closed his fist. I opened up his hand and began to count. I got to five, yes, five. I couldn't remember how many fingers I'd found on my own hand. I put my hand next to his, the same. Good. I raised my other hand. My hand fell from a scream coming from below. There was a prisoner there who had no nails, he lay on the floor and kicked at the wall. I understood, that's it, he's also going mad. I'm not alone, soon there'll be a group of us.

The madman on the floor slowly sat up, his arm straight. I saw he was holding the tail of a fat, black rat. The rat struggled and suddenly jumped and bit his finger. He screamed but didn't let go, even after his finger bled. The rat jumped as if it, too, was about to go mad and the prisoner began to laugh, his mouth wide open, his teeth rotten. He lifted the rat to his mouth and strangled it with his teeth. I turned my head and began to vomit. I was just making a lot of noise, nothing came out.

* * *

And then came another miracle. A sweet, white miracle.

An ordinary person came into the bloc. Wore a long coat, a hat, and leather shoes, a human being like someone I remembered from home on holidays. I stood next to my bunk. Didn't know what I was supposed to do, go outside or climb quickly up into my place. The man with the hat went past everyone once, twice, and finally approached only me. In the meantime, a little bit was leaking into my pants. When he bent down to me, I looked aside, let him go to others, but he whispered, wait for me behind the bloc.

The ordinary man had good eyes. His clothes smelled clean, like laundry taken down from the line. Lifelessly, I dragged myself outside. Darkness fell. I waited alone behind the bloc, my hands trembling. Nose dripping. A few minutes later the three from my bunk were beside me. The stranger approached us, said, I'm from the Red Cross. I've brought you something. He took a large box from his coat and lifted the lid. I didn't believe it. In the box were white cubes of sugar. Rows and rows of cubes arranged in layers like the bunks in the bloc. A box with one or two kilos, I don't remember. The trembling of my hands increased. I pressed my fists into my trousers and hit my flesh. I was afraid of fainting and missing out on the sugar. The man whispered, soon, soon, and divided the sugar into four parts. He gave each one two or three full handfuls, said, put it into your pocket, so there'll be some for later, and he disappeared. I thrust a handful of sugar into my mouth. I crushed the cubes with my teeth and swallowed bit after bit. My gums ached from the pressure. I paid no attention. Finished it all. The others did the same. I went back to the bloc with a sweet smell. I felt good. The sugar gave me a few more days to live.

* * *

A month at Buchenwald and I begin to believe there is a God in that camp, there is.

The most important miracle in my life happened near Bloc 56. I was standing outside sucking on a dry bone. I'd found it behind the bloc. Nothing came of it except scratches on my tongue. But I went on licking. I was starving. I felt as if the skin on my body was like the peel of a hollow tree trunk. I knew, a day or two without bread and I'd crumble in my bunk or in the mud.

Two prisoners with dirty faces stood not far from me, moving like branches in the wind. I didn't know them. One was tall. One was my height. The tall prisoner was missing half his nose. I thought, idiot, instead of eating the rat, the rat ate him. The prisoner who was my height had ears that stuck out and a firm glance.

The tall prisoner pointed at me. The short prisoner took a step forward, put out his hand and whispered something.

I didn't understand the word he spoke, his voice was familiar, but what was he saying to me? I couldn't remember where I'd heard the word, could he be mistaken? Was I dreaming? I threw down the bone. The prisoner who was my height repeated, is that you?

My brother Yitzhak stood before me.

Thinner than he was in the synagogue at my Bar Mitzvah. He had bristles on his head, and a long face, laughter in his eyes. He jumped on me, grabbed me with both hands and hugged me hard, I thought, that's it, now I'll fall to pieces for sure, *ouch, ouch*, came out of me. Yitzhak stood back, holding me by the shoulders, examining me with a piercing glance, said, what have they done to you?

We wept. Laughed. Wept for a long time.

We dampened each other's filthy pajamas. I wiped my face on my sleeve, feeling as if a huge tap had opened in my forehead. My brother's tears left a delicate, clean line on his face. I stroked his cheek, whispered, it's really you, and I didn't recognize you.

He patted my chest with both hands, we're together, don't worry, from now on there are two of us. And then he sniffed and said, Father, Mother, Sarah, Avrum, have you heard anything?

Nothing, you?

Only Avrum, we were together for the first month, then they took him away, are you sick?

I said, don't know, I walked for a few months and I've been finished ever since. He touched me and sighed, there was a dark shadow on his face, and then he took my hand and we went to my barracks.

Chapter 14

Yitzhak

We came to Buchenwald because of the bombing.

The track to Auschwitz was shattered at Zeiss. Airplanes fired volley after volley but didn't hit my car. I wanted to die in the bombing but nothing hit my car. The train to Buchenwald went through Schwandorf. The whole way from Schwandorf I heard a voice that sounded like a father, Yitzhak, jump. Yitzhak, jump.

At Buchenwald I went straight to Bloc 8.

I remembered the doctor with the pleasant face who didn't shout or slap, or hold a rifle with a dog. A doctor with a smile who holds a child by the hand, takes him from the bloc and doesn't bring him back. But first a candy and a pinch on the cheek from Baba Volodya who guarded the bloc. Baba Volodya wanted to make children happy before the injection. Baba Volodya helped me to leave the bloc for Camp Zeiss.

I entered Bloc 8 and didn't see Baba Volodya. I didn't know a single child, no guards. I ran outside.

A prisoner I don't know at all came up to me. He had a yellow face and a crooked hand. He sounded ill, you know you have a brother here, yes, yes, a brother. I felt the blow of a fist in my heart. Cautiously, I approached him, he was clearly mad.

I stammered faintly, repeat what you said.

He began to rock the crooked hand, back and forth, back and forth. Said, you have a brother at Camp Buchenwald. I saw him.

I thrust my head under his chin, whispered, do we know each other?

He sighed, come with me, boy. I saw the two of you together on the way to Auschwitz. I didn't believe him but I followed him. We approached Bloc 56. He pointed out a rather short prisoner with an open mouth, his tongue out. He looked more dead than alive. Weighed maybe thirty kilos, looked like a schoolboy. He was holding a bone in his hand, stuck a nail into the hole of the bone, dug and dug, pulled out the nail and sucked.

The prisoner who brought me disappeared and I didn't see him again.

I approached. Whispered, is that you? The bone fell. He had a hemorrhage in one eye.

He looked at me and immediately tensed like a spring, is that you?

We hugged. Wept. Wept louder. He said, ay, ay, ay.

Dov was skin and bone, pale in the pajamas. I said to him, we're together. We couldn't part from each other.

SSman approached.

SSman in boots with a revolver in his hand. He pointed the revolver at us, his eyes narrowed like a crack in a wall. I wanted to stop crying. Couldn't. SSman yelled: What are you two doing here?

I said, this is my brother, at Buchenwald I've found my brother. The SSman chewed his lower lip and tapped his revolver on the edge of the boot and then, turning around, he went away. SSman Hans Schultz went away.

Chapter 15

Dov

My brother and I talked *organisieren* – organization. We looked for a way to arrange for food. We found no solution. The Germans gave us a piece of bread once every day or two. No soup. I said to my brother, listen, you mustn't leave the bloc area, you mustn't. The Germans shoot anyone who approaches their storage rooms, understand? I noticed that the Germans had become more dangerous since they'd begun to lose the war. They ran about the camp, screamed at one another, there were rumors that American soldiers and Russian soldiers were galloping to Buchenwald. There were rumors the Germans were planning to leave. Vehicles entered, vehicles left, I noticed they paid no attention to us. We no longer stood on parade, didn't go out to work and we were very cautious around the guards. They were at every corner, tracking us like hunters. They had rifles and magazines, a light trigger finger and, most of all, I was afraid of losing my brother. I begged, Icho, don't try and steal food, promise me. He looked over my head, agreed, all right, but you also have to be careful.

We returned hungry to the blocs. Each one to his own bloc. We didn't know what would happen to us. In the following days we mainly hid. Sometimes in the uppermost bunk, sometimes behind the bloc. Guards would catch prisoners and take them outside the camp, we didn't know where.

One morning the loudspeaker shouted, get into rows. Fast. Fast. I thought, a bad sign. I left the bloc and saw bowed prisoners already standing in rows. Some held their bellies, or pressed thin hands to their chests. My brother ran up to stand beside me. Pinched my hand and whispered, they want to get rid of us, they want to throw us out of the camp.

I cried out, how do you know? He gestured with his head, I cried out softly, answer me, who said so.

My brother whispered, remember the SSman who saw us hugging when we met next to the barracks? His name is Hans Schultz. On the way here we met by chance, we looked at each other, it took a second, and then he walked off and began to scream like a maniac, out to the march, idiots, idiots, and he struck a prisoner who fell down near the bloc.

I began to stamp my feet fast, fast, fast.

My brother didn't understand what was happening to me. I couldn't stop stamping my feet. The loudspeaker shouted, stand in straight rows, get in line at once, all of you. I stamped my feet faster, I felt a terrible heat in the hollow of my neck, tiny ants began to run along my forehead and worms ran along my back. My brother tried to stop me, what's the matter with you, talk to me.

I gritted my teeth, I said slowly and clearly, I am not going on a march, no chance, I've done one, can't do another, no.

My brother whispered, *shhhhh. shhhhh.* Calm down.

I shouted in a whisper, don't want to calm down, can't bear to see any more people spread on the road, can't bear the crying and the shouting of the half dead, no, no.

We're together, don't worry he told me and I felt he didn't understand, because he hadn't walked hundreds of kilometers without food or water or a place to lie down. He hadn't heard the bursts of fire, the killings on the roads and he hadn't heard about the surplus of people and the eight hundred bullets that killed them, and he wouldn't understand.

I cried out, no, no, no. Leave me alone, because I'm not moving from here to the gate.

He pressed my neck and said you have to give me strength, yes, yes. Listen to me, you've been on the roads, you know the situations, you have experience, you'll help me, you hear?

I shouted in a whisper, I won't! Don't want to hear German anymore and the whistle of bullets, I refuse, understand?

My brother frowned, biting his lips, he had a scratch that bled. And then he hugged my back, *shhhh. shhhh.* All right, we'll hide.

SSman called through the loudspeaker: Attention, attention, any prisoner who leaves the camp on a march will receive half a loaf of bread. Half a loaf of bread for any prisoner who leaves the camp now. Attention, attention, go in the direction of the exit gate and you'll receive half a loaf. No one went to the gate. The air was electric. I whispered to my brother, I'm not moving.

The loudspeaker shouted irritably: A whole loaf for anyone who leaves the camp, understood?

We remained in our rows. The Germans began to shout and curse. They pushed prisoners by force to the gate, hitting them with rifles, kicking them, prisoners ran to the camp and not to the gate, they scattered like mice with trampled tails. My brother seized my hand, cried, to the German area, quickly, that's the safest place. We ran bent over, we passed several blocs, reached an unfamiliar area, suddenly a trench. We jumped into the trench. After us, jumped other prisoners. We saw Germans approaching. We ran away from the trench to the nearest bloc and hid behind a wall. We heard dogs approaching. We ran round the bloc, reached a door. The bloc was empty, dark. We jumped inside. Again there were bunks. We ran to the end of the bloc and climbed into the highest bunk. We heard prisoners entering after us. We heard shouts, groans, dogs again, and then shots, *pew. Pew. Pew. Pew-pew* and silence. SSman screamed, come out of the bloc or you're all dead. I peeped down. Two SSmen stood at the door. Their guns were aimed at us. I knew we didn't have a chance.

We got down from the bunk.

Dragged our feet towards the door. At least twenty other prisoners left before us, and then one fell. SSman turned round to kick him outside. Another SSman bent down to help. My brother and I looked at each other and jumped into the nearest bunk. We lay close to the wall. We were wet with sweat. My brother moved close to me. He was hot and tense as a spring. I didn't breathe. We heard voices moving away and silence.

And then my head fell.

SSman Hans Schultz stood in front of us. He gave us a dark look. The muzzle of his gun was aimed precisely between us. He made a small sideways motion with the muzzle. Not a muscle moved in his face, he didn't blink. We climbed down. Stood opposite him. My brother Yitzhak looked steadily at him. I looked away. I felt that all my blood was draining away onto the floor. He signaled with his gun in the direction of the door, waited. I was the first to go out. My brother Yitzhak after me. SSman Hans Schultz followed, without firing a magazine. I thought, another miracle, and I don't have the strength for any more miracles, no, no, I want to run to the fence, lie on my back and sleep without getting up.

On the road outside the camp we were several thousand and more, thousands more, like a huge field of thin, black branches bent in the wind of the camp, *hop*. One collapsed. *Hop*. Two. Four. Ten. *Pew. Pew. Pew*. The Germans replaced magazines. They had a lot of them. I raised my head. The mist dispersed, a cold sun stood above. I heard SSmen laughing. I heard dogs running back and forth, happily barking. Like a trip they'd decided to take to an entire town, even a country. There were many, many thousands and I didn't want to set out on that trip in the sun with the happy dogs.

I looked for a German who would put a bullet in my head. I looked back. The nearest SSman was far away. One SSman for every hundred prisoners, maybe more. *Pew-pew-pew*. They fired at anyone who fell. Every few minutes *Pew. Pew. Pew*. Sometimes there was no pause. Sometimes we heard *Pew. Pew. Pew* for an hour or two. Many fell on the road. After the war they showed it in photographs and documentaries. They called it the death march, yes. I looked for us in every place where there were photographs and documentaries, found none. I think we appear in several books and documentaries, I'm almost certain, but not even we know who we were in the pictures, how could we?

Israel, 2001

15:15 Interurban train from Hof Hacarmel to Binyamina.

A group of men are exploding with laughter at the end of the carriage. Evil laughter. A woman with flowers in her hair, says, quiet. A woman pleads in a Russian accent, a little quiet please.

They're jubilant. The woman raises her voice, thick with cigarettes, shut up over there, enough. The men choke, you can hear the tears in their throat. What's going on there for heaven's sake?

The woman shouts, you to stop this, enough already, you make me crazy.

The men repeat her words in a similar tempo, you to stop this, enough already, you make me crazy, enough already, enough already. Their laughter was guttural, ravenous, as if they sensed an easy prey.

The woman jumps up from her seat and walks vigorously in my direction. She holds out her hands as if nothing is right. She has flowers in her hair that waves outward. She is wearing a purple dress, a mini, with a deep cleavage. She's wearing shiny platform shoes. A black shiny bag is slung over her shoulder. She mutters broken words to herself. What had they said to her to make her lose it. I point to the empty seat beside me, but she hurries by, disappears.

Half a minute later and a shrill scream pierces the carriage. People run to the end of the carriage, I join them, what happened, what happened, a female soldier, her hair loose, is pointing to the window, she jumped out of the train, who, who, who.

The woman standing here, she jumped, God, I saw her, a second before, a moment ago, she jumped out, I saw her, she had flowers in her hair, stop the train, quickly, a woman jumped, don't you understand, press the alarm, come on, she jumped, the one in the purple dress, *Mamaleh*, she's crazy, she came from over there, I'm standing here, here, and suddenly, *hop*, gone, how?

A gray-haired man approaches the soldier, asks, are you sure? Maybe you turned away for a second and she went into another carriage?

Wait, we'll ask, have you seen a woman in a purple dress, has anyone seen her? Ask if she had flowers in her hair, ask, have you seen a woman with flowers?

He asked and no one had seen a woman like that.

The soldier looks for a place on the floor, grabs her head, talks to herself: She jumped. It looked as if she was rushing to the toilet. She jumped with her bag, a little black bag, I can't believe I saw it, why did she do it?

All she asked for was a little quiet.

If Dov had been in the carriage, he'd tug at his shirt, smooth his collar, saying, I can understand her, how much can you take without family, without knowing a single person, what could she do with such bastards, eh? And then Yitzhak would thump his knee and say, nonsense, no need to pay any attention, so what if they laughed, let them choke on their laughter, who cares, I would have gone to another carriage at once, that's all. Apart from that, I would refuse to get on a train, can't bear the *choo, choo, choo* of a train, and the whistle, *oy, oy, oy*, that whistle is the hardest, do you know what it is for me to hear a siren, just like the war, I immediately see the Auschwitz train, a few whistles and a loudspeaker, and you're with strangers in the world, surrounded by tall SSmen and dogs, and a crematorium that doesn't rest for a second, ah, better to be silent.

In that time, I would think, better to start a war with an alarm than without, so you can prepare for trouble, and then Dov, who knows how to read my mind, would say, something alcoholic? A Slivovitz or a cognac?

Yes, yes.

Here's to the State of Israel. To life.

Chapter 16

Yitzhak

We left Buchenwald on foot.

The Germans didn't manage to kill everyone. We were too many even for the methods they invented with the crematorium and the pits and the magazines. They didn't want the Russians to enter the camp and count us among the dead. Didn't want it to be known that they'd found tens of thousands of dead in every corner of the camp. The old methods worked vigorously, the pits were dug, the magazines replaced, but they couldn't kill everyone before the Russians entered, not a chance, so they took us out on a long walk so we'd die on the way, on the roads, near villages, and the white snow would cover us and the terrible smell until spring.

I think it was the end of winter. There were clouds in the sky and a cold sun. I saw snow at the sides of the road, sometimes the ground was clean. Beside me, Dov was worn out. He walked and swayed. Walked and swayed. He walked with a bowed back and his tongue out. His head would drop every second. He tried to look straight ahead, most of the time he failed. Dov had already been on one march. For me it was the first. We walked along German roads, sometimes we went by train. We walked from early morning until dark. We wore our usual clothing, dirty, striped trousers and a shirt. Most of the time we were wet from the rain. The soles of our feet slid in what was left of our shoes. Paper-thin soles with torn plastic straps. We had to tie them with something, we were very lucky if we found some barbed wire. We slept whenever it became dark, in forests, at the side of the road, in fields, wrapping ourselves in a blanket we'd carried on our backs, falling asleep immediately, despite the hunger.

Every two or three days they gave us bread. Water we found alone. We ate snow and swallowed drops of rainwater as we walked. Don't remember shitting. We peed whenever, at the side of the road, in our trousers, on breaks, depending on the pressure. We walked from morning till night along the roads of Germany. We walked for about a month, maybe two months. The direction was south. The Germans were running away from the Russians, they didn't want to fall into the hands of the Russians, they wanted Americans. They knew they'd be captured. Until they were captured they wanted many, many Jews to die along the way, and they succeeded. Prisoners went in convoy, fell. Walked. Fell. Fell like flies after being sprayed from a plane. The Germans shot anyone who fell. Shot to kill. It didn't always succeed. Prisoners who got a bullet lay in their blood on the road and wept, begging the SSmen to shoot one more bullet, here. Here in the head. Here in the heart. Begged for a place where death was certain. The Germans refused. One bullet per prisoner, that's it. Whoever died, died. Whoever was wounded was left for the dogs, wolves, jackals, crows, flies, worms and ants.

We advanced slowly, barely speaking.

One day I stopped feeling the toes on my feet. As if they were paralyzed. I had painful rubbing on my thighs. The blood that oozed from the sores stuck to my trousers. I couldn't take my trousers down. When I wanted to take them down, the scabs were removed and the blood seeped out. The clothing was hard as boards because of the blood and the dirt. When it rained it was easier, less painful.

Dov dragged his feet beside me. Dov whispered rhythmically, no chance, no chance, sometimes bending over, leaning on his knees, saying, I'm falling, that's it. I'm ending it now.

I put a hand on his waist. Held him fast by his trousers, whispered into his ear, you aren't falling, we're together, and you're moving on.

He would take a step forward and repeat after me, rhythmically, not falling. I'm moving on, and again he'd stop and look back. Kept looking for a German to put a bullet in his head. I pulled him by his pants and he said, no chance, no chance, and he'd calm down and walk.

My brain beat like a heavy hammer.

Just don't fall. Stay on our feet. Keep a clear mind. I didn't care about dying. I was afraid of being left spread on the road. I was afraid of suffering pain. Afraid of lying with other prisoners on the road and waiting for the dogs, or dying in the ice. Afraid of hearing the sobbing of those waiting to die, my mamaleh, give me water, a little water, Mamaaa. Afraid of dying slowly, hours, days, that frightened me the most. I bit my lips, whispered, no mistakes. Careful. I was only sixteen and I already knew I had to save my brother. He had already marched along roads, my body ached in every place I touched. My skin itched from the lice. I looked for leaves to chew so I wouldn't die of hunger. My mind was empty. Just one channel was working, like a needle stuck on a revolving record, no mistakes. Don't fall. Don't get into the sights of a rifle. Don't faint. Don't strain your foot. Don't stop. Don't bend down. Walk. *Mm*. Walk. *Mm. Mm. Mm.*

And there was also Dov and he was suffering. He wanted to die and I didn't let him so I'd have a reason to live. I agreed to go on the death march because of Dov. I knew that if Dov died, I would die.

Chapter 17

Dov

I told my brother, let's part before the hills.

I was worried about my brother. I was sure I'd fall on a hill and SSman would put a bullet in me and my brother Yitzhak would attack the SSman and would also die. I wanted at least one of our family to survive. I knew that if I died, my brother Yitzhak would go mad. I also knew that if Yitzhak had the ants and worms I had, he wouldn't hold up. I know him, he wouldn't be able to tolerate ants like that in his head, he'd die immediately. That's why I told him, let's part before the hills. We'll meet at the top. Let's part so we don't have to see SSman shoot one of us.

My brother Yitzhak agreed.

We hugged. Looked at one another. Promised, we'll meet at the top. My brother Yitzhak spoke quietly to me, I'll wait for you at the top. You will reach the top. We'll walk down together, understand? Your head will give the order, walk, don't stop, walk, keep moving on, you look straight ahead and don't stop, until the top, promise me, so I'll have faith in my heart.

I promised, we'll meet at the top, and you be careful too, and I felt relief. I was sure I wouldn't finish a hill, but my brother Yitzhak would, at least one of us would survive.

We parted.

Yitzhak went to one side of the road. I to another. There were perhaps thirty or forty prisoners between us. I began to climb the hill. Slowly, slowly. I kept my head straight on the road, didn't dare look right or left. My legs were heavy, as if filled with sacks of concrete. I stepped forward, dragged one leg after another. Closed the gap. Another step. Gap. Another step, break. My mind hammered, don't fall. I leaned on my knees. Breathed in, my mouth open. I heard a whistling sound in my nose. SSman approached me. Go on. Don't fall. Another step, close the gap. My head dropped, dragging my back with it. I had no room in my lungs. We were in nature near large trees, and I didn't have the strength to breathe. *Shshsh*. Breathe. *Shshsh*. Step, close. Step, close. I heard a shot not far from me. Another, two, five shots.

A fat needle pricked my neck, descending down down to my backside. I didn't move my head. I gave myself an order, don't look, don't peep. Don't! Only forwards. Step, close. Left. Right. Left. *Boom*. Another shot. *Boom*. *Boom*. And a scream. Right beside me. I whispered, nothing to do with me, no, no. Moving on. Don't see anyone. I promised not to stop. Step, breathe, close. Step, breathe, breathe, breathe, close.

I heard the sound of weeping near me. I heard coughing and choking, as if someone was drowning in water.

God, he's finished, *aaaah*, walk. Don't look. Step, close. On the black asphalt. The asphalt curves, I curve. Before me another curve. I see the top of the hill, not much left. I feel like singing. I've been searching for a tune since morning, but the ants are biting inside my head, going from one eye to the other, through my forehead, I try and kill them, another thousand ants come along, making holes in my forehead.

I got to the end of the rise.

I was breathing like a tired old locomotive. My heart beat in my chest, pressing at my ribs, I felt as if glue had been poured into me. Pouring, pouring, pouring until it was blocked. I had a stitch in my side. I couldn't bend over because of it. Couldn't feel my legs. They were like heavy tree trunks. I knew I had to find my brother. I looked for him. I crossed the road among prisoners who were barely breathing. Around us there were trees, and water, my mouth was dry. I looked back. On the road were piles of rags that moved slowly up the hill. My brain gave me an order, don't knock into a prisoner. Careful. Don't touch anyone, if you touch anyone, you'll fall. I heard my brain knocking from a distance, as if it was sitting in someone else's head.

Yitzhak stood in front of me, smiling. Nodded. Said, very good. We did it, very good. I smiled at him. Beside me someone was smoking a cigarette. I said cigarette, give me a cigarette, he didn't hear. Fiercely, my brother pulled me back, I heard him say, are you mad? It's SSman, you're asking an SSman for a cigarette, what's wrong with you? I didn't answer, I felt as if someone was trying to get up, straighten up inside me, wanting to leave my body. Again I wanted to say cigarette, cigarette. Yitzhak dragged me to another place.

We continued to march one beside the other.

A uniform pace. My brother breathed aloud as if he was in danger of dying. I had my mouth shut. I looked at him, Yitzhak didn't see or hear what was going on in my head. Good that we were silent. A day and a night, another hill.

We parted at the bottom.

My brother caught my hands. Came close up to my face and said, Dov, open your eyes, close. Open your mouth wide, close.

I asked, can you see ants? There are ants traveling inside my forehead from here to here, can you see them? I pointed to my forehead, yesterday they were in my nose, now they're in my ear, what should I do?

Yitzhak stamped his foot, pinched my chin and said, there are no ants, none, and don't go talking to anyone about ants, d'you hear me? And don't just say things, promise me.

I said, all right, but I also have worms, they go from one place to another, just so you know.

And then Yitzhak hugged me and said we have to get out of this war alive, together, and he'll be waiting for me at the top, like the hill two days before. He took my head in both his hands and turned my face towards the mountain crest.

Drops of blood dripped from my nose.

I cleaned my nose on my sleeve and said to my brother, and you have to promise me that we'll meet at the top, promise. Don't let them just shoot you with a bullet, and wait, before we part, I need a tune, I need a tune to keep pace, what was that song we sang, nu, the song that Vassily would whistle when he rode the horses.

Yitzhak looked upward, dropped his arms to his sides, and said, don't look for tunes now, there's no time.

I said, but I want to play the harmonica, I've got a harmonica in my pocket.

Yitzhak cursed, hit himself on the head and said, oy, I've forgotten, and thrust his hand into my pocket and took the harmonica. He said, I'll keep the harmonica for you, and hide that blood from your nose. We parted.

I bent over to one side and pulled myself along as if I was attached to a hay cart. The blood continued to drip. I stopped. I raised my head and swallowed the blood. I lowered my head and the bleeding went on and on. I thought, I won't have any blood left by the time I get to the top. I closed my nose with two fingers and advanced along the road. I saw a dry stick. I broke the stick in two and stuck them in my nostrils. The bleeding stopped. I felt a weakness in my legs. I gave myself an order to walk. Walk. Step, close. Step, close.

I knew my brother Yitzhak was stronger than me. I knew that my brother and I were perhaps the only ones in our family to survive. My brain hammered, I must not leave my little brother alone. I must succeed for both of us. For Mother and Father. For Sarah and Avrum. For Father. Where is my father, Papaleh, Papaleh, step. Space. Close. Step, break, breathe, breathe. *Boom. Boom. Boom*. Head straight, head straight, and again ants are going down from my forehead to my nose, my mouth. I swallow quickly, and say: Breathe, breathe.

Prisoners fell next to me with their faces in the road, waiting for the bullet. There were prisoners who tried to get up and some did succeed. Half a meter from me one fell. From the ground he held out a hand to me. He had foam in his mouth. He looked and wept without teeth. I didn't give him a hand. I knew that if I did, I'd fall and wouldn't get up. I said to him, listen, my brother is waiting for me at the top, understand? I have a brother, and he needs me, yes? We'll meet in a while. Goodbye.

I continued to climb. The ants descended to my throat.

Only at the top of the hill did I look to the sides. I saw my brother. He smiled at me, pulled the sticks out of my nose and put them in his pocket. And then he held out an apple peel. I asked, where did you get it?

And he said, SSman threw it away. He let me suck on the peel. I sucked a little and returned it to him. He sucked on it, chewed half, took it out of his mouth and gave it to me, eat, eat.

We were told to get in line. They're handing out bread. We took our bread and sat on the side. Next to us sat a tall prisoner who swallowed his bread fast. He looked at the line and called, Father, come and sit next to me. Someone with a red blister under his ear approached. He was holding his bread in his hand. Suddenly the son jumped on the father, grabbed the bread and swallowed it in one go. The father was silent. Then he covered his face with both hands and wept. We left.

We went down the hill together.

I said to my brother, what was that song that Vassily sang on the horse, tell me.

My brother frowned, finally whispered, you mean the song about *Koshot Loyosh*

I cried, yes, yes. Sing me that song, I've forgotten the tune.

Yitzhak tugged his shirt down and said, no, no. I don't want to sing, stop it. I saw he was blushing. The flesh under his eye began to twitch.

I wanted to stop talking to him but I couldn't, then tell me a story, tell me.

Yitzhak looked at me, swallowed, and said, all right, I'm giving you the words to the song and you mustn't ask anyone about songs, or talk about ants and worms, or ask anyone for a cigarette. It went like this: *Koshot Loyosh the Hungarian fought at the front, and if he says again that he has no more soldiers, then the whole nation must join up and go to the front.* That's what I remember.

I cried out, yes, yes, it's a song, and I began to call *Koshot Loyosh* the hero to come to us and save us, why not, we need someone to save us, the Messiah isn't coming, and the Lord left us a long time ago, maybe *Koshot Loyosh* will hear us? Yitzhak caught me by the elbow, approached my ear, opened his mouth,

I said, just a moment, just a moment, I stuck my finger in my ear and mashed all the ants in my ear, now tell me.

He said, Dov, we have to be silent now. *Shhhhh.*

Today, I know.

The decision to part from my brother at every hill gave me strength. We had to analyze the situation. We had to plan, think about how to go on living. I had a goal. I had a reason to make the effort to go up the hill, I knew my brother was waiting for me at the top and that gave me hope on the difficult journey. We talked. We touched. Looked at each other and I saw the concern he had for me. Thousands were left finished on the roads, and one, only one, looked after me, and I looked after him. We were there for each other like a small torch in the great darkness.

Israel, 2001

14:58 from Nahariya to Binyamina. A stop at Bat Galim, in Haifa.

I lean my head on the seat and want something sweet. Don't know how to stay alone with the story.

Their story was becoming difficult, frightening. Yitzhak could still shatter SSman with a blow of his fist, but follows from a distance, waits for an opportunity. Dov is almost finished, he'd already gone through half of Germany on foot and part of Poland.

They are so sad in Yitzhak's living room.

If Dov was with me he'd say, but why are you crying, if I were you I'd be happy, we're coming to the end of the war, aren't we?

Yitzhak would get up and go out into the yard to hush his geese, returning without saying a word.

They'd look at each other for an hour, finally Yitzhak would say, that's enough now, I'm going to my cowshed. Dov would say, do you want to go on? And I'd say, not now, Dov, take me to the station.

Chapter 18

Dov

I could no longer take care of myself on the march.

And my brother Yitzhak became a thief. An expert thief. He knew how to put his hand into someone's pocket and take something without them feeling it. Bread, potato peels, things like that. I saw something in him I didn't see in the camps. He stole food and agreed to share it with me.

We entered a half-empty camp, Yitzhak disappeared and I fell to the ground. Don't remember the name of the camp. Couldn't move. My head hurt. I put a hand on my forehead and it was burning. I felt as if my body was turning into a match and I sank down. I bent my fingers, moved a knee, stuck out my tongue, *aah*, breathed deeply and closed one eye. The second eye burned and burned, I couldn't see a thing. I sat up and thumped my chest. My chest hurt. I felt it was dangerous for me to be in the dark. In the meantime, Yitzhak returned. He had a piece of bread in his hand. Yitzhak cut his bread in half and put some in my mouth. I managed to sit up. I asked, where are the sticks I put in my nose?

He looked at me, what for?

I said, I'm burning, can't open my eyes. Yitzhak touched my

forehead, said, it's because of the fever, eat another piece of bread and we'll look for a tap. I went with him. We found water. I put my head under the tap. It was good. Every time my brother got hold of some food, he gave me exactly half. My brother Yitzhak had the strength to give it to me. Others didn't have the strength to give, Yitzhak did. I saw. Brothers didn't help each other. Father and son didn't share, like the case of the father with the blister under his ear and the son who had his trousers rolled up to the knee. I saw them several times. They walked not far from us on the death march from Buchenwald. The father was maybe forty-five. His tall son looked about twenty. They slept quite near us and didn't speak to each other.

Before entering the labor camp we prepared a place to sleep in the forest. It was cold. Suddenly shouts. The father with the red blister and the tall son were fighting in the mud. The son was holding something in his hand. He was struggling to put it in his mouth. The father caught his hand. The son clenched his fingers. The father tried to open his fingers one by one, screaming, how could you, Ya'akov, it's my bread, mine. The son kicked the father in the belly, speaking through clenched teeth, you're finished, give it to me, give it to me.

The father shrank, stuck two fingers in the son's eyes, weeping, it's mine, Ya'akov, give it back, I'm a father, your father, and I'm telling you to give it to me. The son whined like an animal, bit the father's fingers and covered his face.

I turned over. I heard the father weeping, Mamaleh, oy, Mamaleh, oy gevalt.

SSman Hans Schultz stood near us. In the darkness he looked like a giant with boots and a hat.

He aimed his revolver and shot one bullet, two. One in the father's head. One in the son's head. End. My brother Yitzhak stood near the tree. Motionless. I shivered. I put my face in cold leaves. Pulled the blanket over me. I wanted father. Papaleh. Where is my father. Papa, Papa. I felt a touch on my shoulder. I raised my head. My brother Yitzhak bent over me. He held a piece of bread in his hand. He divided the bread and gave me half. I put the bread next to my cheek. The bread got wet. My brother signed to me to put it in my mouth. I ate slowly.

Chapter 19

Yitzhak

SSman Hans Schultz looked at the dead father and son and signaled me to approach.

The prisoners near me walked away and I approached the dead. I stepped on the blood still oozing from them into the mud. The father's mouth was open. I bent over the son. He had bread in his hand. I took the bread.

I looked at SSman Hans Schultz. He nodded in the direction of the feet. I bent over the feet of the youth. His shoes were ruined and the soles were like paper. I picked up his foot. Felt. Socks. I quickly removed his shoes and took his socks.

The next day I didn't see SSman Hans Schultz. He disappeared forever. After the war, I looked in the newspapers. Looked for his name. I didn't find it in the newspaper. I wanted to see if they found him guilty. I considered putting in a good word for him but in the end decided not to. We must not put in good words for Nazis, we must not, because of all those who died on the roads.

Chapter 20

Dov

My brother Yitzhak took a risk for me.

We reached a German airplane factory. An abandoned factory. It was dark with stars and a scrap of moon like a slice of grapefruit. We were a few hundred prisoners, maybe a thousand, don't know the exact number. A convoy of prisoners in pajamas with the stripes almost erased by dirt and mud. The Germans announced through the loudspeaker, we will spend the night here, and they handed out a quarter loaf of bread to each prisoner. Next to the SSman who was giving out the bread two wolf hounds were waiting. Large dogs with sharp-pointed teeth. Dogs trained to smell a prisoner who got into the line for the second time.

We stood in a long line.

My brother held my trousers from behind. We received our bread and went to find somewhere to sit. We fell to the ground and swallowed the bread in one bite. We looked at each other. My brother frowned, looked into the corners and whispered, now we have to find a place for the night, get up, get up. I remained sitting. I couldn't get to my feet. My brother said, wait here, he got up, walked around and stood in line again for bread.

I looked at the dogs. My heart sank into my soles. I wanted to call him back. I raised my hand but it fell back. I opened my mouth, closed it. I made a decision. I couldn't bear to watch. Fell into a bottomless pit. Got up.

Yitzhak's turn was approaching. Three in front of him. Two. Yitzhak stopped. Gets bread from SSman and barks from the dogs. They smelled him, and as if on command they leaped on him, grasping him in their teeth, *aaah*. The SSman raised his rifle and brought it down on his neck. My brother Yitzhak fell to the ground. The two dogs were on him. I heard the yelps of the dogs tearing at him, *aaah*. I shouted God, where are you, save him, save him. God didn't come. I pressed my hands to the concrete, bent my knees to my belly, flew sideways. I craned my neck and looked ahead, not one prisoner took any interest in my brother. A group of SSmen sat by the door with their back to us. They were eating canned food out of tins. I wept, Papaleh, my papaleh, the dogs are eating him. Father didn't come. Only the SSman took an interest. He stood over my brother his legs spread wide, hands on his hips, smiling at his dogs. I wanted him to die.

But my brother Yitzhak fought the dogs.

I saw his leg fly up into the air. He kicked one of them hard in the stomach. He had a wooden sole on his shoe. The dog howled and flew up to the ceiling. The second dog attacked my brother in the neck. Yitzhak grabbed him by the head and turned it to the side. The dog lay on the floor. And then Yitzhak jumped to his feet, flew towards the factory entrance and vanished. The SSmen continued to eat. The dogs whined and crawled to the boots of the SSman with the bread. He wagged a finger at them, nu, nu, nu, and left the place. I had no air. Began to cough. Couldn't stop. I pressed my mouth, screaming in my mind, you're all right, yes. Your brother is also all right, yes.

A few minutes went by and my brother Yitzhak sat down next to me. His shirt was ripped and he had holes in his elbow and leg. His face was as red as a boiled tomato. His forehead was wet. He wiped his hands and the blood on his shirt, wiping his forehead on the sleeve, put a hand into his armpit and took out a piece of bread. I couldn't believe I was seeing bread. He divided the bread in two and gave me half. I was good, hah? Yitzhak gave a half grin, the other side of his mouth was blue. Another miracle.

When I was strong I had the courage to do things myself.

Night. A German village. Two days walking without bread and water. The SSmen informed the residents of the village by loudspeaker: Organize food for the prisoners. We were a few hundred prisoners, maybe less, maybe more, and we sat down to rest. I saw a horse and cart approaching. On the wagon was an enormous tub. We understood they'd brought us soup. A tall SSman jumped onto the wagon. He held an iron ladle and called out: Get in line, all of you. I saw the long line and realized I didn't have a chance of getting to the soup.

I stole behind the SSman and jumped on the wagon.

I was holding a tin can. I managed to thrust the can into the tub and fill it with soup. The German with the ladle saw me. He thrust the ladle right into my forehead. I heard a *boom* like a bomb and blood. A lot of blood and a mist. I flew off the wagon with the can in my hand. The soup didn't spill. The soup only changed color. I drank the soup with my blood. It gave me strength for a few more hours.

Chapter 21

Yitzhak

The Germans weren't satisfied with our deaths on the roads. Sometimes they loaded us onto open trains. When the American airplanes came they wouldn't let us get off. We didn't ask them, we wanted to live. We knew the war was coming to an end. By the airplanes circling in the skies and shitting on us with bombs. The minute the bombing started we jumped down to look for food. Not shelter, food. We always looked for food. We were willing to eat a scrap of bread, or peels, or roots, even if everything was dipped in blood. There were those who thought that if they'd walk a bit in the fields they'd find real food, others knew there were no miracles and didn't jump to look for something to chew. Their energy to dream was long gone. They lay in the car and waited for bombs from above.

One day we were traveling in an open car in the rain.

We stood crowded in the car, like wet matches without a head. A cold wind traveled between the cars, got into our shirts and peeled off our skin. I wanted to sit on the floor to escape the wind and the cold. The stink coming from below didn't bother me. I dug my elbow into the back of a prisoner standing in front of me, signaled Dov, I'm sitting down, and then the rain stopped.

I raised my head and wanted to shout to Dov, we have sunshine, we have sunshine, and I didn't shout. From a distance a convoy of black dots approached the train. It had wings. A few seconds then a loud *boom*, and a droning, and a dense volley of machine guns, like a rabble of birds with diarrhea.

The train stopped immediately. I rose to my feet and saw that the scenery had changed while I was sitting. We were in a construction area. The German guards screamed something and jumped down. Dov and I jumped after them. We hid behind a brick wall with a pipe at the side.

Not far from us an SSman without a dog took shelter. A fat SSman. I couldn't keep my eyes off him. The SSman heard us moving but couldn't see anything. We stayed close to the wall, thinner than the pipe beside us. The SSman looked and looked, but found nothing. He put some planks next to the wall like an armchair, put a handkerchief on the tall plank and made himself comfortable. After a time, he took out a canteen and drank and drank until he'd had enough and wiped his mouth. Then he removed his backpack. Opened it and rattled about inside. I saw him take out canned food. Looked at the tin and put it back. Took out another tin. I stopped breathing. I bent down, stuck my nails into my leg so it wouldn't itch and I waited.

In the meantime, a bomb fell, hitting the train and the prisoners. I pulled Dov. We lay down and covered our heads. The side of the train shattered, dropping a sea of prisoners on us, pieces of whom came flying, wrapped in pajamas. These pieces fell on our heads and backs, bloody blows everywhere. Blood with pieces of wood and lumps of flesh in pajamas. I wanted to vomit but didn't leave the fat SSman. He was fiddling with his backpack as if he was sitting in a pleasant garden with flowers raining down on him from above. He held the tin and cleaned the lid. My heart was beating like a hammer on a nail. I got up on all fours, my face towards the SSman and I saw Dov also standing. I wanted to tug at his shirt but he had already taken a few steps away from me, he raised his hands and began to make strange gestures. He seemed to be directing the airplanes to the train. He shouted to the airplanes, come closer, closer, closer, signaling to the right. The noise of the airplanes was dreadful, but I still heard him shouting to them, to the right, nu, to the right, don't you understand?

I thought I'd die. I gestured to him with a finger to my head, called out, are you mad, and he smiled at me, continuing to direct the traffic in the sky. In the meantime, the SSman opened the canned food. I looked at Dov. I wanted to shout to him, stop it, stop, but then, about ten meters away, I saw two other prisoners with their hands up. They also began to direct airplanes like Dov. One did everything Dov did with his hands and the other took off his hat, marking a place on the ground for every bomb. He finished marking the place and laughed hoarsely. Another sign and more laughter then, finally, he took down his trousers, showing the bombs the mark of his non-existent ass. I was certain that in a few minutes the plane would take us all. The two prisoners weighed barely thirty kilos each. Their knees jumped as if they were sending strength to their hands, a lot of strength and joy. I saw Dov encouraging them like a big strong king with personality and strength. He became healthy and successful in joyful company. Said, good, good, you're good, good. The best, and he smiled a broad smile.

In the meantime, the fat SSman was wiping a knife and fork on his kerchief.

Another three prisoners came up to Dov and began to direct the airplanes beside him. One of them climbed onto a large stone, making great circular motions with his arms and laughing with a black mouth. A few more laughed with one another, making faces even though the firing was less. Dov was strengthened by his new friends. He shouted to the airplanes to return quickly, you haven't finished with the train, nu, come on, come on and the airplanes indeed came back and then Dov became a Messiah. They said to him, Messiah. Messiah. You're our Messiah.

I left them.

I stuck to the fat SSman. The large box was open on his leg. He lifted the box and began to eat. I tightened the belt on my trousers. Drawing strength from my empty belly I jumped on him. Grabbed the box. Poured the food inside my shirt. Threw the box aside and ran like a madman to the last car on the train. I didn't care about the machine guns. I didn't care about SSmen with rifles. One thing was on my mind. Guard the package smeared on my chest.

I stopped at the last car. Put a hand on my navel. Under my shirt I could feel damp pieces. I looked back. The fat German was sitting on his planks. Held another box on his knee. Dov's friends continued to direct airplanes. I pulled the shirt away from my body. A sharp smell of meat pinched my nose. My nose ran. I was so excited I felt the hair on my body standing on end. It was the first time I'd smelled meat since leaving home. I ran back in Dov's direction. Called him, but he didn't hear. He was stuck to the sky, shouting at airplanes, come back, come back, we aren't done. Then he clapped his hands.

I said to him, listen hard, we need to get onto the train, but Dov didn't move. He'd locked onto the friends who stood beside him, saying confidently, wait a bit, the last plane will come soon. They looked at him and waited patiently. I took out a small

piece of meat, approached him and stuck it in his nostril. He
opened his mouth wide, folded his arms on his chest and stuck
to me. I whispered, I have meat for us, but first we have to go
away from here. Dov thrust his hand into my pocket and began
making sounds, *mmmmm, mmmmm*. I whispered, be careful.
At least twenty SSmen had gathered near the train. They pointed
at the car that had taken the hardest bombing and yelled in
exasperation. I signaled, bend down, and dragged him to a
distant car.

Dov got on first, I followed. The car was empty. We sat close
together. I thrust my hand into the shirt and gave my brother a
piece of meat. He swallowed without chewing and looked at
me. His cheeks were wet. I took a handful for myself and saw
prisoners climbing into our car. At least three had blood on
their faces. I heard SSmen screaming and shooting with rifles, I
knew I had to be careful. In the car were at least five dangerous
prisoners. I signaled to Dov with a finger on my mouth, and we
set off.

I put a hand on my belly and began to itch. I waited. I put a
thumb and a finger into the shirt. Cut part of the meat. I rolled
it slowly like a ball and closed my fist. Pulled my hand out of
my shirt, in the direction of my ass. Waited. I carefully moved
my hand back, found Dov's hand. A warm, trembling hand. I
passed the meat to him and pressed his hand. Whispered, wait.

A tall prisoner towered over me with steely eyes. Dov didn't
move. The prisoner bent his head for a second and Dov raised
his hand and swallowed the meat. I took a piece for myself. I
raised my hand to my mouth and *boom*. A blow to the head.
How could I have forgotten the smell? The meat had a sharp
smell. I stopped immediately. I could feel myself leaking into my
pants and knew that if the prisoners smelled meat they'd tear

me to pieces. I started digging with my foot in the straw on the floor. I wanted to find the smell of shit. There wasn't a strong enough smell. I said to myself, calm down, the car is open and there's plenty of air. We went on eating cautiously until we'd finished the lot.

I felt good.

Dov's cheeks had reddened and I felt like shitting. I held back and managed to fall asleep.

Chapter 22

Dov

My brother Yitzhak fed me like a bird.

The meat tasted like the Garden of Eden and I wanted a few more turns with my hands. The eyes of the tall prisoner opposite me told me I must be cautious. After about quarter of an hour, we finished eating. My body warmed up. I wanted to sleep and saw in my mind a yellow picture. In the picture was a nest of chicks I found on a branch of a tree in the forest. I couldn't remember when it happened. In the nest were three chicks. Three tiny balls of brown wool with a splash of yellow near the beak. I saw myself lying on one of the branches, waiting for the mother.

A medium sized bird arrived at the nest. She held a fat worm in her beak. Three chicks fell upon her, cheeping like maniacs. She tore pieces of the worm and put it into their mouths. The chicks pushed one another, wanting to be closest to the mother. I saw that the fat chick won. He stepped on the other two and grabbed almost all the pieces. I wanted to rip off his head. I didn't interfere. That evening I told Mother what had happened. Mother said the strongest always win. In my heart, I decided to be strong.

I went to the forest, hung from a branch of a tree and did exercises. I touched the branch with my chin at least twenty times. I also did pushups. My muscles swelled in my upper arms and I was satisfied. I began beating up the goy kids who started with me. They'd yell, Yid, go to Palestine, get out of here, Yid. It was on the way to school. I wasn't afraid of them. I beat them up all right. Sometimes I got beaten up, even injured, and didn't tell the teacher at school. I just trained for longer and longer hours. I got on quite well with the goy kids. It didn't help me in the camps.

The terrible sound of machine guns woke us.

The noise shrilled in my ears. Another bombing.

My brother Yitzhak put his hands on my ears, looked steadily at me, and then took my hand and said, we're jumping. The train stopped. The Germans were screaming, you're forbidden to get off, forbidden, and jumped off the train, we after them. A few others jumped. Most of the prisoners stayed on the train. My brother and I hid under one of the cars. It was hell around us. Dense fire sprayed the train. Pulverized trees like a lawn mower. Boards flew up and fell like bombs on the car. I heard prisoners crying, oy, Mamaleh, oy Papaleh, oy Grandma, poor chaps, they remained like that.

And then I saw my brother Yitzhak holding his belly, doubling over and shouting like everyone else, oy, oy, oy, I'm dying of pain. I couldn't see any blood. But I was alarmed, God, he's been hit in the belly.

I shouted, what happened, what happened.

He cried, my belly, I have to shit.

I yelled into his ear, so shit then, and get it over with.

He said, can't, I'm bursting, and pulled down his trousers, sat on the rail, pressing hard, and nothing came out. He wept, I'm dead, dead, screwed up his face and pressed, ay. Ay. His neck almost exploded, his eyes bulged out, his ass was dry. I thought, poor guy, his ass is blocked, what do we do, what do we do. I was afraid, he'd explode inside and his intestines would spill out.

I yelled, no. No. No. You aren't going to die on me here, what do we do, tell me. He didn't say. I grabbed my head and started hitting myself, yelling, you have to save him. And then I had an idea. A stick, yes, I'll find a stick and push it up his ass. Maybe we can free the block with a stick. I yelled into my brother's ear, wait, wait, I'm going to look for a stick and we'll open up the blockage.

My brother grabbed my trousers, weeping, don't leave me, stay with me. And then he stood up and hit his belly hard several times. I caught his hands, held him and we pressed together, ayyy.

Finally, something came out. I looked down. There was a tiny piece of feces, like sheep feces. Yitzhak sighed, it's because of the meat. My body isn't used to meat. All right, doesn't hurt.

I wiped his face with the sleeve of my shirt, said, *phewww*, you scared me. He held my shoulder and laughed.

In those days our bodies were dry as peanut shells. The bread we were given every few days wasn't even enough for one simple bowel movement. Only our guards ate well and would leave whole packages in the bushes. We saw them eating more than they needed. They opened boxes and bottles in piles and we stepped on their packages in the forest.

Chapter 23

Yitzhak

The train stopped around noon. We were given an order, everyone get down, quickly, quickly.

The Germans had to use force for us to agree to get down. We got down near a forest in a place without a name. As we got down from the train, there weren't many of us left, we were less than half the number that left the gates of Buchenwald. Even those who were still alive weren't really alive, but nonetheless they had enough strength not to get down from the train in the forest, in the place with no name. Even the blows from clubs and rifles, the dogs and the curses, didn't affect prisoners whose bodies were already three quarters finished. One prisoner had only half a face. Another prisoner was missing a shoulder. He screamed with pain until a thin SSman spat at him and dug his boot into his face, and pressed, and turned, and that was that. Another prisoner sat on the floor of the car and wept, leave me alone, leave me alone, don't want to get down. He remained in the car, his mouth smashed and his tongue rolling out, without a nose. I lost two nails because of the rifles raining down on all of us.

Finally, we all stood in line.

At first I was hot. Because of the urine in my trousers. We had no bucket for our needs in the car. Then I began to feel shivers, like a fever. Perhaps because of the damp air coming from the forest. Perhaps because of the prisoners who looked as if they were after a pogrom. I wanted to vomit. I breathed deeply, exhaling hot air onto the flesh without nails.

SSman screamed, stand straight, don't slouch.

I saw heavy mist among village houses and a dark forest. The tops of enormous trees touched the sky. The prisoner next to me with an Adam's apple the size of a tennis ball bounced it again and again. He had an abundance of fluids and I wanted to ask him, pray for us, pray, because this will be everyone's grave.

Rain began to fall. The rain was not as dark as the prisoner's tears. My legs began to tremble. I looked for Dov's hand and we held hands.

And then we were given the order to enter the forest.

I was certain the SSmen were preparing us for the firing party. They'd had enough wandering about like idiots, enough. For how long can one wander about in trains, and walk the roads without a reason. We entered the forest maybe a hundred or more prisoners, don't exactly remember. It was rather dark and wet in the forest with a sharp smell like cooked vegetables. After about a hundred meters, SSman shouted, stop. We stopped. The SSman called, don't scatter, don't sit down, and he left. We stood among huge trees that blocked the light. Nonetheless, we felt the rain. On my back I had a blanket. I took it off and gave my brother a corner to hold. I look around.

Dov said, shall we call the brothers to help us hold the blanket?

I asked, what brothers?

He said, the two who lay with me in the bunk at Buchenwald.

I said, what are you talking about, Buchenwald is far away.

He said, nu, so what, they're here, there they are, d'you see the two facing us, near the broken branch, nu, look, I know them. I was sure Dov was dreaming. He caught my head and turned it in the direction of two prisoners as small and thin as us. The two looked at us and whispered to each other. Dov held out a thin hand and called, come, come, this is my brother, have you forgotten? The two approached.

One had a large head, one eye, and a dent in his forehead. The other limped and crumpled the edge of his shirt in his hand. He smiled with his mouth closed and fell upon Dov, hugging him like a papaleh. Dov was alarmed, said, oy, what's this, are you all right?

The brother with the dent on his forehead dragged his brother back, saying, sorry, he's forgotten how to speak. Ask me.

There was nothing to ask. I gave a corner of the blanket to each brother, we stretched the blanket like a tent and crowded into the middle. The rain dripped on the blanket and splashed to the sides. Everything was heavy, apart from my teeth that danced *clack clack* in my mouth. I rubbed my mouth with my free hand. The skin on my palm was as lined as Mother's hands after doing the laundry. I hit my leg. I felt a warm prickling from the knee down. Then came a paralysis that rose and settled in my ass. I felt as if my body began from the waist up. Every few minutes I looked at Dov, whispered, soon we'll go to sleep, we're holding up, yes?

He said, yes. I looked at the brothers. One was silent, his face to the ground, the other smiled. I saw that other prisoners stood like us with a blanket over their heads. Some prayed with their lips. I understood by the motions of their bodies. There were some who slept standing against a tree trunk. Water ran off them like a weak tap. No one sat. The tension was great.

After about half an hour, I couldn't feel my chest or the hand holding the blanket. I tried to fart, nothing. That's it, I'm paralyzed. I glanced at Dov. He was standing a little crookedly, rubbing his forehead, didn't stop. I saw skin missing. The brother who'd forgotten how to speak was crying with a smile on his face. The brother with a dent on his forehead said, soon, soon we'll go to sleep.

Three SSmen were standing not far from us. They looked satisfied. I didn't want to see them. I changed direction and then came a large *boom. Tach.* I jumped in alarm and saw a prisoner lying on the grass beside a nearby tree. He had a huge hole in his belly. He pulled up his shirt and looked at his belly. His intestines were spilling out onto the grass, black with blood. He screamed, save me. Save me. I felt I was about to faint. I made myself bite my hand, I looked at Dov. Signaled, nothing to do with us.

SSman with a rifle in his hand approached the wounded prisoner.

He had a wet cigarette in his mouth. He stood over him, observing motionlessly. Dov continued to scratch his forehead. I glanced back. The limping brother stopped his crying. He opened his mouth wide and rolled his eyes upward, there was white there. I saw his brother putting out a hand to cover his face. The wounded prisoner held out a white hand to the SSman and wept, kill me. Please, sir, I'm dying, dying.

The SSman didn't budge.

The wounded prisoner dug his nails into the mud, pulling up grass, howling like an animal, I can't bear it, press the trigger, please, one bullet, sir.

The cigarette in the mouth of the SSman disintegrated in the rain, fell. The SSman stood like a marble column. Not a muscle moved in his face. He kept the rifle aimed at the prisoner, looking at him.

I felt my temples explode.

Wanted to scream, help him, nu, press the trigger, but I murmured we aren't interfering, understand? Dov understood. I looked at the two SSmen standing five steps from the wounded prisoner. They were leaning against a tree trunk, smoking a cigarette and talking to each other, didn't even bother to look. The prisoner wept soundlessly. Scratched his chest wildly, kicked his legs, stopped. And then he leaned on his elbows, stretched out his chest, slowly sat up, dragging his body forwards. He threw his head on the SSman's boots. Kissed the boots, and begged, kill me, please kill me, I'm burning. The SSman didn't move. He took another cigarette out of a metal box, lit the cigarette and sucked on it. The prisoner raised his head. He had mud on his face, his neck, his chin was jumping up and down, I could hear his teeth chattering. The wounded prisoner looked down, dragged himself away on his elbows. The intestines trailed on the grass, leaving a pool of blood. He made a snorting sound like an animal being choked, *chchchrrr. chchchrrr*. And then he stretched out his neck, screaming at the SSman in German, kill already, bastard, press the trigger, dirty German, your mother's a whore, filth, garbage, son of a bitch, may you rot in hell with your family, kill.

Aaah. I almost fainted. Couldn't believe that a Jewish prisoner could curse an SSman standing beside him. Couldn't believe that a Jewish prisoner with his intestines hanging out had a voice as strong as a loudspeaker.

The SSman's cigarette fell.

Maybe he'd died on his feet? No, no, his eyelids moved, and he was breathing. Yes breathing, his chest was rising and falling,

I saw it. Only then did I understand. The SSman wanted to see how slowly, slowly this death advanced. Yes. The SSman wanted to enjoy the picture. I bit my fingers to stop a scream leaving my mouth, press the trigger, dirty German, press. I looked at Dov. I signaled *shshshsh* with my finger, whispered, dangerous situation, don't move. Dov didn't answer me. I was afraid the SSman would wake up and let go at us with a burst of firing, to see several images of approaching death. I glanced back. The smiling prisoner looked dead standing up. His brother gestured to me, don't worry, we won't interfere. The cursing prisoner dropped his head into the mud. He wept to Sheindele. Where are you, Sheindele, ah, Sheindele, my Sheindele.

I wanted to die.

It started in the belly. Like a ball of fire rising from the belly, burning the chest, choking the throat, and blowing out the cheeks. I pressed hard on my mouth, but a painful weeping came out. My body jumped, shoulders shook, I immediately turned my back on my brother, held onto the branch of a tree, pressing my face into it. I wept for the wounded prisoner, wept for myself and Dov, for Father and Mother, for my siblings. I wept for my home, I wept for my large cat who loved to sharpen its nails on the bed sheet. I wept for a kettle full of boiling water that always stood on the stove in winter. I wept for dry socks in my drawer at home, a warm sweater.

The wounded prisoner continued with his Sheindele, and I wanted to finish my life together with the wretched prisoner, and kill him already, dirty German, son of a bitch, kill us too, yah stinking pedant, piece of shit, *du Arschloch* – you asshole. Kill. Kill.

I felt Dov's hand on my shoulder. He held my shoulder and pressed, didn't let go. I wanted to turn around and tell him, Dov, what will be with us, what will be, I looked at him, no words came out, only weeping, a lot of weeping. Dov hugged me and whispered, we're together, we're together.

If they'd shot me at that moment I'd have been happy. I wanted a bullet in my head, in my heart. If they'd killed me in the forest I'd have said, thank you very much, sir, thank you very much. To this day, in the wind or rain, I hear the screams of that poor man. To this day I see his intestines jumbled together with the grass and SSman standing upright over him. Slowly smoking his cigarette, *aaach*.

Chapter 24

Dov

The dying of the prisoner ripped out my soul.

We stood in the pouring rain for hours, my brother and I, and the brothers I'd known in Buchenwald, Bloc 56.

We'd known one another before one of them lost an eye and the other forgot how to talk. Standing with us were about two hundred other prisoners.

We saw the prisoner quivering, his intestines hanging out, like a fish taken out of the water. At first a lot, in the end, less, and then the ants came and dug into his forehead.

I wanted to go to the SSman, say to him, what's the problem, you hold your cigarette and I'll hold the rifle, finish this, and be done with it! But then I saw my brother Yitzhak weeping and weeping and that weeping in the rain could finish him, so I said to him, look. Here, look, a rabbit, there, there, between the trees, and here's a wolf, do you see the wolf?

He didn't see.

I looked for something else, saw the Germans' packages, a lot of food, whispered to my brother, Yitzhak, look over there, what do you see? He didn't answer me. There are boxes of meat there, you and I can steal together, want to? And stop crying or I'll go mad, I can't bear it, and then we heard SSmen shouting from the direction of the village: *Wer Brot will, wird kommen* – whoever wants bread, come. *Wer Brot will, wird kommen.* They summoned us from the forest with bread, like dogs.

We came out of the forest and received a quarter loaf of bread. Again I swallowed my bread in one bite. I remained hungry and weak. I couldn't straighten my knees. In the meantime, the rain stopped. I looked up.

I heard the cheeping of birds, lots of birds. They were hiding in a huge tree, and I wanted to climb the tree, don't remember why. I thought, you'll never be able to climb, you're lost.

The SSmen shouted, everyone run, run to the village. We couldn't run, it was muddy and slippery. The soles of my shoes sank into the mud, I felt myself sliding and oops, down I went. My brother caught my trousers, pulled hard, stood me upright like a muddy doll, and didn't let go. There were some who fell flat in the mud and stayed down. Someone, not far from me, was on all fours. He didn't have the strength to get up. He grabbed the legs of a passing prisoner, he fell too, dragging several others with him. I heard shouts, and weeping like the cheeping of a bird, and again the blows of rifles, *trach. Trach. Trach.* Other prisoners trampled them where they lay.

We entered the village.

A German village like our own. Small houses with a chimney, a yard with a wooden fence, a muddy path, and awnings over bales of hay. Villagers peered from the windows. The Germans saw them looking at us. They gave the order to halt. We halted next to a huge barn. The SSmen called through a loudspeaker, stand in line. We stood in line. And then they gave the order, now get into the barn. It's a German barn. You have to keep it clean. We entered the barn and the Germans remained outside.

I fell like a sack onto the hay.

I looked at myself and at my brother. The wet pajamas were coming apart at the seams. There were holes, and there was mud, and the terrible itching of lice. Hardest of all was the hunger. I felt as if a fat worm with sharp teeth was eating the flesh on my body.

Prisoners in the barn coughed, spat blood on the hay. There were some who barely moved and left a brown stain that smelled bad. I said to Yitzhak, that's it, we're done. I'm not moving from here.

My brother was silent.

I saw the two brothers from Buchenwald sitting not far from us. The brother who had forgotten how to talk held his chest and smiled, his nose was running. The other removed the scab from a big wound on his hand and licked the skin. I couldn't look at prisoners anymore. I heard three arguing quietly. One said, the war is over, I'm telling you, another two or three days and that's it. One said, agree, pulling out his hair. One scratched his belly and said, what'll we eat in this shitty barn. The first said, we'll eat hay if we have to but the Russians will come, I'm telling you. I decided, the Russians will come when they come, and I don't care if it's in a year or two days, I'm not moving from this barn.

It was dry in the barn.

We dried off in our clothes, and then we saw there was a loft in the barn. My brother Yitzhak said, let's climb up there. I called the brothers from Buchenwald to come with us. I climbed up first, my brother pushing me from below. After us came the brothers. In the loft was a large pile of hay. We dug into the hay. Deep underneath we found wheat seeds. We ate the seeds with their shells and I was still hungry when night came and we covered ourselves with hay. The hay had a clean smell like home, we fell asleep at once.

In the morning we climbed down to relieve ourselves.

I looked at the prisoners in the barn, I was shocked. During that night many prisoners had died. They lay in piles and I couldn't understand how it had happened. I hadn't heard shots, no one had shouted, or cried, or groaned, they died speechless, maybe from cold, and Yitzhak said, they no longer wanted to live.

The Germans were outside. The villagers watched from a distance. They didn't dare approach. The Germans sat under a tree near the barn, enthusiastically singing a German marching song. I listened to the words. It went like this, *the birds in the forest sing so beautifully, in the homeland, in the homeland, we will see each other again*, stamping their feet on the ground, they clapped to the tune, as if they were preparing for a festive march in some stadium filled with people. I thought, let those Germans go to parades. Let them go on marches, I don't care, I'm staying in the barn. I wanted to run back to the loft but we stayed with the dead. We walked from one side to the other, to release the muscles in our legs. I heard the Germans laughing loudly outside, and then they began to sing sad love songs about missing a woman. I was surprised to hear them singing sadly. I didn't know German soldiers knew how to sing tenderly. I said to my brother, I had a harmonica in my pocket, where is it.

Yitzhak looked at me questioningly, said, the harmonica's with me, don't worry, I'm looking after it for you.

Later on, we climbed up to the loft and stayed up there almost until evening. We didn't have the strength to go down. I lay on the hay and chewed seeds. We had no water. I peeped down. Judging by the piles I realized that more had died. Suddenly, shouts from below. SSman shouted through a loudspeaker from outside the barn: Whoever wants bread, come outside.

We peeped from the top. Prisoners with the strength to stand up went outside. The weak remained on the hay. The dead didn't move from their places.

The Germans put the prisoners on a platform with a tractor. We heard the tractor going off to the forest. A few minutes, and then, *ra-ta-ta-ta-tat*. And silence. And again, *ra-ta-ta-tat*. And silence. The Germans wiped out the strong ones with a machine gun.

We stayed in the loft, two pairs of brothers and ants and worms that came only to me. I looked at my brother. I saw he couldn't see. Lay on his back holding his belly. I wanted to tell him, I've got ants, ants are eating my brain. I was silent. Didn't have the strength to speak. I looked at the brothers. They slept next to each other. Looked like a single disgusting body with two heads.

A few hours went by and again there were shouts. Whoever wants bread, come out. I understood they were calling me to come for bread. Finally my turn had come. I got up. Barely got up. I had to hold onto the wall to straighten up. I bent down to the ladder and put out a leg.

My brother Yitzhak jumped up from the hay, said, what are you doing?

I said, they're calling us for bread.

My brother grabbed my hand, pressing hard. Shouted quietly, we aren't moving from here.

I said, no. No. No. They're calling us to come, I'm going down to them.

My brother pulled me to him, I'm not letting you go down there, it's a trap, don't you understand? They aren't giving out bread, they're killing in the forest, you heard it yourself.

I shouted, don't want to give up, going down and that's that.

I took strength from the great hunger, pushed my brother and jumped onto the ladder. In the meantime, the loudspeaker was calling, whoever wants bread, come out. I raised my hands, shouted, wait, wait, I'm coming down. My brother jumped on me and pushed me onto the hay. I got up. Stood opposite him. Screamed, let me go! And then he raised his hand and, *trach*, slapped my face. *Aaah*. It was like a large piece of wood in the face. I flew onto the hay. Holding my cheek I looked at him. My cheek burned as if I'd gone into a fire. It was the most painful blow I'd received in the war. I couldn't believe that my brother Yitzhak had slapped my face. I looked at him. My shirt was wet. The tears fell and fell, taking with them the ants and the worms from my forehead, nose, and mouth. The brothers sat trembling next to each other in the corner, they were holding hands. My brother looked at me, didn't say a word. Just bit his lips.

I curled up in a corner. Suddenly a strange silence fell on the barn. And then shouts, and crying, my brother peeped down, called, they're taking prisoners out of the barn by force. That's it, they're killing everyone. We heard Germans talking under the loft ladder. My brother shouted, dig, quickly, we're hiding. We dug in the hay like madmen. Lay in the pit. We threw the pile on top of us and waited motionless. My brother grabbed my arm under the hay and pinched hard, didn't let go. It hurt and I didn't say a word.

The Germans climbed into the loft.

I heard them talking above us. I stopped breathing and heard a strong blow, and a whistle. Another blow on the hay, whistles, it sounded as if they were loading hay on a wagon. I understood, they're sticking a pitchfork into the hay. They want to skewer us like rats. I heard them going from one side to another. I shrank to the size of a dot. My body shivered. Every stalk of hay was like a needle in my skin. I felt the pricking of a thousand needles. My heart was beating fast and I could hardly breathe. I made sure the hay didn't move above me. Counted the blows. *Trach*. Retrieve. *Trach*. Retrieve. *Trach*. I prayed to God not to let them stick a pitchfork in my ass, back, my head and then they actually stopped sticking the pitchfork into the hay. Maybe because of the shouts down below. We heard the Germans arguing above us then hurried steps going down the ladder, and quiet. I didn't understand the situation. Like being in a pit of the dead.

We didn't dare go out.

For hours we lay there hungry and thirsty and didn't move. We didn't hear Germans calling to come and get bread. We didn't hear shots or the crying of prisoners. Cautiously I made a tiny hole above me. I saw the darkness of night. I peed in my trousers, and checked, maybe the brothers were dead? I knew my brother Yitzhak was all right. His hand touched me. I couldn't sleep. My cheek burned where I'd been slapped, and then I remembered the story about my brother Yitzhak.

One night my father called my brother to the storeroom in the yard. He wanted help slaughtering a calf. The Hungarians forbade us to slaughter calves. We'd slaughter in secret. My brother Yitzhak would hold the candle, the rabbi slaughtered, Father would remove the skin. I refused to enter the storeroom. Couldn't bear the suffering of an animal. That night, a few minutes before the slaughter, Hungarian police broke into the storeroom. Someone had informed on us. They screamed at Father, you slaughter, huh? Ah? Father was silent. They took the rabbi and my brother for interrogation. Yitzhak was twelve years old. The soldiers said to my brother, what did you do with the calf in the storeroom. My brother didn't answer. The soldiers shouted at the rabbi, what did you do with the calf in the storeroom, the rabbi refused to talk. The soldiers stood my brother and the rabbi in front of each other and told my brother, slap the rabbi's face. My brother didn't want to. A Hungarian soldier slapped Yitzhak's face. Slap the rabbi's face. He didn't. A soldier hit my brother over the head.

Another soldier stood in front of the rabbi.

He ordered him, slap the boy's face. He refused, *trach*, the soldier slapped the rabbi. Slap the boy's face. He refused, *trach*, the other side. And then the rabbi said, Icho, we'll do as they say, d'you hear me? The rabbi slapped Yitzhak's face. Yitzhak slapped him back. The rabbi slapped, Yitzhak slapped. Like passing a ball to each other. The soldiers looked at the two and burst out laughing. A few minutes later, they ordered, that's enough now. They said, did you slaughter a calf in the storeroom? The rabbi and Yitzhak made no reply. The soldiers had enough. They sent the rabbi away, leaving Yitzhak.

It was winter. An iron stove burned in the room.

The oven was red hot. Opposite the oven stood a concrete cast at sitting height. The Hungarian officer, tall as an electricity pole, gave the order to seat my brother on the boiling concrete. Yitzhak sat. His buttocks burned. He danced like an acrobat on the concrete. The soldiers laughed. He danced and danced, didn't say a word.

Finally, they let him go. He returned home with burned buttocks and red cheeks. It was the laughter of the soldiers that hurt him most. I told him, that's how it is with the Hungarian police. For the slightest thing they make Jews slap each other.

I knew it was from them Yitzhak learned to slap and he saved me. I fell asleep under the hay.

Early in the morning, we heard a heavy sound outside the barn. Like the noise of a tractor.

We emerged from the hay. Peeped out from the loft. A huge tank stood opposite the barn. On the tank was a drawing of stars. We didn't know if the tank belonged to the Germans, the Russians, or the Americans. From below came screams of joy.

Prisoners shouted, American soldiers, American soldiers, they've saved us, the Germans have run away.

My brother and I and the two brothers began to caper like foals on the hay. We shouted, the war is over, the war is over. We hugged, cried. One of the two brothers held his chest. The one who'd forgotten how to speak fell and didn't move.

We tried to wake him. We failed.

He had a heart attack and died on the spot. Died of excitement. He had a smile from ear to ear.

Yitzhak and I and the poor orphaned brother came down after that. Prisoners were jumping with joy next to a wagon tied to the tractor.

My brother Yitzhak pointed at them and said, look, we saved the prisoners in the barn. The Germans wanted to fill up a wagon and we held them up. They came up to the loft to look for us and didn't have time to shoot those waiting in the wagon.

I didn't answer him. I felt a lump in my throat.

The war was over.

We walked.

Yitzhak walked a bit ahead of me, because I was looking all around. There was sun. A white cloud. It was spring. I saw a flowerbed.

Chapter 25

Yitzhak

We stayed alone in the yard near the barn. A large yard belonging to a German farmer.

Dov and I without the orphan brother. Without the prisoners who'd jumped down from the wagon and disappeared. The air was quite warm and it was muddy. There was the heavy smell of cow dung, a smell combined with the sourness of hay. Just like the day we left our home in the village of Tor'i remeti in the Carpathian Mountains. I heard the tank traveling through the village. I heard a train passing by on the track. I thought, oy, in a while soldiers will come and drag us to a synagogue, and from there by train to some ramp. They'll be sure to find some ramp for Jews who hid. I gave myself a smack on the head. No, no, the war is over.

I saw a cowshed in front of me. It was bigger than the one we had at home.

Beside the cowshed stood a fat brown horse harnessed to a small cart and next to that was a tin box. I lifted the box and approached the cowshed. I wanted to milk a cow for me and my brother. I suddenly heard a knock on the heavy wooden door. A farmer with a mustache and boots came out. He looked at me and Dov, asked in German: What do you want?

I said *Essen und Trinken,* to eat and drink, and I made signs of hunger. He examined me from top to toe, looked at the stripes on the pajamas. He chewed something, spat on the floor and gestured to me to wait. I waited. The farmer went inside the house. Looking behind me, I saw Dov running to the barn. I called him back but he was already at the barn, peeping at me. I gestured to him to come, but he remained standing at the entrance. The German farmer returned with a tin cup and gave it to me. The cup was hot. I took a sip. Coffee with hot, sweet milk for the first time since leaving home.

I drank it all at once and choked.

I began to cough for air and there was none. That's it, the war is over, and I'm dying from a shitty cup of coffee. I defeated the Nazis, defeated their dogs, defeated the hunger in the camps, and now I'm going to die in the yard of a German farmer who wants to help me live. If I had a rifle I'd have shot myself I was so angry. The German also saw I could barely breathe, banged on my back several times, looked at me, then at Dov, lifted me in his arms and tossed me into the cart, sat in front and gave the horse a hard blow with the whip. The horse began to run just as Dov came out of the barn in the direction of the cart. I held my throat hard. Couldn't stop coughing. Snorts came out of my mouth, like the calf we'd slaughtered in the storeroom. I screamed I'm dying, dying.

A few minutes later we arrived at a German hospital, I saw the sign. At the entrance I could hear a language I didn't know and realized that Dov was alone in the large yard. The German farmer lifted me from the cart and carried me in on his back. He shouted, coffee, coffee, I gave him coffee. Three doctors immediately laid me on a bed, forced me to open my mouth and inserted a pipe into my trachea. The coffee spurted out. I could breathe. I was as wet as if I'd had a cold shower. I breathed like a pump with all its blocks opened and looked at the youngest of the three doctors. He put a hand on his chest and said, America, America. He had a pleasant smile and a large ring on his finger. He pointed to a doctor standing beside him. He had a long, unshaven face and he was bald. He said, Poland. Poland. The doctor from Poland didn't smile. And then he pointed at the third doctor. I saw the straight yellow hair and was alarmed. He said, Germany. The doctor from Germany made a sharp gesture with his head in the direction of his chest. My stomach flipped in a second, a German doctor taking care of me? I wanted to shout to the doctor from America and the doctor from Poland, listen hard, German doctors kill Jewish children. I'm a Jewish boy and I'm getting out of here, goodbye. I sat on the bed and saw the three whispering to one another as if they were good friends. I was shocked. I couldn't understand why a doctor from America and a doctor from Poland were amiably talking to a doctor from Germany.

The doctor from Germany looked at me and said in German: You're in a German hospital. The war is over. We're working together. And then the doctor from Poland said in German: Your stomach is constricted and stuck like gum. He made a gesture with his palms and brought them to his chin. And then he stuck a nail under his chin and said, you had no space for a cup of coffee in your stomach and you choked. You're all right now. He pointed at my legs and said, don't worry, we'll take care of your sores. I didn't want the German doctor to touch me and jumped down from the bed. I was dizzy and wanted to vomit. The doctor from Poland said, no, no, lie down young man, you're staying here with us. I remembered the German farmer who had brought me to the hospital, I said to myself, don't worry, a German farmer saved your life, and I got back on the bed. I knew he'd taken care of me because the war was over and he wanted to save himself. I wanted to call the young doctor who'd taken care of me without his friends, but I didn't know American.

The Polish doctor called the nurses. Two women with large breasts approached me and my heart starting beating in my chest. The nurses smelled of good soap, maybe perfume. They had gentle hands and soothing voices. They wanted to undress me completely, held onto my shoes and pulled and pulled and I screamed in pain. The scabs of my sores had grown onto the soles of the shoe. The scabs covered part of the plastic on top. The Polish doctor said, try and take off his trousers. The two good nurses carefully tugged at the bottom of the trousers, nothing. The trousers had also stuck to the skin. The doctor brought scissors, cut away part of the trouser leg and pointed with his finger. I had old sores on my calves. The flesh of the sores had grown onto the fabric of the trousers. I saw the doctor tightly wrinkling his face. He took out a handkerchief and wiped his forehead and neck. One nurse apologized and left. She returned after a few moments with a wet face.

The doctor looked at her, said, all right?

She said, yes, yes, and blushed. The doctor opened my shirt. The shirt was also stuck to my body near my armpit. I immediately understood that I'd be stuck with the Germans' dirty stripes for the rest of my life.

I caught the doctor's hand and whispered, doctor, strip off my skin, I don't care, strip it, and call the German doctor, he already knows how to strip skin and flesh, call him, I beg you.

The nurses filled a bath with warm water. Poured half a bottle of oil into it and put me in with my clothes and shoes. The flesh slowly slowly softened. The pajamas and the shoes as well. After about an hour the nurses peeled the clothes off me, like removing the scales of a wretched, live fish. The water turned red-brown. It smelled disgusting. I felt burning stabs on my skin, but mainly my ass really hurt. I didn't say a word. The nurses finished undressing me, let out the dirty water and filled the bath with clean water. I looked at my small body and first of all covered my penis that began to warm up but cooled when the nurses took soap and a prickly sponge and began to rub my body. Most of all in the place there were lice. I thought, whatever will be, will be and that's all. I let them wander over my body wherever they wanted to and didn't hamper the sponge. I heard heavy breathing, *phoo. Phoo. Phoo*. Like exhaling without whistling. I felt they were taking two or three of the miserable thirty kilos I had. In the meantime, I began to turn pink in the place the flesh hadn't pulled away. It was pleasant and I had a strong desire to cry. I held back. I saw them glance at each other, shamed by my appearance.

I wanted to sleep for a long time.

The nurses put me to bed. They put ointment and bandages on my body. Finally, they brought me real soup with potato and fresh bread. I ate quickly and was soon asleep. I had three days of confused sleep, a sore head and a burning forehead. I had nightmares, mainly about hands. There was a hand that approached me at every opportunity. The healthy hand was attached to a shoulder with the bars of a German officer who stopped at my bedside to take me to a crematorium. I tried to hide behind a pipe but the Nazi's hand held onto me forcefully. I saw an ironed sleeve with a sharp fold like a knife. I called Mother and the hand disappeared and a shiny black boot came. The boot pressed on my chest. I was sure, the German wanted to suffocate me. I opened my mouth wide, screamed, Germans,

Germans, a thick voice came out I didn't recognize. The boot pressed down hard and I had no air. I tried to push it off but couldn't. Suddenly I saw a rifle butt and a tie hanging above me. I jumped out of bed but two strong hands held me. Put me back in bed. The hands were attached to a head without a face. I didn't know if the hands belonged to a German. I heard a fatherly voice.

The voice passed near my ear, said *shhh*, *shhh*. It's me, Doctor Spielman from Poland. You know me. I didn't want to listen. The hands gave me a glass of water, but I didn't drink because of the risk of poison. I even tried to spill the water. The voice quietly urged, drink, its water with sugar. You have to drink. I closed my mouth tight. He didn't give up, said, we met two days ago because of the coffee. He straightened up, put a hand on my chest, saying, here, a hand. Here, a glass of water. Clean water. Drink. I drank and it tasted good. I lay back on the pillow and looked at him. He smiled and said, you have typhus. In a few days you'll be fine.

I whispered, no, no, I have thoughts, and I have images, I'm going mad.

He said, you aren't going mad, the thoughts and images come with the fever. When the fever goes down you'll be on your feet.

I muttered, how do you know, how?

Doctor Spielman said, before the war I was a psychiatrist in Budapest. I know these situations. I didn't know what a psychiatrist was, but I felt better until night came and I saw a white coat. Two. Inside them was an entire body. Head, chest, arms, legs, joined together, the body of a woman. They spoke American. The nurses put wet towels on my forehead, on my chest. I asked for more sugar water. They brought it for me. I asked for more. They gave it to me. I fell asleep. A few hours later I woke drenched with perspiration. It was dark, a darkness with body parts that crawled over me. There were also bags and shoes in a vitrine. I wanted to take shoes. The window was closed but then I saw a pile of suitcases. Like a tower. I climbed to the top. I saw a hand gesturing to me to jump. Didn't move. Nearby was a white glove signaling to me to go left. I didn't know what was best, left or right. I woke up.

I heard myself yelling, left. Right. Left. Right. A nurse came to me with a torch. I shouted, save me, save me.

She changed my shirt and trousers, changed the sheet, gave me medication, whispered, sleep sleep, I asked, when do we eat, ah?

She said, it's night now, and she left.

I couldn't sleep.

I couldn't believe they'd bring me bread in the morning and I began to worry that the Germans were on their way to this place. In an hour or two they'd take us in an open train and we'd travel for a few days, and end with a march to the death. Slowly I got out of bed. Passed among the beds, approaching patients who were asleep. I looked for bread under the pillow, the blanket, the mattress. I collected a few pieces in case we traveled in a cattle train and I went to the toilet. I found a hiding place for bread under a brick in the window. I peeped into the shower room. My heart was beating. I didn't like showers. I looked at the shower and saw a German's hand coming out of it. I recognized the hand by the stripe on the sleeve. I shivered. I was certain the German wanted to cut my hand. I immediately escaped to my bed. On the way, I met other thieves. They walked on the tips of their toes, without disturbing one another. I hid the bread I'd found under the elastic of my trousers. I fell asleep at last, and then crying and screaming.

I jumped up in my bed. A patient, two beds down, sat in his bed hitting his head against the wall, thieves, thieves, where's my bread. Several patients near him began to cry. They didn't find the bread they'd kept for the next day. Nurses came running. They turned on the lights. A patient with a bandaged head stood on his bed, weeping in a hoarse voice, no. No. No. I'm not getting off the car, no. The nurses managed to calm everyone with fresh bread they brought from the kitchen. I wanted to sleep. I heard an American nurse say in German, no need to steal food, there's enough for everyone. Good night. It was no use. I continued to steal food. Others did likewise. I had to keep bread near the toilet, in my pillow, pajamas, even behind my ear.

A few more days went by and my fever dropped.

I rested in bed for a few days longer and then, one morning, I remembered with shock, I had a brother. Where is he. Where is my brother. I couldn't understand how I could forget my brother peeping out at me from the barn.

I jumped out of bed and ran to the nurses who'd taken care of me. I started shouting, I had a brother, what's happened to him, where is he, we were together in the German farmer's yard. The nurses looked at me as if half of my head had flown off. Doctor Spielman arrived.

He hugged me hard with both arms and pulled me back to bed, said, *shhh*, *shhh*, everything's all right, *shhh*, we're going back to your bed, would you like some sugar water?

I cried out, Doctor I'm not mad, believe me, I had a brother, we were together, I'm telling you, listen to me.

Doctor Spielman didn't want to listen, he wanted to bring me sugar water, the best thing for you is rest, yes? He put me into bed, covered me with a blanket, and put his hand on my forehead. I looked at him. He had a deep furrow between his eyebrows. I realized he thought my fever was going up.

I waited for him to take away his hand, said, please, don't go. I need help.

Doctor Spielman stroked my head, said, I'm going to get an injection.

No, no. No injection, no medication, I want you to listen to me, two minutes, no more, will you agree to listen?

Doctor Spielman pulled up a chair and sat next to me. I looked steadily at him.

I stuck my fists under the sheet and spoke slowly: Doctor Spielman, listen, my brother and I met by chance at Buchenwald. Wait. Before that I'll tell you what happened to us. I have a family. Father, mother, and three other siblings. We lived in a village in the Carpathian Mountains. In Hungary. I was silent, my throat closed up.

Doctor Spielman put his hand on mine and said, what happened to your family, Icho? I wiped my nose on the sheet, we were in Auschwitz. Father, Mother, Sarah and my big brother scattered. Only me and Avrum remained together. Then, later on, Avrum disappeared. I was in the camps. In winter I returned to Buchenwald. I found my brother who is one year older than me in Bloc 56. I didn't recognize him. He looked like a tiny sick boy. From Buchenwald we set out on foot to die on the roads of Germany and sometimes we traveled in open train cars. We walked together for hundreds of kilometers.

I raised the sheet to my face and fell silent.

Doctor Spielman pressed my hand, asked, and then what happened?

He and I stayed alive until the American tank came in. We were in the loft of a barn when the Germans ran away. We came down. We came down together with the orphan brother. I'm certain he was standing next to me. And then I drank coffee, and don't remember anything else. Doctor Spielman, where is my brother?

Doctor Spielman leaned back in his chair. He passed his hand over his bald head, said, I believe you, I believe you. I raised the sheet and couldn't stop crying. Doctor Spielman went to bring me some sugar water. I drank the water and then he said, I don't know where your brother is, you must look at the lists. But, you must know, we have many patients here with us, and we don't have all the names. You must look for him yourself. I jumped up from the bed. Doctor Spielman stood up. Held my shoulder and said in a low voice: Many people died at the end of the war, understand?

I shut my ears, shouted, I won't listen. My brother survived all the German roads and he's alive, and I will find him, don't worry. Doctor Spielman smiled, well good, best of luck.

I began to run.

I reached the doctors' room. A nurse with black curls helped me look through the lists. We didn't find my brother. She suggested, look in all the beds, but first ask doctors and nurses. I started running between doctors and nurses. I didn't care that they were in the middle of treatments. I stood next to them and explained slowly, I'm looking for my brother. My height. Brown eyes. Light hair, no, in the camps it turned dark, and he's thin, maybe thirty, thirty-five kilos, have you seen anyone like that in the hospital? The doctors and nurses hadn't seen anyone like that.

I felt I was going out of my mind.

I looked for patients who could talk, I called, does anyone know the barn in the village near the forest, the barn with the tank?

A patient in a bed near the door raised his head from the pillow. He had a dirty bandage on his neck. He said, forest? Forest? I approached him. He caught hold of my shirt with burned fingers and wept, take me to the forest, please, sir, I can't do it alone.

I said, were you or weren't you in the forest before the barn with the tank?

And he with his weeping, forest, forest, I have to go there, the children were left in the forest, Moishe and Yossel.

A nurse came over to us and whispered, no point.

A patient in a cast beckoned to me. I approached. He had a black scar on his bald head. He drummed with long thin fingers on the cast on his legs, he wanted to speak to me and no voice came out. I saw something strange in his face. It took me a minute to understand. He had no eyebrows or eye lashes. I bent down. He whispered, I know the barn in the village. I was there with prisoners who came from Buchenwald.

My voice trembled, the barn with the tank?

He whispered, that's right.

I asked, where did the prisoners from the barn go, where? The man frowned. I shouted, wait, where did you go from the barn?

He whispered, the hospital.

I asked, did you go alone?

He smiled, how could I go alone, can't you see I'm in a cast? They took me in a cart.

I began to sweat, I said, I was also taken in a cart, who took you? He held his throat and asked for water. I said, wait, I'll bring you water but first try and remember, were there other prisoners in the cart?

He said, don't remember, a farmer took me, a fat farmer, he had a pipe in his mouth, bring me water. I brought him a glass of water. He drank and I felt empowered. Thought, maybe my brother also fainted from hunger and forgot his name.

I ran to the hospital entrance and began to go from bed to bed to bed.

I glanced at the faces of sleeping patients. Lifted blankets, pillows. An American nurse said, your brother isn't here, I know everyone. In the meantime, I reached the end of the hall. Began to go through the second row of beds. Some of the patients had blood-soaked bandages, most were without bandages. They lay pale and thin and exhausted, didn't open their eyes when I raised the sheet. Some lay on yellow stains in the middle of the bed, every second I wanted to vomit from the smell. Some dreamed up at the ceiling. Some cried soundlessly. One thought I was the Messiah, put out a hand and whispered, save me, save me. Dov wasn't there.

That night I couldn't sleep.

A faint light made a circle on the wall and I saw my brother thrown in a ditch, with his face in the mud. His body looked like a wet sack. I took a deep breath and shook off the picture on the ceiling. I heard the voices of miserable patients, they were calling for their families, they explained with tears, it's not my fault, not my fault. I heard the steps of thieves among the beds and quick breaths. I paid no attention to the thieves. And Dov again. Lying on his back on a wet road, not far from a burned tank, eaten up by ants and worms. I sat up in bed and pressed a finger to my head, fool, fool, you left your brother at a crucial moment. What did you fight for if in the end you left him alone.

A nurse with a watch hanging from her blouse pocket approached me, do you need something?

I said, just my brother, she left. I didn't know what to do. I got up. I went to the nearest window and leaned my head against the glass. There were a lot of dark dots, like a mosquito cemetery. Suddenly an avalanche of thoughts hit my foolish brain. Maybe my brother ate something and choked. Maybe he ran after the tank and fell under the chains and the SSmen's dogs ate him? Wait, he saw me drinking coffee and choking, he ran away and peeped out from the barn, saw the farmer taking me in the cart, maybe he was frightened and died because he was left alone?

I scraped off lime with my nails and screamed in my heart, not true, no, no. Dov is alive and he was collected with the healthy ones. I didn't know the whereabouts of the healthy prisoners. I went back to bed and fell into a dream. I saw Dov sitting on a blanket. The blanket we held in the rain in the forest. The blanket began to travel like a boat in a river. Suddenly, it rose up in the water. I yelled to Dov, jump, jump, you'll crash. Dov looked at me as if I was a stranger. The blanket was already at my height. I ran after him, trying and failing to hold onto the blanket. I shouted louder, jump, jump, and saw myself in the basement with the suitcases. The prisoner above me was shouting, jump, jump. I jumped and fell to the floor.

I woke early in the morning on the floor. The pajamas were wet and I felt as if I had a scratch in my throat. That's that, I'm about to catch a dangerous illness of my foolish brain.

I checked half of my face with my fingers. And then the other half. My nose was in place. Eyes. I found my right ear, opened my mouth. Went over my teeth, one after another. I counted my fingers. There were five on each hand, ten altogether. *Mmm*, I'm fine and I can get up off the floor.

I got dressed, washed my face and checked the beds to see if any patients had arrived during the night. From a distance, right at the opposite side of the hall, I saw stairs going down. I asked a nurse, where do those stairs go?

She said, the basement.

I asked, and what's in the basement?

She thought a moment, said, very difficult cases.

How difficult? She didn't say.

I held onto the bars of the bed next to me, whispered, breathe, nu, breathe, and began to walk in the direction of the stairs. At the staircase I stopped. I leaned against the wall and counted stairs from the top to the bottom and back again. I put a hand in my pocket and looked for bread. I had no bread. I ran to my hiding place near the toilet and found bread that was two days old. I shoved it into my mouth and went down the stairs. Aha. A huge basement, dark and smelly, maybe a hundred meters long or more, full of beds and patients. Without windows, only rough concrete walls and small lights suspended on a string. Hugging myself I began to walk.

I passed bed after bed after bed, like the hall upstairs, and soon understood why the nurse upstairs called them difficult cases. Lying there were people with swollen bellies and a head like a wheel, sometimes without a face, just a bald head. I approached them. Tried to discover if the body without the face was Dov's. By the fingers I understood it wasn't. One patient sat on the bed scratching the bandage on his nose. The bandage fell, there was just a hole. He threw the bandage on the floor and stuck his fingers into the hole. I wanted to vomit but stopped myself. Another patient sat on his bed telling himself a joke in Yiddish. He laughed *hahaha. Hahaha*. And slapped himself. Began to cry. And then he told another joke. *Hahaha. Hahaha. Hahaha*. Another slap and a lot of crying. I stopped beside him, said, why are you hitting yourself, stop. He didn't stop.

I went on. There was a mixture of the sharp smell of medication and the stink of feces and urine and, in my heart, I hoped

I wouldn't find my brother. I prayed he was healthy and happy and that we'd meet in another town.

One of the patients looked at me. His lips fell inside his mouth, his nose almost touched his chin. I saw he was tied to the bed and I stopped nearby. He smiled without teeth and put out a thin hand, I said, you want to be free, uh? I pressed his hand. He howled in a thick voice, caught my hand and bit it hard. I felt the pain down to my ass. I tried to pull my hand away and couldn't. His gums were like steel pliers. With my other hand I closed his nostrils, pressing hard. He opened his gums, leaving me a deep imprint on four fingers. I was sure the bone was broken. I shouted, are you mad, what's wrong with you. He smiled and pointed at the ceiling. I looked up, a fat fly was stuck to the ceiling, and in an instant the fly flew from the ceiling, alighting on the face of a patient with an open mouth. The fly disappeared into his mouth.

I walked along the other row. There were patients lying under the bed with their faces on the floor. I had to get under the bed and tap their backs. Some didn't answer. I turned their heads and glanced at their faces. There were instances when I touched a patient and the body was cold. I didn't give up on the dead. I turned them over for a second then put them back in place.

I got almost to the end of the hall and there was Dov.

Three beds before the end, I saw him. He lay on his back, looking at the ceiling. Jumping on him I hugged him hard. I cried, here you are, I've found you, oy I've been so worried, when did you get to the hospital?

Dov didn't move. He gave me a brief look then returned to the ceiling. I called, hey, what's wrong with you, it's me, your brother, have you forgotten? We were together, what's wrong, nu, say something. He didn't speak. I lifted the blanket. His body looked whole and healthy. He had a few dry sores on his legs and his hand, but that was all. I felt him, his bones were in place. He looked like someone sleeping with his eyes open. I raised his arm above the bed and let it fall. The arm fell. I raised a leg and it fell. I shut his eye, it remained shut. I held his chin and pulled down. His mouth remained open. I felt as if I was losing all the strength I'd gained in the hospital.

I ran up to the top ward. Looked for a doctor. The German doctor came towards me, I yelled, Doctor, listen, I've found my brother downstairs, in the basement, where's Doctor Spielman, quickly. The German doctor pointed at the office. I ran there. Doctor Spielman was talking to a nurse. I held onto his shirt and pulled him outside.

Doctor Spielman said, what's wrong? I shouted, I've found my brother, I found him in the basement, down there, downstairs. I pointed in the direction of the staircase and began to run there. Doctor Spielman hurried after me.

Dov was in the very same position. I put my hand on his shoulder, said slowly, this is my brother and he doesn't know me. What's wrong with him?

Doctor Spielman folded his arms, said, now I see the similarity between you.

I said, Doctor Spielman, tell me what illness he has, and why is he lying in the basement? Doctor Spielman sat on the edge of the bed, said, I know your brother and I don't have an answer for you. To tell you the truth, we don't really know what's wrong with your brother.

I felt I was about to collapse. Leaning against the wall, I said, what do you mean you don't know, you're a doctor, aren't you? Maybe call the German doctor, he knows the camps, no, no, call the American doctor, in America they probably know difficult cases.

Doctor Spielman sighed, it won't help, we all know this case.

I began to dance up and down. Cried, don't know, well, then I'm taking my brother and getting out of here. Maybe they'll help us somewhere else, tell us what illness this is.

Doctor Spielman raised his voice, absolutely not, he must be in a hospital, I'm sorry.

I jumped on my brother. Shouted, the war is over, do you understand or not, wake up, nu, wake up. My brother looked at me and returned to the ceiling.

Doctor Spielman stroked my hand and pulled me into the aisle. He said quietly, we'll give your brother time, it won't help to shout at him. He doesn't understand you and you need patience, a lot of patience, do you have it?

I fell on my brother's bed and hugged his legs. I couldn't stop my tears. For hours I wept for myself and Dov. Nurses and doctors came and went. Doctor Spielman came and went between the floors. I saw him circling around me. Saw him signaling to the nurses not to approach. After a few hours my brother sat up in bed and took my hand. He examined my palm and turned it up, down, up, down. I saw him focusing on the veins. Cautiously, I sat next to him. Whispered, what do you want, are you trying to tell me something? Didn't answer. Just turned my hand. I tried to stop him and failed.

I felt I wanted to vomit. I pressed my mouth hard and got up from the bed. Dizzy, I fell to the floor. A nurse in an apron immediately came to me. She helped me up and took me upstairs.

Doctor Spielman was waiting at the top of the stairs. He said, you must rest in bed, understand? Leave your brother and go and rest, yes?

I said, it's because of the smell of the medication, if they'd change the smell I could stay with him, he looks healthy, what's wrong with him?

Doctor Spielman threw back his head, I have no explanation, I wish I did.

The patient in the bed next to me woke up. A patient I hadn't seen before. He was a small man without any flesh. He had a large scarf round his arm, it was attached to his neck. He leaned over to me, my name is Isaac, pleased to meet you. What happened to you and why were you crying?

I told him about my brother.

Isaac said, I know the problem, I met prisoners in the camps who didn't know the names their mother and father had given them. *Gevalt Am Israel, gevalt, gevalt* – Oh people of Israel, woe is me. And then he put his hand under the pillow, took out a piece of chocolate, take it, take it, they only give chocolate to difficult cases, take it from me. I took it.

A nurse with lipstick went by with trays of food. I watched her. I saw her going downstairs to the basement. I jumped down from the bed and ran after her. She left the trays on a table in the corner, took one tray and approached Dov. He was in his normal position. The nurse put the tray on his bed, one hand holding the tray, the other thrusting a towel in his pajama jacket and saying in German, *good appetite*. Dov lifted a thin hand and turned the tray of food upside down on the sheet. Hot soup spilled like yellow urine from the sheet onto the floor. I couldn't believe my brother was throwing away food. The nurse was angry, that's the third time it's happened, we'll have to think of another way to feed your brother.

I bent over my brother. I saw a piece of dry bread under his pillow. I couldn't believe it. Dov had hidden dry bread under the pillow and poured hot food onto the bed.

I began talking to him, maybe he'd hear.

I said, you'll get better and the two of us will leave here and go to our village, would you like that?

No, no, I'm not going back to the village, what's in a village full of goyim for us, we'll go somewhere else. We'll go to Palestine, yes, Palestine. You wanted to go to Palestine, a place for Jews. It's best for us to be among Jews, yes. We'll start our lives over in Palestine, what do you say? We'll find ourselves some land, build a cowshed, we'll be farmers like Father. Don't know where Father is, don't know if he survived, but we'll go to Palestine together.

My brother caught my hand and began to turn it, up, down, up, down. My hand again, huh, what do you want, nu, talk to me, but he didn't speak.

I got mad and started shouting at him, I don't have the energy for this, and you aren't going to die on me now, you hear me?

I kicked the bed, almost breaking my foot. I pressed my hands on my brother's face, shouting, I feel like slapping your face, wake up.

I could no longer bear the smell in the basement. I left. I went up to the floor of patients who had a chance to live. There was the silence of the dead there. I felt as if I was alone in the world and held my head. A machine gun started firing in my mind. *Ra-ta-ta-ta-ta-tat-tat*. And again a dangerous silence. My neighbor Isaac called from a distance, come to me, boy, come, I've got some chocolate for you. I ran to him.

Israel, 2001

14:00 Nahariya train platform.

The platform is empty, yellow with dust and leaves falling from the eucalyptus. Linked, empty carriages stand under tight electric lines. The crow threatens from above, *kraa kraa kraa*. A large and impertinent crow. I open the Israel Railway time schedule, and find the 14:18 from Nahariya to Beit Yehoshua written in red. No mistake. Nonetheless, I'm alone on the yellow platform with the *kraa kraa* of the crow above.

If Yitzhak had been beside me, he'd have said, so nerve-wracking this quiet, maybe you didn't see it but a cattle train just went by, taking everyone far away? Nonsense, nonsense. If Dov had been beside me, he'd have said, actually it suits me to be alone on the platform, I don't like being harassed, and be glad you're first on the platform, maybe you'll get an empty carriage, what's wrong with that. I'd say, I wish, I wish.

Black clouds are gathering above, in the meantime, the crow had flown off. My eyes are dry and itchy. I blink to moisten them. Pray, let there be rain.

A man with a beard falling to his chest, a black coat, and a nylon-covered hat enters the station with a crying baby tucked under his arm. Dragging behind him is a woman in a velvet hat with a large fabric flower. She has a huge belly, maybe her ninth month, and her navel is sticking out of the purple jersey falling to her knees. She is pushing a pram with a duck tied on a string, and two little ones, a three-year-old and one perhaps a year older, hold onto to her jersey. The little ones are wearing wide dresses with buttons from neck to waist and a three-quarter coat. One is licking a crusty line of mucus and the other is sucking her thumb.

The baby is kicking its legs out to his mother but his father refuses. Mother says, Menachem, nu, *bring me de kind* – bring me the baby, but the father insists on keeping it. At the ticket counter, the baby already screaming and struggling, and she says in a nasal voice, soon, Shloimeleh, soon. She approaches heavily and holds out her arms to her baby, the father pays the cashier.

She hugs the baby, holding it to her breast oy, oy, oy, Shloimaleh, shhh shhh. The little ones stick to her, they also want a piece of Mama, with one hand she rocks the baby, with the other hand, she holds their heads.

I'd also like a breast to hide my face against, weep the story of Dov and Yitzhak that sticks to my skin like wet clay. Want to peel off the sore, toss off the mud, all before a black scab grows over the mud. If Dov was beside me, he'd say, how good it is that there's a mother who wants to hug her child, it could have helped me in the hospital, and then Yitzhak would make a long *fffrrr* sound with his lips and say, Dov, you didn't want to come back to us, understand?

Chapter 26

Dov

I lay on the bed as if I was in a glass bottle, couldn't remember a thing except veins.

People approached me and I wanted to examine their hands. In my mind, a palm with downward veins was a sign of Jews and a palm with upward veins was a sign of Christians.

And then came the man who spent the most time with me. I saw he had hair on his head. I touched my head, I also had hair, like stubble. In the meantime, my bed began to roll through the room. I wanted to say, give me your hand, hold it, I'm falling into the water, but the words remained in my mind. I was tired, I wanted to sleep. I wasn't sure if I could sleep, or if I had to get out of bed. And then I saw that the man was leaving me, and I realized that I could lie in bed as much as I wanted to and that was a sign the war was over.

When I was alone, I saw veins hanging from the ceiling, sometimes the veins were with worms, sometimes without worms. When there were worms I raised my hand to the ceiling to catch a handful of worms so they wouldn't touch me, wouldn't return to my head after I'd barely managed to get rid of them.

I managed to catch a handful of worms and throw them at

the ceiling and then other worms came. I wanted to shout, bastards, I've got no room in my head. There were times I saw parts of legs, or a foot without toes. Sometimes I only saw toes without a foot. I didn't know if the toes were mine. I wanted to move them, tried hard, the toes stayed in place, so I understood that the toes weren't mine.

One day I saw a knee on the sheet and another inch and a half below the knee. I wanted to put out my hand to examine the place. I ordered my hand to go down, the hand went down and held the knee and then the leg began to grow by itself. It lengthened, grew fatter and took up all the room in the bed, got right up to the bars. At that moment ants came to the knee, going in and out of the flesh, I hit the leg on the mattress, the ants disappeared, taking the leg with them.

One evening I saw my hand scratching my belly and I felt pain. I lifted up my shirt and looked for a bandage. Didn't find a bandage just scratches and a hurting navel. I didn't understand how come a hurting navel got to my belly. Later, I heard a thin *tss, tss, tss* in my mind and fell asleep.

Chapter 27

Yitzhak: You drove me mad with your veins.
Turning my hand up and down for hours.
Dov: I didn't know you, Yitzhak. I didn't know if
you were a danger to me. I was sure there was a difference
between Jews and Christians.
Yitzhak: Of course there's a difference.
Who did they build a ramp at Auschwitz for,
who did they build a crematorium for, if not for the Jews?

Yitzhak

When I sat next to my brother, I was more frightened than I'd been the entire war.

The hospital was in the town of Neuberg von Wald in Germany. I sat next to Dov for a few minutes and ran outside. I'd only sat next to him for a little while and saw that I was already following him into madness and all because of the smell coming from the medications and the patients. There were patients there who wept as if they were coughing without stopping for a minute. There were patients there who wept as if they were vomiting every few minutes. There were some who wept as if they were trying to poop once a day but were crying for half the day as if they had diarrhea. Only four or five patients wept like ordinary people.

There were times when my nerves just finished me, I'd approach the bed of a patient who was weeping next to us, lift him up with his bed and, *trach*, release it, it was the only way I'd get any peace for a while. If I had some peace from all the weeping I'd talk to Dov, even about silly things. I talked about home. About the rabbi who chased us with his belt to the shithouse and wouldn't give up even when our trousers were down. I talked about the neighbor's daughter. Dov liked to play catch with the goy girl. They'd run about the yard and around the house for hours, roaring with laughter. True or not?

Dov fiddled with my hand as if I hadn't spoken.

Once I asked Doctor Spielman, does all the talking help him? Doctor Spielman said, don't know, but it doesn't do any harm, so go on talking.

Sometimes I wanted to knock Dov's head against the wall and sometimes I wanted to knock my own against the wall. I never hit his head – only my own. I'd sit on the floor next to him and put my head between my knees. In a moment there was a puddle there. I felt as if I was losing my family all over again. The nurses never left me. They'd bring me a bowl of soup and say, your brother is young, Yitzhak, he will get over it, have some hot soup, and then come to the office and we'll make you some coffee. I didn't want coffee in the office. The smell was there too. I wanted to breathe clean air, I wanted to count birds on the electricity wires. I wanted to see children kicking a ball and fighting over candy.

Only my neighbor upstairs was normal, and he didn't have a bad smell, maybe because of the chocolates. He'd always hold out a hand to me and say, eat, eat, it's against the smell.

I'd suck on chocolate and hang around the doctors. I followed them about all day. They rushed among the beds as if they had to save as many patients as possible. There were some patients who wouldn't let anyone touch them, but the doctors and nurses wouldn't give up, they'd thrust their hands into bodies, clean up leaks, bandage sores, stroke bald heads and move on. Nurses took care of them while they slept. It didn't help. Bandages and plasters flew onto the floor when the patients woke up. A patient next to Dov with a respiratory problem would pull down his trousers and urinate in the bed whenever an American nurse went by. He'd howl like a miserable wet baby. He refused to let them touch him. They changed his sheets only at night. The smell of urine drove me mad. After a few days he disappeared but the smell remained.

It was the dead that frightened me the most.

Every hour or two there'd be a new death. There were patients who died in the middle of their tears, weeping, weeping, weeping, then *hop*, they were dead, and a moment later they'd fart. Sometimes two or three farts in several minutes and the stink of spoiled meat, or diarrhea. To this day, whenever I hear farts, I check to see if there are any dead, or whether it's just a healthy fart after a good meal. Say, Shabbat *cholent*, or oranges fresh from the tree. The dead changed like travelers at a train station. The nurses would wrap the dead in a sheet and carry them out, to a refrigeration room. From there they took the dead in a truck. Don't know where. Never went near the room of the dead, I'd already seen dead people that made trouble.

In the meantime, nurses would turn over the mattress, put on a clean, sometimes torn or stained sheet, and bring a dying, barely breathing patient. And then this patient would last a day or two, stop breathing and die. I don't remember anyone who actually remained alive. Patients died of typhus, dysentery, pneumonia. Died from the images scurrying about their minds. Died because they slit their wrists with a knife, sometimes with a fork. Some died because they no longer had the strength to breathe. I saw a dead person like this. He stopped breathing and didn't move. After a minute he opened half an eye, closed it, opened half an eye again, waited a little with a half open eye, and that was that. He was swiftly removed and another brought in.

I was afraid for Dov. Afraid he'd decide to play hands up hands down for the rest of his life.

Dov didn't get out of bed. The nurses would turn him belly, back, belly, back. They'd wash him in bed, and all the time he'd check the hands of every nurse. They gave him water with a teaspoon. Sometimes he'd drink. He didn't want to eat. He'd take the bread they brought him on a food tray and hide it under his pillow. I think he ate his bread at night, alone. He relieved himself in bed. There was very little. He had a thick wad of fabric between his legs and it was enough. Dov's body looked like well-arranged bones covered with transparent skin, no flesh. I could count the lines crisscrossing under the skin. They were blue, pink, rather crumpled. I was afraid my brother would die of hunger in a hospital full of food.

All those days I slept at the hospital.

The nurses kept a bed for me even when I was on my feet. I ate at the hospital, wore regular clothes that the nuns brought, I didn't want to shower. Didn't know what might come out of a shower I didn't know. I'd stand at the sink and splash water on myself, in my underwear too, it was enough.

I barely spoke to other patients.

I spoke a little to the neighbor who gave me chocolate. We

spoke mainly about Dov. One day he disappeared. I was sure they'd taken him in a sheet to the refrigeration room. The nurses spoke among themselves, said, no, no, he was sent to another hospital. I didn't believe them and missed the chocolate. Most of the time I sat beside my brother, or ran after Doctor Spielman. I didn't leave him alone.

I constantly asked him what would be wrong with my brother, give me an answer, Doctor Spielman, does he have a chance? I got no answers.

At night I saw patients who could stand on their feet and get out of bed to steal food. They stole from other patients. Stole from the kitchen, from the office, stole from the dead who'd begun to fart. Beds became stores for food and it wasn't enough for them. In their beds, they hid everything that came into the hospital. Coffee, sugar, medication, towels, soap, pajamas, bandages, bottles, plaster, cotton, forks, salt, powder. Piles of equipment. There were those who stole and *hop*, they died. Sometimes they'd die at night on the way to their beds with a bag of coffee in their hands. The nurses would discover the hiding place and ask them to stop. Didn't help. There were patients who used their half-dead neighbors' beds as a store and couldn't fall asleep worrying about their property. The thieves weren't the same every night. Sometimes they managed to steal, sometimes there were blows. Like the camps, when they fought over a potato peel. I realized that the war had ended in the world but not in people's hearts. I knew, the war would never ever leave us. Just like putting a boiling iron with a number on the body of a calf. The calf grows older, the number remains unchanged. I felt I was sinking into a black hole without a floor. I wanted to get out of that blackness and ran outside.

I wandered about the town of Neuberg von Wald. It was

spring outside. Afterwards came summer with a pleasant sun, and blue, and some white, shapeless clouds. Nonetheless, I felt as if a transparent glass was in front of me. Some of the gardens near the houses had flowers. Red. Purple. Yellow. A strong splash of orange. People walked close to the walls of the houses, or near the fence. They barely spoke to one another. They looked as if they were hurrying to finish some task before returning home to lock the door, the window, and stay inside until the following morning. Maybe they didn't want a young Hitler either. There were few buyers in stores. I saw salespeople standing in doorways and playing with coins they had in their pockets.

I walked slowly along the street, I was in no hurry to get anywhere. I always kept to the edge of the road. I left the sidewalks to the Germans. And the Germans left the road to me. Without my brother I felt as if I was the last Jew in the world and it was hard. I swallowed clean air and tapped on the trousers and shirt. The smell of the hospital remained.

One day I passed a display window.

There were trousers in there, a shirt, socks, a tie, and a rather large torch. I approached the window and then *boom*. In the window I see a familiar but strange figure. I looked round, I was alone. I shivered. Wanted to run away. Didn't move. In the glass I saw a thin young man, weighing maybe forty kilos. Taller than I remembered. With gray trousers turned over at the waist under a shabby, colorless belt. The buckle was in the furthest hole. Shoulders grew under the pale shirt, the neck remained the same. Slowly, slowly I looked up, and lost my breath. I had a long, thin, sickly face. I had short hair. Cautiously I touched it, it was prickly. I had lines and tiny sores on my forehead. My nose was long, broad, like that of an adult. Above the nose shot out thick, unruly eyebrows, and I whispered, oy, what have they done to me, not even Mother and Father will recognize me. I gave myself a smack on the head, I forgot I had no mother and father. I thought, maybe because I've changed my brother won't know me, what do I do, what do I do. I put my hand on my chest, my heart calmed down a little and then I began to smooth my forehead. My forehead became red, the lines remained, the sores too, and I could see that I had a smooth face, without any sign of a beard. I couldn't understand why I had no beard, Avrum had a beard at my age and maybe I'd stay with the face of a girl because of the ice in the open trains? I opened the top button of the shirt. I found signs of hair. I said to myself, the beard will grow, in the end it will grow.

My teeth were in place, just the color had changed. I pulled down the skin under my eye. It was pale with spots, same with the second eye, and then I saw the man in the store standing in front of me. He had the face of a giant. He held out a long arm to me and shouted *Raus. Raus.* I understood him. I'd also have been alarmed by me.

Three months had gone by since I'd found Dov, I didn't know what was to come. One day Doctor Spielman came to me and took me to a corner of the basement.

I stood with my back to the wall. With one hand he held onto the wall and with the other he rubbed his bald head. Back and forth, back and forth, and then he fixed me with questioning eyes, thought and thought and thought, and finally said: Yitzhak, listen, I know what you went through in the camps, I was there myself. He had a thick voice I didn't recognize.

I tensed immediately, took my hands out of my pockets, where were you, doctor?

He was silent and then, after a few minutes, he said, your brother's case is a severe one. Very severe. I've decided to try something. Beads of sweat stood out on his forehead. He took out a handkerchief, wiped it and said, if you can get hold of some strong drink maybe you can save your brother.

I stamped my foot on the floor, asked, what strong drink, doctor.

Doesn't matter, cognac, vodka, whiskey, but most important, with alcohol.

I asked, alcohol, like getting drunk? Yes. Yes. Go and look for it in town, you won't find it in the stores, look for it in people's homes. If you find a bottle, bring it to the hospital. We'll come up with some invention for your brother, maybe it will work, but first find some.

I didn't understand a thing. I left the hospital at a run.

It was hot and suffocating outside. I ran along the road. Passed cars, almost stepped on an old woman with a dog, and didn't stop. I heard her curse, then spit, the dog barked, *ruff-ruff*, I was already far away, near a row of houses with dry gardens. I stopped at the first house and tried to breathe evenly. Knocked on the door and didn't wait for an answer. Pressed down the handle. The door opened. I went in.

In the living room sat a fat man in a vest, holding a book in his hand. Seeing me, he jumped to his feet. I saw he was missing an eye and half his forehead. He opened his mouth. I gave him a severe look, he closed it. Pushing his fists into his pockets, he followed me. I went over to the cabinet in the living room. Full of glasses. I opened side doors, opened drawers. There were plates, eating utensils, tablecloths, I didn't find a bottle. I went to the kitchen. The man followed me, two steps behind. In the kitchen was a heavy smell of frying. A small table, four chairs and low cupboards. I opened cupboards, moved tins, packets, utensils, potatoes. I saw no bottle. Near the wall was a large box.

I opened it. Nothing. I left the kitchen. A little girl, maybe six or seven, approached the man. He signaled to her to go and she disappeared from the room. I followed her. Peeped into a room. The girl stood next to a bed hugging a woolen teddy bear. I saw a closet, opened doors, only clothes. I passed into another room. There was a double bed and a closet. I lifted clothes, towels, stood on the bed and checked the closet, nothing.

The girl stood at the door, saying in German, it's forbidden to stand on the bed in shoes, sir, what are you looking for? I heard an irritable clap. The man stood next to the girl. Caught her by the arm, pressing with his nails. I got down from the bed. Looked at his hand. He let go of the girl, and she ran to her room. I went out into the yard. There was a storeroom there. A boy of about ten stood in the doorway. He began cursing. The man made a *tzzzt, tzzzt* sound, the boy didn't stop cursing. I saw he had eyes like a Chinese person and his tongue fell to his chin. I approached the storeroom. The boy didn't move, continued to curse. I went past him and stepped into the store-room. I turned over boxes, looked in a barrel, there were empty bottles there. I went back to the living room. I saw stairs going down. The two children stood beside the man, he held their hands. His face was as white as the wall. I went down into the cellar, it was dark. A small window near the ceiling gave a little light. I waited a few seconds until I got used to the light. I heard the man upstairs talking quickly. He had a voice like a machine gun. I paid no attention. I opened boxes. Lifted a blanket off shelves. Checked the floor. Found no alcoholic beverages. I left and the door slammed. I heard the turn of a key. Saw movement at the curtain.

I went to the second house, the third, fourth.

I'd go straight to the living room without asking permission,

without asking questions. I'd go in and search on my own, as if
the house was empty. The occupants didn't disturb me. Maybe
they were afraid of me, don't know. If I found a house with a
locked door, I broke a window. Sometimes I climbed onto the
roof, and *hop*, I jumped inside. Sometimes I broke down doors.
Nothing stopped me. I walked through the house and left.

In one of the houses, a grandmother in an apron and slippers
followed me, she was crying. As if I was the master and she a
dog. I didn't say a word. I looked in her house too. But I gave
up looking in the yard. She didn't stop crying until I left the
house. In one of the houses, a woman with an infant in her arms
opened the door. She wore an old dress. She had a small face
and rollers in her hair. I wanted to say, don't worry lady, I won't
hurt you, but nothing came out. The woman sat down in a
rocking chair, following me with her eyes. I approached her. I
said, *Trinken, Trinken,* and I gestured with my thumb in the
direction of my mouth. She said, *Nein. Nein.* And slowly shook
her head. I left her and went to the door.

The woman jumped up from her chair and caught my shirt.
She said in German, take me, please, sir, take me with you. I ran
to the path.

I went to a different part of the town.

I knew it was hard to find alcoholic beverages after the war.
People didn't have enough food. But I made a decision, I, Yitzhak
would not return to the hospital without a bottle of alcohol. Even
if I had to go through the entire town. Even if I had to get on a
train to another town. I continued to break into houses. I went
from street to street. In one of the houses I entered, a group of
cats came in after me. They followed me from room to room. As
if we were together. An old hunchbacked woman with glasses
came out of the toilet. Her glasses fell off. She grabbed a rag,

swiped her dress and shouted *meow kishta, meow kishta*. I picked up her glasses and put them in her hand. I began opening cupboards, the cats after me. The old woman picked up a glass of water from the table, and threw it over us. I jumped aside and smiled at her. She shrieked, take your cats, and march outside.

Just a moment, Grandmother, I'm going. I quickly opened a small cupboard in the corner. The cupboard was full of smelly rags. I closed it. Went out into the yard. The cats after me. A medium sized dog on a chain began to bark. I jumped over the fence into the neighbor's house.

In my search, I never laid a hand on anything. If Doctor Spielman had told me to bring gold, bring jewelry, a silver dish, I'd have brought it. No one bothered me. I wasn't interested in gold. I wasn't interested in jewelry. I wanted to save my brother.

Finally I found it. It was before evening and the house was empty. I broke the lock and went in. A few steps brought me to a large, dark living room. It had heavy curtains, a red carpet and a lamp with a glass shade. Above a heavy wooden sideboard with moldings was a magnificent cabinet. A white dancer had one leg in the air and wore a pleated skirt. At first I didn't see anything because of the dress. I turned a small key and opened the cabinet. The good smell of strong alcohol tickled my nose. My heart jumped. And there they stood. Three beautiful, fat bottles on a glass shelf. I put the bottles into my shirt and held them tight. I couldn't help myself and began to shout with joy. I shouted, Doctor Spielman, we have the alcohol for my brother, and he'll get well, *aah*. Suddenly I heard shrieks. Oh. Oh. Oh. I almost fell flat on the floor. I turned round. On a chair in the corner stood a large cage of birds. Inside was a large multi-colored parrot. I approached it and screamed louder, *oho*. *Oho*. I wanted to kiss it. It didn't stop shrieking until I left the house.

I held the bottles close and hurried to the hospital.

Evening was falling. The street was almost empty. The lamp lights drew circles with holes on the pavement. I could barely restrain myself from calling Doctor Spielman from the main road. I ran inside the hospital. Shouted to the nurses, where's my doctor, where is he? Doctor Spielman approached me. I took the bottles out of my shirt and arranged them in a row on the table.

Doctor Spielman laughed and laughed, said: Cognac, whiskey, vodka. Pinched my cheek, said, ay, ay, ay, Icho, none like you, none. I felt as if I had grown at least ten centimeters higher. I even felt as if I'd grown a beard. Doctor Spielman hid two bottles in a cupboard with a key, took the cognac and two glasses and said, come on, we'll go down to your brother. We went down. The German doctor came with us.

We reached Dov.

He was lying there as usual. Doctor Spielman stood beside him. He gave me the bottle and glasses to hold, sat Dov up in bed, clicked his fingers and said, open the bottle and pour into the glasses. Half a glass is enough. I opened the bottle and poured in the cognac. My hands were trembling and cognac spilled on the floor. Doctor Spielman said, one glass for you, Icho, one glass for your brother. Come on, come on, come closer. I came closer. He put one hand on my shoulder and turned me to face Dov. And then he said, wait, a bit closer. I came closer. Dov looked at my hands. And then Doctor Spielman said, you drink first, then give your brother a glass and tell him, drink, drink, understand?

I said, yes, but he can't drink by himself.

Doctor Spielman said, we'll try. Come closer. My foot touched the bed. Dov tried to catch my hand. I didn't let him. I saw

Doctor Spielman take his handkerchief from his pocket and wipe his head. The German doctor smiled at me and nodded his head, wanting to encourage me. The patients next to Dov showed no interest. I counted silently, one-two-three, raised the glass and swallowed at once. *Waaach*, it burned. I felt as if a huge cough was coming but managed to swallow. I gave Dov some. He took the glass from me and waited. *Aha*.

I said to him, drink, drink. He raised the glass, drank all the cognac and began to cough.

Doctor Spielman clapped his hands. The German doctor cried, bravo, bravo and I had an attack of laughter. I couldn't stop laughing.

I fell on my brother and hugged and cried, you will get well, and we'll leave the hospital. I felt as if there was rain in my brain, on my face, my spine, I wanted to hold back, but the rain falling from me wet my brother. He wasn't upset and examined my hand. I said, turn my hand around as much as you like, I don't care. In the meantime, the cognac began to dance in my belly, gallop up to my throat, I clenched my teeth and wanted to run to the toilet. I managed to get to the aisle and then *waaach*. A dark spurt shot out. Dirtied the aisle between the beds. Dizzy, I saw black, grabbed the nearest bed rail and stayed bent over.

The German doctor raised my head and held my forehead, said, you aren't used to drinking, come with me, we'll go to the shower. I didn't move. I don't know why, but the German doctor from Bloc 8 in Camp Buchenwald popped into my mind. The doctor who took healthy children away and didn't bring them back. I remained with my head down and in my ear, I heard danger! I looked at Doctor Spielman. His hand was in Dov's hands. He saw I wasn't standing straight and said, go to the shower, Icho, you have to wash.

I said, how long will it take, and don't tell me a few minutes, I'm not stupid, there were children from my bloc who went with a German doctor to some experiment, so tell me straight, Doctor Spielman, how long will he keep me in the shower.

Doctor Spielman became grave. A thick furrow dug across his forehead. He said, don't worry, Icho, this is a good doctor, you remember him from the first day, go with him. I want to stay a while with your brother.

I began to walk. I had a bitter taste on my tongue and a sour smell. The doctor wasn't revolted by me. He held me by the arm as if we were father and son. I glanced at him. He had a small tic under his eye and a closed smile. We marched with long strides as if we were in a stadium. I thought, in Bloc 8 I managed to escape, I was lucky, and maybe I won't be lucky, and what will happen if something happens to me in the shower, who will notice. Not even Doctor Spielman is paying attention to me. In one of the beds an American nurse was feeding a patient. We approached her. I called her, nurse, nurse, pay attention, I'm going with the German doctor to the shower. You saw, right?

She raised an eyebrow, said, what? And smiled at the doctor. I made sure I told two other nurses.

We came to the shower I knew from the outside. My head was spinning, like a wheel spinning on a road. I leaned against the wall. The German doctor brought me a towel and clean pajamas. I said to him, I can do it alone.

The doctor said, all right, just leave the door open. I went into the shower. Undressed slowly. The clothes had a sour smell. I stood under the shower. I couldn't open the tap. I heard the German doctor behind me, he asked, do you need help?

I said, no, no, I'll open the water, this is the doctors' shower, right?

He said, yes, don't worry. But I did worry until I opened the tap. I poured a lot of water over myself, washing my whole body with soap at least five times. Then I put on the pajamas. The German doctor called me to the office. He poured me a glass of tea and I wanted to check what he'd put in the tea. The doctor put in three cubes of sugar, stirred thoroughly, said, drink, you'll feel good. I drank the tea and my belly fell asleep. We didn't speak again.

Chapter 28

Dov

The cognac I drank made me want to laugh.

No laughter came out of me. My throat burned, my fingers tingled and the veins I saw on the wall thickened. The beds in the basement started moving. Sometimes they twisted. People couldn't walk straight. They had to lean against the wall to advance. A loud buzzing of bees began in my ear. Sometimes it became fainter, usually it got louder. I looked at myself, I wanted to see if I was also traveling in my bed. I traveled rather quickly, like a carousel in a lunar park, I knew everything by a small hole I saw in the wall. I finished one turn and began another.

The cognac I drank made me miss a melody.

I so wanted to remember the melody. Couldn't remember the name, but in my mind there was a melody I had to catch. I'd catch a sound, and the melody would escape. I'd pressure, another sound, and it would escape. I wanted to tell the guest sitting beside me to bring me a harmonica. I wanted to say, look in the pocket of my trousers, there's a harmonica there. I didn't know where my trousers were. I wanted to tell him that we'd drink to life and I'd play the harmonica for him. I pressed his hand and wanted to speak clearly to him, but what I said in my heart traveled, traveled, and returned to the heart. As if the words circled about us and returned to the same place. I said to myself, harmonica. Bring me a harmonica, and it stayed in my heart. In the end, I got tired and fell asleep in a second.

Chapter 29

Yitzhak

We continued with the whiskey three times a day. I drank, Dov drank. I spoke, Dov was silent. I saw that we were about to finish the third bottle, and then what? I'd steal more cognac and we'd drink to life, and more vodka and liqueur, and we'd be stuck in the hospital for a year to two years, no! I don't agree with Doctor Spielman's arrangement, I hate the hospital. I felt I was beginning to catch my brother's illness. Morning, noon and night I'd get a fierce heat in my palms, mainly after we'd had a drink. I started turning my hands over and looking for signs because of the tingling in my skin. I thought, maybe I've got a kind of lice I don't know. Hospital lice. I looked under my shirt. Found no lice. Just red marks and scratches. Maybe my body was beginning to produce special lice? Maybe I have lice eggs from the camps and they're developing well because of the food and the whiskey I've taken three times a day, for a week, two weeks, and I'm full of lice again. I began to check hands, belly and chest after every meal. During the day I went out into the sun. At night I'd take a magnifying glass from the doctors' room and check myself.

One night a nurse with a ponytail and a ribbon touched me, what are you doing?

Looking for lice, can you see anything? She took the magnifying glass and examined me thoroughly. I said, check my back too and I removed my shirt. No need, you're clean.

So why am I itching?

She said, ask Doctor Spielman.

The next morning I went to Doctor Spielman who was standing with several doctors. He smiled at me, how are you Icho, do you have any whiskey left?

I said, the whiskey is almost finished and I'm going crazy itching, what's wrong with me, doctor? I lifted my shirt and showed him the scratches. He frowned and thought and thought, and I was alarmed, maybe I'd caught some severe illness and if he tells me again, patience Icho, I'll slap myself, two slaps, and that's it. Maybe a slap for Doctor Spielman with his bald head and white folded kerchief at the starched collar of his shirt, and one for the German doctor, even for the American doctor who doesn't talk to me at all, for my brother, too, ah. My brother will get ten slaps, twenty slaps, ten on each side, because I'm sick of him and his nonsense. He drinks his whiskey three times a day, eats a meatball, good soup, and doesn't want to speak. Fine. What the hell is he thinking, that I have the nerves for this illness that he's invented, I don't, and I'm getting out of this hospital and that's it. If he wants to rest in his bed for three-four years, let him. I'll have nothing to do with it.

I approached Doctor Spielman and shouted in his ear, I can't bear this itching anymore or the smell of your dead, understand? Doctors in the group stopped talking. A patient with a bandaged head sat up in bed and began to cry. Doctor Spielman said, *shhh, shhh*, and took me away.

In the doctors' room he said, sit, sit down, pointing at a chair. I didn't want to sit down. I wanted to scratch at the floor with my shoe, and at my hip under the belt, and my belly. Doctor Spielman tapped his fingers on the table *tarrarram. Tarrarram.* And said, it's difficult for you and difficult for all of us. And then he gazed thoughtfully at the window, his fingers quiet. Suddenly he turned his head sharply towards me and said, I need a fishing rod.

What?

Find me a fishing rod.

I threw up my hands, Doctor Spielman, sir, what do you need a fishing rod for in a hospital?

He leaned towards me as if he had a big and special secret and said, I'll go with your brother to catch fish. Fish? Is he making fun of me. But his face was very serious. I thought, this doctor has caught an illness of the mind from his patients down below.

I looked straight at him and said cautiously, maybe you have ants? Because I know these ants from my brother, do you have them?

He breathed heavily and said in the voice of a healthy specialist, don't ask questions, first, bring me a fishing rod.

I don't know why, but I was filled with happiness.

Like a burst of warmth in my heart. As if Father had taken me aside and whispered in my ear, it will be all right Yitzhak, don't worry, it will be all right. As if Father Israel had come to the hospital especially for me, and held me in his strong arms without touching, like he did when I was little. I was a little boy, was I? I left the hospital and began to run without itching.

I stopped near houses in the first street and they looked

familiar and happy. I knew they had no fishing rods and didn't know where I'd find one. I didn't believe there was anyone in Neuberg von Wald who felt like going fishing. And then a tremor came into my heart, maybe there is a scrap of river in this town, or a small lake where you could use a fishing rod. Best to look for water and grab someone's fishing rod. I asked people. Didn't manage to get an answer. And maybe I didn't know how to explain myself. I decided to go inside people's houses, as I had with the cognac. I looked for houses I didn't know.

I started going from house to house and knocking on doors. If they opened I quickly went inside and looked on my own. Didn't touch the cupboards, I went round the rooms and into the attic, and out into the yard. No one tried to stop me. The residents followed me about as if I was a soldier with bars on the shoulders and a rifle. I remember my head hammering, idiot, idiot, why didn't you try and resist during the war. I wanted to kill someone.

After two days I found a rod.

I ran to the hospital with the rod. Gave it to Doctor Spielman. I saw he was excited, holding the rod with trembling hands, and said, very good, now we'll see if we succeed, let's go to your brother.

We went down to the basement. We found Dov staring at the ceiling. Doctor Spielman said, stand on the side and don't interfere.

He stood in the aisle facing Dov.

Dov examined his hands. Breathing heavily, Doctor Spielman waited a few seconds and then he brought the fishing rod forwards, flung it back and threw it forwards.

Doctor Spielman said loudly: Bernard, do you want to go fishing?

Dov sat up quickly and said, but there's no water here, how will we fish?

This is exactly what happened, three and a half months after the war.

Chapter 30

Dov

The bald man stood next to my bed holding a fishing rod. I couldn't understand it.

I knew there was no water in the room. I checked because for a long time my bed traveled like a boat in the room. One night I put my foot down and found a dry floor. I felt my pajamas too. The pajamas were dry. I couldn't understand how come I traveled through water and stayed dry.

The bald man approached me. I wanted to take his hand and couldn't remember why. He didn't give me his hand, just threw down the rod and invited me to go fishing with him.

I said, but there's no water here, how will we fish?

How, how can you fish without water? In my village there was a river. I knew fishermen. They'd throw rods with worms into the river and fill buckets, he must be a fool, he also had the laugh of a madman, because I saw him laugh loudly, and beat his hands against his chest, and call to people standing not far from us, come, come, we have a miracle here. I know nothing about the miracle he mentioned, but at least five women in white coats came over, and at least three men in white coats, and they all hugged me, and shook hands with the bald man, and he flung the rod up to the ceiling again and said, miracle, miracle, ach, how fortunate that it succeeded, and he had tears of laughter on his cheek, and one man sat up in bed and began to clap his hands, and another began to sing like a cantor in a synagogue, what is this, are they giving me a Bar Mitzvah, and me in my pajamas, wait, where are the stripes? And why are there beds all around, and where am I? And then I saw my brother Yitzhak.

He stood on one side, his hand on his face. He was wearing clean clothes, and his body trembled like it had when we walked in the snow. Yitzhak looked clean and healthy with hair on his head. I felt myself getting warmer and warmer but Yitzhak didn't stop shivering. What's wrong with him, is he ill?

I wanted to call him, tell him clearly, we're together, come closer. I realized he couldn't hear me because everyone was talking excitedly, joyfully, and the cantor continued to sing with trills. I tried to raise my leg, my leg didn't move. I tried the other leg, the same. And then I saw that the room was full of beds with sick and wretched people, was I ill? I lifted my pajama shirt, saw no signs of illness, and my bed stayed in place. I searched the ceiling, found no veins, and there were no veins in the beds. Where was I?

The bald man approached my brother and hugged him like a father. Everyone fell silent. The bald man said, your brother has recovered, nu, what do you have to say? We succeeded with the cognac and the fishing rod, eh?

And now, with everything behind us, I can safely say: There were days I didn't believe we'd manage to rouse him, yes, I'm overjoyed.

Yitzhak swallowed, didn't say a word.

The bald man approached me, held out his hand and said, I'm Doctor Spielman, a pleasure to meet you. I shook his hand.

What's your name?

Bernard.

What is your brother's name?

Icho.

He smiled at me and said, very good, Bernard, very good. You're in a hospital in Germany. The war is over. You've lain here unconscious for three and a half months, you're all right now. Your brother sat beside you every day and these are the doctors and nurses who've taken care of you.

The people in the white coats nodded hello to me. And then he said, in the coming days we'll help you to get out of bed. You'll have to get used to walking, like a baby. It will take a little time, don't be alarmed. In a week or two you will both be able to leave the hospital. Congratulations, you've recovered and your brother is also healthy.

We heard choking sounds. Doctor Spielman turned around. I saw my brother holding his throat, his cheeks a dark red. The cough became a howl, like the one I'd heard from a wolf or a fox in the forest near our village, can't remember exactly. My brother walked backwards and leaned against the wall, pressing his fist to his throat, and kicked his shoe hard against the wall.

Doctor Spielman's eyes darted between the two of us. I couldn't understand why my brother didn't come to me. I didn't understand why everyone was happy and only his face was sad. I wanted to go to him. I wanted to hold hands, like we used to. I put out a hand to Doctor Spielman, said, help me to get down. He held me and I tried to sit up in bed. All the white coats began to spin. I fell back on the pillow. I was tired. In the meantime, I saw that my brother had disappeared.

From that day onward, Yitzhak did not enter a hospital, not for himself or for others. Even today, yes, almost sixty years after that war, he won't go into a hospital and he can barely see, he has to have cataract surgery, a simple operation for old people. I've arranged an appointment for him, not once and not twice, but he refuses to go to hospital.

There was one incident, after I'd spoken to him a lot, and after his wife Hannah spoke, and the children, when he agreed to have eye surgery. Nu, he got to the anesthetist's office and sat quietly as if he intended to have the surgery. The doctor was already waiting for him, did it help us? It didn't, because Yitzhak ran away. Yes, they looked for him in the hospital corridor, in the toilets, the yard, where was he found? Sitting at home, in his armchair.

I don't know what will be with his sight. He hasn't read a newspaper in ages. He can only see pictures on television, without subtitles. He can't drive. And he loved driving, he has to drive, with cows, calves, hay, after all, he has a truck in the yard. Fortunately he works in the cowsheds with his son. They travel together, otherwise, what? I tell him, go into hospital, I'll come with you, a few hours and they'll solve the problem, does it help me? Nada.

He can't bear anything to do with the infirmary either. I take care of it. I bring him his medications, vitamins. Arrange them in bags according to the day. If he needs special herbal teas, I buy those for him too. May he be healthy, my brother.

Chapter 31

Yitzhak: A new world was born in front of me when Doctor Spielman said, your brother has recovered and is talking sensibly.
My brother has recovered and I have begun to live.
It was as if I had walked out of the darkness and into the light.

Yitzhak

In September we left the hospital and moved to a convalescent home.

The Americans sent us to a monastery in the village of Indersdorf, thirty kilometres from Munich. It was a pleasant day, the air had a festive smell. I remember it as if it were happening today: Blue skies with clouds like enormous, shining, white sheep. I searched the clouds for Father's face. On holidays, he loved to paint the walls of the house with clean, sharp-smelling whitewash.

We wore new clothes. A checked shirt, dark trousers and a gray battledress with pockets and a zipper. We had to make a hole in the belt with a nail to keep our trousers up. The clothes had the smell of fabric that had lain in a cupboard for a long time. I liked the smell. The Americans also gave us new shoes with a strong sole and thick leather with stitching on the side, I'd never known good shoes like those, nor socks of thick, soft wool. I tied the laces with trembling hands, putting a foot on the mattress, smoothing the shoe leather with the blanket, *tshsh-tshsh*. I felt I was smoothing my soul, *tshsh-tshsh*, and went on to the pockets. I had at least eight or nine pockets in all. I put my hands in the pockets and waited a while. The pockets were empty, but I still felt as if I had a private place, just for me.

From the pockets I went on to the zipper of the battledress, *zip-zap*, and again, *zap-zip*, *aah*, I couldn't stop. Dov said to me, you'll spoil the zipper, what's wrong with you, and I said, did you see how many pairs of underwear they gave us, did you see? I made a fine pile on my bed, there were at least seven pairs of underwear and another seven pairs of socks, just for me, *aah*. I remembered the wool underwear the Germans gave me at Camp Zeiss, it was the only pair I had in the camps. The lice loved the wool of the underwear. They sucked my blood and got fat, and multiplied, and sucked even more, I went mad from the itching and didn't throw them out because of the cold. Only a jet of boiling steam I sometimes found in the topmost pipe room would kill the lice. Hot water would only hurt them and then they'd get even more edgy. The steam released me from them for a day or two, and then other, stronger lice would come.

Dov and I set out from the hospital with a bag in our hands. We looked like two strangers cut out of a newspaper. We laughed, pummeling each other's heads. Then we walked along the road, stamping on the asphalt like soldiers on a march. We wanted to hear the sound of shoes with soles from a factory. It was a strong, confident sound.

From the hospital they took us to the monastery, a gray

building with a lot of windows. I was given a clean bed in a room with Dov and a few other refugees who were left from the camps. Some were Jews, some were Christians. The Americans sent us to the monastery to put flesh on our bones. Everybody looked as if they'd come back from the dead. Their eyes were uneasy and their movements sharp. They'd sit on the edge of the bed, chew their nails, or smoke a cigarette, and suddenly jump up and go outside. Outside, they'd wander the length and breadth of the yard, examine the road and look for flies. If there was the slightest noise, say a window banging in the wind, or a bucket overturning, they'd lie on the ground with their hands on their heads, or they'd hide.

At night, I couldn't sleep. I'd get into bed with my clothes and shoes on. In one hand I held bread, in the other I held the handle of the bag I'd received at the hospital. In the bag were other clothes, underwear, socks, two towels and a small plastic bag for toiletries. After a few sleepless nights I put the bag under my pillow and finally managed to sleep but got up in the morning with a stiff neck. During the first days my brother and I took turns guarding our bags. Some went everywhere with their bags. I saw them going into the toilet and sitting down with their bag on their knees or on the floor. There were some who sat on their bags in the dining room. In the yard they looked like passengers on a train platform without a train. One of them wore all the clothes he had in his bag, he was swollen and nonetheless still thin.

At the monastery there were nuns and female British and American soldiers on behalf of *UNRRA*, the United Nations Relief and Rehabilitation Administration. Most of the female soldiers were Jewish. We suddenly had a great many young women with breasts, and beautiful long hair, and a narrow belt at the waist, and legs in nylon stockings, *mmm*. A pleasure. Suddenly red lips were smiling at me, and there was a black line above the eye, and hands touched me with well-done nails and soft skin scented with good soap, like perfume. The soldiers would go by and I'd get dizzy. One poor fellow would walk about the monastery with a towel in his hand. Every time he saw a beautiful soldier approaching, he'd spread the towel in front, and run to the toilet. It took him almost a month to get used to it.

The nuns wore black cloaks to the floor and a white head covering. I didn't see hair, just a warm, loving glance as if we were a Hanukkah miracle.

The nuns and soldiers spoke patiently to us, they didn't need to hold a loudspeaker even though they worked very hard with us. For instance, they wanted to teach us to hold back at the dining table. Take food in turn. Leave something in the main dish for others, bread, fruit, vegetables. This was a big mistake. The main dish was emptied in a second. Because of this the lesson on holding back was repeated from the beginning every morning. The soldiers are talking and I see a fellow with a wet nose descending under the table with his plate. I saw his neighbor and understood the reason. His neighbor had the look of a plate-snatcher. I peeped under the table. There were at least four or five fellows, plate in hand. They sat on the floor and took large bites, eating with their hands. And then what a laugh, I saw a large hand going down under the table, wandering cautiously over several heads, then, *hop*, it grabbed a chicken leg with mashed potato. *Oho*, what a commotion down there. All five under the table threw away their plates, grabbed the hand of the thief and pulled him down. It was the plate-snatcher. He fell with his ear in the mashed potato and began to curse, bastards, bums, leave me alone idiots, they didn't leave him alone but pulled even more strongly, and potato got inside his nostrils, but he didn't let go of the chicken leg.

A big female soldier came over at a run. Her black ponytail jumped like a horse brushing away flies. She stood next to the fellow with his face in the plate and said, Yosef, I'm waiting. Yosef didn't hear. The solder leaned down near Yosef's ear and whispered something. Yosef straightened up. He wiped his hand on his trousers, and held his neck. And then the soldier bent down under the table and said politely and respectfully, everyone will now come out from under the table and sit nicely in their places, understood? Eight fellows came out from under the table, sat down looking at their plates. In the meantime, the fellow sitting next to me jumped back as if he'd been stung in the back. He had an old face the color of a well-washed shirt. The dark fellow next to him began to whistle a cheerful tune and *hop*, quickly grabbed his bread. *Oho*.

The poor man began to shout, help, thieves, help.

The dark fellow stopped whistling and said, shut up, little girl, stop whining. The fellow with the old face didn't want to stop whining. What he wanted was to attack the thief and take a bite out of his cheek.

In a flash all was bedlam. Three soldiers came over at a run. Shouting, sit down nicely, friends, everyone sit down nicely. Didn't help. The soldier with the ponytail grabbed the fellow with his mouth on the cheek of the other fellow, lifted him above all the heads, pressing him hard to her breasts. She had huge breasts.

She said, enough Miko, enough Miko, and at that moment I was sorry I wasn't mad Miko. Miko didn't like her breasts. He kicked, threw himself on the floor and cried continually. The dark fellow shouted, crazy, crazy. He had nice red teeth marks on his cheek.

He returned to his chair and said, I knew we had an issue with a baby here, *meeyow, meeyow meeyow*.

A nun with a rather large blond mustache approached with a tray full of meat. She offered the tray to Miko and said, take two, nu, two just for yourself. Miko didn't want to.

I said to the nun, his bread was taken, do you have any more bread?

They brought him bread and he actually calmed down. The soldier with the ponytail said, bon appetite everyone, and now listen carefully: You don't have to grab food from one another, you don't have to take food in your pockets to the room, and why do you hide bread in your beds, we serve you three meals a day, true or not? Everyone was quiet. She said in an even clearer tone, answer me, true? Someone farted, *broooom. Brooooom*. Everyone began to laugh. The soldier with the ponytail went scarlet. She looked at the small soldier next to her. She had a braid down to her bottom.

The soldier with the braid smiled at her and shook her head, as if to say, never mind, pay no attention, and called out, quiet, quiet. And there really was quiet. The speech of the soldier with the ponytail continued: There's no need to steal food from the kitchen. The food in the kitchen cupboards and in the pantry is for you. The boxes delivered in the truck are also for you. And a fellow at the end of the table shouted out, what happens if the Germans take the truck, eh? I know them, they'll take the truck, and then what will you do, eh?

Several fellows began to hammer on the table with their forks, shouting, yes, yes, yes, the Germans, damn them to hell, will come and take us to the crematorium as well.

The soldier said, no, no. The Germans won't come, understand, the war is over.

We couldn't understand anything. Neither could we understand the words of the American doctor they brought especially from the hospital. Nor the American officers with bars on their shoulders. We didn't understand anything. Anything. As if we had a block in our minds.

I remember four tall, good-looking officers they brought to the monastery to talk to us. They didn't know everyone had blocks in their minds, and explained to us in professorial tones that the war was over, Germany was beaten, and there was enough food for everyone. We didn't believe any of them. We'd sit at the table and check to see what fresh food could be hidden in a pocket. That could last for at least two days. The officers talked about peace in the world and we were in the war.

The soldiers and the nuns wanted to restore us to a normal life.

They taught us to bathe with soap and sponges. Wash our hair three times, yes, scrub our ears. Brush our teeth. Put paste on the brush, not eat it and spit it out in the sink, yes. They taught us to go into the shower, take turns, room by room. We didn't want to wash. They didn't give up. They stood us in a line for the shower and watched us so we wouldn't run away. Sometimes that line didn't end because they didn't manage to shower everyone from evening till morning. They'd get one in and three would run away. There were some who refused to go into the shower before they looked in through the window and saw that water really was flowing from the tap. I understood them. I would also go into the bathroom and very carefully check the shower. When I looked, the thought always ran through my mind, what will come out of that shower. Hot water or gas, and maybe powder. I'd undress and wait. Sometimes I'd go in and immediately escape. There were many times I was certain there was gas there.

The soldiers wanted us to go to bed on time. To get into bed without our clothes on, without shoes. They'd beg, take off your shoes at night, you're dirtying the sheet, take them off, take them off, and wear pajamas, here, choose, there are lots of pajamas in two colors.

The soldiers taught us to play the piano and sit nicely at a concert. They wanted culture for us, and that was hard for me, very hard, because they busied us with nonsense. They had a daily program for us. One day a trip. One day a play in Yiddish. Then a circus, or a concert. *Aah*.

Seven in the evening. They seat someone at the piano in a large room in the monastery. I sit quietly as they told us, as if I was a normal human being, hands crossed on my chest, or on my legs, or with crossed legs, head up, yes, the most important thing was head up, two ears to the piano, yes, no going to sleep, we could lean on one another. I sat as the soldiers told us. The piano moves and I hear the *tach tach* of a rifle. *Tach. Tach-tach. Tach-tach-tach-tach. Tach*. Many rounds. My shoulders fall, and I weep, I weep from nerves, and I glance at my brother, and at other friends, and say to myself, am I the only one who's going mad? And suddenly I see another friend weeping, and another wiping his face, and at the side another looks down at his shirt and pinches his leg, *aah*, the piano is also driving them mad. I look at the soldiers, and I see they are happy, smiling at one another, nodding, yes, yes, weep dear ones, it's healthy. Fools, fools they thought we were weeping because of the piano they'd brought us.

The next day they brought two more pianos. I wanted to leap to the ceiling, and then they brought us a play in Yiddish. An actor with a hat and a scarf around his neck told us about Feigele – young girl – who wanted to drink water from a puddle.

Ah. He's talking about Feigele, and I hear, Shloimeleh and Saraleh, and afterwards a terrible noise in the ears. Like a broken radio. The actor makes faces with his mouth, his hands, according to his face I understand we have to laugh, and we didn't laugh, we wept a lot. And then he left. The stage was empty, soundless. And that was the most dangerous thing for me. Because every silence would bring me Germans with a machine gun. And after the machine gun came the powerful silence with the strong feeling. The silence of death. I couldn't bear that silence. I had to be in an environment where there was life, so they wouldn't make people disappear into some crematorium and leave me alone in the world.

One day they took us to a circus. A clown with lipstick stamped his enormous shoe on the floor. He had ringing bells on his sleeve. He went *ring-a-ding-ding*, and I heard *tach, tach-tach*. And I saw blood, a lot of blood pouring onto the bells on the sleeve. Then they brought an acrobat on a rope. Everyone watched that happy acrobat, and I examined the black hole in the stage that produced Germans: Ten Germans in a line like a ruler, and twenty more Germans with rifles, and thirty more Germans with steel helmets, and finally, a thousand Germans screaming *schnell, schnell*, and we've been dead for over an hour.

I couldn't tell the women soldiers about the hell going through my mind. Couldn't talk about the film running through my mind, like an enormous wheel, turning, turning, back to the beginning. Turning, back to the beginning. Turning, back to the beginning. Like The Muselmann movie on the train. Prisoners trampling him and he opens his enormous eyes at me. Doesn't shout, doesn't cry, just waits for his life to end. And there was a film about a prisoner who stood near the door of a barracks in the camp, nibbling a hole in the door. Nibbled, nibbled, *trach*.

Got the butt of a rifle. His brain fell and scattered. And there was also the film about the prisoner who danced in the mouth of a large dog. Danced like a rag doll. Because three other dogs wanted pieces of him. Films with a bad ending.

Only occasionally did the film with the German girl come to me, the one who gave me food at Camp Zeiss, the girl with the braids, one tall, the other shorter. That girl brought me the most weeping of all.

I felt that life at the monastery wasn't good for me. I had more and more blocks in my mind because of all the films I saw while sitting nicely at the table, or at the piano. I told the soldier with the ponytail, I need to work because I'm in great danger. She wanted to know, what work, Icho, tell me.

I said, teach me a profession, teach me to be a butcher, like my father.

They sent me to a German butcher. He had a back as broad as a table and a small fixed smile. I traveled with the butcher to fetch animals for slaughter. He bought cows from local farmers and slaughtered them in the yard. I loved the journeys to the villages. Loved seeing large cowsheds with dairy cows and calves. For the first few days I had a hard time. We'd arrive in a village and I'd feel suffocated. I saw that the butcher noticed me. He spoke to me and I couldn't answer. I was sure that if I began to speak a huge flood would follow. I pinched my leg and ordered myself, control yourself. After a few days it got better. I began to take an interest in the price of cows, calves, the farmers' hay I saw. The butcher taught me to cut meat in the right direction, to take care of the meat and what to do with the internal organs. In the meantime, I learned German. He spoke to me in a soft, pleasant voice. For me it was like a new language. I didn't know

German without screams and orders like a hot nail to the brain. I didn't know words in German like, how are you, be careful, cut slowly, didn't know German gladness in the morning just for me. He called me boy. Come here, boy, do you understand, boy, now, boy, you do it. Sometimes he put his hand on my shoulder. His hand was wet from the water. Nonetheless, I felt a pleasant warmth on my shoulder.

One day I cut myself with a knife at the butcher's store.

A deep cut in my finger. It bled a lot. The German butcher took me to a doctor who said, broken finger. He put a board under the finger with a large bandage. The wound didn't heal well. I didn't return to the German butcher. My finger is crooked to this day.

Shaleachs from Israel – emissaries – arrived at the monastery.

Shaleachs from the Jewish Brigade. They wore ordinary clothes. They were suntanned and healthy, with strong hands. I wanted to be close to them, hear stories about Eretz-Israel. The Shaleachs asked us, where do you want to go after the monastery, to America or to Israel.

I spoke to Dov. We said Israel, but first to our home, in the village of Tur'i Remety in the Carpathian Mountains.

Chapter 32

Dov

The monastery was good for me.

At night they gave us chocolate to get us to go to sleep. We didn't want to go to sleep. We'd wander round the room, the yard, the room, sit on the beds, lie down in our clothes. Get up. Start conversations, drop them in the middle, go back to them. There was one fellow who after ten turns in the yard would stand next to the wall, and *boom-trach* he'd bang his head against the wall. He was given a whole bar of chocolate. At first he refused to eat it. He said to the soldier, you first. He was certain the chocolate was poisoned.

There was one who sat with us in the yard every morning and plucked out his eyebrows with his nails. He went from the eyebrows to the eyelashes. Finished with the eyelashes and went on to the hair on his chest. He'd take hold of a handful of hair on his chest and *hop*, pull it out with the skin. Disgusting. Then he'd throw up his hand with the piece of skin, as if he was flying a plane, *mmm. Mmm. Mmm*. He'd call us to watch. The soldiers dabbed on blue iodine, put on a large bandage and cleaned under his nails. Then they brought scissors and cut his nails. In the meantime, one soldier with a braid down to her ass quietly,

quietly sang him a song. I heard it. He'd go, *mmm. Mmm. Mmm.* And lick a candy. Don't know where the soldiers got so much candy. They had a store of candies in their pockets. They'd thrust candies at us at every opportunity. For instance, if they found a wet bed in the morning. Sometimes they found three or four wet beds at a time. Mainly after nights with barking dogs. Some fellows go into a frenzy if a soldier even unintentionally touches them, on the elbow for instance. One fellow locked himself in the shower and stood under the shower for a whole day because a soldier touched his shoulder. They shouted through the window, Moishe, open up, open up. Only that night did he agree to come out.

We barely spoke among ourselves at the monastery.

They spoke a bit about home. A bit about the village, the town. We didn't ask questions. Most of the day we'd follow the nuns around to see what was happening and what the plans were and I was uneasy because of the large dresses they wore. I didn't want anyone to see what was going through my mind and, by everyone else's gestures, I realized that they, too, didn't want anyone to see what was going through their minds. There was one fellow who liked to follow the fattest nun. She had a wide pleated dress. He used to hide behind the trees and run after her, his back bowed. He was certain she was hiding grenades or a little Kalashnikov under her dress. He'd say, why does she have such a big dress, if not for bombs, eh? Why does she have a head covering like a sheet from her head to her neck, if not for a chain of bullets?

One day the fat nun had enough of the fellow. She took him to her room. Don't know what they did there, but he began to visit the nun's room regularly and stopped talking about bombs.

There were days we'd mess around with the soldiers. We'd

measure their waists and breasts with our fingers, measure the length of a leg from the middle of a skirt down, always arguing about where the groin actually started from, we also weighed each of them with our hands. We'd laugh a little, then fall silent. We'd usually count fingers, back and forth, back and forth. Count up to a thousand and start again.

Nobody at the monastery knew where any of us came from.

Stories about the camps passed only among us. Through faces, hands, the smell of the skin. In line for the shower. At the dinner table, or when we sat on the wall, looking into the distance, or when someone's nose ran without his having a cold.

The hardest of all were the rumors.

Every day there were different rumors. I thought I'd go mad. It was enough for someone to say he'd seen doctors in white coats, or mention a gas truck that had come to the monastery, and no one would take a shower. Everyone ran away to the yard and the poor soldiers didn't understand why we didn't go near the showers for three days. Finally, the soldiers said, you'll get lice, do you want lice? According to the rumors I knew which camps the refugees had come from. For instance, when they said truck, one of the fellows cried out, uprising, uprising, as he'd seen in his camp. He shouted to the soldiers, fetch rifles, everyone, take shelter, quickly, quickly. It took an entire bar of chocolate and a handful of candies showered over him to stop the uprising in his head.

One fellow used to make a high pile out of all the bags he had in his room. He collected bags from the neighboring room as well. At first he got beaten up. In the end they left him alone, they even let him open the bags and arrange clothes in groups. Because he always put things back in the evening. I knew, that fellow came from "Canada" Commando at Birkenau Camp, we might have been there together, but I didn't know him. Another fellow would wander about the toilets all day with a brush, a rag, and a bottle of Lysol. He cleaned the toilets from morning till night, poor fellow, he got sores from the Lysol. One day I said to him, Simec, your poor hands, what are you doing.

He said, I'm working.

I asked, what work did you do at Auschwitz?

He said, poop and pee, took the rag and walked off.

When a train went by the monastery for the first time, everyone ran away to the forest. Three trains went by and we remained in the forest. Only at the fourth did we agree to come out.

One day a group of doctors arrived by train. They wore ordinary clothes, no white coat. There was a stupid nun who blurted out, the doctors have come to see how you are. Nu, within a second not one was left in the monastery. Everybody ran away to the forest. We were certain the war had started again. We were certain that the doctors were hiding white gloves in their pockets and would soon line us up on some ramp and start directing us, left, right, all with white gloves. During the first weeks we ran to the start of the forest. The more we ate, the farther into the forest we ran. Some ran to the forest, some ran on the spot and waited to see what would happen. Some climbed onto the roof of the monastery and kept watch from above. Sometimes we waited for a signal from someone who'd climbed up onto the roof. According to his signals we'd decide whether or not to return to the monastery.

And there was one day when they gathered us together to go and see Yiddish theater, the early show. We stood reluctantly, hands in pockets, waiting for the vehicle. Suddenly a rumor spread, Germans. Wow. All of us ran to the forest. By that time, we'd put a little flesh on our thin bones so we ran far. I was strong and immediately climbed a high tree. I thought, today no one will get me down from this tree. Not even my friend Vassily. Vassily, my best friend in the village. Vassily with the coat, one sleeve long, one sleeve short, and high shoes without socks. Vassily with the straight yellow hair like stalks of mid-summer wheat and brown eyes like mine. Vassily who came to look for me in the forest when Hungarians came to take my family to the synagogue. Vassily wept under the tree, Bernard, if you aren't back by nightfall, they'll kill your family. Your father said, remember the young man from Budapest, remember Shorkodi's friend, the one who promised you work in Budapest. They stood him up against a wall. Ten rifles were given an order. Ten rifles all at once. Bernard, listen to me, they'll put your family up against a wall, do you understand or not?

The rumor about the Germans kept us in the forest for hours, and then we heard the women soldiers calling us, we have hot meat for you, we have bread for you, and you have beds with sheets. Five or six fellows left the forest at a run. A few minutes later we heard the fat nun saying over a loudspeaker: Listen, listen, the war is over. The war is over. There are no Germans at the monastery. None. Please come back to the monastery.

We slowly left the forest. One by one, heads down. We were ashamed.

After a month, maybe a little longer, the boredom at the monastery began to annoy me.

I went out to wander around Indersdorf. I walked fast for a hundred steps, a hundred slowly. I ran for half a street, and for half I walked slowly. I found an inn. There were cars there, mainly the American soldiers' command cars. They'd park their command cars next to the inn and go in for a beer. I liked their command cars. Sometimes I'd run up to them. Stop. Approach slowly, walk around, choose the best looking command car and get closer and closer, touch the steering wheel and run away. Because I remembered the rifle butts on my back. A few minutes later I'd stop, and immediately return to the command car. I was excited by the steering wheel in my hands. By the clocks and the smell of petrol in the tank. I spent hours sitting near the inn and dreaming of holding the steering wheel in a traveling command car.

In the meantime, I received piano lessons. A soldier with curls tried to teach us simple tunes on the piano and for six months I failed to learn how to play "*Ha-Tikvah*" — the Jewish anthem. And I had a lot of time to practice. I said to her, I know how to play the harmonica, do you have a harmonica? She didn't. I dreamed about the command car.

One day my brother Yitzhak said, it's time we went to the village.

I said, yes, it's time to go home.

Yitzhak said, to the village, to the village.

I repeated, yes, to the village.

We left for Prague. By the falling leaves and the leaves on the pavement, it was autumn. I almost peed in my trousers with excitement. Mrs Fischer from UNRRA, a small woman with powdered cheeks and white beads round her neck, gave us papers in English with a red stamp. She said, if they stop you at the train show them these papers. Do not under any circumstances agree to go with soldiers.

I began to chew my nails. I asked, what soldiers, Germans?

Mrs Fischer said, no, no, there are no more German soldiers on the train. There are Russian soldiers.

I asked, Russian soldiers who fought against the Germans?

She said, yes.

We had no money for the journey. Yitzhak said, I don't like trains. Maybe we'll hitchhike and have done with it.

I said to him, we won't reach Prague before the snow.

He said, but I still don't like trains, and he chewed on the zipper of his battledress.

We went to the train station. In my heart I asked, which train will come for us, a passenger train or a cattle train, and then came the whistle. *Aah*. I wanted to run. I looked at Yitzhak. His face was white, as if he was on the ramp at Auschwitz. I came up close to him and we held hands. Our palms were warm and sweaty. I cried out, it's an ordinary train with windows, look.

The train stopped. We ran to the locomotive and went around the train. We checked here and here and *hop* we climbed in through the window. We sat on a seat. We didn't talk. I closed my legs and arranged my head as if I was used to traveling by train with seats and a window. As if I was used to breathing normally and had plenty of air. *Mmphaa, mmphaa*. And there is no smell, none. Why not? Because people didn't urinate or poop in their pants and there was no one to die on the shoulder of a neighbor.

Mmphaa. People sat quietly, one read a newspaper, another slept, someone else ate a sandwich, and then I heard a baby crying. I jumped up and my brother caught hold of my sleeve, said, sit down, sit down, and don't turn around. I sat down. I was confused and all the more so when the conductor approached. I kicked my brother and we got up together. We walked slowly to the end of the carriage. We left the carriage and hid in the space between the carriages. The conductor passed by. We went back to our places.

Two people behind me began to talk as if there was about

to be a serious disaster. I didn't know that Germans could be afraid. One said: Russian soldiers take people off the train if they don't have papers. The other said: Take them off, what for? The first one said: They send them to a labor camp in Russia, Siberia I heard. The other one said: Siberia? The first one said: Far away, in the snow. They need laborers, do you have papers?

My mouth went dry, did you hear, did you hear, my brother asked me not to worry, our papers are all right, Mrs Fischer said so. I put my hand in my pocket and held onto the papers. I didn't stop worrying. At the entrance to Prague, a Russian soldier boarded the train with a rifle. An *oy vei* escaped me, and my brother made a *shshsh* sound. We're all right. I urgently needed the toilet and didn't dare get up. The Russian soldier pointed at me and said in German, papers, papers. I took my papers from my pocket. My hands were shaking. The soldier examined the papers from top to bottom. I saw he couldn't read English. I didn't know either. I saw that the red stamp on the paper satisfied him. He returned the papers to me and left. I fell back against the seat. Said to my brother, and what will happen if the red stamp doesn't satisfy the next soldier, what'll we do then?

My brother said, it'll satisfy him. I got a stomach ache and regretted leaving the monastery.

We reached Prague before noon. It was a little cool and my brother said, I'm going to find out about the train to Hungary. We decided to meet at the station in two hours.

I wandered the streets. People in the street were wearing wool coats and hats. They smoked a lot of cigarettes and stood in groups to see what was new in the newspaper. I put my hand into my pocket, waited a few minutes, and then took it out, put it back. I repeated this several times.

I reached the municipality building. Saw people standing in a long line. I asked, what's the line for?

They told me, they're handing out a free cup of coffee and a sandwich. I was hungry and stood in line. I progressed slowly. At the allocation table were Russian soldiers. Two were handing out sandwiches, two stood on the side with rifles. My stomach constricted, I took out my papers just in case, and whispered *shshsh*. Calm down. I got a sandwich and a cup of coffee. I ate the sandwich in one gulp and was still hungry.

I stood in line a second time. I approached the table. The soldier with the rifle pierced me with his eyes. He had a nervous mustache. He raised his Kalashnikov and aimed it at my forehead. I immediately left the place. I wanted to run and didn't dare, I was sure he'd put a bullet in my ass. I quickly left the municipality. Aha, a Russian soldier was willing to kill me because of bread, and Mrs Fischer said the war was over and there was peace in the world. A shitty peace.

I decided to return to the monastery.

Two hours later I told my brother, I'm not going on to the village with you. I can't be afraid anymore over bread, you understand me? Yitzhak didn't say a word just sat down on the pavement.

After a few minutes, he stood up and said, I'm going by myself. You go on back to the monastery and wait for me there. When I get back we'll go to Palestine. And listen to me carefully, if you feel bad things then go aside and pretend to shout at someone, loudly, d'you hear me? But aside, so nobody sees you.

We stood together on the platform to Hungary.

Me with my light hair, about fifty kilos, my brother with black hair, maybe fifty-two kilos. We both had soft bristles on our cheeks and a battledress with a wool lining, without a bag. My brother jumped onto the train the minute it entered the station and stood at the window opposite me. I put my hand in my pocket and took strength from the papers. My brother said, it'll be all right; I had asked. Be careful. He said, don't worry. I'm going away and I'll be back.

The train left. I didn't leave Yitzhak until the train had disappeared.

Chapter 33

Yitzhak

The train left the station in Prague, I was on my way to Hungary.

Dov stood on the platform, I couldn't take my eyes off him. Even when he was the size of a dot I went on looking, even when I felt burning and itching.

On the train I sat, stood, wandered around a bit, sat down again, and got up to wander through other carriages, because most of the passengers were asleep and it was hard to be alone. On my way through the carriages I hoped to find some Jews from Hungary, maybe one or two from my village, or the market in the town of Perechyn.

I didn't find any familiar faces on the train. I went back to my carriage, and tried to doze off with one eye open, one eye closed. A woman in a theater dress and a beribboned hat smiled at me and began to wink. *Aha.* I closed the open eye. A few minutes and *hop*, my head fell forward. I jumped to my feet. Gave myself several slaps and sat down on the edge of the seat, one foot in front of the other. The woman with the hat put her hand on her breast and winked. I closed my eyes leaving them open a crack. She licked her lips with a pointed tongue and played with an earring at the edge of her ear. I felt a tingling along my spine. I wanted to tell her, leave me alone, I have no patience for your nonsense, none, and I moved to another carriage. I'm walking among the packages and bags when suddenly I hear Icho, Icho. My stomach turned at the sound of that Icho. Slowly I turned around. A short man with a paunch and a dark face fell upon me. We almost fell on the floor. He seized my hand enthusiastically, how are you, Icho, don't you remember me?

I didn't remember. He said, I'm Chaim from Humenne, nu, Humenne, Humenne, in Slovakia, what, have you forgotten me already? His face took on a muddy color and I didn't understand. Chaim was a Jewish name, and the man looked fat and normal with normal hair and a strong hand.

I asked, really, you're Chaim from Humenne?

He said, yes, yes, I remember you this small, and raised his hand to his hip, I remember when you used to come and visit your grandfather and grandmother.

My throat closed up in a second. The village, Humenne, was where my maternal grandmother and grandfather and three of Mother's sisters lived. I'd travel to Grandmother and Grandfather for the school holidays. I loved being with them. They had at least ten cats and a lame horse.

I got a buzzing in my head, no grandmother, no grandfather, no aunts, you're alone and you're going to Tur'i Remety. I pinched the top button on my shirt. Swiveled it and swiveled it, the button remained in my hand. Chaim pointed to his seat, we sat down. He said, you know that your aunts came back from the camps, the aunts are now in the village, Icho, they're living together in the same house, what about your mother and father?

I scratched the button, said quietly, don't know, we parted at Auschwitz, Mother's sisters came back? Came back from Auschwitz?

Chaim said they'd come back. Putting a heavy hand on my knee, he said, you've grown, Icho, you're a young man now, why don't you come and visit your aunts, then go on to your village.

I got off at Humenne.

It was night and it was cold. He pointed out a window with a faint light, that's the house, and off he went. I approached the house. In the window I saw the shadow of a paraffin lamp. I peeked in through the window. There was a curtain like a sheet and it was impossible to see anything. I approached the door. I put my ear to the keyhole, heard voices. I knocked. They didn't open the door for me. I knocked louder, nothing. I put my ear to the keyhole and couldn't hear a word. I stuck to the crack in the door, calling, Aunts, Aunts, it's me, Icho, open the door. They didn't answer. I knocked louder, calling, Aunts, it's me, Icho, and I got off the train on my way to Tur'i Remety. Chaim was on the train. Chaim told me everything.

A few seconds went by, and then the aunts called, Icho died, died, what do you want, have you come to frighten us, go away from here.

I shouted, Icho isn't dead, Icho is alive, I'm Icho and I'm cold, nu, open the door now. And then I heard a sound like weeping, no, no, no child from the camps was left alive, you're lying, go away, you rascal.

I bent down to the lock of the door, spoke quietly, I can't go away, the train left and I have nowhere to go.

I walked round the house. I hoped to find an open window or the kitchen door unlocked. The window and the door were locked. I could have broken the window, as I did when searching for a bottle of alcohol. I didn't want to frighten the aunts. I went back to the path. Sat down and waited. I thought, maybe they'll look out of the window and one of them will recognize me. But how will she recognize me, idiot, it's dark outside. I didn't even have a match in my pocket. I called out loudly, pity I got off the train, pity I listened to Chaim, at least I was warm on the train. I wanted to sleep. A tired dog barked from across the road. I heard three barks, a pause, another two, it fell asleep, and then I heard steps at the door. Cautiously, I approached. One of the aunts said: What is your mother's name?

Leah.

What is your father's name?

Israel.

I heard them whispering and breathing fast, fast, as if they were running on the spot.

Three heads peeped through a crack in the door.

Three heads covered in colorful scarves and tied in a firm knot in the middle on top. One aunt held a paraffin lamp at face height. Six large eyes examined me from top to toe and the crack in the door widened. They wore dark dresses with collars and an apron. One was small and thin. The second tall and thin with a long face and dark circles under her eyes. The third was small and plump, with a heavy chin, no neck.

I held out my arms to them, Aunts, it's me, Icho, nu look, you know me. Together, holding one another's hands, the aunts took two small steps forward. The paraffin lamp swayed between us. I heard them arguing in a whisper. I approached the light.

The plump one caught me by the arm, saying, Icho, is it really you?

The plump one and the tall one fell upon me together.

The paraffin lamp fell to the floor. I followed with the aunts on top of me. It was dark and there was a smell of paraffin and a smell of sauerkraut. I heard, oy vei, oy vei, and heavy breathing, and throats clearing, *cach. Cach. Cach.* I felt four hands holding my shirt and *hop*, they stood me on my feet. And then came squeezes on my neck, my shoulders, pinches on my belly and pinches on my backside, I felt the aunts measuring the thickness of my flesh. Suddenly the plump aunt caught me and threw me up in the air and said, not enough, not enough.

I began to laugh, enough Aunt, put me down. She didn't listen and I fell with my belly on a soft chest, and was bounced up and down, up and down, *tchach. Tchach. Tchach.*

The plump aunt said, this child weighs nothing, and dragged me into the house.

We wept together, the tall one, the plump one and I.

The aunts wiped their faces on their aprons, beat their breasts, opened their arms wide, crying out, our Icho has come back, oy, Icho, Icho, the little aunt stood on the side. She was twisting a crumpled scarf in her hands. After about an hour the aunts' weeping became a wild, rolling laughter, with slaps on their knees and on the scarves on their heads, then more great weeping, and then the plump aunt said, what did you do to stay alive, eh Icho'leh?

I sat down on a chair. I said, I didn't do anything, just went wherever they sent me, what's wrong with her? I pointed at the little aunt.

The tall aunt said, she received a gift from Mengele, pay no attention, what about your father, mother, your brothers and sister?

I said, just Leiber for the time being, and looked at the little aunt. She had a pretty face, like delicate, milk-colored glass, she had thin, pale fingers. She stopped twisting the scarf when the plump aunt said, now let's eat.

The table in front of me filled with food. There was meat, potatoes and sauerkraut, slices of bread, and sausage, and jam and apple and cakes, and eat, child, eat. The little aunt didn't come to the table.

I ate a slice of bread and jam and pushed away the plate. My throat was blocked. I said, I'm tired Aunts, dying to sleep.

The two aunts at the table said in unison, very well, Icho, and they stood beside me and began to pull at the sleeves of the battledress.

I said, I can do it myself.

They said, very well, Icho, and whispered among themselves, and then the plump aunt took a pair of pajamas from the closet. She gave me pajamas with thick gray stripes. My ribs locked and I stopped undressing. The tall aunt said, sorry child, we have no other pajamas. From the corner of the room came the sound of crying, like a hungry infant. The little aunt was crying into her kerchief. I approached her. Putting out my hand I touched her shoulder. She jumped as if she'd been stung by a scorpion. The tall aunt whispered in my ear, leave her be, Icho, the poor thing will calm down.

She didn't calm down. She lifted up her head, pointed at the pajamas, making strange sounds in her throat, like a cat caught in a trap. *Hisss. Hisss.* Her finger drilled a hole in the air, there was fire in her eyes, *hisss. Hisss.* The two aunts jumped towards her, grabbed her arm. They couldn't lower her arm. They shouted, *Genug!* – Enough! *Sha. Sha. Sha. Sei still* – be quiet. You're scaring the child, and she with her *hisss*. She had tiny drops on her forehead, her nose. I took the pajamas, opened a window and threw them outside. The little aunt fell into a chair.

I got into bed in my clothes. My eyelids were heavy, my body too. I wanted to say goodnight. My cheeks filled with goodnight but my lips were like glue. I saw Dov fading away on the platform and prayed he would reach the monastery safely. I heard faint breaths, like a train in the distance, my brother on a train? The breaths intensified. I heard small groans, and *tch, tch, tch*, and a long *shhhhh*. I opened my eyes and the two aunts were standing over me. Their arms were folded on their chests. The little aunt stood one step behind them. The plump aunt whispered, sleep, Icho, sleep, we're standing here, we won't bother you.

I closed my eyes. Loud breaths sounded above me. With difficulty, I raised my head from the pillow, leaned on one elbow and said tiredly, I can't sleep with you standing over me like that.

I fell back on the pillow. A headache climbed from my forehead to my hair. The tall aunt raised her arms and pushed the two away behind the table. She said, very well, very well, we're going to bed, goodnight, we'll talk tomorrow.

Two minutes went by and again the loud breathing. I saw three dresses flying to the corner of the room.

I got out of bed and returned to my chair. I received a glass of milk and a teaspoon of jam and cookies. The aunts said, eat, eat, tell us everything from the beginning.

I began to speak. I spoke about Auschwitz, about Buchenwald, about Camp Zeiss. About the meeting with Dov. About Doctor Spielman at the hospital. About the monastery. The two aunts sat opposite me, nibbling on cookies and wiping their faces that grew wet again and again. A pile of handkerchiefs collected on the table. Two hours later they brought a large towel from the closet instead of the handkerchiefs. The little aunt sat in the corner. She held a chicken egg in her hand. She passed the egg from one hand to the other, her eyes fixed on me. I beckoned to her, come, come closer, sit with us. She didn't want to come closer.

I asked, and you, Aunts, where were you during the war?

The plump aunt murmured Bergen-Belsen. Bergen-Belsen, we were together. But first in Auschwitz. I asked, and Grandfather and Grandmother, what about them?

The tall aunt said, don't ask anymore, Icho, don't ask.

I didn't ask.

In the morning people came.

The aunts took chairs out into the yard. There weren't enough chairs. People sat on stones and planks. They played with their hats in their hands, or scratched at the earth with a stone. Some people stood with a bag in their hands. They took out cookies and sandwiches. Some took out photographs. Maybe you know them? There were young faces, old faces, the face of a boy, a girl, a baby, have you seen them? This is Zelig, Zelig Abraham. This is Elisha Kramer, this is Irena, have you heard anything? Maybe my Golda'leh, huh?

I wiped my face on my sleeve. The plump aunt gave me a glass of water. I said, put some sugar in the water, a lot of sugar. I asked, more water. I drank three glasses of sugar water and my throat was still dry. People in the yard pointed at pictures and began to talk about the families that had disappeared. There was one with large hands and a thick neck. He spoke chokingly. Said, they took my Yelena out of my arms on the ramp at Auschwitz. She was barefoot with yellow curls and a broad ribbon. I didn't want to hand her over. The SSman hit me with a rifle butt. Yelena fell, began to run barefoot on the ramp, crying Papaleh, Papaleh. I began to run after her, shouting Yelena, come, come. Dogs came. From a distance I saw a bowed grandmother seize Yelena's hand, hold it firmly. She didn't have the strength to pick her up, and so they went in a line to the crematorium. I heard my Yelena, Papaleh, Papaleh, that's all, that's all.

The man held his head in his hands. His weeping drew others after him and then he raised his head and said, my Yelena loved soup. My Yelena used to ask for a song before going to sleep. Every night she wanted the same song. That was the song I sang to her in the dark car on the way to Auschwitz. It was hot, it was terrible. My little girl wept, Papa, water, water, and all I had to give her was a song, d'you understand, Jews, a song instead of water. And then he began to sing an old lullaby. People in the yard sang with him, *hi-li-lu, hi-li-lu, schlaff shoyn mein teyer feigeleh* – sleep now my precious bird.

And I wept and wept, the aunts wept too, but the little aunt didn't cry. She lifted up her apron and chewed on the corner. Someone shouted, now you, Icho, where were you.

I told my story from the beginning. People added the details they knew. Said, Buchenwald, oyyy, oy, oy, maybe you saw Marek, I think he was there. Zeiss, where is Zeiss, in Germany, oy, oy, oy, did you hear about Herschel, Herschel Miller.

A day later more people came. The group in the yard grew larger and larger. By sunrise the path was filled with people. They apologized, fixed pleading eyes on me, and threw names into the air. I had nothing to say. My aunts served tea and cookies and poured water on people who felt faint. I asked for sugar water. People pleaded, again, Icho, tell us about you. I was hot, hot. My shirt stuck to my back. I began to speak, took shortcuts. People didn't give in. There were some who knew my story from the first day. They called out, wait, wait, you forgot Bloc 8 at Buchenwald, how could you, Icho, and at once restored what I'd left out, with their own additions. My story grew longer and longer.

On Tuesday after sunset there was no more space. People were sitting at the side of the road. I had to shout for them to hear. They couldn't hear. And then some of the people at the edge of the path began to pass on the story to the audience behind the fence.

I felt exhausted. After a week I told the aunts, enough, I'm going to the village of Tur'i Remety. We hugged and I promised to return.

Chapter 34

Dov

My brother Yitzhak went to Hungary and I experienced a miracle.

In Prague, I met my Vassily. Vassily Korol. My best friend in the village. I met Vassily where the hungry met in Prague, near the municipality, before noon. First I wandered the streets and touched houses with a door and a handle. Sometimes there was a number on the door, sometimes a name. I knew, soon winter would come, and snow, the sky would fall on the road and I had no home to go back to. I felt lonely and wretched. A woman in gloves came out for a walk with her dog. A tiny dog with a ribbon tied round its neck. I thought, the dog has a home and a plate of food, and I don't even have an address to send a letter to. If I had an address I'd write: Hello, I'm Leiber, and I'm alive and hungry, when will you come and fetch me? P.S. You won't recognize me. In the camps I stopped growing. I think I've stayed as small as I was in *cheder*, maybe even a little smaller. See you soon, your loving son, Leiber.

My throat constricted, my heart too. I swallowed and went aside. I opened my mouth wide and screamed loudly, *aaaah.*

Aaaah just as my brother Yitzhakhad told me to, if you're in pain, scream, but don't talk to strangers.

My belly was bothering me. I approached the municipality building.

First I made sure that the soldier with the Kalashnikov had been replaced. I stood in the long line and saw someone familiar. Three people ahead of me stood someone in a short coat to his waist. I saw only a head, an ear and half a cheek, and it looked like Vassily. I bent down and saw that the person was wearing good trousers. His shoulders were wide apart. Not like him. But the hair, the hair was Vassily's, hair like yellow stalks in a wheat field. I closed my mouth with half a fist like a trumpet and called in a low voice, Vassily? Nothing. I called louder, Vassily? The man turned around, wow, of course it was Vassily, but with a mustache. At least half a head taller than me and clean shaven.

He stopped and called, Bernard?

We hugged. Laughed. Like madmen we laughed and wiped our tears. He said, you're alive. Father said no Jews were left, and you're alive.

I lowered my head to my chest, said, barely alive, Vassily, and don't stand twice in line for a sandwich, you hear? The Russians will put a bullet in your head, do you have stamped papers in your pocket?

We took a sandwich and sat on a bench in a small park. Vassily said, you're so thin and where is your hair?

I muttered, where, where, better to be silent, and I made a hole with my heel under the bench.

Vassily said, remember playing hide-and-seek in the forest, you were always on the highest tree, weren't you?

I said, remember, remember, and how come you're wearing

socks, huh? And Sabbath pants, and a mustache, hey, you're a young man now Vassily, d'you have someone?

Vassily reddened. He chewed on the end of his mustache and said, what about your father, mother, your brothers and sister, we've heard terrible things. Saw photographs in the newspaper, a mountain of dead, all without clothes, did you see?

I got up from the bench and began to walk away. Stopped. Came back. I sat next to Vassily and said, I've found Icho and we're going to Israel together, understand? He's on his way to Tur'i Remety now. When he comes back we'll travel far away from here, that's all. But first to the monastery.

Vassily caught my hand, very good, very good, no good going back to the village, there's not enough work, no market for goods, people have no food, Bernard, that's why I came to Prague, can I come with you to the monastery?

I put my arm around Vassily's shoulders. Said, of course you can come. We're together Vassily.

And when you go to Israel, you'll take me with you? I didn't answer.

Vassily said, we're brothers, I wanted you to stay in our home but the Hungarians said they'd kill everybody, we're like brothers, right?

I got up from the bench. Vassily got up after me. He combed his yellow hair with his fingers. I also wanted to comb my head, but I had stubble. Vassily touched my cheek with the tip of his thumb, said, not shaving yet, huh? And where are the curls?

I said, they took a train to Germany. He caught my hand and pressed it hard. I felt a pleasant warmth in my chest.

We wandered through the streets together.

Two Russian soldiers stood at a table on a street corner. I saw they were handing out something to people in the street. It didn't look like a sandwich. We approached, and they beckoned to us, come here, come. I whispered to Vassily, be careful, the Russian soldiers are very dangerous. We approached cautiously. The soldiers smiled at us as if we were good neighbors. The bearded soldier held out a fist in front of him, bouncing his hand and making faces like a magician wanting to surprise. I heard coins clinking. Ah, they have a few crazy people too. He carefully opened his fist and laughed with a mouth full of teeth, the middle one on top was gold.

The soldier's hand was full of tin badges. He took one of them and said, Stalin. Stalin. And turned the badge over, Lenin. Lenin. And then he bent down under the table, put his hands inside something and I heard a lot of clinking. He stood up, winked at us, and held out two handfuls of badges. We didn't move. The soldier nodded his head, take, take. I took one Stalin. The soldier held my hand and gave me more badges. To Vassily as well. The soldier pointed at Vassily's little suitcase. Vassily opened it, it was rather empty. He dropped in four more handfuls and closed the suitcase. The soldier approached me unsteadily, he smelled of vodka. He took a Stalin badge and fixed it to the pocket of my shirt, and one to Vassily's. And then he belched, took an unsteady step back, raised a straight arm and saluted us as if we were soldiers. I didn't know what to do. Suddenly he gave a whistle and farted like a canon. Vassily and I jumped together. The drunken soldier began to laugh, and then the other soldier got mad, pulled his shirt, and laid him down on the ground. I saw them struggling. Two seconds, and three soldiers with rifles arrived at a run. I whispered to Vassily, quickly, let's get out of here, but walk slowly. We walked away from them. I looked back, the soldiers were dragging the drunken soldier along the pavement. I heard him shouting, Stalinka, Leninka, babushka, hee, hee.

Who's Stalin.

I said, maybe he's an important man if there are so many pieces of him, we'll give them out at the monastery. From a distance I saw another distribution point.

Vassily said, let's have another turn. My heart beat, but we did go over, because I wanted to bring gifts from Prague for my friends, I also wanted to give some to the female soldiers and to the nuns. We took the badges off the pockets on our shirts and approached the soldiers. They welcomed us and put badges on our shirts, our collars, the belts of our trousers, and a few more handfuls in the suitcase. I understood, they want to get rid of the quantity they'd brought. I saw they had full boxes under the table. We passed three or four distribution points. The suitcase filled up, we were pleased.

We left Prague towards evening.

We wanted to cross the Czech border and arrived at a train station. We had no money for food. A rather neglected man was sitting on the pavement, he had a backpack. Peeping out of the backpack was a parcel, it looked like a bread wrapping. I said to Vassily, I'll talk to the man and you steal the bread. He agreed. I went over to the man. I asked in German about a train to Germany. He began to answer, he had a loud, officer's voice. The hair on my body stood on end and I listened to the explanations until Vassily took the parcel out of the backpack and off we ran. We stopped at a safe distance. The German didn't move. He cleaned his teeth and watched us. We got nothing out of it. In the paper were dry chicken bones. We chewed the bones and were still hungry.

We decided to leave the train station.

We went on foot to the fields. I said to Vassily, maybe in a farmer's field we'll find some vegetables to eat. The sun set and

I didn't know who would give my brother food when he arrived in the village. I was worried about him. I asked Vassily, is our neighbor Stanku still in the village?

He said, yes, Stanku is in the village, what are we looking for?

I said, don't know, we'll find something. We walked for about an hour through a bare field. Suddenly, in the middle of the field, I saw a large airplane with a lot of small windows. I didn't see any people. I nodded to Vassily, we bent down, and approached the airplane at a run. We heard no voices. We peeped inside. Saw empty seats. We climbed into the airplane. Looked for food among the seats. Found nothing. We climbed back down into the field. I asked Vassily, isn't this a cabbage field? Vassily bent down and began to dig in the earth. We dug together. We found cabbage roots. We made a large pile, climbed into the airplane and sat in the seats. We ate it all and I felt like a king. We held each other for warmth and fell asleep in a second.

The following evening, we arrived at the monastery.

The fellows at the monastery gathered round us. They stroked the badges on our clothes, and I said, we have some for all of you. We took the badges out of the suitcase and gave three badges to each one. The fellows did what we had done, put badges on their shirts, belt and hat. Stalin and Lenin took over the monastery. There were some who didn't want to take them. They wanted to spit on the badges and they spat on the floor. There were some who stood to attention and saluted each other.

The next day, the yard was cheerful. Each one who appeared decorated with badges was laughingly spat on or saluted. The female soldier with the ponytail said to me, you've created a real mess with your badges.

I said, it's better than your Yiddish theater, at least we aren't dying of boredom.

One evening my instructor came into my room. Her eyelashes were blue. She said to me, you must come with me. I got up from the bed, arranged a few badges on my shirt and followed her to the office.

Four American soldiers were sitting in the office. The silence in the office frightened me. One of them pointed at a single chair at the table and said, sit down, please. I sat down. The soldier with the bars on his shoulder began to question me in German.

Where did you get the Stalin badges?

I brought them from Prague.

Who gave them to you?

Russian soldiers.

Where did you meet Russian soldiers?

In the street near the municipality. In other places. They were standing on main street corners and handing out free badges.

Who did they give them to?

To anyone going by in the street. They even gave them to children.

Why did the soldiers hand them out for free?

My mouth went dry. I didn't understand why an American officer was taking an interest in Russian badges. I leaned towards them and said, I can give you all my badges. Lots and lots of Stalin, Lenin on the other side.

The soldier with the bars sat up in his chair. His forehead was thoughtful and I was alarmed, he'll turn me over to the Germans. He'll say something about me to the Germans and they'll put me on a truck. They've probably hidden some little crematorium in the mountains, maybe even in a nearby forest. I wanted to run away. Holding onto to the table, I jumped to my feet. The officer said, sit. I sat. I felt a tingling in the back of my neck. I got up. My instructor gestured to me to sit quietly. I couldn't without bouncing. I wanted to shout, leave me alone, where's my brother?

The officer said, Bernard, did the Russian soldiers ask you to hand out badges?

I leaped to the door, no! Why should they? I don't speak Russian and Russian soldiers frighten me, I saw them taking people off the train for no reason, just because they didn't have papers in their pockets. One man cried, caught hold of the window, it was no use, they hit him on the back with the butt of a rifle, and sent him off. They were like the SSmen at the camp and a Russian soldier aimed his Kalashnikov at me because of a sandwich.

The officer pointed at the chair. I scuttled between the door and the window. The officer whispered with the soldiers next to him in a language I didn't know. My instructor observed me. She had wrinkles between her eyes. She tried to smile at me and her face came out all crooked. I bent down to her and whispered, and if the Russians had asked me to hand out badges, d'you think I'd have listened to them? Suddenly, *pak*. My heart fell. I understood that the Americans suspected me of spying for the Russians. I understood that the Americans hate the Russians and that's why Mrs Fischer warned us not to lose our papers. She knew the Russians were dangerous.

I felt I was about to faint.

Finally, the officer said, now bring the suitcase from your room.

Shakily, I ran to my room. I held my ass tight so it wouldn't run away to the forest. Vassily was sleeping in Yitzhak's bed. I pulled the suitcase from under the bed. Tore badges off the shirts I saw in the room and returned to the Americans. They opened the suitcase and emptied the badges onto the table. The officer said to the soldiers, the Russians want to take over Prague. And then he said to me, sit down and he began to ask all his questions from the beginning.

I thought about my brother Yitzhak. He'd probably be angry with me. Think for a moment, who took care of us in hospital, the Russians? Who sent us to a convalescent home? The Russians? The Americans are taking care of us. The Russians send people to Siberia.

I was ashamed that I hadn't understood it myself. I was young. For me the war was over. I believed my troubles were over.

After two days of interrogation, the soldiers released me. Not before I'd collected all the badges in the monastery. I didn't even leave one badge as a souvenir.

Chapter 35

Yitzhak

After a week I left the village of Humenne and felt relief. Local people continued to come to the aunts' house looking for relatives. I could no longer bear listening to people weeping for Roza, Sida, Shura, and Hannah, Lenna and Feige, Hershi, Martin, and Gerti, she was three, Gerti, she had a small bag on her back, like the bag you take on a trip to the mountains, did you see her, did you see? I was sure their ashes were scattered across the Wisla, what could I say?

One day a small, white-haired man arrived. He may have been thirty. He began with Mira'leh, and Moishe'leh, and I shouted, I don't know Mira'leh, and Moishe'leh, I know 14550, I know 15093, do you understand, ask me numbers, sir. The plump aunt immediately brought me a glass of water with five teaspoons of sugar. That evening I told the aunts, I'm leaving tomorrow, tomorrow.

From the village of Humenne I went on foot to Brezna. I didn't want to board a train because it crossed the border under Russian control. People in Humenne said the Russians were taking people who were alone off the train, whether they had papers in their pockets or not.

From Brezna I took the train to Perechyn.

In Perechyn was the market where my father sold cows. I knew the market well. I knew the vendors. I didn't go to see the market. I knew I wouldn't find Yenkel, Simon, Jacob, or the Klein sisters from the dress store. I knew a dirt road in the mountains from Perechyn to Tur'i Remety. Dov and I used to take cows from the village along this road to market. Father would promise to buy us ice cream in Perechyn for each cow we took on foot.

I found the way and began to walk with the good smell of wet earth and hay. The path looked just as I remembered. Rather narrow, exactly wide enough for two people and a medium sized cow. Alongside the path were thorns and bushes full of snails. Under the bushes was a carpet of black pebbles. I picked up a handful of stones and threw them into the distance. Two birds flew off in alarm. I remember thinking, the path, the mountains and the sky all look the same, if I close my eyes very tightly, and open them, I'll see Dov walking beside me, a cow between us, and we'll tap the cow on her hindquarters with a stick, nu, nu, cow, this is no time to graze, we're going straight to market now because Father is waiting for us, and he'll be glad and say, very good, children, very good, now run along and buy ice cream, and he'll give us a coin and we'll race each other to the ice cream and Dov will win, he always won, and each of us would have an ice cream in our hands and we'd lick it pleasurably and wander round to see how Yenkel, Simon, and Jacob were doing.

I closed my eyes. Stood still. Waited.

And then came a shout from the core of my belly, *aahhhh*, *aahhhh*, and the kicks. I began to kick stones, kick the bushes and fling away branches with crushed snails, and I bent down and picked up a handful of earth and flung it on the path, and let out another scream, *aaahhhh*, and warm tears fell on my cheeks, wetting the battledress, and I wiped my face on my sleeve, and my nose ran like water, *aaahhh*, and I continued to walk.

I reached the village towards evening.

I stood at a distance. The houses in the village had stayed as I remembered. Rows of small, dark houses made of mud mixed with hay, a chimney on the roof, and a large yard. In the yard was a cowshed, behind it a haystack, beside the cowshed were vegetable and flower beds with apple trees at the end. I saw yards with a stable and horses, yards with one horse and no stable. Three hay-laden wagons traveled along the road, a long *mooo* of cows heralded the night.

I sat on the ground and put a hand on my chest. I felt as if my heart wanted to jump out and I began to count, one two, three. I reached fifty and my heart still hadn't calmed down. I spoke to myself, now get up and start walking, one two, one two.

I approached until I was two houses away from ours. The house was at the corner of the street. There was light at the windows and a woman's voice and the voice of a child and from the direction of the cowshed came the sound of a pitchfork shifting hay, I wanted to tear out my hair. I leaned against a tree trunk and held my belly. My mind was pulsing, those bastard goys hadn't waited until the end of the war. Those bastard goys hadn't waited to see if we'd return home. We boarded the train to Ungvár and they'd leaped on the house like wolves on a carcass, damn them. They sit like a good, loving family at our table eating dinner with our utensils. They wash in our bathroom, and soon their damned children will get into bed, and Mama will come in to say goodnight with a kiss on the forehead, and I need a Kalashnikov in my hand, I want to break down the door and spray all of them, *ta-ta-ta-ta-ta*.

I didn't know what to do with the rage in my body.

Chapter 36

Dov

After Prague I landed in the hospital.

One day I was waiting at the inn. Don't remember where Vassily was. A cold wind blew leaves from the trees onto the road. Spun them like a carousel. An American soldier arrived in an open command car. A freshly painted command car. The soldier went inside the inn and I went up to the command car. I stroked the clocks and the steering wheel, grasped the seat, jumped in and sat down, pressed the clutch, then rushed away behind the fence. I was alone. I returned to the command car and tried to turn the steering wheel. *Brrrm. Brrrm.* The gear stick was stiff. I stroked the armrest of the seat, the command car had a good smell and I really wanted to travel in a command car. *Brrrm. Brrrm.*

After almost half an hour the soldier came out of the inn. I jumped down. He looked at me and smiled. I smiled back. The soldier said, want a ride!

I choked, whispered, yes, yes, I've never traveled in an open command car.

The soldier said, but we'll be cold, boy, what do you say?

I said, cold doesn't scare me and I remembered the open

trains and the wind like a razor blade, without coat or gloves, just stinking pajamas and the newly dead to hold onto and keep warm.

I got into the command car with trembling legs. The soldier gave me a can of beer. I drank it in one gulp. Wow, it was as cold as ice. And then he said, hold tight, he pressed hard on the accelerator and we shot out onto the road. My heart wept with joy. I saw fireworks and prayed my friends at the monastery would see me in the command car. I prayed that Vassily would be standing on the road and I could wave to him. I didn't see friends.

We went into the fields and the soldier accelerated. He called out, are you all right?

I shouted yes, I feel wonderful, and heard my teeth dance in my mouth. I was freezing and I felt on top of the world. After two hours in the fields we returned to the monastery.

That evening I developed a high fever.

They immediately sent me to a hospital in the town of Deggendorf. American and German doctors worked there. An American doctor examined me with a stethoscope. He fell asleep on me while listening to my lungs. After pressing my chest and back he woke up and said: You have pneumonia, you're staying in hospital. I pulled down my shirt and stood up. I was alarmed, hospital? I refuse, no, no, I promise to stay in bed at the monastery for a long time, two weeks, a month, even two months, and I promise to drink hot tea, and you can give me an injection in my backside, but I'm going back to the monastery. The doctor wrote something. I understood from him that there was no chance of my leaving. It was all I could do not to cry.

In the coming days I burned with fever, I felt like a rag.

They stuck a needle in my back and drained water from the lungs and gave me a lot of medication. I lay in bed and called the doctor, I need matches.

The doctor asked, what for?

I said, for my eyes, otherwise I'll fall asleep for three months. Where were you during the war?

Don't remember, Doctor, do you have a match? He left me and whispered something to a nurse. I didn't get any matches so I started to talk to myself to stay awake, I said, listen Vassily, I sat next to an American soldier in an open command car, and he went *zooom, zooom*, with his foot on the accelerator, and I was on top of the world in the fields with a cold beer, where are you, Vassily, and where is my brother, I want my brother. My head fell back on the pillow. I pinched my belly and tickled my navel and armpit until I fell asleep.

Two weeks went by, my fever went down, but I didn't have the strength to wander around. One day I was lying in bed and began to tap my fingers on the iron railing of the bed, like the British soldier taught me to play the piano. I failed at the piano. I remembered the harmonica I had at home. I had two. Father brought me one from Perechyn, and I got a smaller one from my grandfather in the village of Humenne. I'd dreamed of a harmonica ever since I was in *cheder,* because of the goy children. I saw them playing the harmonica and the mandolin. They'd ride their horses, one hand holding the rein and the other a harmonica. They played songs that made people joyous and happy. I wanted to be like the goy children. I said to Father, buy me a harmonica, and I started learning to play on my own. I didn't succeed. And then they tested our singing at school. A woman with a loud voice said to me: Sing. I sang.

She stuck her finger in her ear and said, you don't have to

sing anymore, it's not for you, understand? Maybe she was right. Maybe I didn't have a musical ear. I hid my harmonica inside a drawer and covered it with a towel.

One day I saw my neighbor, Ilona, stopping in the middle of her game of catch to look at a goy lad riding on his horse. He was holding a harmonica and playing a polka. I called out, Ilona, Ilona, catch me, nu. She wasn't interested. She wanted to follow the tune. I felt lonely. I ran home, took the large harmonica and tried to play a cheerful polka. Don't know why, but what came out was a sad, tuneless polka.

At the hospital in Deggendorf there were too many German soldiers.

German soldiers with half a leg, or two half legs, or without an arm and a leg, like that. They had no prostheses. They crawled on all fours to the shower and the toilet, the stump trailing after them. Sometimes the stump was bandaged, sometimes not, sometimes I couldn't see a stump just empty pajama trousers tied with a thick knot. I looked at their faces. Some of them had strong faces with a direct, steel-like gaze. They crawled along the floor, holding onto the legs of the beds in order to advance one meter then another. I saw a wounded German dragging his short leg in the direction of the toilets. An American nurse going past held out a hand and said, get up, get up. I'll help you. His head reached her knees. He stuck out his neck and continued crawling to the toilets.

It was the young Germans who looked different. They crawled along the floor groaning in pain. Sometimes they'd stop mid-way, hold onto the stump and shout for a nurse. Some would drop their heads to the floor, I heard them weeping.

Their weeping brought me to tears.

Friends from the monastery didn't come to visit me. Vassily didn't come either. I didn't understand why. It was only when I returned to the monastery that I understood. They didn't know which hospital I was in because I was taken there at night.

After a month I decided to run away from the hospital. One morning, I jumped out of the window and went back to the monastery.

Chapter 37

Yitzhak

I decided to go to our goy neighbor, Stanku's house. Stanku, who'd come to us the day we left our home and wanted to know where the Jews were going. Stanku was the neighbor who made us take fresh Easter cakes so we'd feel good during that Passover in 1944. I went into his yard. At the gate, I stopped for the first time. I took a breath from the deepest place in my body and approached the door. I stopped for the second time. I heard the sounds of a home, a chair moving, the bang of a pot on the stove, I heard Stanku, where are my slippers? I wanted to die.

I knocked on the door. Stanku stood in the doorway. He looked as I remembered. Apart from his height. He was shorter than me. He had a red, furrowed face and a large nose. He wore a blue, peaked cap, I knew the cap. Stanku muttered something, I saw his pupils darting in his eyes and then he fell upon me with hugs, calling Ichko, Ichko you've come back to us, I didn't believe you'd come back, how are you, we haven't heard anything since you left, where's your father, where's your mother, where is everyone?

I stood back.

Who is living in our home?

A family from the village, you don't know them, he cleared his throat.

Who?

I'm sorry, but I couldn't stop them.

When did they move in?

Not long after you left.

How long?

Stanku moved his head, his cheeks whitening under the tears. I said slowly, don't cry, it won't help, and the cows? Stanku whispered, everything belongs to them now. I caught hold of his shirt, saying, and my cat, where is my cat, at least the cat, you promised to look after my cat.

Stanku wept more loudly. My head fell on his shoulder. We wept together.

Stanku's wife came to the door. A small woman with brown hair. She embraced me and said, oy, yoy-yoy, oy, yoy-yoy, they've come back.

I entered and immediately held onto the back of a chair. I didn't know what to do with my nerves.

Stanku said, sit down Ichko, sit down, and pushed me into the chair. Stanku's wife went into the kitchen and brought a pot of food to the table. I smelled meat. I pulled the chair to the table, and saw Michael, Stanku's son, standing in the doorway. He had one leg. He had a burn mark on his temple. Leaning against the door frame, he held a stick. Stanku said, you remember Michael, he was in the Russian army, see what they did to him.

We sat down to eat.

Stanku's wife filled my plate three times, Stanku cut bread for me, Michael didn't stop talking about the battles he'd fought in Russia and I was silent, I hadn't seen them for a year and a half and felt like a stranger. Stanku said, enough now, Michael, let's hear something from Ichko, nu, tell us where you were, have you heard anything from your father, your mother?

I said, I'm tired Stanku, we'll talk tomorrow.

Stanku's wife jumped up, I'll make up a bed for you right now, you're like one of our own. Come, come.

I couldn't sleep. I thought about the sounds coming from Stanku's cowshed, perhaps our cowshed.

Early in the morning, before sunrise, I went out into the yard. Geese wanted food, a farmer spoke to his horse. I approached our house. Pressed fists against my trousers, saw Stanku standing next to me. A dog barked behind the house. The door opened and a man and a woman stood in the doorway. Behind them peeped two small children in pajamas. The man looked about thirty, my height, his face unshaven. He wore a sweater with patches at the elbows and leggings to the knee. The woman was pretty and wore an apron. The man and the woman looked at me. The man shouted at the dog, quiet, quiet, approached me, scratching under his chin.

Who are you?

I am Yitzhak, son of Israel and Leah, and this is our house.

You are a Jew.

Yes, and this is our house.

No.

Yes.

But on the radio they said there are no more Jews. They said no Jews were left. They also said there'd be no more Jews, ever. Because they killed your babies.

Your radio is mistaken. We're alive.

We saw pictures in the newspapers. Lots of dead Jews in heaps. Didn't you see the newspaper?

I did, but many Jews were left who weren't photographed in the newspaper, and this is our house.

I saw in the newspaper that none were left, Stanku saw it in the newspaper, didn't you, Stanku? Our whole village saw it in the newspaper. That's why we're living in Jews' houses.

Not because of the newspaper, because you didn't have a home and it was easier to take everything from the Jews.

Not one Jew has returned to his home, right Stanku?

I've returned.

Wait a minute, where is your father?

Don't know. I am Israel's son and this is our home. I know every room in the house, I know where the closets are, the beds, the kitchen sink.

The farmer stuck his finger in his nose, scratched something and shook his finger, like a nu, nu, nu, to a naughty child. And then he winked at Stanku and said, but the mayor of Perechyn said there are no more Jews in Hungary, right Stanku? He said there are no more Jews in Europe, he said there is no such thing as Jews. The mayor's wife also said so. Everyone knows it, right Stanku?

Stanku stuck his fists in his pockets and didn't answer.

There is no such thing as Jews, ah, I felt my jaw closing like a steel door. I wanted to leap on him and take out his eye, I wanted to choke him until his white tongue dropped and rolled on the path. I walked hurriedly behind the house. The dog was frantic, it was a large wolf hound. I wanted to leap on the dog and rip its mouth open, Stanku and the farmer arrived at a run. The farmer cursed and kicked the dog. The dog crawled into its kennel, whining like a cat. I pointed at the yard, saying in a choked voice, that is a Jewish cowshed, understand? And that is a Jewish storeroom, and over there was a Jewish butcher shop and I am wholly a Jew, and there are many more Jews at the monastery, and your mayor is a great fool, so what are you talking about, huh?

The farmer looked down and began to cough as if he had tuberculosis. His wife hurried up, followed by the two children in their pajamas. The farmer saw his wife and children and waved them away. The woman disappeared with the children. Stanku stood between me and the farmer and chewed his hat.

The farmer put one hand on his chest and approached me. Stanku tried to stop him. I said to Stanku, don't interfere. The farmer stood a step away from me. He had spit on his chin and smelled strongly of tobacco.

He said, listen, Jew, it's not good that you're here. You shouldn't be here. It's not good for you. In this village there are no more Jews, understand? We're done with Jews, and on the radio they also said the Jews in Hungary are *kaput*, d'you want to be alone here? He bent down and whispered, go to a place for Jews. It's better for you, understand? I took a step back from his smell.

The farmer spread his hand above his eyes as if I was a blinding sun, saying, now what do you want?

Nothing.

What do you mean nothing?

Nothing means nothing.

He cleared his throat and said, are you staying in the village?

No. I came to visit.

A visit, and when are you leaving?

We'll see.

Not coming back?

No.

Stanku said: He's going back to Germany. From there to Palestine.

Where is Palestine?

As far away as possible.

Stanku said, it's a place for Jews.

The farmer said, you're going away to a place for Jews, very good, so maybe you'll come in and have something to drink?

I said, have you seen a black and white cat, I had a cat before we left, a large cat, have you seen it?

The farmer laughed, no cats here, just my dog, maybe it went to the neighbors, Stanku, have you seen his cat? Stanku said, no, I know Ichko's cat. The farmer held out his hand, please, come inside, have something to drink.

I stayed where I was. Stanku said, Ichko, he's inviting you into the house. Let's go in together.

I wanted Mother and Father and I went into the house.

My family's dining table stood in the entrance. I pressed my fingers to my throat, gave a platch to my trousers and came to a decision in my heart: I, Icho son of Israel and Leah, stand upright in this house and draw down a steel screen, yes. I'm a stranger, and this house is not mine, it belongs to goys, yes. I don't belong to this village, and I have no connection with this house, ah, I came in by chance and don't recognize anything, and if I feel like it I can kill everyone with an ax, *trach*. I can cut this bastard peasant in two, *trach-trach*. See half a body fall to one side, and half a body to the other side, *trach-trach*.

I approached Dov's and my room. There was a buzzing in my head like a bothersome fly. I said to myself, there are flies in this house and I don't care, may the house burn down, may the cowshed burn down, may they cry until tomorrow and even longer.

Nonetheless, I peeped into the room. Under the window were two small beds close together and covered with a wool blanket.

On the closet I saw a scratch I'd made long ago with a nail, I whispered, don't recognize it, no, no. I went to the other room, I fell upon the curtains Mother had sewn for Sarah's room. The flies in my head grew louder, I shouted in a whisper, don't recognize, don't recognize.

The farmer's wife stood beside me. She held a glass of water and a saucer with a teaspoon of white jam. She smiled at me and said, please, taste the jam. The farmer said, please sit down, pointing at an armchair.

I stayed where I was. I looked for a place to look at, every place I looked at, burned, oy, the armchair, and the little carpet at the door, and the large pot on the stove, oy, I want, what, what, what, not a thing, I don't need anything. I went back to the farmer.

I wanted to sit on his neck and shout into his ear, the Germans killed us, and you killed us too, and your death is more painful, go to hell, we were neighbors, we brought you gifts on holidays, helped you cut the corn, Mother knitted a coat and hat for your babies, how can you say there is no such thing as Jews, you bastards. The children held hands and watched me.

I wanted to find family pictures.

I knew that without pictures I'd forget Grandmother and Grandfather's faces. I wanted at least one of Grandmother and Grandfather with Dov during the years he lived with them. Those were years they wanted to help Mother, I thought, Grandmother and Grandfather were good people and we mustn't forget the faces of people like that. I wanted pictures of Mother and Father and Sarah and Avrum, I wanted to take pictures with me to Palestine, and we had an album, where is our album. I remembered the first page in the album. There was a picture there of the whole family. Sarah and Avrum standing next to Father. Dov and I sitting on chairs next to Mother. We were four and five years old. Dov held a bell in his hand. Years later, I asked Mother why Dov was holding a bell in his hand, Mother said, so he'd agree to be photographed. He didn't want to sit on the chair next to you and the photographer said, bring a bell, it helped. I remembered the photographer who came every summer to our village. He had a camera on long legs with a covering of black fabric. On the day we were photographed, he took kitchen chairs outside and positioned us all in the yard. He asked Mother ten times to raise her head, to smile. Don't know why she didn't listen to him.

I pulled my hair and said to the farmer in a clear voice, in my mother and father's room, in the bottom drawer was an album of family photographs. I want the album, where is it, and in my heart I said, if he doesn't give me the photographs I will stand his children one after the other and *trach-trach*. Cut them in half. Yes, I have to leave here with at least family photographs to remember them by.

The farmer said, we didn't see any photographs. The gendarmes came into the house before we did, right, Stanku? Slowly I approached the back of the armchair. I took a penknife out of my pocket that the aunts had given me and opened it under my battledress. I pressed the penknife into the back of the armchair and made a hole. I returned the penknife to my pocket. Stanku said, it's true, Ichko, the gendarmes were the first to enter the house. They took a lot of things.

Took where?

Took them away. They also burned some.

What did they burn?

Maybe they burned photographs, I don't know.

They burned pictures.

Yes.

Did the pictures make a large fire?

Don't remember.

And what did they do with the ashes, throw them into the Tur'i Remety river?

I went out into the yard.

The farmer's wife followed me with the water and the jam. I heard the farmer telling her to come back. She said, I'm sorry about your cat, our dog eats cats, look in the village. I looked at her. I wanted an ax for her too. The farmer approached. Said, do you want to see the cowshed?

I said, I do, but alone. The farmer and his wife returned to the house. I took two steps and saw three chickens and two geese pecking at the dirt in the yard. And then I closed my eyes and Mother was calling to the geese, *piu. Piu. Piu. Piu. Piuuu.* She stood near the wall of the cowshed, scattering seed from her apron, *piu. Piu. Piu. Ahh.* My throat filled up. I threw my head back and whispered, you are in a stranger's yard and you don't recognize the chickens or the geese, and you don't recognize the cows in the shed, enough, nu. I swallowed and gazed at the sky. It was gray and tipped with yellow, like Auschwitz, but without the smell. Right in front of me was Father's butcher shop and it was open. I didn't approach. I went to the cowshed. Father had said to me in the train to Auschwitz, if you go back, look on the lintels above the cowshed door, I hid several pieces of Mother's gold jewelry there, from the wedding. I said to Father, why are you telling me this, we'll go home and you'll give the jewelry back to Mother, and Father said, don't forget Icho, and I remembered his gentle voice.

I didn't find lintels. I found a hole in the wall.

I said to Stanku, let's go.

The farmer and his wife followed us to the road. I heard him call, Ichko, in a hoarse voice, and I didn't stop. He ran up to me and said, is there any chance that your father and mother will return? I stopped. Turned to him.

I gave him an evil look and said slowly, yes. They will come back. Father will come back first, then Mother will come back. You took our home and Father will take the house and the money you owe him. The woman dropped the saucer with the jam and began to cry. I said, you should cry and it's good that you're crying. Cry until my father returns.

The farmer scratched his trousers and said, your brothers, will they come?

I said to him, look at your wife and see for yourself.

I knew that none of my family would return. I knew they were dead. I wanted the farmer and his wife to toss and turn on their pillows all night until the night was over, and may their hair turn white on all the other nights. May they never forget that this house belongs to Jews.

I wanted to get away from that village forever.

I said to Stanku, I'm leaving.

Stanku said, wait a while, Ichko, you're my guest. That evening I heard people were looking for me. My godfather was looking for me. He'd returned from a labor camp. He was the first Jew to return to the village. He went straight back to his house and found it had remained empty. I moved in with him. He was tall, thin. His black hair had vanished, only gray stubble remained and there was a great sadness in the house. We didn't tell each other where we'd come from. He didn't ask about Mother and Father or my siblings. He didn't ask anything and I didn't ask about his wife or his three children. Sometimes we'd look at each other and understand on our own.

My godfather said, Icho, you'll rest here with me for a few days and then leave. I stayed.

People from the village came to my godfather's house and stood near the path.

They could see my comings and goings. Goys I knew waited half a day before daring to walk along the path and enter. If they entered, they'd greet and wait politely. They always waited for me to begin speaking. I asked about the market in Perechyn and my heart was screaming: All of you hate Jews. All of you, hate, hate. I asked about the price of a calf at the market and all the time my brain would disconnect and spin like a carousel. They'd say something and I'd fall upon them with an ax. *Trach.* One blow for every Jew they handed over to the Hungarians for a kilo of sugar. *Trach-trach.* I knew the truth. Goys in our village handed over Jews for one kilo of rice. For one kilo of flour. They were paid by weight for every Jew they handed over. Jews hid in the village and goys informed on them and made a living on the side. There was one family in the village whose son was in the SS. He was happy to receive information about Jews. And he received it, oh yes he did, as much as he wanted. And who informed on Dov when we were at the synagogue, who told the Hungarian soldiers that one child was missing. Who told the Hungarian soldiers that Dov had run to the forest to hide something, maybe gold, maybe money, which is why the soldiers almost beat him to death.

I wanted the traitorous guests with their traitorous children to leave quickly. I wanted them to leave me alone. But first I wanted to see them axed in their chairs. Each one with a fine thin cut in his chair. Half the body sitting, half the body oozing onto the floor.

In the evenings I went walking alone in the village.

A wind whistled in the chimneys. I met young people from school, we'd studied in the same class. We said a few polite words and I walked on. I got to the main road as if I had a purpose. As if people were waiting for me at the end of the road. I was in the village where I was born and I felt alone.

To this day, I've never been near my home again.

Israel, 2001

The 14:18 interurban train from Nahariya to the center.

I want to get as far away as possible.

The sea appears in the window. Brief waves attack the shore. They make a nervous sound and I can guess the nervousness by the motions on the shore. The flamingo stands out on one slender foot, maybe two, and looks into the distance. The flamingo has a steady, peaceful stance, long neck, majestic head. The battle between the sand and the waves makes no difference to her. She is alone, and I think, what's happened to that bird, standing there alone, and where did they all go in the light, any minute now the sun will fall into the sea, and what will a bird do alone in the dark, die?

If Yitzhak was beside me he'd say, it's not a sign of anything, and then Dov would ask, what's not a sign? And Yitzhak would say, it's not a sign that the flamingo will die, death has no signs. And then Dov would say, death has signs, I've seen a few. Yitzhak would get angry and Dov would respond to me, I like being alone, don't feel comfortable if people want answers from me about everything and I have no answers. And then Yitzhak would say, they can ask me a thousand questions, what do I care, but remaining on a large beach without the flock, that's dangerous, Dov, an eagle with claws could devour her. I don't agree, Dov would say, she has healthy wings, she could easily get away.

Nu, so what, and Yitzhak would get up, she'd fly for an hour or two, in the end she'd get tired, and then she'd have to put her head down, how would she know where to land? And maybe four more eagles waiting for her in the skies, no easy matter, is it? And then Dov would say, she could always dive into the water, she'll manage.

I might say that the bird is happy. Why happy – they'd both say, because she's beautiful. A beautiful bird has less to worry about in life.

Chapter 38

Dov

The soldiers at the monastery in Indersdorf looked for an occupation for me.

It was after I'd had pneumonia and returned from the hospital. They sent me to the garage of a German without an eye to learn how to fix agricultural machines. At the garage worked a disabled man who had no stick, he had one high shoulder and one short leg. The German laborer was glad the Germans had lost the war because they disliked the disabled of their race. The laborer and I became friends. One day I said to him, I'm dying to learn how to drive.

The garage owner had a car without tires in the yard.

The German laborer said: Get hold of some petrol, we'll fix up that old jalopy and I'll teach you to drive. I barely managed to finish my workday. I ran to the inn and waited outside. Just then it began to rain and I ran to the tree nearest the inn and watched the door. The strong smell of wet earth tickled my nose and made me shiver. I put my hands in my pockets and ran on the spot. In the meantime, I heard my teeth chattering in my mouth. I said, you'll get pneumonia for the second time. I took my hands out of my pockets and held my nose. With my other hand I pressed my backside. A few minutes later I shifted to my ears, stuck my fingers in my ears, closed my mouth and returned to my nose and backside, my ears and mouth. I thought, I won't let infectious germs enter my body, no, no, I'm not going back to the hospital, that's for sure.

After about an hour, an American jeep arrived at the inn. A soldier got out of the jeep. Holding on to his hat, he ran to the door. I got to the door after him and tugged at his sleeve.

He turned and asked, what are you doing out in the rain?

I said, I'm from the monastery, please, could you give me some petrol, I must have some petrol.

What for?

For the jalopy at the garage, I'm learning mechanics and want to hear the sound of a working engine, it has no wheels, it's just an engine and a steering wheel.

The soldier pinched my cheek and said, but be careful now, and ran to his jeep, gave me a can with two liters of petrol. Holding the can I ran to the garage. The disabled laborer was waiting for me. He poured the petrol into the engine of the jalopy, connected some wires, *tttrrr. Ttrrr. Tttrrr*, the motor was working. Wow. I jumped on the laborer and gave him a kiss. He was pleased and said, come and sit down, we'll begin our first lesson. He pressed the clutch and *hop*, put it in first gear. Left it. Pressed the clutch and *hop*, second gear. Left it, now you, slowly, Bernard, slowly, the gear mustn't screech.

Afterwards we went on to the brakes. I pressed, pressed, until he said enough and then we went on to the steering wheel. He taught me to turn right, left, straight, straight and again left, right, stop. I was overjoyed.

At the end of the second lesson the German laborer said to me, that's it. You're ready now. From now on you can drive a regular car, you have my word. I kissed him twice and looked for a regular car.

One day I was waiting at the square.

Between the monastery and the inn was a square. American soldiers would park their automobiles there. In the middle of the square stood a statue of the Holy Mary. Around the statue was a fence. I stood in the square and waited for an opportunity.

There was no rain the day an American soldier arrived at the inn. He parked his command car in the middle of the square and went inside for a drink. I jumped into the seat of the command car and did what the German laborer had taught me. I started the engine, pressed the clutch, put it into first gear, and accelerated, the command car choked. My heart started to beat fast. I said, from the beginning, and be careful with the clutch, it's sensitive. I rubbed my hands and started the engine again, oy, oy, oy, the command car began to move. I turned the steering wheel to the left and proceeded slowly, not daring to shift into second gear because of the square, I needed to turn left all the time. The command car traveled around the Holy Mary and I yelled, Icho, listen, I'm driving alone, I have a steering wheel in my hands and I'm driving around the Holy Mary. After a few turns I managed to take one hand off the steering wheel. I waved to Mary, yelled aloud, look at me, I'm a Jew, do you see me? I felt strong, especially in front of Mary.

I only had one problem. The German at the garage hadn't taught me how to stop. Nu, I've been driving around for about twenty minutes, and have no idea how to stop a traveling command car. I began to sweat. Yelled, save me, save me, I don't know how to stop, save me.

The soldier at the inn heard me. He ran out to me, jumped

into the command car, turned off the engine and said, hey, what do you think you're doing, who are you?

I began to stammer. My face was burning, I whispered, sorry, I'm from the monastery, you won't tell the Germans, will you?

He began to laugh and finally said, get out of here boy, nu, be off with you.

I ran happily to the monastery. My whole body felt warm, I called out, I love American soldiers and I want to be a soldier like them because they don't shout or hit or say dirty Jew.

The rumor that I'd driven a command car spread quickly through the monastery.

I became known as a car expert. I felt as if I'd grown twenty centimeters taller. As a matter of fact, I began to give Vassily driving lessons. He'd wait for me at the garage in the evening. I taught him to drive the jalopy, and also gave him lessons on car mechanics. From that day on, we waited together in Maria's Square.

One day we saw a heavy tractor approaching the square.

A German farmer was sitting on it. He had an enormous face and a broad neck. He left the tractor with its motor running next to a burned wall and went into the inn. I said to Vassily, I'm going first, you're next. We got up onto the tractor. I said to Vassily, push here, push there, we shifted gears and the tractor began to move. Oho, my heart sank into my underwear. Vassily was the first to jump, I jumped after him. The tractor went into the wall and stopped. The wheels didn't stop. They continued to turn and made a huge hole in the wall, but we'd already fled from there, only Jews from the camps know how to run when they're in danger, and that's very, very fast. I don't know how come the heavy tractor didn't knock down the wall or go into the houses standing there.

For a whole day we hid from the German farmer at the monastery. I was sure he'd take us to a German camp and they'd put us in a closed vehicle with a pipe connected to the engine and we'd die and my brother Yitzhak would go mad.

From that day onward, I didn't dare practice driving.

In Indersdorf, I got acquainted with a man who rang the church bells.

He let me ring the enormous bells. I hung on the rope, a carefree bird, singing loudly, ding, dong, ding, dong. Sometimes my throat closed up. *Din . . . cach. Din . . . cach. Dong . . . mmm.* I saw myself swiftly climbing a tree in the forest near my village and shouting to the skies *yoohoo, yoohoo*, and afterwards eating nuts with green peels. The nuts made my tongue rough as sandpaper. *Ding . . . dong . . . cach.* I saw myself chasing my friend Ilona around the house, deliberately not catching her, because we loved to run and laugh, making sounds of great pleasure. I missed the laughter of children, not for any particular reason, I missed the laughter that rolled out of the throat just when Mama and Papa were in the vicinity. I missed being a boy in a family, agreeing to my big brother smacking my behind and running away from him to my room, hiding under the bed and hearing Avrum say, where is he, and my mother's voice saying, leave him alone Avrum, he's a little boy, now go and take a shower. I wanted my mother.

I often think about Indersdorf.

Chapter 39

Yitzhak

After three days in Tur'i Remety, a young goy ran up to me like the wind.

I knew him. He was my sister Sarah's school friend. He was holding a letter in his hand and shouting, I got a letter from Sarah, your sister Sarah is alive. I opened the letter with trembling hands. The letter fell to the floor. I bent down to the floor and said, you read it. Sarah wrote she was now in Sweden. She'd gone to Sweden at the end of the war and wants to know if anyone from her family has returned to the village and if there's any news. She asked her friend to write back to her and wrote the address in large letters.

I hugged the letter and wiped my face on my sleeve. My sister's friend put his arm around my shoulders and laughed. I said to him, the Germans didn't manage to kill Sarah, she survived and, in the meantime, I have half a family. And I'll write to Sarah, when I have an address in Israel.

That night I couldn't sleep. I saw Sarah. She was twenty when we left the house. She was small, thin, weighing maybe forty or fifty kilos before the Germans, I didn't understand how a girl with that weight had managed to survive winter in a labor camp.

I understood from stories I heard in Humenne that women's conditions in the camps were like ours. Thoughts of Sarah made a wound in my mind and brought on a bad dream.

I saw her standing barefoot in the snow in pajamas without stripes. She was holding a tin pot and crying, Icho, I'm hungry, Icho, help me, but I continued to walk, and then I got to a station and boarded a train. I stood at the window and saw Sarah. She continued to cry, Icho, help me, and I left. I woke wet with perspiration. Couldn't talk for three hours.

Finally, I said to my godfather, I must go to Dov, I want to tell him about Sarah.

My godfather said, a few more days, Icho, stay with me for a few more days.

One day I heard a loud drumming from the direction of the path.

The village drummer stood near my godfather's house. He was wearing a black coat with metal buttons. He held thin sticks and beat a drum hanging from straps over his belly. *Poom, pooroom, poom, poom pooroom, poom-poom*. Drumming in the street meant there was mail and I went out to him. He gave me a note, on the note was a message for me: You must report immediately to the NKVD at the police station.

I handed the note to my godfather. Said, what's the NKVD? I don't know the place.

My godfather read the note and paled. He turned it over, sat down on a chair and said, sit down Icho, sit. The NKVD is the Russian secret police. They came to the village at the end of the war. They're located in the large building near the synagogue.

My heart sank.

I said, what does the Russian police want with me and how do they know I came to the village, I haven't made any problems, or asked for anything, tell me, what do they want from me now? My godfather didn't know what the Russians wanted from me and then, stunned, I cried out, the goys informed on me, yes. They're used to handing over Jews, true or not? My godfather said, I don't think so, Icho, everyone knows you're leaving the village. And what about the farmer who took our home, could he have informed on me? Maybe he thought I'd stay, understand, he's afraid of losing the house. I began to itch. My godfather brought me a glass of water. I said, do you have any sugar, I need three, even five teaspoons of sugar.

I remembered Dov's story about the Russian soldier who aimed a Kalashnikov at him because of a sandwich. The aunts in Humenne also said that Russian soldiers kidnap people who are on their own and send them to labor camps in Siberia. I got up from my chair and said, I'll run away and that's that. I don't want anything to do with Russian soldiers, I had enough with the Hungarians and more than enough with the Germans. My godfather said, it's not worth it, Icho, they have soldiers everywhere, they'll catch you and you won't be able to escape, I'm sure there's some mistake, you should go over there.

I went to the window and asked, this NKVD building, does it have bars, or not? My godfather said, no bars, just glass. I said, excellent, I'll go to this secret police place, and if they arrest me I'll escape at night through the window.

I washed my face and changed my shirt. Made a decision: No one will send me to Russia or load me onto a truck, and no one will put me on a cattle train, yes, no one in the world will make me dig pits in the snow or insulate pipes.

I went to the police station. At the entrance stood a soldier with a rifle. I showed him the note. He put me in a small room, pointed to a chair and left. I sat back in the chair as if I had time, patience, and good thoughts. My mind was exploding: The Russians know I'm alone. The Russians know that if they make me disappear, there isn't anyone to weep for me. Aha. They've heard I traveled by train without paying for a ticket. No, no, it has to do with our home. The farmer told them some story so they'd arrest me. I got up from the chair and thrust my hand into my pocket. My UNRRA papers are fine. I approached the window. I measured the distance from the window to the gate. Tried to open the handle on the window. The handle opened. I could breathe. I returned to my chair and saw a soldier standing at the door.

He had a closed face and a mustache straight as a ruler. He wanted me to go with him. We went along a narrow passage and reached a large room. In the room was a wide table with six chairs. A Russian officer stood at the window. He looked about twenty-five or so. He had stars on his shoulders. He wore an ironed uniform with a stripe down his trousers and sleeves, and high boots. A peaked cap sat on the table. A good sign. The officer asked the soldier to leave the room. He approached me and I saw blue eyes, neither good nor bad, light-colored hair, a small nose and high forehead. A scar the size of a key ran from the end of his eyebrow to the middle of his cheek.

He examined me and asked in Russian, what's your name, young man?

Icho.

Sit down, Icho, sit down.

I sat down. He pulled up a chair and approached me. I pressed my back against the chair and he said, tell me the names of your family please, and where they all are.

I didn't know what to say after Dov and Sarah. I said they're there, I mean, they were there, and maybe they aren't there anymore, I don't know.

The officer leaned back. He said, Avrum is young, he might come back, how old were you when you left your home?

Fifteen.

Fifteen and you remained alive. Children didn't survive the camps, how did you manage?

I didn't know what to say.

The officer leaned forward and said quietly, Icho, I want you to tell me what you've been through. It's important to me to hear everything, and start from the day you all left your home, but first a cup of tea and cookies. At the door stood a soldier with a tray. He put the tray on the table and left. The officer gave me a cup of tea and sweet cookies and I was sure I was dreaming, yes. And in the dream there's a Russian officer with bars on his shoulders, and he's giving me tea to drink and cookies to eat, and he's taking an interest in my Jewish family, that's it. I put a hand under my leg and pinched it, my leg hurt. I realized I wasn't dreaming.

We finished drinking the tea, I maintained eye contact with the wall opposite and began to speak.

I spoke slowly about the ramp at Auschwitz. The officer wanted me to give him a precise picture, where were the Germans standing, and where were the dogs, and where were the prisoners with the pajamas standing, and then he said, one moment. He opened a drawer and took out paper and pencil and gave them to me, can you draw it for me, Icho?

I said, no, no, I don't want to draw. He took the pencil and drew circles on the paper, some with x's some without x's, and there was no room for children with grandmothers and he took out another sheet of paper, and drew a long convoy on the path, in the meantime, some of the children and grandmothers rested in a wood, as if they were on a picnic, and then I put a finger on his paper and said, put the orchestra here.

He tossed away the pencil and cried out, orchestra? You mean an orchestra that plays music?

I said, yes, yes, marches. There were also happy songs, depending on the time, we went with marches to work, to the crematorium we went with a happy song, or the opposite, the Germans wanted to please the people on their way to death, nice huh?

The officer took out a handkerchief from his pocket and rubbed his forehead and I thought, oy, the Russian officer is also beginning to itch, poor man. And then he said, go on, go on. He wanted to know exactly where the showers were, and where they put the suitcases, and tell me, what color was the smoke from the chimney?

I said, you have no color for that, and the smell is missing from your drawing, yes, yes.

We were in a bloc. I'm talking and I see the bloc in the drawing filling out, the bunks like sardines in a tin, and he says, but there's no more room, Icho, and I say, push, push, now you can take them all out for a parade. Prisoners stand in straight rows, some fall to the ground, and there's already a huge pile behind the bloc, and I tell him, add rats, but what comes out is a small mouse, and I say, Mr Officer, a rat has a huge belly, and I want to vomit but I hold back, and on the fourth sheet of paper naked prisoners stand for *Selektion*, and there are already three prisoners on the fence, and on the fifth sheet, I'm on the train to Buchenwald, and I'm thirsty, and hold my throat, and the Russian officer says, have another cup of tea, eat cookies, and he trembles and swallows, coughs, takes out his handkerchief, gets up to the window and *boom*, bangs his fist into the wall and immediately comes back to me, go on, and I went on.

After a short bathroom break I still didn't understand why

the Russian officer wanted to hear about the fate of wretched Jews. After four or five or six hours, the Russian officer stood in front of me, slightly stooped, slightly tense, gave me a long questioning look and I didn't know what to do, so I stood in front of him, a little tired and tense. Suddenly, I saw his eyelids beginning to tremble like the wings of a butterfly about to die, and then it happened. He fell on my shoulder, and began to cry, *aaah*.

I froze on the spot.

Then I raised my arms, lowered them. Raised them again, and stopped three centimeters from his back. He sniffed on my shoulder and said in Yiddish, Icho, I'm a Jew like you, I'm a Russian officer who is Jewish like you and it's a secret. And then he left my shoulder and said, I fought against Germans on several fronts, doesn't matter, the Russians believe I'm a Christian.

I choked, a Jew, a Jewish officer?

He sat down on the chair and wiped his face. Said, my parents are Jewish. We're Jews living in Russia. I joined the Russian army and hid the fact that I'm Jewish from my commanders. After the war, they posted me to your village. I'm in charge of the whole area. I heard you'd come to Tur'i Remety. I called you in because I wanted to see a Jewish child who survived the camps. I heard hard stories about the Nazis, I also saw things, I didn't understand how you managed to hold on, I wanted to meet you, Icho. He got up and hugged me hard, his weeping increased.

I didn't understand a thing.

A Jewish officer. In uniform. A Jewish officer in a goy army. I couldn't believe such a thing existed. After all, a Jew was nothing, a cockroach, a rag. A Jew walked in a convoy to the crematorium. A Jew was a blue number on an arm. A Jew was a slave for soldiers, and here was a Jew in charge of soldiers, with bars on his shoulders, and stars on his chest, telling me in Yiddish that he's a commander of the Russian secret police in my village, it's impossible for him to be a Jew like me. He's tall, good-looking, he has light colored hair and blue eyes, like a successful goy, no, no, it's a mistake, but why is this officer crying on my shoulder as if we were brothers, and why is he hugging me with his strong arms, aah, my father used to hug like that, Papa, where is Papa, I want my papa, I . . .

And then it came.

A great weeping from the throat, chest, shoulders, belly, a terrible weeping. As if I was weeping for every hour, every day, month after month, for almost a year and a half. My nose dripped like a tap on the officer's shirt and he didn't let go. Held me hard and said, we're both Jews, Icho, we're like family. He gave me a handkerchief he took from the drawer and stroked my head.

I fell into the chair. Said, forgive me, Mr Officer, I'm not used to crying. He put a finger on my mouth and said, thank you, Icho, thank you for telling me your story, it was important to me to hear you, I'm glad we met.

I went to the door. The officer stopped me, saying, I want to help you, just tell me what you need, do you want your house back, I'll have them out in a day.

I said, no, no, I'm going away from here.

He said, you're sure Icho, I can arrange it.

I said, sure, but maybe call the farmer and his wife in for questioning, yes, Papa hid Mama's jewelry on the lintels of the barn, I didn't find it, you won't either, but bring them in, let them sweat a little.

The officer, said, do you need money?

I said no, no, I don't need anything.

Well, food maybe? Clothes? What do you need?

I told him, nothing.

He didn't give in and thrust money into my pocket, for the train, and buy yourself food. And then he said, do you need help crossing the border, wait. Maybe you want to live in another village in the area, I can easily arrange that, what do you want, boy, just tell me.

I took the letter from Sarah out of my pocket and showed him the address in Sweden. I said, I wrote to Sarah and told her to come to Israel. My brother and I are going to Israel. I'm done living among goys, don't want to live in Tur'i Remety anymore, don't want another village in Hungary, don't want Germany, I want to live in a country of Jews, things will be good for us there, I'm certain of it.

The officer put his arm around my shoulders and we went out to the path. The soldier at the gate saluted him and he didn't remove his arm. We stood on the road. He hugged me and said, look after yourself, and remember, if you need something, I'm here. Opposite, a minute's walk away from where we were standing, stood a group of villagers, and they looked at us.

I said to the officer, maybe call in the neighbor who didn't look after our house or my cat, ask him if he received money, and what he did with the money, and maybe, in the end, call the entire street in for questioning, call them in maybe once a week, or once every two weeks, can you do that?

The officer smiled, I can, I can, it will be an honor to call them in and question them on how they took a house without paying for it, and I felt like nice hot oil on a sore, and my tongue filled with the taste of hot, sweet chocolate, and I thought, at last I can throw away that damned ax and I never ever want to hold an ax in my hand and chop people in half again.

I returned to my godfather's house. I couldn't speak. I lay in bed and pressed the pillow to my head. After a few hours, I heard a knock at the door. My godfather stood in the doorway. He called me to come outside.

In the yard stood a wagon and horse. Two farmers began to unload things from the wagon. Chairs, food utensils, a scale, a sewing machine, blankets, candlesticks. I knew these objects. I thrust my fingers into my hair and shouted, I refuse, no, what do they think they're atoning for? How dared they break up our home while we were stinking on the trains, huh? My godfather said, they're afraid. Maybe they hoped the Russian officer would put you and me on trucks, or on a train to Siberia, and they'd get rid of the last two Jews. Maybe they're in shock. They thought you'd cry and pray and they came to see the final performance of the Jews. They took tough punishment right in their ugly faces because they saw the police commander hugging you and now they're praying and weeping for themselves. I said, excellent, and I don't want anything from them, tell them to go away.

My godfather watched the farmers' every movement, they're groveling to you, Icho, don't you understand? They're used to groveling. First they groveled to the Hungarian soldiers, then to the Germans, now they're groveling to the Russians and their friend, you. Grovelers.

Another wagon came into the yard. Two farmers from the end of our road unloaded Mama and Papa's beds, a third farmer unloaded pillows with embroidered slips. I went into the house and slammed the door. I felt my heart shatter in pieces. I sat on the floor with my head between my knees. My godfather stood beside me. He said quietly, what should I do with the things in the yard?

I said, nothing in the meantime. Let the goys sweat for a few moonless nights and we'll see. I'm leaving the day after tomorrow, you can have everything.

A few hours later the farmer who lived in our house arrived. He came in with a cake and wine and a jar of pickled cabbage, put them on the table and wept that they'd called him to the police station. He rolled the edge of his hat and wept louder, I told them at the station that I was willing to leave the house, if they'd just give me a few days to get organized, but the secret police told me, stay there for the time being. What will happen, I don't know what to do, you tell me what to do, are you staying? Are you coming back?

I didn't reply. I left through the back door of the house, passed quickly through several yards, reached the field in front of the forest, began to run, just run and run.

I returned towards evening. My godfather was waiting for me in the backyard. He said, come, you have to see this, and pulled me into the house. My godfather's kitchen was full of things. Jars of jam, bottles of wine, loaves of bread, a bag of corn, a tin of sauerkraut, a pot of eggs, smoked meat, a piece of fabric tied with a ribbon. All the gifts were spread over the floor. He held his head and said, they've blocked up my house. I asked, who, who? The people from your street, they say they've been called in for questioning, what can I do with all these things?

And then we heard a knock at the door. My godfather said, you open it. I didn't move. My godfather opened the door. An old farmer stood at the door with a chicken under his arm. The chicken's legs were tied together. My godfather whispered, this man barely has enough to eat, look what he's brought you. I jumped over the package of sugar and the sack of potatoes, approached the door and said to the farmer, I don't want your chicken, take the chicken and go back home. Next time help Jews in trouble, do you hear me? And tell this village that Jews are returning and they're not to inform on them, it's disgusting, do you hear me?

The farmer smiled shyly and held out the chicken, I said, no need, there's no room. He lifted one leg over a jar of jam and a can of oil, put the chicken on a sack of wheat and looked for the way out. I told my godfather, go after him and tell him I'll try and tell the Russian officer to leave him alone. My godfather took a bag of sugar and ran after the farmer. I saw him thrusting the sugar at him, he didn't give up.

I looked at the packages. My belly hurt. I said to my godfather, I'll tell the Russian officer that if any more Jews come back from the camps to the village, he must help them, but that he shouldn't stop his interrogations for at least three months, even half a year. Let them cry. Let them sweat. Let them pray in their church.

I left Tur'i Remety forever.

I left the way I came. With a small bag, a coat, and a hat on my head. I got onto the train and bought a ticket with the money the Russian officer had given me. I returned to my aunts in Slovakia. Ate chicken soup, rested and, two days later, I parted from them. Went on to Indersdorf in Germany to meet my brother.

Chapter 40

Dov

I was so happy when my brother, Yitzhak, returned to the monastery.

I wasn't worried about him. I knew he could manage. I was sure the Russians wouldn't hurt him. My brother Yitzhak had endured Germans and dogs, would the Russians be a problem?

We prepared to leave the monastery. Vassily, my friend from the village, begged me to take him to Israel. I didn't take him. I didn't know a goy could come to Eretz-Israel. I think I made a big mistake. Today, Christians come to Israel. I could have brought him. He'd have been circumcised and lived with us in Israel. I'm sorry he didn't come. Vassily was a born farmer and we loved each other.

Vassily ran away from Tur'i Remety to Prague because of the tuberculosis. All his brothers in the village died of tuberculosis. There were thirteen children in his family. His parents and sisters were unharmed. Just the boys. They didn't know there were tuberculosis germs in cows' milk. Every year or two one of his brothers died. It affected him. Vassily wept when I parted from him. We wept together.

Vassily left Germany and went to England. He wrote me and

my brother a letter. He wrote about his life in England and wanted to know about us. I don't know why we didn't reply. I regret that too. Vassily Korol was his name. He was my best friend and I miss him.

From May 1945 until August 1945, I was in a hospital in Germany. From the hospital I moved to a convalescent home at a monastery near Munich. While at the monastery I was hospitalized again. At the end of March, 1946, we left the monastery. We left with a group of Jewish youngsters. They took us to France, to Lyons, and from there to Marseilles. We left on a ship called the *Champollion*. We reached Israel legally and went straight to Camp Atlit.

Chapter 41

Yitzhak

On the ship to Israel, I felt like an idiot.

I couldn't understand what was wrong with me. I had no contact with anyone, not even the youngsters who were with me at the monastery. I was anxious from the moment I woke up in the morning. We had no family, no language, and no profession. We had no money in our pockets. Nonetheless, I was glad I'd chosen to travel to a country of Jews. I dreamed of a farm. I dreamed of a dairy farm of my own with dairy cows, like my father had.

Our instructors on the *Champollion* taught us Hebrew songs. They were cheerful young men with strong hands, and they insisted on singing. Reluctantly I pretended to sing so they'd leave me in peace. Dov also pretended to sing and clapped his hands, more or less. After the Hebrew songs they told us about the country, about Haifa and Tel Aviv. I listened to their stories. I knew that if I wanted a good life in their country I had to do what they told me. Dov didn't have the patience to listen to stories. He went to the stern of the ship and gazed at the sea.

One day Dov found a girl and wanted to be alone even more. I wandered among the instructors and asked them if there were farmers in Israel. They said, there are lots of farmers and they told me about life on a kibbutz, like a commune. I asked, and are there single farmers, not together? They told me, there are, on a moshav – a farmers' cooperative – and don't worry, everything will work out.

I couldn't stop worrying.

Mainly because of peoples' nerves on the ship. People walked about the deck as if they had a screw loose. They'd quarrel over nonsense, like where they'd sleep at night. They slept crowded together in storerooms below deck and I couldn't understand why it was important to sleep on the right side of the storeroom or the left side of the storeroom. People would fight over the line to the toilet, it was always dirty there. They'd fight over the line to food, and there was enough food for everyone. People would hide bread in their pockets like thieves. We could stand in line for food and suddenly I'd see two people attack each other, and for what, because one had unintentionally touched the other's foot, or one had spoken loudly near his neighbor's ear. One fellow ripped a plank out of the deck in order to hit the man standing in front of him over the head, why? Because he left a gap in the line for food. There were men and women who stuck close to one another and were inseparable. They even stood together at the toilet. At night they slept close together under the blanket, as if an SSman might come to the ship and say: Men to the right, women to the left. I remember catching cold because of all the worry, how could we become one people with all these nerves.

And there were hours I gazed at the sea. I planned my farm. I didn't know where my farm would be, but in my mind I could see a home in a yard with geese, and a cowshed with dairy cows, and a barn full of hay, and a green field near the house. In the meantime, I followed our course. We sailed out of Marseilles. We passed Bizerte in Tunisia. From there we went to Alexandria in Egypt and, finally, arrived in Haifa.

Chapter 42

Dov

I almost got married on the ship to Israel.

We left Marseilles on a ship with many decks, and below there were storerooms. They made place for us in the storerooms. We slept on the floor, without mattresses, just blankets.

We sailed for seven days. There was tension in the air, there were high waves. People walked about the ship in groups. Some asked questions, and some made up answers. Anyone who walked around with a cigarette behind his ear and who had a loud, deep voice could usually be found next to people with questions. He'd listen to them with a serious face and nod his head, finally answering everyone as if he knew. I wandered around the deck with a few friends I knew from the monastery and prayed, just don't let us capsize at sea. And then a miracle happened to me.

I was eighteen and I fell in love with a girl.

One day I was sitting on the deck with friends, counting waves. There was a cold wind. A man and a woman I didn't know approached us. The man pointed at us and asked in Yiddish, which of these young men do you like? I remember deciding, this man lost his mind in the camps if he thinks we're goods in a market. He must have been in Auschwitz for a long time.

The woman looked at us for a long time. Every minute she settled her beauty on someone else. Finally, she pointed at me. Ah? The man said, this is Betty, and you are?

I looked at her and a pleasant warmth spread through me, to my neck, my feet. I forgot my friends from the monastery, forgot about the high waves at sea, forgot about myself. I was transfixed by Betty's face and I was happy. Betty smiled at me. I saw that one of her teeth was bigger and covered another tooth, cute, and I smiled back. Betty approached, I rose as she came up and we shook hands. Her hand was gentle and moist.

Oh, lovely Betty. I liked her from the very first moment. She had shoulder-length hair and green eyes. She had a rather narrow nose and had pink lipstick on her lips. She was a little plump, my height, wore a light skirt and a jacket drawn in at the waist. Her full breasts spilled out of her jacket. She was my age, a girl from France who spoke Yiddish and who hadn't been in the camps. She was traveling to meet relatives in Israel and wanted to remain in the Jewish land.

We sat on deck wrapped in a blanket from morning till night, every day the same, and Yitzhak saw and said nothing. We whispered secrets into each other's ears, mainly funny things, counting in Yiddish until the globe of the sun fell into the sea. Sometimes we sat silently before the sunrise, even when we couldn't see it for clouds. In the line for food, Betty explained to me about French baguettes and cheese with mold, and how much she longed for a glass of red wine. I taught Betty the Hungarian names of trees. She drew the Eiffel Tower on my leg and wanted to know where I'd been during the war. I told Betty, I was born on a ship, now sing me a French song. She sang *Frère*

Jacques, Frère Jacques and taught me to French kiss. I'd lie hidden under the blanket and feel her fingers gently traveling over my hand. She'd cover me with tiny circles like a massage, oh, God, the hair on my body would rise in a second, but not only there. Sometimes my hand would begin to jump by itself, and there'd be electricity in my skin. I'd be alarmed and close my hand in a fist, and then she'd whisper, what's wrong, my Bernard, and go on with the tiny circles of her fingers, on my neck, ear, barely touching, and every part of me would fill up.

One day she found a scar like a hole in my arm. She looked at me sadly and said, does it hurt? Burn? And immediately began to cover the scar with little kisses, as if the hole in my arm was my mouth. Betty whispered, I love you, *mon amour*, love, love, and we began with a long, airless French kiss, *ach*, Betty, Betty.

I wanted time to stop forever. It didn't stop. We approached the shore. Betty said, I want to stay with you, Bernard, I have family in Israel, they're waiting for me to come to them, but I want to go with you, the place isn't important to me, it's you I want, *mon amour*, let's get married.

I was confused. My chest hurt and I didn't know what to do. I went to my brother. I found him in the lowest storeroom below deck. He was talking to one of the group instructors. I took him aside, told him quietly: Betty wants to get married and I don't know what to do. My brother shouted, what? And frowned, what do you mean get married, what do you know about life, you have no home, no money, you know nothing about Israel, and you want the burden of a wife at such a young age, what do you need it for. I realized my brother was right. Betty didn't belong to the group of youngsters from the camps. They'd already told us on the ship that our group would remain together. She couldn't come with us. She said, I'm going to my relatives in Tel Aviv, will you know how to find me, Bernard?

We parted. Betty wept when we parted, and I did too.

Betty *mon amour,* my first love. Afterwards, I missed her very much. I'd dream about her before falling asleep. I didn't have the money to go looking for Betty. I heard that a year later she got married. I never saw her again.

Chapter 43

Yitzhak

We reached the Port of Haifa in mid-April, 1946. I was seventeen and a bit. It was towards noon. The sky was a special blue I'd never known before, a clean color. At the port a large band waited for us. The players wore a dark uniform and held strange instruments in their hands. Pipes with small holes, fat complicated pipes with large holes. The band played cheerful tunes, like the ones I'd heard at Auschwitz. One man held a small stick in his hand, gesturing as if to shoo them away. I didn't see any dogs. Behind the band and on the side stood men, women, and children. They had happy faces. They waved to us as if we were family. They stood with their legs apart, like people who knew the land belonged to them.

The band irritated me.

What were they hiding from us behind the band, what. What were they hiding? They had to be dumb or stupid or both not to think we wouldn't think of bad signs. I asked one of the instructors, what's the band for?

He clapped me on the back, smiled at me with his white teeth, said, they're giving you a festive welcome on behalf of UNRRA. You're the first youth immigration, refugees from the Holocaust.

I asked, what youth.

He said, you're refugee youth, you're from a camp in Poland, aren't you? Refugees.

I didn't understand what refugees were. However, I asked, will more refugees come?

He said, many Jews will come. Ah, you could see he doesn't understand the ramp at Auschwitz, he doesn't know that the chimneys devoured almost all the Jews.

And will they have a band at the port for everyone?

He said, don't know, we'll see.

The band played marches and people began to move, clapping their hands to the tune. I was sure they'd come to blows any minute. They'd hit each other, run away, look for a forest. I began to sweat and then I saw there was confusion, like Auschwitz: People who'd left the ship began to walk in different directions, not understanding what healthy people were telling them, and there was a long delay disembarking from the ship. From where I stood, I could see that some wanted to return to the ship. I think because of the band. It made us all very nervous, that band, playing march after march. The healthy people of Eretz-Israel continued to clap in time. They looked like good, happy people, and the babies in their arms also looked healthy and happy. They looked educated, too, I thought, they're probably good merchants with lucky lives. By the length of their sturdy legs, I was sure they could catch a colt with no problem at all. Don't know why, but their happiness brought tears to my eyes. Beside me several other youngsters were in tears.

The sunlight was strong. Without smell or smoke. I felt my body gradually releasing my nervousness. From the port, they took us to Camp Atlit.

Again there were lists and names. They had loud voices in

Hebrew, even without a loudspeaker. Some had huge forelocks that fell nicely on their foreheads. They'd read two or three names, raise their heads, and *hop*, toss the forelocks back. The young men from Eretz-Israel wore khaki trousers and shirts with the sleeves rolled up in a broad band where their muscles were. And what muscles they had, they could lift a calf, even two on their shoulders without any problem at all, they were broad and well-padded. They could even catch chickens or a duck with their little finger, and carry at least three or four sacks of hay on their backs.

I remember, when they called my name, I straightened my shoulders and neck, thrust out my chest and called out, yes, in my strongest voice. My voice sounded as strong as theirs, I was pleased. There were some who didn't answer when they were called. Sometimes they had to repeat a name three times before other youngsters in the group said, it's him, it's him, pointing at someone. There was one who refused to answer to the name they'd called.

The young man with the lists approached him and said, tell me, what's your name? The youngster put out a hand, tugged at his sleeve and pointed at the blue number on his arm. The Israeli coughed and said, forget your number. In Eretz-Israel you are Ya'akov Mandelbitz, is that clear? Now repeat after me, Ya'akov Mandelbitz, Ya'akov Mandelbitz. The youngster just mouthed something.

The young men finished reading names and then sprinkled powder over us, I think it was DDT. *Waachch*. What a stink. They said it was against itchy disease. I was sorry I didn't have a few bottles in the camps. Then they took us to wooden huts. Each one was given a bed to himself, a blanket, a sheet, and a pillow. The blankets smelled of DDT. The smell didn't bother me, I was glad I didn't have lice.

The next day they told us, now we have to wait until each of you is sent to a settlement in the country.

I asked, how long do we wait?

They said, a week or two, no longer.

And what do we do in the meantime?

They told us, we'll sing a bit, tell you about Eretz-Israel.

I immediately began to itch. I said to the young man who'd read out the names, I need some more DDT and can you perhaps give me a bottle for later? He refused.

The young men gathered us together in one of the huts and told us about the kibbutz and the *moshav*, and we sang songs, *"Anu banu artzah"* – We came to this country – *"Se'u tziona ness veh degel"* – Carry a flag to Zion – *"Hatikvah"* – The Hope – the country's anthem. The young men from the country sang enthusiastically, the youngsters from the camps in Poland did not. Those sitting in the first line sang all right. The second line not so well, from the third line, nothing. Some mouthed the words, some looked into the corners or at the ceiling and didn't even mouth the words. I mouthed the words. Dov confused the words, too.

The young men from Israel stamped their feet on the ground, clapped their hands, and tirelessly sang many songs. One of them put two fingers into his mouth and gave a whistle that almost burst my eardrum. At least five or six youngsters from the group jumped up from the bench and ran outside. There were times when in the middle of the *yula, yula, yulala*, my head began to throb, *tach. Tach. Tach-tach-tach.* But I stayed in the happy hut and whispered to my brother, we're staying till the end. Dov was one of those who constantly stood up and sat down, stood up and sat down, took two steps and returned to their chairs. They made all the healthy people from Eretz-Israel dizzy.

There were several healthy people from Eretz-Israel who stopped the tune because of those who got up and were confused: They couldn't find the door, wanted to open a window, they were tired and wanted to lie down on the bench, all in the middle of the great happiness.

When the healthy young men went on to sad songs, they'd put their hands behind their backs and hug and sway and gesture to us, you hug too, and everyone together, *"Hinei ma tov oh ma naim, shevet achim gam yachad"* – How good and pleasant it is for brothers to be together – sing with us, *"Hinei ma tov oh ma naim, shevet achim gam yachad,"* and, interestingly, this line made some weep at all this togetherness, but there were some with weak nerves and they kept getting up from their chairs. They'd tell them in Hebrew to sit down, sit down, soon we'll have refreshments, but many got up and left, not understanding one word of what was said to them, and so they missed the refreshments.

In the happy hut I loved to sing *Hatikvah* most of all. When we reached the line, "To be a free people in our land, the Land of Zion, Jerusalem," I'd shout loudly as if I had a loudspeaker in my mouth. It made me feel good to shout out that line.

Dov had a very, very hard time in Atlit. Hardest of all was the happy hut. Sometimes I pulled him to a chair, telling him there'd be wafer cookies or plain cookies and oy va'avoy, if they didn't hand out candies at the end. Dov was unhappy, I think mainly because of the girl from France who'd wanted to marry him. I couldn't agree to such a plan because that girl didn't know anything about what we'd been through. We spoke like normal people, smiled when appropriate, but our hearts were broken, and this she neither saw nor felt, we were chronically ill in a way, and ordinary people didn't immediately see it. I was so fearful for us. I knew that if Dov married, he'd commit suicide within a week. I was glad he agreed to give her up, but I worried about what I saw in his eyes. I saw him sitting with people and not hearing what they said to him. I saw he wanted to be alone and I was worried. I refused to let him be alone. I would go to him, take him by the hand, and bring him back to sit with everyone until refreshments.

Two weeks at Camp Atlit and then they took us to a small village in Lower Galilee, opposite the Kinneret – Sea of Galilee. Thorns as tall as our heads and heavy black mud. In this village the roads were narrow, the work hard and our pockets empty. A collective, we were told, I didn't know anything about it. Friends said, if you mix kibbutz and private *moshav* together in a large pot, you get a collective *moshav*. I imagined a large pot, mixed and mixed, and remained hungry. In the very first week I didn't understand what I was doing in that collective village.

Chapter 44

Dov

We were twenty-five young men and women who arrived at a small collective village that was ten years old.

A youth group, mostly from Poland, Holocaust survivors, as we were known in the village, I didn't know exactly what I'd survived, but neither did I ask.

It was the month of April. We walked along a muddy path with the heavy smell of wet grass. Alongside the path I saw small, black stone houses with empty yards. Men and women of about thirty were waiting for us in a rather large building they called the Members' Hall. The men wore simple clothes, khaki trousers, blue shirts. The women wore short skirts, some wore trousers. They had red embroidered x's on their shirts. Near several women was a pram with a baby. The people looked at us and sang together, *"We've brought peace upon you, we've brought peace upon you, peace upon you all."* Some clapped their hands and nodded to us, nu, sing along with us, but I stuck to a chair and the huge belly of a woman in a sweater who was sitting in the corner. She was holding the very bottom of her belly and I wanted to flee.

I got up from the chair, but my brother, Yitzhak, grabbed my trousers and pulled me back into the chair, he whispered, what's wrong with you, sit still. I couldn't sit still because of the picture in my mind: The picture of a pregnant woman's huge belly, she was maybe in her ninth month, and she was flying into the fire, *aah*. I said to myself, pull yourself together or you'll be done for. The woman with the belly smiled at me, she looked happy.

People in the hall talked and they talked in Hebrew, we didn't understand a word.

I bent down as if I had to tie a shoe-lace, took a large step, and went outside. I looked for trees. Didn't find any. Opposite the entrance was a row of small pine trees in round holes, they looked half alive, half dead. My brother stood beside me. He looked at me with a long face and beckoned with his finger, we're going back into the hall.

I went back to my seat and then someone at the central table with protruding teeth stood up and said in Yiddish, hello, my name is Issasschar, and I'm your instructor and translator. He welcomed us in the name of the members, said a few words about the collective, and explained our daily routine in the village. Issasschar constantly looked for words in Yiddish, nonetheless I managed to understand from him that we'd start work early in the morning, continue until noon, and every afternoon we'd study in a classroom with a teacher.

He says classroom with a teacher and my mind goes *pak*. I whispered to my brother, ask which teacher, quickly, because maybe we need to return to Camp Atlit now, before the truck leaves the village. My brother said, excuse me, sir, what do you mean a classroom with a teacher, you mean like a school? Issasschar said, yes, and approached us, because in the meantime, people began to talk among themselves, and we couldn't hear a thing. He said, we've organized a special classroom for you, there are books, notebooks, and we have an excellent teacher in the village.

My brother said, and what will we learn in school?

You'll learn Hebrew, reading and writing, history, Bible, and . . . that's it.

I understood there were several other things we had to learn, and he couldn't find the words in Yiddish. I whispered to the instructor, tell me, are there return ships in the country, yes or no, and where do your ships leave from, and where do these ships go, and how many times a week. The instructor didn't understand a single word.

I had to have something sweet in my mouth.

Women gave us a glass of lemonade and a slice of cake. A brown cake with soft chocolate icing on top. I put the cake in my mouth and my nose ran colorlessly. That cake tasted like the cakes Mama made for Shabbat. I liked being with Mama in the kitchen. I'd help her beat the egg whites, slowly fold in the sugar and flour and put it in an iron stove that stood on two metal plates. I wanted to swallow the entire cake that remained on the table and grab some from the others who were eating slowly and politely. I said to my brother, if, in this village, they make good cakes like Mama used to make, we'll be all right. I'm still worried about the lessons, what do you think?

My brother smiled at me, said, we'll be all right because we have no other place, understand? And then Issasschar said, now we'll go to the rooms. He took us to two single-story buildings, divided us up, three or four to a room, with beds and a small cabinet, boys and girls separately. We were given clothes and high work shoes and a new name for the group. Buddies, Issasschar called us. Come on, buddies, get up, buddies, no dreaming, buddies, and time for bed now, nu, buddies.

That first night I couldn't fall asleep. I pursued the stripes of light cast into the room through the window. I got to the ceiling and began to descend. I wanted to go back to the ship, to embrace Betty.

The next day we were examined by a doctor.

A man with glasses and greasy hair without a white coat. He cleared his throat. Every minute or two he'd clear his throat. *Cach-cach.* In the meantime, he examined chest, back, ears, and even inside underpants. My face flushed in an instant. The doctor didn't say a word. Neither did I. The doctor didn't look me in the eye. And I didn't look at him.

A few days later, Issasschar came to my room and said, Dov, you have an appointment for surgery.

I felt I was about to faint. Yelled, what surgery, what do you mean surgery, I'm not in any pain and I decided to run away.

Issasschar sat down on my bed and showed me a letter. He said, this is from the hospital, I'm sorry, but I don't understand what's written in the letter. I said to him, I'm not going anywhere, I'm healthy.

My brother immediately agreed, saying, I won't permit my brother to go to hospital. We had enough hospital in Germany, understand? The instructor left.

A day later I was called to the doctor.

My brother didn't want to come with me. His mouth was white, he struck his leg with his fist and told me, be careful Dov, be careful, and don't go anywhere alone with the doctor, d'you hear me?

I said, very well, don't worry, and gave him a candy I'd hidden in my pocket.

The instructor and I went into the infirmary. The smell of medication made my body prickle. The doctor spoke to the instructor. I realized the doctor knew how to talk. The instructor translated. There was only one problem, the instructor didn't know how to say hernia in Yiddish. He told me to remove my trousers. I did so. The doctor pointed to my groin. I knew the place. Sometimes it hurt there. It began in Hungary, on nights when Father, my brothers and I dragged heavy logs to train cars. We did this work for food. The instructor took a stick used to examine the throat and broke it in two. He said, hernia, hernia, I didn't understand. Finally, he said, we have to operate, I'll come with you.

I went with the instructor to the Italian hospital in Tiberias. My third time in hospital in a year. We waited on a bench and I wanted a plane to come from the skies and hurl a bomb on the doctors' room. I rose from the bench and went to the toilet. Returned and sat down. About twenty minutes later I went to the toilet again. I had a lot of urine because I was afraid of the anesthetic that would keep me in hospital for three months.

I couldn't explain to the doctor what I'd gone through. The instructor's Yiddish wasn't sufficient for my troubles. I said to him, tell me, how do I get to the nearest ship to Tiberias, ah? He hugged me and I was called inside.

I lay in hospital for ten days after surgery.

I had a lot of pain in my leg, belly and head. They placed a heavy bag of sand on the wound to fix it in place. I couldn't move. The nurses washed me in bed with water and soap, dried me with a towel, bandaged the wound, talking and laughing loudly, all in Hebrew. They were nice, those Hebrew-speaking nurses. One was red-haired with red skin as if she'd lain in the sun for two months. She'd purse her lips and let the air out like a tune, *ttshshsh ttshshsh*, and smile at me. Another one gathered up her hair behind like a black banana with a lot of pins in her hair. I was ashamed to say in Yiddish, ouch, I'm in pain, and take away this bag. I felt like a wretched, weak old man. I had another problem. In the bed opposite was a young man who made me laugh. His name was Maurice and he had enormous ears. He knew how to move his ears up and down and turn his lips over like a sock. He'd pout with his lips and turn them inside out. The worst was during the doctors' rounds. A doctor would stand next to my bed with a few nurses, and read my card, and in the meantime, from the side, I'd see Maurice turning his lips in and out. I couldn't stop laughing because of him.

When I laughed, the place of the surgery hurt even more. I begged him, enough Maurice, enough. Maurice ignored me. I started lying with my face to the wall. It didn't help. He'd say something, just a word, and I knew he was talking to me with his lips inside out.

I had many visits in hospital. Issasschar visited me almost every day. As well as other friends from the group. My brother didn't come to visit. I wasn't angry with him. Today, I know: My brother Yitzhak will never set foot in a hospital. Not even for himself. The three months he spent looking after me in the hospital in Indersdorf at the end of the war were enough for him. I remember when they wanted to give him an injection and he fainted.

Ever since the surgery in Tiberias, I've had two more operations on my groin. My wife, Shosh, visits me, the children visit, friends come, Hannah, Yitzhak's wife, also comes to visit. She always says that Yitzhak follows her around the house saying, go to Dov, go on, go. He doesn't come, he can't set foot in a hospital.

After the surgery in Tiberias, I realized another miracle had happened to me. A day after the surgery I was told that the doctor who did the surgery on my groin was a spy and they

caught him that night. He'd spied for Lebanon. He was immediately imprisoned. At first I was alarmed. He could, after all,
have killed me with his knife. These thoughts brought iciness
to my back in the middle of a heatwave.

I called out, miracle, miracle. Someone is looking after me
from above. When my brother Yitzhak heard the story, he immediately looked for a chair to sit on and asked for water with five
spoons of sugar. I gave him water and a piece of bread I had in
my pocket. He threw away the bread, got up and put his fist
through the glass window.

The glass broke with his shouts, I told you not to go with
doctors, I told you it was dangerous.

However, I was satisfied with the surgery. The pain in my
groin stopped and in my heart I came to a decision, I, Dov, will
be a good laborer in this village, and it was all because Issasschar
said, in Eretz-Israel, the most important thing is to be a farmer,
like the goys in your villages in Hungary, or in Poland. And then
he asked me, what is your profession?

I said, mechanic, just as I said on the ramp at Auschwitz,
without meaning it. But in the meantime, I had experience from
the garage in Germany. In the village they were glad. They needed
a mechanic for their garage.

I got out of bed at four in the morning. I remember a loud
knock at the door. I put a foot out of bed and went outside. I'd
gone to bed in my work clothes. I'd woken at least an hour before
four and counted the stars at the window.

The guard who called me had a gun on his shoulder. He
nodded goodmorning and accompanied me to the garage. I
felt like a certified mechanic with a diploma from Germany,
and it made me want to cry. I wanted to say to the guard,

thank you, sir, for accompanying me to work and making sure I find the way. I didn't say a word. I knew the guard didn't understand Yiddish.

I parted from the guard near the garage. The head mechanic was waiting for me. He stood half asleep, yawning loudly. His yawns smelled of coffee. He wore a cap on his head and smiled pleasantly in between yawns. A dog ran between us, licked my shoes and wagged its tail. I took a piece of bread from my pocket and gave it to the dog.

The mechanic took me round the garage and explained things in Hebrew. I didn't understand a single word. I nodded and stroked the dog that ran after us. In the meantime, we finished our round and he gave me a heavy container and showed me an automobile on the side. I opened the lid of the container and smelled it. The smell of oil. I didn't know what to do. I spoke Yiddish, Hungarian, Russian, a little German and I had no words for him. I waited. He opened the bonnet of the engine, pointed at a hole like the opening of a pipe, and gestured with his head. I understood that he wanted me to pour the oil into the pipe. I lifted the container and poured the oil – straight onto the ground. The mechanic grabbed his head and flung off his cap, he shouted something, and gestured to me in the direction of the path. I understood him and left the place.

Four-thirty in the morning and I'm alone on the path.

It was dark and I was ashamed. I stuck my hands deep in my pockets and began wandering about aimlessly. In our building the buddies were asleep. I didn't know anyone else in the village. I walked for another fifty meters and then I heard the mechanic shouting, Dov, Dov, I stopped. I turned back. He was standing under the lamp at the garage and beckoning to me to come back. I went back. I realized I'd made a mistake. Realized I'd wasted very expensive oil. I didn't know how to apologize in Hebrew and I was sorry. I looked for words that were familiar to the mechanic. And then I had an idea. I started to sing *Hatikvah* to him. I remembered some of the words. He stood straight as a flag, I also straightened up and we sang together. Then he put a hand on my shoulder and began to explain about engines. His motions were delicate, and I understood that he'd forgiven me. From the car we went on to a wood panel like a table. He took out paper from one of the drawers and drew me an engine, naming each part and marking it with an arrow. I realized that in the village they believed I was a professor of tractors. They were sure they'd received a certified mechanic from Germany. I couldn't say that I'd learned mechanics on an old jalopy in a small garage. And I couldn't tell them in their language that I was hungry. Constantly hungry.

During the first weeks we had a common kitchen. We ate as much as we wanted. Well, more or less. In the village they decided to close the kitchen. They allocated us to families. The food they put on the plate was a quarter of what I really wanted. I was ashamed to ask for more. When they put a bowl in the middle of the table I took the same as everyone else, two or three spoons, but I could have eaten the bowl by myself. Even two bowls. There was *tzena* – austerity measures – in the country. Moshav members ate what there was during the *tzena*, bread, cheese, some vegetables, sometimes eggs, barely any meat at all. They thought we were like them. We weren't like them. I couldn't tell the family about the hunger I'd known in the camps, and shout, the food in your bowl isn't enough for me, I need ten bowls, I have to eat meat, lots of helpings of meat. And then I had bad thoughts, if there wasn't enough food in the village, the members would start shooting, start to reduce us, yes. They'll wipe out some of our group so there'll be enough food for everybody.

I said to my brother, Yitzhak: I can't bear thinking of bread all day. The dreams at night are bad enough. I can't go back to potato peels, understand?

My brother looked down. Made a small hole in the ground with his heel and said, so I'll get bread for you. And Yitzhak did, because Yitzhak knew how to get hold of bread, and no matter how much he brought, I wanted more, but most of all I wanted to run away.

Chapter 45

Yitzhak

We came from the Holocaust to a new hell.

Again songs and clapping. Again the smiles of regular families with a father and a mother, small children, a nicely set table, and a mother taking a handkerchief from her sleeve to wipe her child's nose, and afterwards a hug. We saw a father who drove a combine, who at night was a hero guarding a post with a gun. And what were we, they burned our father and mother and they burned our grandfather and grandmother, and they burned our siblings and aunts and uncles. We were ashamed. They talked and talked and I didn't understand a word. I kept checking with the others, did you understand what they said to you, did you? Nothing.

When we began to understand their language we began to understand what they were saying about us in this country. They called us *soap,* said *you went like sheep to the slaughter and didn't resist. You didn't fight like men. There were thousands of you in their trains, why didn't you revolt. You could have grabbed their guns, at least wiped out a few Germans before the crematorium.* Aah. We felt new enemies had risen against us. For the Germans we were garbage, in Eretz-Israel we were sheep. This talk wounded my heart. Pain in the morning, pain in the evening, and at night, most of all. I wanted to erase Auschwitz, Buchenwald and Zeiss from my mind, and I couldn't. And then came the nerves, because I realized that the hell wasn't over. Sometimes I wanted to bring down an ax on the natives of this country. Chop some of them in two. Maybe just a blow to the head, without chopping.

They put us to work from the first day. They allocated us several places, like the cowshed, chicken coops and fields. They told us, do this, do that, a lot of explanations and hand gestures, because they wanted everything to be just right, and it was hard for me. They taught us to carry a sack of mash on our backs, hold tight with both arms, walk bowed from the truck to the storehouse, and we saw the crumbling bodies of prisoners to be dragged to a large pile. They gave us a shovel to dig a hole for a tree, and we saw a pit for the dead. They played classical music for us in the village on a cello and we heard the orchestra of Auschwitz and the screams of a mother, Golda'leh, Golda'leh, they've taken my Tuvia. They wanted us to sit in an ordinary classroom to learn Hebrew and flames and fire came out of our ears. Issasschar, the translator with the protruding teeth, said, come and learn to dance the Hora, come on buddies, let's go, kick your legs up high everyone, to the side, and now stamp your feet three times, *tak*. *Tak*. *Tak*. And under my feet, I saw a face like dirty dough. Hardest of all were the fires. The village bell would ring and everyone would run with wet rags, or a pail full of water, or a special bat to put out the fire in the fields or the woods. People would shout, where's the fire, where is it, and I would stand stock still. Because just seeing the smoke would bring pressure to my ears. It was the same with the bonfire and the song *Hinei Ma Tov* – Brothers Sitting Around the Fire Together. The flames were high and there was smoke and I saw my family disappearing into the smoke. I'd hear the *pak-pak-pak* of branches, and remember the *pak-pak-pak* of the lice cooking in the steam.

And there was the urgent need to get used to life in a collective.

I didn't understand their economic method. A cowshed the size I remembered from home, and it belonged to everyone, the chicken coops belonged to everyone, the vegetable garden to everyone. I asked, and who gains in the end, everyone, and the losses, everyone, who covers them?

Nobody, we write it down, and then what, we continue working and hope for the best, what do you mean hope for the best, hoping for the best is . . . nu, what's wrong with you, why are you so worried, Yitzhak.

I said, because I want to understand, ultimately, who gives. They said to me, God gives, all right?

I worried even more.

We worked physically hard, the pocket was empty. I asked, where will I get money to buy things.

They asked me, what do you need, Yitzhak.

I said, work boots, for instance.

They said, go to the store.

But they don't have any.

They said, order shoes and they'll get them for you.

When will they get them.

At least two to three weeks.

I said, where will they get them, from the market? I know a very good market, and I want to buy them myself.

They said, what do you mean a market, we buy them from a proper store.

I went to the village store to order shoes.

Prices at the store were fixed. I couldn't feel the goods or weigh them in my hands. I wanted to lower the price of sugar. They said, you need to understand, we don't bargain here.

Why not, because everyone's equal in a collective, there's no difference, all members earn the same. I couldn't understand how the hell people earn if they have no money in their pockets, they explained to me that each member has a budget, everything is written down in a book in the office.

I asked, and if a member wants to buy something.

They said, he buys it.

And how does he pay.

No problem, they reduce the numbers in the book.

I said, and if I feel like working double the hours, to earn more money.

They told me, that's fine, but the budget doesn't change.

I went back to my room and banged my head against the wall.

I really missed the Perechyn market. The barrels of fish and sauerkraut, sacks of beans and rice, packages of spices, colorful pieces of fabric, lamps, work tools, and the cries of vendors. I missed standing with a good joke or some story, there was always time for small talk in the market, no one was in a hurry. At the store I realized I had to hurry because there were other people there and everyone was buying from the same vendor.

And there was the problem of food.

The food they gave us wasn't enough. They put half a tomato, onion, a piece of cheese, a few olives and a slice of bread on the plate. That's all. There was barely any meat. It brought despair and a lot of anger. Our bodies began to live. We were hungry even when we were full. My brother Dov received a loaf of bread per day at work in the field. He'd finish the loaf at breakfast. There was no bread left for lunch. The members demanded hard work from us, they needed us as laborers in order to work the farm, and we worked hard, but the food they put on our plates drove us mad. We were ashamed to complain because the members of the village ate as we did. They gave us what they gave themselves. They had no knowledge of the enormous hole we had in our bellies.

We began to run wild in the dining room. We fell upon the poor vegetables on the table, on the margarine and jam. We'd grab margarine and smear it on each other. We'd have water fights with water from the jugs. We laughed like madmen so we wouldn't cry. Don't know why. Maybe we were releasing nerves from the war. We were like a bottle of soda that had fallen to the floor with a closed cork. Maybe we needed to pour out our hearts, but we were ashamed of our past. And even if we hadn't been ashamed, how could we have explained without language, how?

I felt I was beginning to go mad.

I wanted to peel off my skin.

Dov said, I can't live in a place like this, understand.

I said to him, it's hard for me too, believe me, but let's give the place a chance. I started to make a plan regarding the food. I made a map in my mind of the places where there was food. I got out of bed in the morning for work, and I searched, yes. In the chicken coops there were eggs. In the bakery there was bread. Vegetables in the vegetable garden. I planned what I should take at night when nobody could see. And so we began eating on the side. I saw other members of our group also making plans. We started wandering around at night in groups. Each group ate in a different place. Some ate behind the chicken coops, or near the pen. Some went down to the woods. It was the first time we felt free. When we sang *Hatikvah* in the hall, *Being a Free Nation,* we didn't really feel free. Only when eating with our group, in our language, did we really feel free. After a night like that, there were some who didn't want to get up for work in the morning. In the village they thought we were lazy. They didn't know we wandered around at night looking for food.

I made a plan regarding the food but I also came to a decision in my heart.

I decided that I, Yitzhak, son of Israel and Leah, would begin a normal life in Eretz-Israel. Yes, yes. Because I was tired of being angry. Tired of wandering through the world with an ax and chopping people in half. I said to myself, I will build myself in this country, even if I have to eat a lot of shit. I said to myself, I have to succeed in a country of Jews. I have no other place, this is it. And in my heart, I knew that I wouldn't be able to live the life I wanted in that village.

Chapter 46

Dov

M y brother told me, we'll give it a chance, Dov, and I suffered. We felt like slaves. They didn't like us. And I didn't like them. We were their strangers and they were our strangers. We were bored by their cello, their talking and their laughing. We missed the simple things we had at home before the camps. I like simple songs and short stories. I wanted to hear stories but there was no time for stories. There was hard work and that was all.

We started to go wild.

There were youngsters who had fist fights. They threw out some youngsters in our group for fighting and this didn't help our boredom. Those who remained and who didn't fight began to give up. I remember the first day they put black olives on our plates. We weren't familiar with olives. We thought they were candies on the plate. We put them in our mouths, they tasted bitter, salty. We spat the olives onto the ground. We made vomiting noises, *waaach*, *waaach*, and we threw olives at one another, and at the wall. We got into a state of camp-survivor excitement, as they whispered about us. They whispered and whispered and we collected olives from the floor and shot them at the kitchen workers. The women in the dining room put their heads in their hands. We were wasting food during the *tzena* and it killed them.

Finally, they closed the dining room and distributed us among the families and so there was more suffering, apart from the cello and their irritating comments. I'd eat everything they gave me and was still hungry.

One day the woman I ate with said: I'm going away tomorrow. I'll leave you a pot of soup. Come home, Dov, come into the kitchen and eat by yourself.

I came at noon.

It was a hot summer's day and, like their cello, the flies stung my ears. I breathed with a dry mouth and knocked at the door. There was no answer. I took off my shoes and entered quietly. I looked for a pot of soup. I saw something that looked like soup in a pot on the counter. I lifted the pot and drank what I found. I remained hungry. I scraped at the bottom of the pot with my nails and put it in my mouth. It tasted like burned tin. I put on my shoes and left.

The next day at noon the woman was waiting for me.

She said, Dov, why didn't you eat the soup in the pot, I left you a full pot of soup.

I said, but I did eat.

She asked, which pot did you eat from?

From the pot on the counter.

She was alarmed, just a minute, did you eat from the pot next to the sink?

I said yes, that's the pot I saw, it was standing here. I pointed at the counter.

The woman put her hand on her chest and said, oy, that was the dirty pot after I cooked, I filled it with water and didn't have time to wash it. Did you really eat that?

I said, yes, it was a little salty, not a bad taste.

The woman raised her eyes to the ceiling and made a *cach-cach-cach* sound, but the soup I prepared for you was in the airing cupboard, why didn't you open the cupboard, you know we keep our food there, look, the pot's been here since yesterday, you probably went hungry, what a pity.

I was ashamed to tell her that dirty water with a few little bits on the bottom, if I was lucky, was my usual food in the camps. Neither did I tell her about the decision I made on the path in her yard. I didn't tell her that I, Dov, was done being hungry all the time, done. I, Dov, was done with scraping bits off pots for food. And then I myself began sneaking into the village chicken coop. I held a kilo bread pan I found in the bakery. I collected twenty-eight eggs. I went to the sheep pen. There was an electric stove there. I broke the eggs into the bread pan. I stirred it well with a stick and fried myself a huge omelet. I ate the omelet without leaving a crumb. I felt good. I went to work picking vegetables in the vegetable garden, some went into the box, some I ate in the bushes, tomatoes for instance, cucumbers, cauliflower. I took potatoes to the room. I cooked them in the yard. I took bread from the village bakery. I'd sneak in like a cat, take a fine smelling fresh loaf of bread, hide it under my shirt and leave. I didn't like going into the bakery. Luckily, someone from our group always worked there and we had an agreement. He would throw three or four loaves of bread out of the window, one of us would wait under the window and we'd share it.

I didn't like going into the bakery because of the oven.

There was a large oven inside the wall. A large fire. And there was a baker in a dirty apron who would use a stick to put the pans of dough straight into the wall. Whenever I entered the bakery I'd remember the SSmen who caught one of our relatives, a woman in her ninth month of pregnancy. The woman was weeping and calling out to God. God didn't come, only the SSmen, may they rot in hell. One of them caught her by the shoulders, the other by her legs. They managed to pick her up a little and she fell. They cursed and spat on their hands, the woman began to kick, I heard a lot of farts coming from her behind. One of the SSmen slapped her face. She froze for a second. They bent down and lifted her with difficulty. She swung in their hands, and then one of them said, one, two, three, and they threw her into the fire. To this day I can hear her screams, I think I also heard the screams of a baby, or maybe I just seemed to.

I thought a lot about what the farmer from Budapest said to me at Auschwitz. He said, Bernard, steal, kill, but most of all save yourself, you have a chance, understand? It hurt me that I had to steal food in a village of Jews, but I stole and suffered less when they whispered insults about me or the group. I never stole chickens from the chicken coop, even if the whispers were loud. I didn't want to kill animals.

Members of the village knew about our stealing. Eggs were missing from the chicken coop. The baker counted the number of loaves. Issasschar was angry with us, he said we were ungrateful. Yes, ungrateful. We knew they were right and we wanted to be good. We saw how hard they worked to hold onto their young farm. We saw they were hardworking people with beautiful intentions, but we couldn't help ourselves. To this day I regret throwing olives and taking eggs for omelets in quantities they'd never have allowed themselves because of the *tzena*.

*   *   *

In the village they wanted us to learn Hebrew and I was tired from labor that began early in the morning and from wandering about at night in order to feel full. I was most tired on days I worked as a porter. They'd tell us to unload sacks of corn and barley from trucks. I saw that my body was falling to pieces under the sacks. The *moshav* members were strong. Their muscles stood out under their skin, I didn't have muscles that stood out. I barely had any flesh at all under my skin. I managed light work, like mixing mush with my hands, or feeding the chickens, or milking cows, work like that. Nonetheless, I was tired at noon and didn't want to go to their classes that began in the afternoon. Issasschar didn't give in. We'd go to the class-room and pray our teacher would be ill, but we had a very energetic teacher.

Safra the teacher knew a little Yiddish and he knew how to knit socks. He'd manage at least nineteen rows while we copied words from the board. He had a round face and his eyes were always smiling. Even when he was counting rows on a sock, his smile remained. He taught us history and Hebrew in funny Yiddish. I didn't understand anything I wrote in my notebook. Just like *cheder* in Tur'i Remety when our teacher shifted from Yiddish to Hebrew. *Vayomer, gesukt* – he said, *Vayedaber, geredt* – he spoke, *nu shoyn* – Okay.

Our teacher wanted us to learn reading and writing, but I found Hebrew difficult. Certain letters don't exist in Hungarian. I kept confusing the letters. In the end, I despaired, to this day I write with mistakes. How do I write "weep" in Hebrew? How do I write "piano"? How do I write "lupine" or red "anemone"? Hyacinth? I managed loquat and poppy.

The teacher gave us Hebrew names. He said, what did they call you at home?

I said the Christians called me Bernard, at home they called me Leiber.

He said, Leiber means lion-bear – Arieh-Dov – choose, Arieh or Dov?

I said, Dov.

And then he said to my brother, what did they call you at home?

My brother said, Icho. The Christian neighbors called me Ichco.

The teacher said you will be Yitzhak, we'll learn about Yitzhak in the Bible, all right?

More than history and Bible, the teacher taught us to be human beings. To greet an adult, to say please and thank you. To eat politely and wash our hands before a meal. To wash our ears really well so there'd be no yellow inside them.

The teacher, Safra, loved us. I agreed to sit in his classroom because of this love. I was willing to sit for four hours straight and hear how to talk to an old man. I was willing to hear ten times over what to say to someone sick, to the weak, to all those sitting *Shiva* – the seven days of mourning for the dead in Judaism.

If this teacher had continued to speak and tell us, I would know how to weep about my life, but the teacher spoke less about the dead and comforting and a great deal about Hebrew grammar, *go, went, stroll, was, were, will go, we'll go*, and I wanted to shout, we'll all go to hell long before we know how to say *Kaddish* – the Hebrew prayer for the dead.

He'd talk about God in Genesis, and I couldn't bear that God, was he at Auschwitz?

* * *

The evenings in the village broke my heart.

The sun would set and I'd feel full of sadness and sorrow. There were no youngsters my age in the village. There were only families with small children. There was no dining room like kibbutz where people could gather, meet someone. The families withdrew into their homes.

We were left alone.

Sometimes things were good. In the group we had a few regular clowns, mainly Shimon and Eliyahu who came with us on the ship. They made us laugh with their stories and vulgar jokes. They gestured with their hands, imitated members on the farm, like the first milking lesson in the cowsheds, without speaking, yes, or a visit to the doctor in order to get out of work. We rolled on the floor from their descriptions. But most evenings our clowns were silent and we followed suit. We were silent because of our dead, each one carrying his own burden: Longing for Grandmother who kept a burned sugar-coated apple in her apron pocket, and a handful of sweet almonds, *aah*. Longing for a cousin who loved to turn cartwheels and sing aloud, and for his beautiful sister who played the violin. *Aah*. Missing friends from football games in the street. Sweet Shloimeleh, the neighbor's son, he was just three years old, Shloimeleh, and wanted to hear a thousand times over the scary story about the lion who liked to gobble up children. He would burst out laughing, particularly when the lion roared, *raaaaar*, and gobbled up the child.

In the end, Hitler gobbled him up. *Aah*. The noise of firing would reach the village every evening, the smell of the dead, the shouts and hungry dogs, everyone, everyone would gather in my ears, ringing *trrrr. Trrrr. Trrrr.*

Even after we'd finished frying omelets on the stove in the

pen and sat down to eat, the dead were waiting for us with their final moments on the road, the path, on the floor of an open cattle car.

I was tired of this life and of the noise that came from the dead and I was tired of stealing and eating in the dark with SSmen who were suddenly standing there when I opened my mouth wide. I wanted to run away from myself, pretend I'd been born in Eretz-Israel near the Lake of Galilee or Safed. Be like those perfect young men we saw on the ship, at the camp in Atlit, the young men with their crests of hair and a *kaffiyeh* wound round their necks. I wanted to do things, like walk confidently into a place I didn't know. And if someone asked me a question, to answer quickly without looking at the floor. I wanted to be happy with all my heart. How I envied their free, open-mouthed laughter with their heads thrown back, slapping one another on the back and feeling as if they'd vanquished the Germans with their own hands.

And I wanted Betty.

I missed her flower-like perfume. I missed the kiss, tongue playing with tongue. Hear her whisper *mon amour* and feel a thousand bees in my ears. Just the thought of Betty made me want to suck something sweet. There wasn't anything sweet to steal in that village. Sometimes I'd pick at a scab on my hand or leg, let the blood run, for no reason, no reason. And we had couples in our group. They'd meet in the room, each one in turn, sometimes in the fields. Some of them had sex. We all knew the news. Yitzhak had a girlfriend. Don't remember her name. And there was Sonya with the lipstick. Sonya had three fingers missing from the camps. Sonya followed me everywhere. Walked behind me almost weightlessly. Sometimes with rollers in her hair. Sometimes with dark lipstick that smeared on her teeth.

Whenever she laughed I'd get a fright. It looked like blood on her teeth. I fled from Sonya. I had no interest in the girls of our group, not even the nice, pretty ones. I missed Betty *mon amour*. There was no money to go and visit Betty and no nearby train one could sneak into through the window and travel far away.

I wanted to run away before I died.

I said to myself, I have no hope in this village.

The girls left first and were immediately taken. There weren't many marriageable girls at the time. A girl who went to Tel Aviv to visit relatives, returned with a wedding date. On her next holiday she stood under the *chuppah* – Jewish wedding canopy. I remember at least three or four girls who got married in a month. The girls were in a hurry to marry so they wouldn't have to return to that village. In the village, people didn't understand these weddings. They suggested the girls wait a bit, get to know their grooms better. The girls didn't give in and said, if we have to wait, we'll wait in Tel Aviv. Sonya who pursued me also left. Sonya begged me to marry her. I didn't want to marry. I wanted to eat well without the noise of the dead in my ears. I wanted to eat a filling breakfast and a four-course lunch, and a full supper, and I wanted money in my pocket.

The boys left after the girls.

One by one they left. Stealthily, alone. Without a word, in the morning they simply saw someone was missing at work on the farm. They looked and looked, didn't find him in the room. Two days later another took off. Three days later, two more left. The village families couldn't understand why they left them. We couldn't explain it to them. It was as if our train had stopped at the small village by chance.

* * *

I arrived at the collective village in April, 1946. I was eighteen and a bit. I left the village on my own after less than a year. My brother Yitzhak remained and left after me. I moved to a small private *moshav* not far from the collective village, on a hill overlooking the Sea of Galilee.

It had as much food as I wanted and I had money in my pocket.

Chapter 47

Yitzhak: Dov, do you remember the crying of
the baby girl in the home where I ate?
Dov: No. I remember the crying of a girl
in the house near the hall.
Yitzhak: It was because of the crying baby
I liked going to the family.
Her crying reminded me that life exists.

Yitzhak

I decided to give life in a collective village a chance.

I went through a crisis when we stopped eating in the dining room and they divided us among the families. I didn't want to go to a family. Issasschar came to my room. He said, Yitzhak, they're waiting for you, everyone's gone to a family, come on, I'll go with you to the family. His pocket was full and I also wanted a pocket filled with a sandwich for later.

I said, I'm not going to a family.

He sat down on a chair, aren't you hungry?

I said, very hungry. Give me money and I'll buy myself food.

No, no, I have no money, and you need to be like everyone else.

I took a step in the direction of the door and grasped the handle. I said, don't want to be like everyone else, and leave me alone.

He left. I fell on my bed and covered my head with a pillow. I wanted my mother and father but saw that I couldn't remember what they looked like. It alarmed me. I stuck my fists into the pillow, and couldn't see a thing. I called, Papa? Papa? Mama? Nothing. The pillow grew wet. I grabbed the pillow, threw it at the wall and heard a knock at the door. I quickly wiped my face, stood up straight. A member from the farm stood in the doorway. I knew him, I worked with him. He wore dark work clothes and his laugh and yell were the loudest in the village. He had a plate in his hand that was covered with a towel. He said, we waited for you, Yitzhak, eat my friend, good appetite, and come tomorrow.

I didn't go.

Issasschar arrived with the Hebrew teacher. He talked and talked, it was no use. They left. And then a small woman arrived with a plate in her hand. She had green eyes and a round moon-shaped face. She gave me the plate and put a small hand on my shoulder. I felt a pleasant warmth and she said, come tomorrow, the children at home are asking about you, we all want to see you at home.

I went to them. There were three children, one was a baby. I liked hearing the baby cry, I liked seeing a living baby in a mother's arms, even when it made my belly turn. Maybe because I saw a mother, a father and beautiful children, sitting together at a table set for a first course, a second course, and a sweet dessert, and a father who kisses the mother and pinches her bottom, and she blushes and giggles and immediately begins to collect the dirty dishes and put them in the sink, and what sticks in my mind are those dirty Passover dishes. And I didn't know what would happen if Hungarian soldiers came into this collective village and said, one hour, and everyone outside. My heart began to race, and I whispered, *shhh. Shhh*. Calm down, in this village no one will chase Jewish families from their home, fact: There was a large rifle on the cupboard and lots of bullets.

I ate with the family and remained hungry. I was ashamed to take as much food as I really wanted. The head of the household took three slices of bread, would I, a guest, take six?

The families in the village tried to make us feel good and maybe they didn't try hard enough. Why else would we have felt so ashamed of what we'd been through. The families didn't understand what we lacked or why we were leaving. And maybe they refused to admit we brought too many problems with us. And maybe we were tired of hearing whispers about our problems and we also felt bad because we stole food from them, and couldn't stop stealing.

Dov was the first to leave. I decided to leave after he did. I didn't tell anyone. One day I took a bag and went to Nachlat Yitzhak, even though I had a girlfriend, Bracha, who was two years older than me. When I left the village Bracha left too. She wanted to marry a millionaire so we parted.

Chapter 48

Dov

The words a-Jew-who-works-the-land made my heart feel good.

The words a-Jew-with-a-tractor-and-a-plow gave me hope that maybe we'd be a nation in our country, maybe a small and complicated nation with problems of the dead in our ears, but nonetheless a nation.

I had a lot of respect for people who had a connection to the land. They reminded me of the goys in our village in Hungary, and I loved the life of a farmer. When they served me eggs from the farm and home-made cheese and bread with wheat they'd harvested from the fields, I got the shivers. I wanted to hold the bread up high in my hands and say aloud, this is bread made by Jews alone. Jews plowed the field, Jews sowed and harvested with a combine, Jews filled sacks of wheat and barley and stood stacks of hay like a tower in the barn.

I decided to be a tractor driver.

On the small *moshav* I fled to from the collective village there were seven families and one tractor, a tractor that crawled on chains. The farmers took me on as a tractor driver for everyone. I had a regular work schedule. I plowed, sowed, harvested in

order. I earned ten sterling a month and was a millionaire. I had
as much food as I wanted, a room of my own, and I was happy.
At the *moshav* they gave me a special certificate, that of a tractor
driver and a soldier. During the day I drove a tractor, at night
I guarded. I had a rifle and I was responsible for a guard post
and other Jews. I remember that my beard grew faster at the
time and I even grew five centimeters taller.

I ate lunch with the families on a rotation basis. They gave
me four helpings of food at every meal. I waited patiently for
each helping and always had eye contact with each one. If they
gave me three helpings, or even two, I paid no attention. Why?
Waiting in my room for me was food I bought myself: Canned
food, sausage, biscuits, wafer cookies, fruit, vegetables, candies,
I had at least five loaves of bread even before sunrise. I bought
quantities of everything and I bought a motorbike. I rode along
the narrow roads and I was happy.

I found new friends on the little *moshav*.

They were all young, my age, and born in the country. In the
evenings we'd sit on a eucalyptus log and they'd tell stories. I
liked hearing their stories, we laughed a lot. I didn't tell stories
and they didn't ask anything.

I remember envying those born in the country. They had a
large watch on the wrist with a broad strap and a brown leather
lid that closed on top. They'd make a *tick* with the strap, check
the time, and *tack*, to close, I liked hearing that *tick-tack*, it was
the *tick-tack* of brave men. I envied their courage to do things.

One day I went with one of them to Tiberias on the tractor,
his name was Shalom and he wore a red *kaffiyeh* wound round
his neck, and a thick belt with a design on the buckle. I stood
behind Shalom who drove the tractor. Green grass and red
anemones grew like a carpet at the roadside. The Sea of Galilee

was a bit smooth, a bit rough, with small foaming waves. In the middle of the descent into Tiberias stood a command car. Shalom slowed down. We saw that the command car was British and empty. Shalom said, the command car looks as if it's broken down, we got down to take a look. He opened the bonnet and began to fiddle with the wires.

Let's steal the command car. Huh?

I swallowed and held my hands behind my back. Said, are you sure?

He laughed and said, lucky we got here first, in a minute we'll travel in style, d'you want to?

I didn't know what to say.

He sat on the seat in the command car, connected some wires under the steering wheel and managed to start the engine. Wow. I sat next to him and we turned off the road into the fields. Shalom accelerated, didn't take his foot off the accelerator, the command car bounced and bounced over the holes in the track. I held onto my seat, and began to sweat. I didn't have the energy to be sick. I looked back. Saw a command car with two British soldiers chasing us. I shouted stop, stop, they're chasing us. Shalom stepped on the brakes, we almost flew out of our seats. We jumped out of the command car and began to run through the field. The British soldiers also stopped, got down from the command car and began to chase us. I remember running through the field as I ran from the twenty prisoners with a loaf of bread in my hands. I knew the British soldiers would never catch me. The space between me and Shalom grew. Shalom cut to the right and ran off in another direction. The soldiers stopped. I saw them returning to the command car, each of them getting into a different command car. We circled the field and returned to the tractor.

Shalom said, Dov, you know how to run, where did you learn to run so fast? I was silent. But my heart swelled and swelled.

Three months passed and I had an accident.

The British Mandate came to an end, without my feeling the pain of a stick. The British hurried away from the country. They left their horses at the police station in Tiberias. The young people from the *moshav* immediately traveled to Tiberias to take the horses. They invited me to join them and having a country of my own gave me a pleasant rush in my body.

We arrived at the police station, we didn't see any people, just horses. The horses, noble and beautiful, stood in a long line as if waiting for us to take them home. I almost had diarrhea from the pressure of the currents reaching my belly. I chose a white, particularly beautiful horse. He had a long tail and smooth skin. I jumped onto him and galloped bareback to the *moshav*. I wanted to sing aloud, shout, look, I have a horse, I have a horse. I was embarrassed in front of the young men riding beside me so I sat straight and arrived at the *moshav* tall and manly.

Near one of the cowsheds I stopped to give the horse a drink, I also brought him hay. I stroked him gently, whispering, we'll be friends, my horse, and I remembered the horses the goys brought to the races in my village in Hungary. I said enthusiastically, ah, life is finally beginning to bless me, and I love Israel. In the meantime, a water cut was announced because of a fight. I was dirty, sweaty. I decided to gallop on the horse to the collective village to wash in the building where I lived. I wanted to show off my white horse to my friends in the village, mainly to Yitzhak. I jumped on the horse, made a *click-click* sound in my throat, hugged his neck and we set out at a gallop to the road. At the entrance to the village is a water tower. There are two roads around the tower. A road on the right and one on the left.

The horse galloped to the tower. The horse saw two roads. He didn't know which road to take. Maybe he was waiting for a sign from me. In my excitement, I forgot to give him a sign. And then, when he was almost at the tower, he swerved right and I flew off, landing on my head.

The end of British rule and I got a head injury.

I lost consciousness exactly as I did at the end of the Nazi regime. Members from the village carried me on their backs to the infirmary. They lay me on a stretcher and called the doctor. I lay unconscious for three or four hours. When I came round, I couldn't remember anything. It took me a whole day to remember the horse. I wanted to get out of bed to go and look for my horse. The doctor refused to let me get up because I had concussion.

I said to the doctor, but I have a white horse, where is my horse?

The doctor said, you must rest.

And then a friend from my group said, your brother Yitzhak asked me to tell you that shots were fired from the direction of the Arab village of M'rar. Your horse got a fright and ran away into the fields.

I sat up at once. I felt as if my brain was floating in a barrel of water. I shouted, and you didn't go after him?

The friend was sorry. We didn't have time, Dov, Yitzhak said they saw the horse galloping towards M'rar.

I lay in bed for three days because of the concussion. My heart ached at losing the white horse. I didn't understand that I could have been killed.

Chapter 49

Yitzhak

I looked for work in Nachlat Yitzhak.

I remember a winter's day that came in the fall. It stepped on yellow leaves that lay dead on the ground looking like dirt in the camp because of the mud. I wore a light battledress and trembled in front of a store window. I wanted to tidy my face and messy hair. In the window were flannel shirts, trousers with turn-ups, and three sweaters. On the wall at the side hung a brown coat with a wool lining, a coat in my size. I went into the store and put out a hand to the coat. My hand remained suspended mid-air because of the shout in my mind, idiot, you have no money, and you don't need a lined brown coat to live.

A man with a paunch approached me. I said, excuse me, sir, do you know of any cowsheds in the area? He went to the door, pointed at a tall cypress and said, next to that cypress, you'll find a cowshed.

I straightened up and went into the cowshed. Another man with a paunch and small forehead fixed his eyes on me. He asked, what are you looking for, young man? He had the accent of a German Jew.

I saw that his cowshed was clean and orderly and regretted not wearing a good coat. I said, I'm looking for work with cows.

He asked, do you know how to milk?

I said in German, I know how to milk very well, I milked in my father's cowshed in Hungary and I've milked here too. I like milking, and I'll have a large dairy farm someday.

He smiled at me. A good sign. He rubbed one boot against the other, removed some mud and said, do you want to start tomorrow?

I said, today, I've nowhere to sleep.

I milked cows, cleaned up garbage and took full milk containers by horse and cart to the Tara Dairy in Tel Aviv. I slept in a small room next to the house of the orderly farmer, Joseph Stein, and I loved my work at Nachlat Yitzhak. It was a great relief not to have to worry about food and a bed. I had as much food as I wanted. But in the evening, when the sun set and I went into my clean room, the smell of Auschwitz came to visit my nose and sometimes my throat. I was already used to this hour when the scorched, sweet smell didn't leave without a bottle of wine or vodka that I bought from the store and poured into my heart, which trembled every time Auschwitz entered my mind.

Mina, farmer Joseph's wife, invited me to eat lunch with them. A small woman, she was almost hairless and had a thumb with a wart and no nail. She always had a slice of bread in her pocket. Sometimes she said a few words, but most of the time she was silent. She'd put a spoon of mashed potato with a chicken leg on my plate and keep her eye on me until I finished wiping my plate with bread. I always left her with something in my pocket, nuts, an orange, or cookies made by pressing a glass into dough. There were times she said, there's only bread left, take some for later and she'd give me a slice. I didn't want to take it because

I was earning money. I could easily sit in a chair after a day's work, take off my shoes, undo my belt and drink a glass or two, and be calm. If I wanted a good coat, I had a good coat. If I wanted to crack seeds, I did. If I wanted to eat a cream cake with sugar sprinkled on top, I did. If I wanted a girl, I had one. I felt good at Nachlat Yitzhak, but I wasn't at peace. The smell of Auschwitz didn't leave my tongue or my nose and I sometimes heard evil voices in my ears.

One day two young men from *Hahagana* – a Jewish paramilitary organization in the British Mandate of Palestine – arrived in a truck.

It was raining, I had just finished milking. They were tall young men, one had a deep voice and one had a narrow beard around his jaw. They said to me, Yitzhak, we need you for the *Hagana*, and I wanted to cry. These tall young men had made the journey to Nachlat Yitzhak on a rainy day especially for me, *aah*.

I was moved and said, give me a few minutes to get ready, as if I was used to young men from the *Hagana* coming to look for me.

I collected my clothes from the room, parted from the farmer and his wife and went with them. In my pocket were three sandwiches wrapped in a napkin. One with sausage, one with jam, one with margarine and salt, and another three slices of bread without anything.

I sat in the cabin of the truck between two young men and their strong muscles pressed against my shoulders. We turned onto the road and the windscreen wipers of the truck weren't adequate for the rain. The driver with the deep voice said, oy, I can't see a thing, I need to turn left, and he pulled a small handle. I saw he was checking to see if the little arrow-shaped blinker had jumped out to indicate a turn.

We approached a windowless building on the right. The head of the young man with the beard fell back and rolled onto my shoulder. The head dragged the knee, I was hemmed in on all sides and the building on the right set my nerves on edge. I thought, maybe it's a small crematorium. And these two, whom I don't know, are taking me to the Gestapo. I at once hit myself on the forehead, there's no chimney, no smoke, stop being such an idiot, and *mmm, mmm*, came out of my mouth.

The young man behind the steering wheel said, are you all right?

I said, everything's all right and in my mind I wrote a Hebrew sentence, without mistakes, Israel is a wonderful country, with many strong Jews but what came out was *mmm, mmm*. In the meantime, we reached the cinema in Ramat Gan and the rain stopped.

A truck covered with a tarpaulin stood to one side. Standing on the pavement were fifteen, maybe eighteen young men. Most looked over twenty. Some were strong, some thin, like me. They held a backpack or a bag, I saw no bundles wrapped in a sheet and no grandmothers in scarves or small children.

The young man with the deep voice said, Chaim, get up, let him out. I got down. Both shook my hand, said good luck, young man, and went off. I approached the group near the truck. Asked, anyone know where they're taking us in the truck? A strong man with red eyelashes said, to Shavei-Tzion, a small place near Nahariya.

I was last to climb into the truck, on purpose. If I had to jump off it was important to get on last in order to jump in time.

We sat on the floor and set off. I didn't lose sight of the road, fixed my eyes on the asphalt. Some of the young men spoke among themselves, others arranged their backpack under their heads and fell asleep. We traveled about an hour, maybe longer, and then I saw a eucalyptus wood on the left. I don't know why but the woods next to Crematorium IV at Auschwitz-Birkenau jumped into my mind and stabbed everywhere. The woods of disaster. Mothers and children sat in those woods as if they were at a picnic and waited their turn for the crematorium because of the overload at the doors, and the lines of people weren't getting shorter.

Again I became nervous, and fell upon the sausage sandwich.

We arrived in Haifa and the first thing I saw was a chimney with smoke climbing upward. I looked at the people in the truck. They looked untroubled, as if a smoking chimney was normal in human beings' lives. Only one young man with glasses and a runny nose opened a large eye. His glance was fixed on the chimney and he chewed his fingers. I tried to catch his eye, thought, three eyes are safer. I leaned forward and backwards with the turns of the truck on the road, failed to catch his eye. He was like a paralytic with a cold. And then the evil smells came into my mind and everywhere else and I fell upon the jam sandwich and margarine and salt sandwich, and also on the three slices of bread without anything. It was only when we approached the port that I calmed down and breathed normally.

At Shvei-Tzion they trained us to shoot: Hold the rifle straight, put it on your shoulder, yes, don't move, look through the sight, don't close your eye, right, both eyes open, put your finger carefully on the trigger, slowly, hold your breath, don't breathe, don't breathe, fire! I became a military convoy guard. Yes, yes. I was at Auschwitz, I was at Buchenwald, I was at Zeiss, two years later, and I'm invited to be an armed soldier in the State of Israel, to accompany convoys from Nahariya to Haifa and Akko and guard Metzuba.

I walked hungry for kilometers to die on the roads of Germany, and two years later I'm asked to bring food in a backpack to heroic friends on Kibbutz Yechiam. *Aah*. I'd only hold my rifle for three minutes and my eyes would begin to moisten. I'd hug my rifle hard, hard, and say, oy, oy, oy, Mamaleh, and then my hands would start to tremble and in my heart was something like the IDF band on the parade ground that I like to watch on television, *pom-pom, pom-pom, prooompompomppom*. A trumpet band, and drums, and meter-sized cymbals, and flutes with a button. The band that welcomed us at Haifa Port was meager in comparison with my band. Because I am Yitzhak, son of Leah and Israel, known as Strul, I never dreamed I'd hold a rifle in my hands. The Hungarians had rifles, the Germans had rifles, and what did I have? What? And now, three years later, I have a state. *Aah*. By the number of trains, and by the number of dead on the roads of Germany, I was sure that my people were finished, best case scenario they'd learn about us out of books. No, no, they burned the books as well. Maybe they'd learn about us in cemeteries, no! They broke headstones to pave roads. Yes.

The hardest punishment was not being allowed to participate in some operation. I knew, if I didn't protect myself, who would protect me? And I knew I could be killed. I didn't care about being killed, I was willing to die for my country, it was a great honor.

In Eretz-Israel I was the complete opposite of a humiliated Jew. I was a proud Jew, a free Jew. The fact that I, Yitzhak, load a gun, receive an order, and *hop*, shoot my rifle, *aha*, if anyone in Germany had said to me, take a gun, shoot, I would have shot all the Nazis who took my people to the crematorium. But

I had no gun or water or bread. I was 55484 sewn on my pajamas, and it was only by chance that I didn't reach the Wisla as dust.

When I stood in front of the mirror with my rifle and saw protruding muscles and shoulders that filled any jacket I wore, the healthy color in my face, and heard the voice of a man, my eyes wept at this wonder, yes. And what hurt most of all was that my mother and father weren't beside me in front of the mirror. I so wanted them and Avrum, Grandfather and Grandmother, all my uncles, aunts, and cousins to stand in front of the mirror, all of us together, looking at this wonder, I, Yitzhak, son of Israel and Leah, a soldier growing stronger in Eretz-Israel.

Chapter 50

Dov

When you're young it is easy to move from one place to another.

I spent about a year in the collective village and every morning I got up and saw I was alive. I'd touch my body, my arm is in place, I have two whole legs, I have an eye. The scariest thing was not being able to open my eyes because of an infection or some other block. Finally, I'd get up. First of all I'd check my drawer. There's bread. I always kept a slice for the next day.

The transition to a private *moshav* was a great joy for me.

I'd go to bed at night and not be able to sleep for excitement. I couldn't believe I had money in my pocket. I'd put my hand in the pocket of my trousers, take a handful of coins and let them jingle, *gling, gling, gling*, until I'd fall asleep. Afterwards, I looked for pajamas with a pocket. Sometimes, in the evening after work, I'd make coin towers in the air and then, *phoophoophoo*, and listen to the sound of coins rolling on the table, onto the floor, *mmm*. A sound as tasty as ice cream. I had as many tins of food on the shelf as I wanted. I had my own motorcycle on the path outside my room. In the evening I'd sit with my *Sabra* – Israeli-born friends, each and every one of them great people. We laughed without a care.

One day I realized that two years had gone by, and I found myself moving for the third time. The War of Independence had come to an end and my brother, Yitzhak, established a *moshav* in the Western Galilee with a group of friends from the battalion. Yitzhak had a dream about a large dairy farm with a high barn in the yard, and I had a problem being far away from my brother. I could be a five-minute journey away, a ten-minute journey from him, no more. I had to know that if there was a sudden disaster, say, someone would decide to send us on foot along the roads, we could immediately meet and walk together. I decided to move to the *moshav* he established, and I wasn't happy.

In the beginning we lived in tents. There was an old concrete surface in the place. We put tents on it. After several months the concrete sank. We dug around the concrete and deep down we found boxes. Boxes of dead bodies. Don't know which period the bodies were from but it was clear to me that the dead always came out to meet me: Sometimes I have the dead at night, in the middle of the day, sometimes I have the dead in boxes underneath a tent. For two weeks I had a migraine from all these dead, even after we put up the tents in another place. Afterwards we moved into tin shacks and managed quite well. We had cows, horses, and a tractor from the Jewish Agency. I worked outside on the tractor. My brother, Yitzhak, worked on the farm and we lived together.

Every morning I'd get up before my brother, get into the bathroom first, stay in there for as long as I needed, then I'd make the bed, and hand wash a few of our shirts. We drank our first coffee in the communal dining room, the young women on the *moshav* prepared it. And then I'd make fat sandwiches for me and my brother, a large pile of fat sandwiches, and wrap each one in paper and write in pencil on the paper what was in the sandwiches, cheese, or sausage, or jam. We worked hard on my brother's *moshav*, but we weren't hungry.

In the evening I'd shower first, but before that we'd kill bugs. We had a lot of bugs in the tin shack. We'd collect them on the floor, pour paraffin over them and burn them.

And then I had an accident, I broke my arm. The car of a *moshav* member stalled in the middle of the road. He asked me to turn the crank while he pressed on the clutch. I held the crank in both hands and hit it hard. The bone broke in two places. They took me to hospital and I felt as if my brain had turned to liquid, what the hell is this with me and hospitals, and why are the bones in my poor body like matchsticks, *chic*. Broken, *chic-chic*. You need a cast, said someone in a white coat, and I felt like slapping his face, breaking down a wall, and running like a rocket to find a forest to stay in forever.

I left the tractor and guarded with a cast on my arm, barely able to hold a rifle.

Afterwards we got separate houses and land. My home was near Yitzhak's. We worked from morning till night and didn't make a living. We barely had anything to eat, and then a lot of members left the *moshav*. My brother Yitzhak managed well. Maybe because he was good at reading numbers and he knew where luck lay. He was five steps ahead of everyone, already knowing where the luck would fall.

My brother also married quickly. Hannah, his wife, came to visit a relative on our *moshav*. Yitzhak met her on the Friday.

The next day, on the Sabbath, he said to me, I'm going to marry Hannah. It took him a night and half a day to decide that he and Hannah were suited. I said, all right.

One day, three thug-like officials came to my house. They wore good jackets and shoes. I saw them approaching the yard and my heart sank. I put a slab of chocolate in my mouth, and went out towards them as if I was used to meeting Jewish thugs in my yard. They were looking for something in the yard, said something, and finally gave me a notice. I understood they wanted to throw me off the *moshav* because I owed money to the Jewish Agency. I had no money to pay the Agency and decided to leave the *moshav*.

My brother Yitzhak remained. Yitzhak had Hannah. She washed shirts and cooked food and she made sandwiches. I could leave without worrying.

I rented a room in Nahariya, a five-minute journey from my brother's *moshav*.

I learned to operate an excavator and mainly dug water lines. Then I became a crane operator, which I enjoyed.

The moment I'd hear they were establishing a new town in Eretz-Israel, I'd be the first there. I felt at home in these places. I'd rent a room or live in a hotel near work and eat in restaurants. I made sure to eat four full courses every noon. Something light for the first course, a pie, or a piece of fish, or a plate of salads. Second course, soup. Main dish, meat, a thick steak, or half a chicken and mashed potatoes, or rice or noodles. For fourth course, something sweet, stewed fruit or ice cream, or strudel with nuts and coffee. When I finished the work in the new town I'd go back to Nahariya.

* * *

When I was a crane operator, I volunteered to work in dangerous places, like the northern or southern borders. I'd sit on the digger, my head visible, knowing the Syrians or the Egyptians could shoot me. The rifles of the Syrians and the Egyptians didn't bother me. I was willing to give up the restaurant with four courses and a good pie with rice, I ate enough. I knew that if I didn't dig fortifications on the border there'd be an Auschwitz here.

My brother Yitzhak told me I should marry.

He looked very hard at me and saw that crumbs were beginning to fall on my shirt, that I went out in the evening with an unironed collar and stains that didn't come out in the laundry I did alone. I wanted to marry Betty whom I'd met on the ship. In the meantime, I sat in the Penguin Café in Nahariya and the years went by. Betty didn't stay in my heart and there was no one else. One year then another, and for many years I'd sit in the Penguin Café with friends every evening, listening to laughter, jokes and stories, drinking cold beers, or vodka, according to mood or the women at the table. My brother Yitzhak persisted. He'd say, listen to me, after a certain age you don't marry, you get used to living alone and that's a bad habit. You have to marry, this is what he said, and in the meantime another ten years went by.

My brother Yitzhak might not have understood that thoughts about family gave me sleepless nights, that I'd wake up one morning and there'd be no one beside me, because maybe they'd take everyone to some forest, or that my child would get pneumonia and die and it would make his mother sick and she'd also die, and another brother would die, and one Sunday morning I could find myself without anything.

Twenty years went by before I agreed to marry.

When I met Shosh I had no intention of getting married. Shosh persuaded me, and I had Yitzhak on the other side. Finally, I married at the age of forty, and at sixty, when I wanted a rest from this life, I had daughters the age of the Twist, rock 'n' roll, and the noise coming out of the loudspeakers.

I married Shosh because she had laughing eyes. Because she had a joy about her. But also because she took charge of papers, identity cards, arranged things at the Office of the Interior, the rabbinate, a wedding hall, flower store, an invitation store, a photography store and a clothing store – she arranged everything, and without this I wouldn't have married. My wife Shosh was born in 1945 – just as I came out of hell, she was born. I left for a new life and so did she. I met her through her friend, a waitress at the Penguin Café. I didn't believe I'd take an Iraqi woman to be my wife. You have to get used to Iraqis. They'd invite me to lunch. I'd arrive at noon, they'd serve food at five. I'd be dying of hunger by five.

It's good that I married. Good that I have a family. Don't know what I'd have done with this life on my own.

Chapter 51

Yitzhak

My dream of establishing a dairy farm almost shattered during the War of Independence.

By chance I was saved from almost certain death.

It was spring. I was on a Sabbath leave from the battalion. I went to my adoptive family in the collective village. I kept in touch with them. On the Sunday I was supposed to return to the battalion. I couldn't return. There was a war. The roads were blocked and I had a fever. But, nonetheless, I intended to return. I packed my backpack but my adoptive mother refused to allow me to leave. I said, I have to, they're waiting for me. She wiped her wet hands on her apron and said slowly, you are not going, Yitzhak, I've had a bad feeling all morning, and you're staying here. Her face was red and she had a handkerchief in her sleeve. I went on packing. She stood at the door and said, wait here, don't move, and she ran to the village doctor.

Ultimately, I obeyed her. The convoy to the besieged Kibbutz Yechiam was blocked. We had forty-seven dead. I should have lain dead among them. I'd remained in the village and wasn't in the convoy of the dead. I began accompanying the village supply-truck driver with my rifle. Later I became a combat soldier and fought in all the state wars. When I was young I was a machine gunner, a good one too, without dreams or nightmares. Screaming loudspeakers didn't frighten me. Then I was a driver, a hard-working one, as long as there wasn't a fire near me. I just had to smell smoke and my eyes smarted, or I'd get an ear infection. It was like that for years.

I knew that if I didn't marry after the War of Independence, I'd swell up with alcohol.

We lived a sloppy life on the *moshav*. There was no one to take care of us. I had no clean laundry. No organized food. I'd go to Nahariya to eat. I wasted the money I earned at the *moshav* on alcohol. I liked to drink cognac, vodka, and I'd get drunk and talk nonsense. Sometimes I'd throw glasses, lie on the floor and kick my legs, and scream and laugh like a madman.

Dov also drank. He liked whiskey, gin, Slivovitz. But Dov would drink and be silent. I made a lot of noise when I drank.

At the Penguin and the Ginati Café there was a band. I liked the band. I'd stick money on the musicians' foreheads so they wouldn't stop playing. I stuck a lot of money. I felt they had to keep playing, or the darkness and suffocating smell would come.

I knew, on my own, I'd be lost.

I was twenty-one and I wanted a family. The decision to marry was quick. The moment I saw Hannah I knew she'd be my wife. She was tiny, and lovely. Hannah knew what I'd been through without our talking about it. We'd look at each other and under-stand everything on our own. Hannah was born in Romania in 1932. When she was seven her family was sent to the Ukraine, to Ghetto Vinoj. Her mother and three siblings. Her father remained in the labor camp. She had a hard time in the Ukraine.

They'd leave the Ghetto to beg. For four years they looked for food in the streets and people would hit them. Afterwards the family returned to Rumania. They met her father. Five years after the war they emigrated to Israel.

The day after the wedding I left Hannah and disappeared for three days. Don't remember where I was. I think I went to look for something related to the dairy farm. I forgot to tell Hannah I had errands to take care of. I wasn't used to having a wife at home. Hannah went to our neighbor on the *moshav*. He harnessed his horse and cart and they set out to look for me.

It took me time to get used to being with a woman at home. It took me a very long time to get used to coming home late at night and finding a woman waiting for me, a tidy home and the smell of good food. It took me time to get used to waking up in the morning and finding another pillow and a woman beside me. I needed vodka and cognac to get used to seeing a clean towel, a woman's underwear and lipstick near the mirror in the bathroom.

After a hard day's work, mainly after a good commercial deal, I'd go to a restaurant with friends and raise a glass to life. What I enjoyed most was the owner of the restaurant saving us the internal parts of the cow. He'd fry the meat for us and we'd toss back tots of vodka, cognac and whiskey, *mmmm*. A pleasure. We spent a lot of time at Tuti Levy's café. In the end, I gave up drinking. I think because of age and responsibility. I had Hannah, there were children, we had a roof over our heads, I earned a living, it was wonderful. I didn't want my liver spoiled by cognac. We came from nothing, we wanted to make it and we succeeded. The most important thing was that I managed to raise a family.

Chapter 52

Dov

My sister Sarah came to Israel after the Declaration of the State.

She was twenty-four when she came to Israel. She came from Sweden after being in Bergen-Belsen. My brother was the first to hear about Sarah and we both wrote to her. We asked her to come to Israel. We didn't hear from Avrum, we didn't hear from our father, we didn't hear from our mother. Later we heard something of father. We heard that our father was released from a labor camp, don't remember the name, and he died because of food. Zalmanowitz told me. He said that several released prisoners slaughtered a sheep and ate too much meat. Father was one of them, can you believe it?

My brother Yitzhak and I missed Sarah. We'd drink coffee and say, Sarah. We'd sit in the room and say, Sarah. We remembered Sarah locking us in our room because she wanted peace and quiet in the house, so she could do her homework without our bothering her. Sarah was a good student. She studied at the Hebrew Gymnasium in Ungvár. She knew how to sit at her books and notebooks. We didn't. Sarah wanted to be a teacher or a head teacher of a school. Sarah studied at the Gymnasium for a short time and then they threw her out because of the laws against Jews. She stayed home and helped Mother wash and fix the clothes of Hungarian soldiers so there'd be food.

When we met Sarah at the Haifa Port we barely recognized her. She was smaller and thinner than we remembered. Her head came up to Yitzhak's and my shoulders. She had a long face the color of the wall and pale lipstick on her lips. Her hair was very short and a color we didn't recognize, black mixed with smoke. The expression in her eyes hadn't changed, she had a questioning, steadfast look.

Sarah looked at us and cried out, are you my little brothers? We cried a lot.

From the Port of Haifa I took Sarah to the little *moshav* where I was a tractor driver. She lived with me in my room. I didn't talk about my camps and she didn't talk about hers. I didn't talk about my daily routine and she didn't tell me what hers had been. I didn't tell her what I ate in the camps and she didn't tell me what she ate. I saw that Sarah turned her head away when I put a slice of bread in my pocket. I also turned my head away when Sarah hid bread under a towel in a drawer.

There were a lot of bachelors on the *moshav*. One of the young men really wanted Sarah. He spoke to me. Sarah refused and decided to move to Tel Aviv, where she met Mordecai who had emigrated to Israel on the ship *Altalena*. Sarah and Mordecai married and went to live in Be'er Sheva. It was hard for them to make a living in Be'er Sheva. Four years went by and they left for Canada and from there to the United States of America. We stayed in touch and speak on the telephone. My brother Yitzhak and I didn't travel to visit Sarah in America because we don't travel anywhere. We know that at the end of the day we have to go home, because one doesn't leave home. Not even to visit our sister Sarah. Not even to visit one of our children who lives far away. Sarah has visited Israel twice. I don't know what Sarah went through during the war and she doesn't know what we went through.

Chapter 53

Sarah

Queens, New York City

After the war, Yitzhak only returned to the village because of his cat. He looked for his large cat with its black and white fur. Yitzhak loved his cat very much, did he talk about it?

It was the first day of Passover, 1944, I was twenty. Father returned from the synagogue and said, we have to pack, they're sending the Jews away from the village.

Gendarmes took us from the house.

Until that morning, the gendarmes were like our friends because we brought them clean laundry that Mother and I washed and mended for them. Some of those gendarmes liked drinking coffee in Mother's kitchen and chatting to her in Hungarian. They also agreed to exchange clothing for food because Father wasn't working. The gendarmes turned their faces away on the path and I saw they were a danger to us. Nonetheless, when we came out, I whispered to one of them, the pocket I sewed up for you, is it all right? He turned his back and pointed his rifle in the direction of the synagogue, where they immediately took me behind a curtain and ordered me to strip. They searched me for jewelry. I was twenty and had to stand naked in front of soldiers. Afterwards it was dark outside, barking dogs, and the lowing of suffering cows in the cowshed, my brothers said to the gendarmes, we have to milk the cows, let us go, we'll come back. The nearest gendarme raised his rifle and played with the bolt.

We got ready to sleep.

We divided the synagogue benches among the families and arranged blankets on them. The gendarmes told us to tell jokes all night, they wanted us to keep them amused so they'd stay awake. We took turns to make up jokes. If a Jew choked in the middle of a joke, there was already someone there to tell another joke.

After two days in the synagogue they took us in trucks to Perechyn, a town near our village.

The villagers accompanied us until we got on the trucks and I felt my heart break. I was born in that village, all my brothers were born there. Father and Mother came to Tur'i Remety after their wedding. We had school-friends in that village, Father had connections with the goys, none of the villagers moved, not one of them spoke up. Some waved goodbye, I didn't respond. I wanted to shout, a good play this, huh? You've got a Jewish play as well as gifts to take home, I didn't know then that they'd take homes and cowsheds.

I looked at the sky and vowed, I, Sarah, will never ever return to this village.

In Perechyn they put us on a train to Ungvár. They took us to a brick factory belonging to someone called Moskowitz. It was a huge quarry, like a pit dug in the ground. Trains came, trains went, bringing more and more Jews. There were thousands of Jews there, men and women, children, grandmothers and grandfathers, all with yellow patches on their coats and bundles on their backs. We crowded together in the quarry because of the rain. We had no roof to hide under. We walked in mud, sat in mud, slept on boards and blankets in the mud. It was cold and stinking of peoples' excrement. They gave us one meal a day and this is how they began to close our minds. We received only potato soup cooked by Jewish women volunteers. I also volunteered to cook. People stood for hours in line for food, and there was shouting and pushing, a lot of nerves, in the end everyone was left hungry.

One morning I went to peel potatoes. I saw a grandfather with a white beard fill a plate with mud and eat it with a teaspoon. The woman standing next to him shouted, Grandfather, Grandfather, spit out the mud, spit it out. He laughed and the mud dribbled out of the sides of his mouth and reached his beard. He wiped his mouth with his hand and wiped it on his coat. The woman began to weep. Two men caught the grandfather by the arms. They lay him down on a board and covered him with a blanket. It was no use, he stuck a thin hand out of the blanket, took a handful of mud and put it in his mouth. In the morning they took him, wrapped in a blanket, to the truck.

The Hungarian gendarmes looked for money and jewelry.

They'd drag Jews to one of the corners of the quarry, mainly those they knew were rich. There, in the corner, they'd beat them with a stick, shouting, where is the gold, where is the money. Sometimes they'd stand an entire family in a row, and give just the father a beating with electric shocks, the screams of the children made us all jump. Afterwards we got used to it. The women were in another corner, near a blanket they stretched on a rope. The gendarmes or goy women would search the vagina of Jewish women for gold and jewelry, one woman didn't stop bleeding after they stuck their hands into her body. I saw them putting a large bowl between her legs, it took her three hours to die.

We were left without Father.

The gendarmes took the men right at the beginning. They loaded them onto train cars that stood permanently on tracks at the edge of the quarry. They said the men were communists and a danger to the government. I stole from the soup I cooked at lunch and brought it at night to Father's car.

One day I got a high fever and a cough. I was shivering and couldn't get warm in the wet blankets. I heard a bearded religious man near me say: If on one day we have a wedding in the quarry, a funeral and a circumcision, the Hungarians will release the Jews. Two days after I heard him, it happened. A rabbi married a young couple in the quarry. The same rabbi performed a circumcision on a baby eight days old and there was also a funeral, like every day, but we weren't released.

Just before we left Ungvár, my fever dropped and Father returned. They told us we'd be taken to labor camps in the east. We were glad to leave the stinking mud. One man, with a large body and long arms, didn't stop calling aloud, what are you so happy about, Jews, weep, weep, the soldiers are sending you to die like fleas, weep, weep, your turn has come and time has run out. People began to shout at him, shut up, idiot, you're frightening the children. The man shouted louder, children, weep, Mother, weep, you too Father, Grandmother, why are you silent, nu, start weeping. A Hungarian soldier dragged the man behind the train. There was a shot and the children calmed down.

In the car it was dark and crowded. Any child that wasn't picked up and held, stopped breathing. Children screamed, babies cried, people called out to God and I stuck fast to a crack I found in the door and peeped through it. A passenger train went by on a nearby track. The passengers were sitting in chairs. The passengers looked at us, I saw them cross themselves.

We didn't know where we were going. We didn't know if it would take hours, or days. We had a little bread we'd hidden in bundles before the journey. We'd got the bread from peddlers, we gave them utensils from home. In the car were two buckets, one was full of water, the other was empty, to relieve ourselves. The water in the bucket was gone within less than an hour. It was suffocating. People were begging for water. Small children wept and died. One woman thrust her finger into the mouth of a child who didn't stop crying. The child sucked and wept. Sucked harder, finally fell asleep. A drop of blood created a thin red thread on his chin.

We had to relieve ourselves in the small bucket in front of everyone. I held it in until I could no longer. I pulled down my underwear, opened my legs, stood over the bucket and held my dress away from my body. The bucket was almost full. I tried hard not to dirty myself with other people's excrement. I felt as if my stomach was rising, I wanted to vomit. I tore off a piece of my dress to clean myself. Women who were menstruating ripped strips off sheets and put them in their underwear. After a few hours the stinking bucket began to overflow. The stink was appalling. A tall man with a mustache volunteered to pour out the bucket through a tall, narrow opening near the roof. There was barbed wire over the opening. He stood on a suitcase and tried to pour out the bucket without touching the barbed wire. The wind outside flung the dirt back in his face. Small, black mud-like pieces stuck to his mustache. He didn't let go of the bucket until he'd managed to empty it completely. Afterwards he took out a handkerchief and cleaned his face. I pressed hard on my mouth, breathed deeply, and asked God to help me hold it in.

Two days in the car and a young man of twenty from my village died beside me. He died quietly. He was ill in Ungvár. His mother insisted on taking him on the journey. We rolled him into a corner and covered him with a blanket. His mother sat beside him, took off her kerchief and tore out her hair.

We reached Auschwitz at night.

The door opened with a blow, soldiers yelled, everyone out, quickly, everyone out. I could barely get down. Everything hurt: My back, legs, neck.

A projector-like light hurt my eyes. After the line of light came darkness, as if the entire world ended at Auschwitz. I heard instructions over the loudspeaker. I saw black uniforms and green uniforms, and boots, and a belt with a revolver, and many hard hats. Some had rifles on their shoulders. Almost all of them held a stick in their hands, like the stick used by old people. Beside the soldiers stood large dogs. On the side stood people in pajamas and striped hats. In the air was the sweet smell of burned meat. Like a barbecue feast for a hundred thousand people.

The soldiers waved their sticks, shouting quickly, quickly. Leave your possessions on the train. People in the car were blinded and tried to advance, but their legs had forgotten how to walk. They fell and got up and held onto one another's coats and pushed forward, like a confused river current. My heart was pounding, pounding, the woman pressing against my shoulder shouted, I'm losing my little girl, Tibor, the girl, where is the girl. She was a tall young woman, maybe twenty-three, with a white, pretty face, and long hair black as coal. Her hair fell on her shoulders like heavy ropes wet with perspiration. She wore a coat down to the floor that clung to her waist. The man beside her tried to catch hold of the little girl, and was pushed back. The woman threw herself forward and managed to catch the hand of the little one, maybe three years old. With her other hand she pressed a bundle with a baby to her breast. And then I saw a stream of people push the mother back and the little one disappearing. The woman called, Mariska, Mariska, where are you, God, they'll trample her underfoot. The woman got a blow from a rifle butt on her back but didn't notice. She stretched her neck high, her eyes almost bursting from their cavities, screaming, Mariskaaaa, Mariska disappeared.

I saw the Germans were separating men and women. I heard the Germans shouting to young mothers to give their babies to grandmothers and old people. But the old people couldn't take anything. Exhausted, they sat down on the platform. Some of them tied a towel round their chins because their beards had been cut off and they were ashamed.

A soldier with a rifle stood near Mariska's mother. The baby in the mother's arms was whimpering. Its voice was like a chick about to die. I saw the soldier wanted something. He was the mother's height. They looked the same age. The soldier said loudly, give your baby to an old woman. The woman didn't move. The soldier yelled, give your baby to an old woman fast and go with the young women. The woman held the baby more tightly to her chest, judging by the movement of her head she was refusing. Her face was full of sorrow. The soldier approached the mother, almost touching her and, then, holding the rifle butt between his legs, he held out his arms for the mother's baby. He screamed, give it to me, stupid Jewess, give it to me. Their heads were almost touching. The loudspeaker called, men apart, women apart, quickly, quickly. The mother looked straight at him, whispered, no, no. She had a strong chin. The soldier dropped his arms, took half a step back, opened his mouth, closed it, made a small gesture with his head, as if to say, as you wish, and walked off. Mother and baby were pushed in the direction of the old people.

Two other little girls, one seven, the other maybe five, were holding hands, without a mother. They wore white fur hats over their ears like Purim costumes. The older one had a bag on her shoulder and an embroidered coat, the little one had an embroidered coat without a bag. Three other boys were pushed toward the old people. One wore a woolen hat and coat with a cup tied to a coat button. Two others wore coats with shiny buttons as if they were before Bar Mitzvah. Everyone wore a yellow patch on their coats. Mother and I stood next to each other.

And then the Germans separated me and Mama. I know they took my mother straight to the crematorium. They thought she was a grandmother. My mother was young, forty-two. She had black hair. A smooth face, my mother was a strong woman. She was used to hard work. Nonetheless, they took her from me as if she was a grandmother who had to die at once. I saw her walking away with the grandmothers in the direction of the crematorium, maybe a five-minute walk from the ramp, in a place where there stood a Red Cross ambulance. Her back was straight, her head to the front. Her arms swung at her sides. She walked as if the end of that world was waiting for her there.

The Germans were looking for professionals.

I said I was a seamstress. I knew how to use a sewing machine, I helped Mama mend clothes. They took me in a line with other young women. Some wore scarves, some a hat gathered or knotted in the middle on top, or two protrusions on the sides.

Some of the women wore dotted or checked dresses and a coat with a fur or woolen collar, some wore a jacket and a coat. Some held bundles, or a cup, or a bottle or a bag, some wore shoes and rolled up stockings, some with socks to their knees. Some women wore lipstick, most didn't, and all had serious faces.

In the meantime, morning came. I saw a tall chimney, even two, and brown-colored barracks. Rows and rows of barracks with narrow windows at the top, and then I heard cheerful music and I saw a photographer. The photographer, a uniformed soldier with a hat, photographed us from the front, from the side, from the top, even from the roof of a train car. The women beside me looked gravely at him. One woman with a pretty face arranged her hair, bringing a cute curl to her forehead, straightened her dress and stood ready for a photograph. I realized that death at Auschwitz was like a wedding. There's an orchestra, a photographer, people, but at Auschwitz there was no food.

We were taken into a large hall and I no longer saw my family. There were rows and rows of long benches. There were women in striped dresses and black aprons. They wore polished boots. Their hair was short and tidy, and their bellies were swollen. I heard a language something like German-Slovak. There were several soldiers there. They looked drunk and happy. We were ordered to strip, quickly. We didn't move. The soldiers attacked us, we were slapped, cursed, cow, fool, filthy Jewess, strip, quickly. We stripped. We arranged our clothing in a pile on a bench. I made a sign on the wall, and hid my body with my arms. One of them didn't want to remove her panties and bra. A soldier with a scratch on his cheek approached and grabbed her breast. He had a pen knife in his pocket. He stuck it under her bra and ripped it. The woman fell to the floor and began to shriek. The soldier screamed, strip. Some of the women nearby began to cry, Tzili, Tzili, Tzili, one of them bent down and pulled down her panties. They were bloody.

In the meantime, they shouted at us, run, quickly, quickly. We got to the barbers. They shaved our heads with razors, they cut long hair first with huge scissors, like the ones used for sheep. The barbers didn't stop their work for an instant, they were perspiring, their hands hurried. Some girls left the barbers with cuts on their heads. Then they disinfected us. Soldiers held large cans of spray and sprayed us with a burning disinfectant. On our shaved heads they smeared a stinging substance. I felt as if my head was on fire. From there they hurried us to the shower. A flow of boiling water blistered our skin. And then they gave us a short-sleeved gray garment of rough material, a pointed collar, three buttons and a rope belt, and I felt naked. They returned the shoes we'd brought from home, they smelled of chlorine, and then they took us to the barracks. The orchestra switched to cheerful songs. The photographer, without a rifle, photographed as usual, the loudspeaker shouted something, the sweet smell grew stronger. I asked one of the women in the apron and boots, what about our clothes. She wrinkled her nose, laughed aloud and said, what do you need clothes for, fool, soon you'll get to the chimney, and she pointed with her stick in the direction of the smoke. There was cruelty in her teeth. I felt faint.

I whispered Mamaleh, and fell over the legs of the woman in front of me. My garment pulled up. The woman behind me stepped on my belly and jumped aside. I shouted with pain, pulling the dress down. A large woman grabbed my arms and stood me on my feet. She didn't let go of my hand, afterwards we went hand in hand like two sisters. We were taken to Bloc A, Barracks 20, Camp Birkenau.

We entered the barracks. It was dark brown and built with rough logs. There were no windows like the ones at home. There were just narrow openings near the ceiling. On the wall of the barracks were steel rings.

A senior prisoner with breasts to her waist and thin legs said, the steel rings are for tying horses, it's a horse stable, I asked, how many horses, she said, fifty-two German horses, five hundred, six hundred, seven hundred Jewish women can get in here, depending on the season. I felt alone at the long stove in the middle of the bloc. I asked, do they heat in winter? The prisoner said, of course not, do you see any horses here? Along the walls were wooden bunks, three stories, without mattresses. On each bunk was a thin blanket.

Edit Elifant, a beautiful, blond Slovakian with high cheek bones and broad shoulders was our Kapo. The Germans put her in charge of the entire bloc. She held a stick with long, delicate fingers. I knew Edit came from a piano playing family with at least three servants. She wore a striped dress and a black apron made of lining fabric. On her sleeve was a red ribbon embroidered in white, and she had a blue number on her arm, like a tattoo.

Edit Elifant had several aides who knew German, they were beautiful or particularly tall. Each aide was responsible for a number of beds. Above her were the Germans. She had her own room in the front of the bloc. One day I peeped into her room. There were curtains, an embroidered cloth on the table, and colorful cushions, and a lamp decorated in gold, it was like the room of rich people.

Edit Elifant gave the order for us to stand next to the cubicles, and then she divided us into groups of five. She stood with her stick on the stone stove in the middle of the bloc and said loudly in Hungarian, here you obey orders and if you don't obey orders, you'll get it, why did you come?

One of the girls said cautiously, what could we have done, thrown ourselves under the train?

Edit Elifant sighed and said, better under the train, the only exit from this camp is through the chimney. She had the soft voice of a mother and I fell onto the stove. I managed to grab the bricks and hold on and then hurriedly pressed my knees and pushed myself back. The girls standing beside me pulled my dress, and stood me in place. Later, we fell onto the bunks and were asleep in a moment.

Several Kapos from neighboring blocs passed through our bloc looking for relatives. They also wore a striped dress and black apron. One Kapo found her cousin, a gentle girl with long lashes and transparent skin like glass. She lay on the bunk next to mine. The Kapo brought us blankets and whispered, in Camp Birkenau they take women from the ramp to the gas. From the gas they take the dead to cremation in the oven. That's why there's a smell of burned meat. Afterwards they scatter the ashes to the wind, and we don't know each other outside the bloc, is that clear?

I began to tremble. I hugged my body, I felt small, weak, and I trembled. The Kapo had a broad face and a huge chest and she had confidence. However, I didn't believe her and was glad when she went, but I couldn't stop trembling. Edit Elifant looked at me and said, you can change places and you can choose five girls who want to sleep together. I joined up with four girls from Ungvár. I didn't know them before but we had common acquaintances. And then she showed us how to fold blankets. At noon prisoners came with a large pot and poured soup into red tin bowls. The soup smelled bad and we didn't eat. Edit Elifant shouted, why aren't you eating?

We told her, because we have no spoons.

She kicked the bucket in the corner and screamed like an SSman, so eat without spoons, you spoiled Hungarians, eat. We drank the soup from the plate and ate a piece of bread. They put Bromine in the bread to stop us menstruating. The belly swelled and menstruation stopped.

Early in the morning we heard shouting.

The Kapo called, roll call, get up quickly, everyone outside for roll call. In the distance we heard the ring of a bell. We went outside to the empty ground between the two blocs. Five hundred women in a thin dress, without a sweater, without a coat. There were stars in the sky, and I felt the sting of a thousand pins in my flesh.

We stood in fives. I stood in front with the shorter girls, the taller ones stood at the back. I knew that without food they'd think I was a child in kindergarten and was very worried. The Kapo's aides began to count us. In the middle of the count there was confusion and they began the count from the beginning. The aide who was counting my row, a particularly tall young woman with the face of a Cossack, went on counting and made a mistake. She cursed as if she was in a market and then she brought her stick down on several heads, *hach, hach, hach.*

They finally finished counting. But the numbers didn't match the lists they had in their hands. I heard arguments and feet stamping on the ground, and then the Kapo screamed, idiot, idiots. I realized they were afraid of a mistake, and again they began to count as if they had no other plan for us. An hour passed, two hours passed, three, we were yelled at, stand straight, Jewish cows, straight as a ruler. The aides' sticks flew indiscriminately about heads. I heard weeping and suffering. I felt as if a butcher's knife was flaying my skin, strip by strip. I could no longer stand straight and was afraid of the Cossack's rage. I saw wet marks on the ground. There was a sharp smell of urine in the air. Suddenly shouts, sport! Sport! Everyone down on your knees, down, stinking Hungarians, hands up. We went down on our knees. The bones in my body hurt. I couldn't stretch my hands above my head. The Cossack approached me. She had white balls at the edges of her mouth, and a cold fire in her eyes. She raised her stick and hit me on the elbows. I felt an electric shock to my brain. After a few moments we heard an order: Get up. We got up. Sit. We sat. Get up. Sit. Get up. I couldn't get up. And then came the order, straighten up, quickly, quickly. Some of the women in the group began to shout at one another, go back, go forward, one of the girls screamed at me, nu, get up, get up, it'll be your fault if we never get out of here.

In the meantime, morning came and a bright light covered the barracks. They looked like heavy, frightening lumps in the mist. In the distance I heard the orchestra of Auschwitz with their marches and the female SS guards who arrived in gray uniforms, with a hat and red ribbon on the sleeve. On the ribbon was the symbol of the swastika in a white circle. The female German guards raised the left hand in a diagonal salute with Heil Hitler as we'd heard on the radio, and then the SS guards began to count us again. The mouth of the guard at my row turned down as if she was disgusted, she screamed, the row is crooked, crooked, and she strode off to Edit Elifant.

The Kapo paled, leaped up, and began to hit us with her stick.

Finally, the roll call ended and we were told that all the prisoners were to receive a tattooed number on the arm. We didn't receive a number. Edit Elifant made sure they didn't come to tattoo our arms. We went back to the bloc. I fell on the bunk and was asleep in a moment.

One of the girls in my fivesome was a painter. She knew how to draw faces. She drew Edit Elifant's face and gave it to her. She was happy with the drawing, and gave her a kerchief in return. Afterwards she took the kerchief, divided it in two and left. Then she came back with two more kerchiefs. And she cut up another kerchief, and returned with two more. Gradually she dressed all the girls in the bloc with the kerchief. At least our head and ears were warm. We saw that Edit Elifant wanted to help us. She sometimes brought us food in secret, potatoes, bread. We felt we had a bloc supervisor like a mother, on condition there were no Germans in the area.

One day they took us to the shower.

We went into the shower where we stripped and were given soap. The shower supervisor, a fat woman with sores on her face, shouted, wash thoroughly, and use soap in all the stinking places of your bodies. I'll smell each and every one of you after the shower. She shook a fat finger in front of our faces and went out. I thought, another disgusting Slovakian house-cleaner, and I began to pray. I was sure she was lying and gas would soon come out of the shower-head.

I looked at the women beside me. They all had thin, white bodies with sharp bones, some had blue marks on their body, some had sores from scratching. Even breasts shrank in Auschwitz, only the belly was swollen. The women wept, shouted, one of them began to eat her soap. She had a long, ballerina-like neck, long thin legs. She shrieked, you won't kill me, filthy Germans, I'll die alone. Someone tried to take the soap from her. She bit her on the hand, took another bite and vomited. Another young woman lay on the floor and began to kick. Weeping, I don't want to die. I want to live, why won't they let me live? We wept with her. Next to her stood a young woman of my height with a flat chest and two dark nipples. She bent over the woman on the floor, pressed her forehead, and slapped her face hard. I don't know where she got the strength in her hands. The woman on the floor fell silent, we all fell silent in turn. And then the young woman with the flat chest put out a hand and helped her up. My head began to spin like a carousel. I leaned against the shower wall, closed my eyes, and saw my mother. She was walking along the ramp, swinging her arms at her sides, and she walked away from me. I wanted to call her, Mama, wait for me, wait, and then came the water. Hot water. We hugged, jumped, soaped ourselves quickly, helping each other soap the back, laughing aloud, I was still worried because I looked so small.

After the shower I saw a man come to visit Edit Elifant. He entered her private room at the front of the bloc. I think the man was Mengele. He came several times. Sometimes he brought Maryanka with him. A small Polish girl, Maryanka was beautiful with blue eyes, a small nose, cheeks like red apples, and straight blond hair. Mengele asked her to look after the girl. I saw that Mengele loved Maryanka. He'd look at her with soft, laughing eyes. I saw that Maryanka wasn't afraid of Mengele. She had the smile of a woman who knows how to manage. She smiled with a closed mouth. Her eyelashes fluttered delicately like small butterflies. She'd put her small fingers on her belly and stroke it gently.

One day, Maryanka was left with Edit Elifant and Edit made her braids. Maryanka sang Polish songs to her. She had a thin voice like a bird. Edit liked to listen to her. Sometimes they sang the refrain together. The songs we heard from the front room made us weep onto our dresses. I missed my family, Grandfather, Grandmother, uncles, aunts, everyone. One of the girls in the bloc was left without eyelashes and eyebrows because of Maryanka's songs. She would fall upon her eyebrows mainly during the trills. Then she'd go on to the hair on her head, it had just begun to grow and she already had holes in her bald head. The young woman who slept underneath my bunk didn't have a smooth place left on her breasts because of those songs. One morning the two were taken in the *Selektion*. It was after an evening when Maryanka had sung and sung, unceasingly. They were actually happy songs.

Edit Elifant saved us from certain death.

She had her ways. The Germans wanted to separate us in the *Selektion*. She said to Mengele, I have an older group of women who can work, what shall I do? Mengele said, put them to work. She took us for small, unimportant jobs, like cleaning, carrying pots, things like that. I worked fast, I volunteered to carry large pots as if I was strong. One day they did a *Selektion* and Edit Elifant couldn't interfere. An enormous SS soldier held a stick and gloves in his hand. We stood in line next to the bloc. He signaled me towards the old women. I went towards the old women, knowing in my heart that this was the end for me. In the meantime, they shouted at the women who had passed the *Selektion* to stand in lines of five. Not far from me stood a foursome of young women. I waited until the soldier turned and jumped into the middle of the foursome. I stood on the tips of my toes, filled out my chest, raised my shoulders. I straightened up as if I was tall and strong. The women began to walk. I remained among them. I was saved from the gas, for the time being.

A few days went by and another *Selektion*.

We stood in line on the way to the crematorium. Beside me stood several other girls, the thinnest in our bloc. Our Kapo approached us. She said to the German soldiers: I need women to bring soup from the kitchen. Let me take a few women. The

Germans agreed. She took women from our group, I was one of them. She took us back to the bloc and I was saved for the time being. Edit Elifant saved more and more women. She cut the gray hair that had begun to grow on some of the women. She gave us ointment to rub into a bruise or rash on our skin. Sometimes women were sent to the crematorium because of a small bruise. She'd move us from one place to another and invent jobs for us to do, so we'd be away from evil eyes. She'd get girls out of the clutches of soldiers on all kinds of pretexts. Sometimes, she'd save Jewesses close to the crematorium, where the death ambulance stood with its red cross and boxes of Zyklon B. Near the Germans she screamed and used her stick, but I saw the great sadness in her face. She had large, brown, moist eyes like a woman who loves. She could have been a nurse or a good doctor in a hospital.

At Birkenau they forced us to write postcards to our villages. They forced us to say that we felt good. We wrote lies. Many lies. We wrote about good food. We wrote about barracks with beds and a blanket and a sheet. We wrote that we had good work, trees and birds, and beautiful gardens with sweet-smelling flowers. We didn't write in the postcards that the sweet smell had nothing to do with flowers.

Ever since Auschwitz I can't go anywhere near a barbeque. In America they eat a lot of barbeque. I keep away from it. I eat gefilte fish, meatballs, and cholent, and a lot of vegetables, and bread. I always have reserve bread in the drawer, always. I also have two rows of sliced bread in the freezer, want to see?

Sarah laughs, and she has mischievous eyes and the laugh of a girl. And then she gets up from her chair, washes her hands, says, and now a break, let's have some coffee.

* * *

New York City, 2001

11:00 coffee break in Sarah's kitchen.

I look at Sarah. Sarah is seventy-nine, a small slender woman, with an upright back, straight white hair, her eyes are wise and her gaze is sharp and relentless. Sarah talks and wipes the table and her fingers draw large circles and small circles, and the circles blend into one another, and sometimes the fingers move away to the edge of the table and then she tugs at the edge of the tablecloth, and returns to the middle, and again wipes the floral plastic tablecloth, starting other circles, as if the oilcloth is an enormous camp, requiring more and more circles in order to live.

If Dov had been in Sarah's kitchen, he'd have said, oy, Sarah, Sarah, what our sister went through, and she was so small. If Yitzhak had been in Sarah's kitchen, he'd have said, Sarah was alone, and Sarah went through many *Selektion* and she defeated the SSmen, damn them, why? Because she had brains, and luck, a Kapo like Edit Elifant is great good luck in life. And then Dov would have said, pity we didn't have a Kapo like her with us. And then Yitzhak would have said, Dov, we were there for each other, Sarah was alone.

Chapter 54

Sarah

O ne day we were told to leave Birkenau.

We didn't want to go, we were certain it was a trap with an opening to heaven. They sent us by cattle train to Gelsenkirchen in Germany. It was a sunny day and the clouds were like crumpled cotton wool. Yugoslav and German SSmen traveled with us on the train. German SSmen weren't as hard as Yugoslav SSmen. The German SSman could hit a girl and go. Yugoslav SSman would beat a girl until she fell to the floor and stopped moving, and then he'd send his hungry dog to the girl.

In Gelsenkirchen we worked cleaning up ruins.

The Americans bombed German factories, and we carried large stones to a pile. Our hands were full of scratches and sores, our backs burned and we couldn't feel our feet. I was worried my legs would break and I'd find myself lying in the rubble. I remember walking with a stone in my hands and sometimes, just from the rustle of an SSman passing by, I'd fall. Sometimes I'd just fall and I saw that actually nobody had passed by, and then I'd say to myself, Sarah, you didn't have to fall. Sometimes I'd hear a shout, or the thud of a stone that fell from someone's hands, and I'd fall, and if I didn't get up quickly enough, they'd aim a rifle at me. That's why I learned to get up right away, let's say I was lying on my back, or on my belly, or on my side, I'd immediately bring my leg up to my belly, stick my fingers in the ground, and push hard with my hands, and jump straight into a standing position.

After a few weeks in Gelsenkirchen, they sent some of the prisoners by subway to Essen in Germany, don't remember how many girls. They sent us to a military camp to work in the munitions factory. We had to check the strength of metals with a special machine. The Germans took strong metals to build tanks. Naturally we also sent weak metals to their tanks. I remember that at work I felt the hunger was dissolving my mind, there were times I couldn't remember what to do with the metal because of the hunger. I'd be thinking of something, and suddenly it would be erased in the middle. Let's say I didn't know whether to cut a piece of the dress I wore for a handkerchief and a kerchief, or whether it would be better to leave a three-quarter skirt because of the falls and sores on my knee. I had a constant problem with bread in the morning: Leave a piece of the bread I got in the morning for later, or eat it all at once, and just like that, in the middle of the thought, there'd be a white screen in front of my eyes and I couldn't remember the question.

Women began to steal bread. Women would fight over a cabbage leaf. Women would fight with their fists or bite a back to get to the bottom of a pot of soup. Many women fell ill and died. I saw them on their bunks in the morning. They looked like a pile of dirty garments before laundry. I only thought about one thing, how would I, Sarah, die: By a bomb from a plane, illness, gas in the shower, or hunger. I didn't know what would be better for me. With a bomb, one could finish in a flash, for instance, if a plane reaches our factory and drops a pile of bombs, and then the concrete ceiling falls on my head, that's good. But what would happen if a piece of concrete fell on my leg, and I'm caught there and don't die? Would someone save me? Not a chance. And maybe illness is better, an illness that ends quickly, dysentery, or typhus, maybe pneumonia. And what would happen if the illness progresses slowly and I'd be half dead? In my heart I asked for gas. Best to die by gas, like my mother. A few minutes and that's it, but gas revolted me. Gas went together with cremation in an oven, and the smell of burned flesh, that's what Edit Elifant said, and I didn't want to end like a chicken. I was twenty and I wanted to live.

I had almost no flesh on me, I was bone and dry skin, thin as a piece of paper in a notebook. I so badly wanted bread and water. I couldn't push in the line, the slightest touch and I'd fall to the floor. I tried to stand aside and wait for my turn for soup that was salty. The salt burned my throat, and we got no water. One day I couldn't bear it any longer. One of the girls in the camp approached a German soldier with a gun and a water canteen. She said to the soldier, give me water or shoot me with your gun. The soldier screamed at her to get back in line. She didn't move. Stood up straight, looking right at him. Said, give me water or shoot me now. The soldier gave her water and she got back in line.

Prisoners of war worked in the camp next to us.

Russian, Italian, and French soldiers. The Germans forbade us to talk to the prisoners of war. We ignored them and went to the prisoners of war. A French prisoner of war made head clips out of wire and smuggled them into the women's camp. Our hair had grown a bit and we began to wear head clips, above the ear, on the sides near the temples, where there was a small ponytail, or a fringe. We stank with filth, with infected sores on the soles of our feet, our arms, and we insisted on clips in our hair. We blew kisses to the French prisoner of war. Italian soldiers gave us soap. Some women exchanged soap for bread. Sometimes we found a water tap in some corner, we'd have a quick wash under the tap and hide the soap under our arms. We didn't go near the Russian prisoners of war. Their glance was evil and suspicious.

One day the Americans bombed the factory in Essen.

The siren sounded just as they called us to eat. We ignored it, maybe because it was a beautiful, moonlit night. The Germans took no interest in the moon, nor did the Russian prisoners of war, they wanted to eat. The Germans had to kill several prisoners of war to get them into the bunker.

I sat hunched up in the bunker, my heart pounding from the bombing that rocked the walls like a ship. After a few minutes the bombs got nearer the bunker, like a hundred-ton hammer on the head. I felt pressure and pain in my ears, and heat and moisture on my whole body. I remember calling out to God to be there. To take the time to look down on the suffering. I whispered, help, God, help, and I promise to be a good Jewess, a Jewess who observes the Mitzvoth with Shabbat and the holidays, just get me out of this hell.

The bombing ended and I remained alive, but the factory was completely destroyed. The soldiers returned us to the camp in a small train. We waited at the camp for a few days and then they returned us to the factory to clear away the rubble. One group worked during the day and another at night. We were about a hundred in each group. It was winter with snow and storms, nonetheless they forced us to walk a distance of a few hours every day. We'd wrap ourselves in blankets from the night and set off. It was one fine day when I noticed that even the beautiful women had stopped being beautiful and had blemishes on their skin and blue sores around the nose and mouth. However, there were still some particularly beautiful women, I was the smallest with the most blemishes. As we walked along the road, someone would always fall, and I wondered how I, Sarah, still hung on.

One day I saw a long, lovely woman on the snow. I stopped beside her to rest. She had two five-centimeter ponytails with two clips and a ribbon-like belt for her dress. Most painful of all was seeing a lovely woman die in the middle of the road, it touched my heart and sometimes I could have wept. I knew that if I died in the snow and a woman stopped beside me all she'd see would be a few spots and red blemishes on disgusting skin. SSman screamed behind me, walk, walk, and I fell into the snow. I tried to jump up, but couldn't. My legs were tangled in the blanket I wore, it was wet and heavy. I saw the barrel of a rifle aimed at me from a distance of six meters and my ribs shut down like a door. I threw the blanket off me, stuck my heels into the snow, leaned on my palms, raised my backside and jumped to my feet. I walked upright as if my dress and I got along fine in the snow. After a few steps, I turned around, grabbed the blanket from the snow and covered my head with it. That night I couldn't sleep for the cold. I was certain I was getting pneumonia and would slowly begin to die like some poor souls the previous week.

One day the storm was particularly wild and the soldiers couldn't bring us soup in the wind. Almost a whole day went by without food, and then we were told that the Essen municipality had invited us for supper. Trucks with tarpaulins arrived at the camp and by the whispers of the girls near me I realized they were also thinking of the crematorium. Nonetheless, we got onto the truck. The soldiers took us to a large hall and we were given good food, bread, meat, potatoes, vegetable soup, cakes. We were overjoyed. We returned to the camp with good color in our faces and a great swelling between the *décolletage* and the belt, and all because of the food we pushed inside our dresses. We received life for the time being.

They hadn't taken us to the shower for a long time.

In some of the barracks were ovens. We'd strip and put our clothing into a large pot on the stove to get rid of the lice. The lice would die with a *pak* sound. *Pak. Pak-pak-pak*, from the beginning of the boil. What I liked best was wearing clothes directly from the pot, it helped me to sleep even if my body was dirty.

I didn't dream at night. I craved a little quiet, I could no longer bear the constant buzz in the barracks: Whispers, crying out to God, Father, Mother, Rosie, Ester'keh. I couldn't bear hearing the whistling and wheezing of the poor souls before death. I'd already realized that death had an early sound. People usually didn't weep before they died. First they'd whistle through the nose, then through the mouth, finally dying with a dry throat. I wanted to flee far, far away from the barking of soldiers and dogs accustomed to eating human beings. I longed for the quiet of my room at home, when everyone was outside, mainly the little ones, Dov and Yitzhak. They always made a noise, those two, and I loved reading books without other sounds.

One day they took us on foot to a place we didn't know.

They didn't tell us in advance. They told us to stand in line like any other day. We thought, we're going out to work. Trembling, we stood wrapped in our wet blankets. My nose dripped like a tap, my fingers and toes were paralyzed. I looked at my shoes, there were holes in the leather, and there were also holes in the scuffed soles. I always slept in my shoes, mainly since Gelsenkirchen, when I saw a woman eating her shoe.

At roll call, I saw the SSmen turning in another direction from the one we usually took. And then they shouted, walk, walk, indicating the opposite direction. We didn't know where they were taking us and I understood that the time had come to part from the world. I looked up, there was ordinary snow. We progressed slowly in a line and there were gaps. I felt my mind leaving me as well as the desire to fight for my life. My feet walked by themselves, following the feet in front of me. I knew that if the woman in front of me fell, I'd fall after her. If she stayed on the snow, I'd also stay on the snow, that's it. And then I saw a lace on the snow. I don't know why but I felt a little joy in my heart. I bent down cautiously and picked up the lace. Behind me I heard a woman cry, it was the whistling cry through the mouth before dying. I said to myself, stay away from that woman, or you will fall onto the snow from her whistling without pulling yourself together. I managed to persuade myself to stay on my feet a little longer, and then I tightened the blanket round my shoulders, tied the lace round my head, the knot in the middle on top. I arranged my only clip in my hair, rubbed my lips hard with my finger, pinched my cheeks, and then I whispered, there you are, Sarah. Now you can lie on the snow forever.

I didn't fall. We continued to walk and walk, we reached places without snow. At night we slept at the first place when night fell. Sometimes there was a roof in some building, or barn, sometimes we slept without a roof, sometimes under a tree or bush. Women around me were dying like the rain. They put down their heads and *tak*. And *tak*. *Tak-tak*. The Germans killed some with a rifle, don't know why. Afterwards they loaded us onto a train. We traveled for several days without food. There were times the train stopped in the middle of a field, as long as they grew their local vegetable there. This vegetable was larger than a sweet potato, but not sweet. Not everyone could get down into the field. The German soldiers helped us, they got down from the train and brought us the vegetables, because they knew us from the camp, they particularly wanted to know the educated girls, the kind and polite girls among us. When we left the camp they stopped shouting and hitting and looked for an opportunity to talk to us. I saw they were glad to bring us the vegetables, bringing and bringing, until we were full. I looked at the Germans, and didn't feel anything, I was tired.

We reached Bergen-Belsen and the first thing I saw were tents.

In the tents there were only human bodies, layers and layers of bodies stinking of rotten flesh and disease. I looked for Jewish prisoners and saw none. I remember thinking that there were no Jews left in the world, and if there were, then only a few poor Jewish women. From where I was standing I could see a small group of Jewish women beside a tent. They wore dirty dresses, two had blankets on their backs. Each one of the women faced a different direction, they weren't speaking, they had died on their feet. Near the path I saw another group, some stood barefoot in their dresses, their feet black and dirty, and some sat bent over like stones near the path. I approached two women who were standing near the barracks. One was missing a shoe, the second held a small empty bag. I asked what's happening in the camp, is there food? The woman with the bag saw me and didn't answer. The woman without a shoe scratched a little at her belly, didn't see me standing beside her.

* * *

At Bergen-Belsen I saw that the German soldiers were closed up in the guard towers. They didn't move around the camp. Sometimes they fired a few rounds into the camp and fell silent again. Maybe they were afraid of germs and disease, maybe of cannons. We heard the sound of cannons in the distance, prisoners said, those are the Russians and they're getting closer to Bergen-Belsen.

Hungarian soldiers did wander around among us, mainly guarding the central kitchen that was no longer in use. Near the kitchen was a huge pile of rotten food. Prisoners tried to steal potatoes or cattle beets from the rotten pile, but the Hungarian guards were waiting patiently there with guns aimed, may they rot in hell. The prisoners in our group looked a little healthier and then a Hungarian soldier with a hateful expression approached us and said, women are needed to dig graves for the dead, whoever digs will get bread, d'you want to? We dug graves and dragged the dead there from the tents. I tied a rag around my face, and I still suffocated, the smell was like a sharp poison that burned the nose, throat, and chest. Sometimes I'd take hold of a body and pull, pull, and suddenly find myself with just an arm or a leg. Sometimes I put the leg on the belly and continued to pull the head or neck. I didn't think of anything, I wanted to get bread.

At Camp Bergen-Belsen I met Aunt Yuli Levkowitz.

She was Mother's sister. Mother had three sisters. Yuli Levkowitz, Sari Levkowitz and Margaret Levkowitz. Margaret was deaf and dumb. Aunt Yuli was thin, bent, with a hole-sized sore on her leg.

At first I didn't recognize her. She was standing next to my barracks. I approached her. Her face was pale and a bone stuck out like a ball under her neck. I stammered, Aunt Yuli? She looked at me, her face remained frozen. I came closer, Aunt Yuli, is it you? I'm Sarah, Sarah, Leah and Israel's daughter.

Aunt Yuli opened big eyes, hid her mouth with fingers as thin as matches, and said, Sarah? We hugged, wept and wept. Aunt Yuli hugged me and pulled me into her barracks. It was dark with the heavy smell of excrement. The floor of the barracks was full of excrement. Women with huge eyes lay on bunks, held out a thin hand from the cubicle, saying water, water. Aunt Yuli quickly took a small parcel from under her blanket and showed it to me. She said, its tobacco, let's go. We went in the direction of the fence. On the other side of the fence stood dirty prisoners. I thought, ah, so there are more Jewish men in the world. Aunt Yuli shouted something, and threw the parcel over the fence. Several minutes went by and someone threw her bread. Aunt Yuli gave me the bread and said, you must finish the bread now. I finished it at once. She asked me about the family, I didn't know what to say. Aunt Yuli and I didn't live in the same barracks. We'd meet during breaks when I wasn't dragging the dead to the pit. One day I came to her and she'd disappeared, don't know where. My brother Yitzhak met her and her sisters after the war in the village of Humenne. I didn't meet anyone. Didn't return to Hungary.

Bergen-Belsen was a place of germs and disease.

Most of the women with me in Bergen-Belsen were ill with stomach typhus, dysentery, fever.

Those who could stand on their feet and walk would leave the barracks to look for bread and marked their way with drips of diarrhea. It was impossible to stop the diarrhea in the camp. Sometimes, to clean up, some would rip off a piece of the dress they wore. There was no running water in the camp, just a few puddles of dirty water near each barracks.

Day and night you could hear howls like wretched animals and a lot of wheezing prior to death. There was a woman who raised her hand, pointed at the sky, and murmured words I didn't understand as if she was having an important talk with God. There was a woman with a ribbon on her bald head who held a dirty plank wrapped in a blanket. She coughed, spat blood, and sang a lullaby to her blanket. I saw her lifting her dress and looking for a breast. She had no breasts, just two empty sacks. She began to howl, the coughing increased, she still held the plank to her chest, patting it with her weak hand as though she were holding a baby who needed to burp. There were two women who lay in each other's arms in the cubicle like mother and daughter. One was long, the other small. They looked like two old women of sixty. The as-if-mother barely moved. The as-if-daughter scratched herself on the back, neck, legs, scratched the mother's back too.

When a woman died, the lice on her body would leave the cold body and look for a warm one. That's why I tried to stay away from fresh bodies. I had enough with my own lice. Sometimes I talked to my lice. I said, if I die in the crematorium or by gas, you're finished too.

Fresh bodies were dragged from the cubicles to the corridor at the end of the bloc. From there to a large pile, then to a big pit dug by the healthy ones behind the bloc.

One day we heard shots and cries of joy I'd never heard before.

I lay on the bunk without strength and the shots and new cries approached the barracks. I soon grabbed a bone in one leg and then a bone in the other leg, got down on the floor and from there dragged myself outside. Apart from myself, a few other women went outside. The two who held each other like mother and daughter went out before me. The as-if-daughter had her arm around the waist of the as-if-mother who was very tall and she supported her head on her shoulder.

Beside me was the woman with a ribbon round her bald head, she left without the plank she called Yoszi, just with a blanket tightly around her chest. She coughed and held out her arm in the direction of the shooting. After her came several other women. Some stood open-mouthed, another just wept, one sat on the ground and covered her head with a blanket. It happened in the afternoon, as light was fading. I leaned against the wall of the barracks, the shots stopped but not the cries of the prisoners who ran together, some limping, some jumping, everyone hurrying to the gate, and then I saw that all the Hungarian guards had vanished and the guard towers stood empty. I wandered about the place like an airless ball and didn't understand anything. I stood on a box, raised my head and heard shouts of joy from outside the camp. I approached and saw prisoners throwing their arms in the air, come on, they shouted, the British have arrived, the war is over. I ran with everyone without knowing where, and I felt my heart fly out.

I found myself in the German part of the camp, near huge storerooms of food. I didn't know there were food storerooms in the camp. The gates to the storerooms were open. Prisoners grabbed heavy sacks of flour, sugar, rice, and dragged them along the ground, Sometimes a sack tore, and everyone leaped on what spilled out and filled their pockets. I saw canned food, jams, bread, oil pouring like water, prisoners rushed about like madmen, grabbing more and more cans, some left the storeroom unsteadily with a bottle of alcohol. I found bread, there were piles of bread loaves. I sat on the side and ate bread. I looked up at the guard towers and again saw they stood empty. I saw no Germans. Saw no Hungarian soldiers. Only British soldiers, tall, clean, with a beret on the head and a three-quarter coat. They looked at us in astonishment, as if they'd never seen the standing or walking dead.

One woman shouted, clothing store, and immediately a few more dead straightened up with cans and bread and cartons in their hands and began to run in the direction of the storeroom. I approached and saw prisoners putting on one sweater then another, a coat and another on top of that, they put on an entire wardrobe. There were some who stripped completely and put on clothing they took from a large pile. Everyone put on a whole wardrobe, holding another in their arms. Some grabbed something, quickly dropping it. I took a clean dress and a thick sweater and returned to the barracks. On the way I saw a woman without a scarf, in prisoners' trousers and a long Pepita coat, opening a private kitchen not far from the pile of the dead ready to go into the pit. This woman collected a few planks and paper, lit a fire, opened the canned food and poured it into a large tin container that she put on the fire. She had at least six portions in the container.

And then I saw another long line. The British had brought us clean water in special tanks. I didn't have the strength, but my throat was burning with thirst so, with difficulty and in pain, I stood in line. In the meantime, I saw prisoners who, without being ordered to, began to drag bodies in a large piece of fabric hung on sticks instead of a stretcher. They dragged the bodies into a big pile, then they laid them in a common grave, without names.

In the meantime, the area between the barracks was filled with rags and boxes, and spilled wasted food. The camp filled with colorful garbage and weak prisoners who walked about dazed, wanting to understand what had happened in the camp. There were some women who dragged buckets of water to the barracks and began to give water to those in the bunks who were unable to get up on their feet. A group of at least ten women dragged a large pot of soup, some went to the barracks with six or seven loaves of bread and returned with more and encouraged those who lay exhausted. Anyone who could walk dragged something into the barracks, the storerooms of food moved into the barracks and those about to die were given another chance.

I couldn't sleep that night because of the block in my chest. Although I understood that the war was over I knew I wouldn't live, that I'd die with joy, a thick sweater and a few blemishes on my face. All around was the sound of cans opening, the rustle of paper, the taps of forks on a plate, and women chattering. Beside me was someone who called out Gretti, Gretti, Gretti, and wept, and again Gretti, Gretti, Gretti. Finally I fell asleep.

The following evening, the British brought us canned meat. By the color I saw it was fatty meat. Women who could get down from their bunks shoved large chunks of meat into their mouths and swallowed without chewing, taking more meat and more bread and more meat and more cakes, they didn't talk, just swallowed and swallowed. The chin was oily and shiny, eyes moistened, some got a strange purple rash on their cheeks. The barracks filled with inhalations and exhalations and swallowing sounds like a huge vacuum cleaner. Afterwards they brought us thick cocoa mixed with sweet condensed milk like jam. The women drank one cup of cocoa and asked for another. I ate a little. I just put something into my mouth and immediately wanted to vomit because of the smell of the dead. There were a few other women who refused to eat. The woman who pointed at the sky didn't leave God. They gave her food, she grabbed the food, hid it under the blanket and continued to talk nonsense with a white tongue.

After the food I felt faint and dizzy. I thought, I have bread, I have water, and I'm getting weak. I was sure I'd caught an illness and I would die in Bergen-Belsen. I wanted to sleep for at least a week. I couldn't sleep because the women next to me began to cry and shout, oy, my belly, my belly. Some got down from the bunk and pressed on their backside, they wanted to relieve themselves outside the barracks but didn't have time. A stink we didn't recognize settled in the barracks like a heavy moist cloud. I blocked my nose with two fingers and the dizziness in my head increased.

The next day, towards noon, I woke from the smell of goulash. Was I dreaming of my home? I got down from the bunk and saw real goulash with a real smell. Women were sitting with a plate full of goulash hurriedly swallowing potatoes and meat that the British had brought. I saw several women with stained trousers asking for another helping. I tasted a little goulash and went outside. People continued to wander about the camp like a dirty market, each one holding something in their hand, a parcel of clothing, or a loaf of bread, or a plate of food, everyone looked busy. There were people standing in groups, some smoking cigarettes, some holding a bottle. There were people who sat alone with no teeth in their mouths, staring ahead and I understood that they'd left a long time ago.

I couldn't stand in the sun and returned to the barracks.

And then came a disaster we didn't know. One woman shouted save me, save me, my belly's on fire, Mamaleh, I'm dying. There were several women who began crawling on the filthy floor, crawling, crawling, and they died. Others died in their bunks, some died with a plate of food in one hand and a good coat in the other hand. British soldiers came into the barracks. They held a handkerchief to their noses and passed among the bunks. Their faces were the color of whitewash and their eyes were shocked, and they spoke fast, fast. One of them said in German, go outside, everyone outside. I dragged myself outside. The British soldiers told us to sit down, everyone sit down and they pointed to a place not far from the barracks. They even carefully took out women who couldn't walk and lay them all down in the sun near me.

After about half an hour, they brought in local Germans who wore regular clothes and had no rifle, no stick, and no dog. The British handed out a bucket, a rag, and a broom to each farmer and ordered them to clean the barracks. I couldn't believe my eyes. Germans with blond hair and strong muscles, like the pictures I'd seen, sat on the floor of our barracks and scrubbed every centimeter with a rag, while we, thin Jewesses with lice and flaking skin, warmed ourselves in the sun as if we were in a convalescent home. I thought, you're dreaming, Sarah, you're asleep and dreaming. It wasn't a dream. Fact, I pinched my leg and it hurt. Time passed and every few minutes one of the Germans ran outside to vomit on the sand. The British didn't relent, when they finished vomiting they signaled to them to continue cleaning. There was sunlight and soldiers who took care of food and water and, nonetheless, at least seven or eight women died next to me within a few hours.

After a thorough cleaning by the Germans, the British disinfected the bloc and laid whole sacks of clean hay on the floor. In the meantime, young, local German women arrived, healthy young women with washed hair, smooth-skinned faces and full breasts. Some had lacquered nails and plucked eyebrows and lipstick. The British told the German women to wash us, and several women in the group began to cry. One wrinkled her clothing and cried out, no, no, no. Some spat on the floor. Some of the women lay quietly, I was among them.

Two German women approached me. One had thick hips and pearl earrings in pierced ears. Another had a chain with a cross round her neck, her hair was cut with bangs. I put up a weak hand to feel the holes in my ears and they were closed. Then I felt the clip in my hair. I removed the clip and closed it in my hand. The two young women smiled at me and carefully undressed me. They smelled of perspiration under their arms. I looked at my body, I saw bones and yellow skin full of scales like a dry fish. The eyes of the woman with the cross on her chest filled up in a moment, she bit her bottom lip, took a handkerchief from her pocket, but she still wet the cross. The young woman with the pearls scolded her and gently began to soap me. I saw she was making an effort to breathe normally, by her breaths I knew I didn't have a chance. After thoroughly washing my hair, they patted me dry, as if they were doing it with cotton wool, and they dressed me in a clean dress. Finally, they combed my hair and took me in their arms like a sweet baby and laid me on a large mattress in the barracks. I felt good.

A few more hours went by and they brought us dry crackers and a cup of tea, and then a bespectacled British doctor arrived and said, eat only crackers, you mustn't eat fatty food.

It was no use. Women continued to open canned food and the pile of dead near the barracks was as high as a mountain. I ate crackers and a little bread, I felt weak, but I didn't give up on fresh air. I'd drag myself out of the barracks with difficulty and lean against the wall for a few minutes.

One day I saw an open truck enter the camp. There were

soldiers on the truck. Within minutes a rumor spread that they were German prisoners. People in the camp began to run after the truck, shouting, cursing, throwing bottles and stones. The prisoners were hurt. I saw faces full of blood, I saw one falling from a blow to the head. I didn't throw anything, I could barely stand on my feet, and if I had thrown a stone I'd have flown with it to the prisoners. Afterwards I saw those prisoners wandering around the area. I recognized the strong faces, light hair, and the expression of superiority. Also by the ballooning of their trousers above the knee, their shirts untucked, without belt or gun, without boots, without a hat. They passed among the blocs and loaded the dead onto a broad wagon and, taking the place of horses, they dragged the dead to a pit at the edge of the camp. I looked for happiness in my heart but found none.

The days passed. Released prisoners who could manage alone moved to a large, German military building. There were some who organized themselves in groups and left the camp. They had somewhere to return to. I had nowhere to go. The Jewish women who lay next to me also had nowhere to go. I felt myself growing weaker by the day. Women continued to die in the barracks and we were moved to another barracks. I saw the British burning emptied barracks. Seeing the fire made me feel good. I wanted all the barracks in Bergen-Belsen to be burned with nothing left to remember them by.

One day the British doctors passed among us. They were looking for sick women. They said that sick women would leave Bergen-Belsen to convalesce in a hospital. Two women lying next to me, Rissi and Hanchi, knew English. Rissi and Hanchi told the doctors we were ill. The doctors asked, Sarah, what illness do you have? I didn't know what to say, but I felt I was dying, as if I was being eaten up from within. The soldiers found hundreds of sick women in our barracks. And then people dressed in dark overalls, a hat on their heads, and fabric-covered shoes, came and took us away from the barracks on stretchers with blankets. They covered our faces and sprayed us with DDT. And they loaded us into ambulances and trucks. I saw black smoke all around, I remember thinking, German barracks burn black, Jews burn gray-white.

We left Bergen-Belsen.

They took us to a place called The Round House, a large, two-story building with a sloping roof, it was a Nazi club. The British filled the club with hundreds of crowded beds and turned the place into a hospital. They gave me my own bed with my own pillow, two clean sheets and a blanket. The sheets smelled of a mixture of soap and moth balls. I pulled the blanket up over my head, hugged myself and whispered, Mamaleh, Papaleh, and wanted to die. English-speaking nurses approached me. One of the nurses pulled the blanket off me, spoke quietly, I didn't understand a word, and then she put her hand on my head, and caressed, whispering, *sh, sh*. Then she brought me another pillow and I put the wet one underneath.

The hospital was noisy during the day and at night, an irritating noise. There were patients who constantly called out, Nurse, Nurse, there were patients who talked loudly to the wall, morning, noon, and night, the same thing, there were some who conversed between the beds, sometimes the third bed from the entrance took an interest in the seventh bed from the entrance, what are the plans after the hospital. There were also some who lay curled up in bed, like an exhausted baby. They neither spoke nor wept, after a day or two I saw the bed was empty. The empty beds were immediately filled. A few more days went by and a group of doctors stood at my bedside. One of them was a British doctor with a small ginger beard and a large gap between his two front teeth. Beside him stood two other young doctors. By their questions, I understood they were medical students. And there was also a nurse I didn't know, with the hips of a girl, and two nuns. The nuns pointed to themselves and said Belgium, Belgium. The doctor examined me and said, well, she has typhus, and raised his chin as if there was nothing to be done, and I understood him without knowing any English, and I asked in German, how much time do I have left, Doctor? He didn't say anything and went on to the next patient.

My body burned. I threw off my clothing and lay naked under the sheet and waited for the end. At one point I removed the clip from my hair and gave it to the woman lying next to me. I whispered, look after the clip, it's a keepsake from a French prisoner of war, look after it.

I was calm. I didn't care if I lived or died. I regretted only one thing, I regretted that I'd never see my brothers Avrum, Yitzhak, and Dov again.

A few days went by, I saw that I wasn't dead.

The first thing I did was to take back the hair clip from the woman next to me and put it in my hair. I stroked it as if the clip and I had been together for life, and then the nurse from the first day approached me. She smiled at me and said, you will get well, Sarah, and she helped me to get out of bed and changed the sheet, and dressed me in a clean nightgown. The nightgown was enormous. I weighed about twenty-seven kilos. From then on, that nurse fed me porridge with a teaspoon, and water with a teaspoon, and a lot of medication. I ate like a bird but I knew I'd get well.

One evening British soldiers arrived at the hospital to cheer us up. They brought a record player and records and taught us how to dance an English hokey pokey. The girls who could get out of bed danced the hokey pokey with them. Even though I was stronger I didn't get out of bed, I was sure my legs would break in the middle of the dance.

A few days later, the doctor with the gap between his front teeth came over to our beds and said, now, girls, we have to decide, you can go home, or you can go away to convalesce.

I asked, where is the convalescence?

The doctor said, in Sweden.

I said, why Sweden.

The doctor said, Sweden is good. I thought, maybe because it's far away, and I quietly asked a British soldier who came to visit a pretty nurse, if there were dogs in Sweden, and if there were guns there, and he laughed.

I said, why are you laughing, and who did Sweden fight with during the war, ah? And then I informed the doctor, put me on the list for Sweden, and I signed papers.

Doctors from Sweden came to visit us. They were the height of the ceiling. They thoroughly examined all the women who said Sweden. They put a device on the chest, back, examined eyes, throat and ears with a light, felt the stomach, I immediately constricted down below and began to sweat, finally they gave us a note and a slab of chocolate, waffle cookies, good soap and hand cream and said, two days.

The day came.

Stretchers again. Soldiers, prisoners of war, were ordered to take us outside. I immediately saw they were Hungarian. They had faces like the soldiers who took us out of our home, who ordered me, strip, stupid Jewess. I saw them in Bergen-Belsen too. They stood with their rifles not far from a huge pile of garbage near the kitchen and shot prisoners who came near.

The Hungarian soldiers lifted the stretchers and fixed their eyes on the handle. They were submissive and polite, like dogs who were cautious with their master. They carried the stretchers carefully, primarily at the door where the British soldiers were standing. The Hungarians covered me with a blanket and measured the distance between the stretcher and the doorway, breathing as if they had to carry a large man with a belly. And then I saw a group of ambulances with the sign of the Red Cross. I remember crying out God, they're lying to us, maybe Sweden is crematorium in German? I held onto the stretcher and sat up, the soldiers called out in Hungarian, lie down, Madame, lie down, and I shouted, stop! Stop! And then behind me I heard a shriek like a frightened animal, I turned around for a moment and saw a woman in socks and a nightgown throwing herself from the stretcher, and beginning to run. She ran aimlessly looking for a place to hide. She was followed by several other women who scattered in alarm, and then I saw women running out of the hospital, and they also began to flee. The Hungarian soldiers began to chase the women, they were even more alarmed because of the Hungarians, screaming, save us, save us, one of the women got into an empty barrel standing next to a tree, two disappeared into a pile of cartons. A strong soldier caught a woman, hugged her shoulders, tried to talk to her, it was no use, she wept and lifted her nightgown over her head. In the meantime, doctors and nurses arrived, they had a great many soothing words in Hungarian, finally the women agreed to get into the ambulances. I remained sitting on the stretcher. I knew that if I began to run I'd fall and my body would break in two.

To this day I can't bear ambulances. Every ambulance in the street makes me want to flee to the underground. An ambulance once came to our building to take someone who'd had a heart attack. I was just returning from the market. I wandered through the neighborhood for half a day with bags of food in my hands, and it was a hot day, the middle of summer, like the day I left Germany.

The ambulances took us to the Port of Lübeck. They put us on board a ship and allocated us crowded cabins below deck. My nightgown was wet with perspiration, I could find no air. I went up on deck and leaned against the railing. The ship left the port and the first thing I saw was a huge ball of sun embracing the water, painting the waves red. My throat closed, I thought, a year alone with the Germans, without Father and Mother, with the body of a ten-year-old girl, and I'm alive, alive. I stayed on deck until dark and didn't turn my head round. I didn't want to see German soil, and ever since, I haven't wanted to see it, not even on television.

We arrived at the Port of Kalmar in Sweden after a two-day voyage.

It was July, 1945. The port was full of happy people. There were women with beautiful smooth skin, a special hat, and a dress with décolleté, sometimes one with a pattern, sometimes the fabric was cut straight with a broach or embroidery in the middle. Everyone had a huge smile for us. We disembarked thin and pale, some had no hair, I had short hair with a clip on the side. Some of the women were on stretchers and some stood on their feet wrapped in a blanket. People waved hello with handkerchiefs, and in their happy faces I saw how wretched we were.

From the ship we were transferred to a hospital, they checked us for infectious diseases. Three weeks of pricks and X-rays and taking temperatures every two hours in the German language. The German language made me go hot and cold, maybe Sweden was part of Germany? And maybe they do special experimenting and in the end they'll take all of us to a crematorium? Beside me I saw other pairs of eyes darting about and tiring of that German. A woman not far from me jumped off the bed, ran outside and returned after two minutes. All right, there's nothing outside, she said and sat down to eat. We were only given one meal a day, because the doctors didn't want us to die from food. It didn't bother me, because I always had bread under my pillow, others also had bread. And then, without discussing it among us, we arranged a roster. Every morning one of the women would go outside the hospital to check if they were building or organizing something outside, if they were changing the environment. Nothing was happening.

Three weeks went by and they found I had no contagious diseases. There were twenty or thirty young women with me who could leave the hospital. They gave us a suitcase with three bras, four pairs of underwear and socks, two dresses, a sweater, a coat, shoes and a dressing gown, and they said, tomorrow to the convalescent home. That night I saw several young women going with their suitcases in the direction of the shower. They laughed behind the door, called out, help me, fasten my bra, tell me, how do I look, things like that. I didn't go and try on. I knew two Sarahs could fit into the bra and underwear they'd given me, and that three like me could fit into the dress with space to spare.

From the hospital they transferred us by bus to the convalescent home in Ryd. An energetic albino social worker said in German, we're going to a convalescent home especially for survivors from Czechoslovakia, nice dresses! On the bus, the women laughed at their appearance, some opened up suitcases, comparing clothes, touching the fabric, measuring the length and hemming. In the meantime, the bus entered a large pine forest and then everyone fell silent. I sat fixed to the window and began to whistle. One of the women on the bus began to cry. The social worker approached her. The woman wept, take me to the hospital, don't want to be here, don't want to. The social worker soothed her with kind words. After about an hour we saw two-story buildings among the trees, no chimneys. Next to the buildings were yellow and orange flower beds, nevertheless we refused to get off the bus. The social worker went from one to the other. The director of the convalescent home, with her starched collar and tightly gathered hair, helped her. The nurse had a kind smile. Some agreed to get off with the nurse, and I was among them. Some waited on the bus until we'd finished seeing the rooms. Only when we beckoned did they all agree to get off.

We were given a clean room for four girls, each with a bed and small cupboard of her own, but I didn't unpack my suitcase. I wanted my suitcase ready for any event. The bell rang three times a day, inviting us to eat from beautiful china plates on embroidered table cloths. Waitresses with an apron and cap passed among the tables with full trays and served us good food. The waitresses had ringlets and curly hair. We also wanted ringlets and curls. One of the women in the group said, what's the problem, she taught us to make paper rollers on her finger. Our hair was short, but we tugged, and tugged, and made rollers at night. In the morning we had ringlets and little curls.

Next to the dining room was a room with a piano, a stage for plays and a special hall with exercise equipment. The convalescent home staff were very good to us. They made sure we were constantly occupied, they taught us to speak Swedish, invited us to dance, or listen to concerts, to choirs, we sat in the hall like ordinary women taking an interest in music, but we weren't ordinary women. Actually, the first thing I saw when I opened my eyes in the morning was my mother's face in our home in Tur'i Remety. I never left home, I always helped Mama with the little ones, and then, in one day, one moment, everyone disappeared on the ramp at Auschwitz, and I didn't know if they were living or dead. I only knew about Mama. I missed my mama. I continued to sit through concerts and choir performances by sweet girls with embroidery on their sleeves and braids with ribbons. I clapped them, but sometimes, in a flash, all the girls in the choir would fall naked one on top of another, and their bodies would shrink on the stage and their sweet braids would drop to the floor, and I would close my eyes in fright, open them slowly, and the sweet girls would be bowing before the audience, and I'd clap even harder, and again the sweet girls would fall naked, and fat rats would come to the faces everyone loved so much, oy my mamaleh, and I'd call out to God, or run outside.

After almost a year in the convalescent home, I reached the normal weight of a slender young woman of twenty-two, and then, in the spring, they transferred me and several other girls to a Czech refugee camp called Robertshöjd, near the town of Gothenburg in Sweden. Around the camp was a barbed-wire fence, at the entrance stood a guard who examined papers. I saw the fence and wanted to flee, but I calmed myself, stop, Sarah, stop, there isn't a crematorium, no electricity in the fence, the Swedes are good, rest. I found the strength, held tight to the suitcase, put my other hand on my chest, straightened up and entered the camp as if I was a tall, normal woman. I was taken to a bloc with two-story beds, twenty girls to a room. I said to the director, dear woman, I can't fall asleep in a two-story bed, either a floor or a regular bed. I was given a regular bed in another room.

There were goy men in that camp.

The goys lived next to the kitchen and were always first in line for food. We received food through a hatch in the wall. There were times the Czech men didn't want to wait in line and then they'd push one another, cursing and hitting. The blows of the Czechs weakened me, I would quickly go to the end of the line. There were times I'd go without food because of their shouts on the path.

One day we were told they'd found work for us and I registered at once. I set off to work at the Lessly factory, where I learned to sew dresses. I earned well and began to feel I had a chance in this life, especially after receiving a telegram from a young woman who was with me in the camps. She was in another town in Sweden. In the telegram she wrote that two of my brothers were alive and living in Israel. Her brother had met them in Israel. I sent her a telegram, writing, but I have three brothers, who is left? The young woman responded by telegram, two, Sarah, don't know the names. And then came the letter from Yitzhak and Dov. They asked me to come to Palestine. I so wanted to meet my brothers. I decided to travel to Eretz-Israel.

On the day I heard that Jewish men from Eretz-Israel had come to the camp, I went to meet them. They looked strong and healthy. They spoke the Hebrew language among themselves, a confident language, unlike the Hebrew my brothers brought from *cheder*.

The minute I saw them I fell in love with them, I could barely refrain from giving them a kiss. All the Czechs in the camp looked at the handsome men from Eretz-Israel, and I straightened up, and in my heart I shouted, you see, there are Jewish heroes in the world, and they've come from Eretz-Israel especially for us, to take us away in a plane.

That night I couldn't sleep, I felt as if a hundred sewing machines were at work in my mind, lasting until morning. The heroic men told us that we should take five things to Israel: Blankets, clothing and towels, a sewing machine, and a folding bed. I bought an old sewing machine and a folding bed. A friend who lived with me got me a trunk, I packed my things in the trunk and parted from the people I'd met in the camp.

The following night the strong young men took us in a truck to the airplane. It was a military plane with a Danish pilot. We flew to Marseille. There were problems on the flight. We were told to sit on the right-hand side, and they suddenly said, everyone move to the left. A few minutes later, to the right, and again to the left, we moved from side to side the whole way, I was worried the plane might fall to earth and we'd burn to death.

Marseille smelled of rotten fish and perfume.

In Marseille, I saw a black person for the first time. As if he'd been burned in an oven and didn't look good. Even his hair looked as if it had been in the oven. Apart from being black, he wore a coat and tie and he had a briefcase in his hand and he blew his nose on a handkerchief, like the French woman standing beside him. That night we slept in a hotel. Before going to sleep I bought perfume. I put perfume behind my ears, on my neck, under my chin, and on my wrists, I couldn't sleep for the smell and the excitement. In the morning they took us to Palestine in another airplane. The plane was steady, we didn't have to move from side to side during the flight. Not far from me was a woman with a pleated skirt and she was holding a crying baby in her arms. She moved around the seats, trying to calm her baby. Another woman with a beret and a burn-like mark on her cheeks walked beside her. The two looked related. The woman with the beret peeped over the mother's shoulder, made faces and sounds at the baby. The woman with the baby turned to her and said, do you want to hold him? And she gave her the baby.

The woman with the beret sat down in her seat, said Yanu'leh, my Yanu'leh, and sang him a lullaby in a deep, hoarse voice. The baby was alarmed and began to scream, I saw the hand of the woman pressing hard on the baby's chest.

The mother stood beside her, said gently, maybe I should take the baby, he's tired.

The woman with the beret didn't hear the mother, said, Yanu'leh don't cry, nor did she hear the man with the hat sitting beside her.

The mother bent down to the woman's ear, and said loudly, give me back the baby. The woman bent forwards, pressing the baby's face with her chest. He began to cough and the mother screamed, she's suffocating my baby. One of the heroic young men ran up and moved the mother aside. He bent over the woman with the beret and whispered things in her ear. In the meantime, other people jumped up and gathered round the mother and then I felt the plane fall and stop as if it had been struck. It happened twice, and people began to shout, the plane is falling, the plane is falling.

It took four forceful young men to restore the baby to his mother and calm everyone. The woman with the beret wept and the man next to her pleaded with her. She knocked off his hat and continued to weep. I went to her. I took the perfume I'd bought in Marseille out of my bag and gave it to her, take it. She didn't want to take it. The man without the hat whispered to me, she had two, twins, a son and a daughter. I lifted my hand with the perfume and began to spray. I sprayed the aisle, I sprayed the people, above my head, I went to the front and sprayed that part of the plane. Only when the perfume was finished did I return to my seat.

After about seven or eight hours we saw shore lights through the window.

The young men said, that's it, we've reached Haifa. I said to one of the men, my brothers won't recognize me and I won't recognize them because four years have gone by since we parted. Leiber, who became Dov in Israel, was a boy of sixteen, and today he's a man of twenty, and Icho – Yitzhak, was a boy of fifteen, and today he's nineteen. The young man said, don't worry, they'll help you. I knew my brothers had been in Israel for two years and, in my heart, I worried, maybe they look like the brave young men bringing me in the airplane? And how will I recognize them if all the young men in Israel look the same? I took a piece of bread out of my pocket and put it in my mouth.

We reached Haifa after the Declaration of the State, in October or November, 1948.

They took us to an immigrants' camp. There were a lot of people in the camp. They looked old to me. Maybe seventy, or a hundred. They had red marks on their cheeks and short jackets. Their collars were half in half out and there were papers in their pockets. They took their papers out of their pockets, looking for a way to understand something. I saw they didn't understand anything. I didn't understand either. The women wore dresses a little below the knee. They had rollers in their hair. When they took out the rollers their hair turned nicely upward. I had thin, short hair. All I had to do was run a comb through it and that's all. If I pulled hard on my hair, I could make a few ringlets, but I didn't feel like ringlets in a camp full of immigrants. I didn't like looking in the mirror, the young woman I saw in the mirror gave me nightmares because of the black smudges around the eyes and because of the thin face, and the thin line where the mouth should be. I had to puff out my cheeks and give myself a light slap to restore the lips to their place.

I sent Dov and Yitzhak a telegram from Haifa.

The telegram said: A message to my brothers Dov and Yitzhak. It's me, Sarah, your older sister. I came by plane to Haifa. I'm waiting in an immigrants' camp. When will you come? P.S. Have you heard anything from Avrum or Father?

One day people came to call me, they said, Sarah, Sarah, come, you have visitors. I went to the gate, my legs gave way, and I fell twice, for no reason, but I got up quickly and continued walking. Two young men stood before me, they were at least a head and a half taller than me. They had shoulders, and a neck, and a broad jaw like strangers, but I still recognized them by the smile and the eyes. Dov was the first to smile, he had a head full of brown curls, and a brown sadness in his eyes. Yitzhak smiled after him, he had a knife-sharp glance. They wore black trousers and pale shirts with a collar. Dov wore battledress. Yitzhak had a sweater thrown over his back.

I called, almost shouted, is that you?

And I began to laugh. I laughed like a mad woman, and then we wept. We wept a lot.

They said, Sarah. They choked, Sarah, Sarah, and I touched them, murmuring, I've found my brothers, I've found them. We embraced. Held hands. A lot of people stood around us. They held notes in their hands and wept with us. Beside my brothers I felt like a small, happy woman. Dov said, Sarah, we've come to take you, and I agreed, yes, yes, and I stood between them and we began to walk. They had large steps, my brothers, one was a soldier, the other a tractor driver and responsible for a post with a gun. They spoke fluent, strong Hebrew to each other, I said, wait a minute, have you forgotten Hungarian? They both laughed and shifted to Hungarian but they spoke quietly.

Dov took me to the little *moshav* where he worked, Yitzhak returned to the army. I lived with Dov in his room. He had a lot of food in a cupboard and he persisted, eat, eat, I couldn't eat because of the blockage in my belly. At night I couldn't sleep, the quiet in my brother's room made an explosion in my ears.

The next day Dov went to work, not before he set out on the table five canned foods, two loaves of bread, a jar of jam and a jug of milk. I ate a little and went back to sleep. That evening, Dov said, Sarah, there's a fellow on the *moshav* who wants to marry you, come and meet him. I didn't want to meet an Israeli fellow and I didn't want to get married.

A few weeks later I went to Tel Aviv and met Mordecai the soldier. He'd emigrated to Israel on *Altalena*. I married Mordecai because of his eyes. When he stopped near me I'd feel a pleasant warmth in my body. Mordecai was in the camps. I didn't tell him where I was and Mordecai didn't say where he'd been. After a few months we moved to Be'er Sheva. I worked in a kindergarten. I was a kindergarten teacher's aide. I had experience with my brothers at home. We didn't manage financially. We barely had enough to eat. We ate bread and radishes. In 1952 we left Israel for Canada, we said, maybe we'll manage better in Canada. A few years later, we moved to the United States and our two sons were born, and I never ever fell again. Even when I had images in my mind, every day with its images, for instance, the image of a woman my height who hid a baby under her coat. She tucked him into the elastic of her trousers and he began to cry. A German soldier with a hole in his chin ran in her direction and looked for the baby. He went from one woman to the next until her reached her. He held the rifle in both hands, took a step back and thrust the butt of the rifle into her belly. The crying of the baby stopped. The woman's face went green, but she didn't move and the soldier walked away. The woman took a tiny bundle out of her trousers, threw it onto the pile of suitcases and stood in a line of four.

There were other images that returned again and again like a giant wheel turning very, very slowly in my dream, and sitting in a chair, I'd want to flee, but couldn't get up.

I spent a year in the camps.

Since then I don't trust people. It doesn't matter what people say, I don't trust. I don't trust the government, I don't trust strangers. I decided that I would never ever trust anyone, only myself and my closest family. I live frugally. If I grow old and ill I will take care of myself. I try to be a good Jewess. For me being a good Jewess is eating kosher food, keeping the Sabbath, celebrating the Jewish holidays. I give as much as I can to charity, even the Arabs in Queens have learned to go past the houses calling, charity, charity. I try and stay in touch with good friends nearby.

I haven't talked to my two sons about the camps.

I don't know why I've kept silent all these years. Lately, my grandchildren want to know. They say, Grandma, Grandma, tell us about the camps, and I tell them, a little. I only began to take reparations two years ago, 200 dollars a month. I live primarily on social security.

When I was in the camps with other young women, we said revenge! Revenge will be bringing Jewish children into the world. I have children, thank God, and that's the revenge.

Chapter 55

Yitzhak: They killed six million Jews, six million!
Could three million of them have fought?
Of course they could. But they told us
wait for the Messiah, and the Messiah didn't come.
Dov: That's why I don't want to speak Yiddish.
I want to forget Yiddish and the Messiah.

Yitzhak

Today, I know: We should never have left our home.
We should either have died at home or escaped to the forest. If I had known of the plan to annihilate my people I would never have gotten on any train. But the rabbi took the Bible and led us in rows, yes. He led us, as if the walk to the gas chambers was the most normal thing in the world. What, didn't the rabbis know what they were doing to the Jews? We stood at the entrance to the shower in Auschwitz, two lines of naked men, and instead of shouting, resist, the rabbi shouted *Shema Israel*. We should have attacked them. We should have caused havoc, stopped those convoys walking and walking to the crematorium as if they were handing out candies on sticks in there. They'd have fired their rifles, so what, was gas any

better? At least we'd have stopped the pace of death, I think about that and go mad.

Sometimes two SSmen led a thousand hungry Jews. What, couldn't we have killed two SSmen? And if a hundred had come, couldn't we have kicked them to death? We were many thousands and they were only a few, we could have. Before the hunger we could have risen against them. The hunger weakened our minds. A hungry person can't think about anything, his mind is stupid. The Germans took care to make us stupid in the camps, so we wouldn't notice the convoys going to the crematorium, is it any wonder that we were silent? People didn't even have the strength to commit suicide. The mind needs a lot of strength to think it's better to die. We preserved our remaining strength to survive the hunger and the frost, not in order to think. It was the strong who committed suicide. The strong ran and threw themselves on the fence, or hanged themselves with a rope. The strong stopped eating because they'd decided to die. Do you know how much strength it takes to step out of line and do things alone?

I remember having only one thing on my mind: More bread in order to live. I wanted to get more bread so my brother Dov wouldn't die beside me.

Chapter 56

Dov

I try not to think about what happened to me in the camps. I have friends who have lived with the camps every night for over fifty years.

I don't dream. When I open my eyes in the morning, I don't pass my hand over my body to see if I have a leg, or nails on my fingers. And at night when I go to bed, I don't see a cart with the dead, their arms dangling down over the sides. But what I went through at sixteen still affects me today. Let's say, when I see a television program about food in which the chef produces goose with a special spice from Spain, I watch and am eaten up inside. My fingers immediately begin to tap on the table and my coffee spills, and cake crumbs drop on the carpet and I feel like firing a bullet into the middle of the screen because I can't bear talk of special spices.

In the camps every stinking rotten peel helped me live for two days. I'd pray to God to give me bread ten times a day. When I found moldy bread, it was as if God was telling me, Dov, you will live. And here they are, talking to me about a powder from China, grains from Paris, and mushrooms from the Himalayas, why are they telling me this? I can't hear chatter like that.

Sometimes I see a movie in which a child throws dough at another child. It kills me, I can't bear to see food being thrown around. Sometimes they throw whole cakes in someone's face, just like that, for a laugh, and it irritates me. Isn't that a waste of a cake? How many people could have eaten pieces of it?

At home I'd die rather than throw food. Sometimes the girls can eat a third of a pita and throw the rest into the garbage. It affects me. I feel my blood pressure rising, my forehead gets moist, and I boil inside. And nonetheless I explain to the girls that food shouldn't be thrown away. Sometimes I call them to come and watch a television program about children in the world who are dying of hunger, and here we are throwing food in the garbage. Not sure they know what I'm talking about.

Hotels are the hardest of all for me.

I am incapable of going into a hotel and being waited on. My wife says to me, everyone goes away for a weekend, let's go to a hotel. I don't want to go, don't like someone serving me food at a table. Those waiters stand at my table and say, it's special food, and that's a delicacy, and this is imported wine, and I want to get up and leave. I get nervous right at the entrance to the hotel. The reception clerks tell me, you'll sleep in a luxury room with air conditioning, a Jacuzzi, a view of the sea, and a bar, and your own private dressing gown for the pool, and I feel a heat in my body. I don't enjoy talk like that. I say, as long as I have bread and a tomato and a roof over my head, I'm in paradise. Not long ago we were dying of hunger and now I miss a liquor bar? If I had to live for a week in a hotel I wouldn't be able to bear it. I went overseas once in my life, my wife wanted to, I was in Turkey on behalf of the company I worked for, all the luxury I saw there got on my nerves.

Chapter 57

Yitzhak

The camps are in my thoughts.

I look at my grandchildren and can't erase what I went through at their age.

The camps affected my relationship with my children. Our family is not united, why? Because on the ramp at Auschwitz each one in my family went in a different direction. If today my family is not united, it's because each one is going in a different direction. As if some SSman is traveling above our heads and dispersing us. As if he were saying, you go south, and you go far east, and you stay here in the north, and all these thoughts are because of that ramp and those trains and the loneliness everyone is living with. As if the Nazis have got us accustomed to being each one for himself and that gets on my nerves today as well.

Look, I don't go to visit my daughter who lives in the south of Israel. And I have grandchildren there. Why don't I go? How can I explain the anxiety of returning and not finding my home? How can I speak about the fear of returning from a trip and instead of my home there's a train standing there, the one that goes from Haifa to Tel Aviv. How can I explain that every day I am likely to feel that a train is standing on my home with a ramp larger than yesterday's ramp. I can't even spend one Saturday with my children, and my wife wants to go. She says to me, Yitzhak, let's go and see the children. And I am incapable of leaving the house for more than a few hours, not even at Passover, and it burns me up inside, but I can't move.

It could be that I can't move because a large part of myself was left in the camps, damn them to hell. And it could be that not even once, not even at Passover, have we told the children about our own exodus from Egypt, and that may be because a large part of the soul is still there, and there is nobody to tell them how hard it is to be connected to someone who is neither Yitzhak nor Dov. Only Dov and I stayed together. It's as if we have a mountain to climb. As if we haven't finished climbing one of the hills on that terrible death march from Buchenwald to nowhere.

Chapter 58

Dov: For me, God is earth, air, water, nature.
Without it I don't exist.
Yitzhak: Before the Holocaust I knew there was a God.
Afterwards, I didn't know, should I believe or not.
When things were hard I prayed to God.
Today, I think my God is the State of Israel.
If I have the security of Israel, I have God all the time.

Dov

In the camps I had a habit of not jumping first.

I did things according to fate. I didn't raise my hand and didn't volunteer to be first. I thought, what needs to happen will happen. It was a sacred rule for me in every camp. Let's say there was a truck at Auschwitz. They told us to get onto the truck. I never jumped first. I waited at the side. Suddenly the truck left. It was those who jumped first who got to the crematorium and those who moved away were sent to work. From 1944, I decided to take fate as it came, without maneuvering the situation. I let fate lead me, I wasn't a commentator.

It was here in Israel that the great change took place.

I did jump first. In the beginning. Because it was for my

country. In fact, I volunteered for dangerous work on the border. Why? Because of Hitler. I said in my heart, the most important thing in life has already happened to me. I beat Hitler. Now all that is left to beat is the possibility of being a living dead man. I am a living Jew, and I love my country, and I am enthusiastic and excited about contributing to my country specifically on a dangerous border, yes. Afterwards I stopped jumping. Look, with my girls, I see them throwing away pita, and I don't jump. I see that the youth of today have no respect for an adult, and I am silent. I'm glad I have bread to eat and water to drink and that Jews are not sent to the crematorium just because of our father Abraham and circumcision.

I often talked to God.

I asked him to help and advise me. Should I go right or left? I looked upward and asked for direction. I think I received direction. I also talk to God today. I ask Him for health and respite from the images tapping in my mind, I ask that we not lack for food, that we never lack for food.

Sometimes I have images with sound from life in the camps.

The images and sounds come like thieves in the day. Sometimes I hear the painful noise from the ramp at Auschwitz, and it's a hard sound because of the searing pain. Here I am, in a convoy on the ramp. And that line is advancing slowly, slowly, one step after another. And soon I approach the point at which SSmen decide with a finger, to the right, to the left. Yes, like that, a small movement with a finger, to live or to die. To go to a bloc or become dust in the garbage.

By chance I didn't go to the gas chamber. By chance they needed laborers on the day I stood on the ramp, why? Because of the large transport from Hungary, my transport, yes? The

Germans needed us to sort through our clothes and so they sent me to Camp Canada. And if I'd been a year younger? The SSmen were looking for children all the time. And what chance did I have of staying alive if I hadn't met my brother?

I want to tell you something that happened in my village in the Carpathian Mountains.

In the village there were Jews who went to the synagogue every day and there were Jews who went only on the Sabbath. On the Sabbath everyone went and who didn't go? Disabled Friedman didn't go to synagogue on the Sabbath. He was the older brother of Friedman who threshed the grain for the village farmers. Their family had a threshing machine, a saw mill, and a large house near the road.

Every Sabbath when we'd come out of the synagogue, disabled Friedman, about fifty at the time, would be sitting opposite us on a bench in his cap and smoking. He smoked on purpose. It went on for years. A Jew smoking on the Sabbath. It's hard to explain. He was an aberration. Out of bounds, unfit.

Why did Friedman smoke on the Sabbath? I thought about it a lot. Why did that Jew smoke on the Sabbath of all days, in front of people coming out of the synagogue? And two days before they took us to Auschwitz, that Jew died and was given an honorable Jewish burial. It was as if he was telling everyone, don't waste time on trivialities. There are more important things to do. Save yourselves. And he was an educated man, not a fifteen-year-old. With his behavior, he was telling us, Hitler is screaming on the radio, Europe is smoking Jews, while you go to the synagogue to pray, and weep for the Messiah to come, and call out to God, begging him to save us, save us, and nobody says, Jews, flee, live.

And that drives me mad. Friedman of all people, who left Adonai, who smoked against God, against everyone, he was blessed. He didn't lie in the stinking mud in a brick factory and wasn't pushed in the line for food. He wasn't thrown onto a stinking cattle train, without water, without air. He didn't stand on the ramp at Auschwitz and didn't see his family scattered to hell. He didn't go in a convoy of weeping elders and children to the crematorium. And he would, of course, have gone with the elders, because he was old and disabled. Feet didn't trample on him and his head wasn't crushed in the gas chamber during the last moments of life. Yes, Friedman was blessed.

Sometimes I think about the death march from Buchenwald.

When they drove us out of Buchenwald at the end of the war, German families walked with us on the road. Women, children, youth, prams with babies. They fled their homes so they wouldn't fall into the hands of the Russians. We walked on the very same roads. The roads were full of Flüchtlinge – Refugees – and German families. I saw their convoys, we almost intermingled.

I looked at them and thought, we are driven out and they are leaving of their own free will. So what was the war about, what?

Chapter 59

Yitzhak: I think about this sometimes.
If I were to meet the German girl who gave me food
on the way to Camp Zeiss, I'd bring down stars
from the sky for her and make her a queen.

Yitzhak

Sometimes when I'm tired I dream of being young and jumping on a moving train as if it were real.

I'm wearing a short coat, gray trousers and a woolen scarf. I sit on a bench near the aisle and lean against the window. The train rattles, *shak-shak*, *shak-shak*, like a tune stuck in your mind, *shak-shak-shak*, the head gets fuzzy, *shaaakkk*, *boom*.

The head drops and I wake up, jump to my feet, open large eyes and go to the end of the car. And return. Go to the other end, return. Sit on the bench and get tired and fall asleep until morning.

The train stops at Camp Zeiss, and I get down at the station and don't know whether to go right or left.

Right, to work underground insulating pipes deep beneath

the earth, and right is also preparing for certain death at the hands of the Germans who haven't yet completed their programs against the Jews.

Left is to the village of the girl with the braids and the sandwiches, and the great hope of living.

Behind my back the locomotive puffs and pants and an old woman with two baskets heavily boards one of the cars. The train left with all the sighs of the old woman with her baskets, I was left alone on the platform. Opposite me, exactly as I remembered, stood little houses with tiled roofs and a chimney on each roof. There was also a yard and a picket fence and dark curtains at the window.

I put my fists in my pockets, and whispered, now cut to the village by road, nu, walk, but my legs were like lead, stuck in the track. The mind buzzed, do something, man, take one leg and move it, and then another leg, nu, nu, nu. The leg moved forward, the other leg following, and I find myself proceeding along the track. The mind shouts, good, have you come to the village to count train sills, and soon another train will come, and then what?

I go on skipping sills and examining the houses. There were houses with dark stains on the wall, others had been re-painted. The bushes near the houses had grown, the thick tree remained the same, and then, in a moment my heart plummeted. Behind the tree I see the tower with the green point from which hangs a rope ladder. I remember the tower, the girl with the braids always stood in line with the tree and the tower and I fall and get up, straighten up, and wait for the girl to come out to the path so I can hug my savior, but the girl didn't come out to the path, no one came out to the path.

I want to go back to the station, but then, in the distance, I see a girl in a red dress with loose hair to her shoulders. She'd come out of the last house in the row of houses and was coming in my direction, stopping a few steps from me. Her blue eyes were brighter than I remembered. Tiny sores covered her forehead and her cheeks. I swallowed, was it her?

I approached the girl. Put out my hand and stammered in German, hello, I'm Icho. The hand remained in mid-air.

She took a step back and said, I'm Gertrude, who are you looking for?

You, perhaps, I don't know.

Gertrude said, me, excuse me, have we met?

And I say, Icho. The prisoner during the war two years ago in the convoy to Zeiss, and a girl with braids waited for me on the road with food, was that you?

Gertrude folded her arms on her chest and said, excuse me, I didn't understand you.

And I say, I came to thank you, you saved me, I mean, if it was you.

Gertrude said, when was this?

During the war.

During the war, were you a camp prisoner?

I was.

Then I pointed in the direction of the road and said, that's exactly where you stood, opposite the tower, don't you remember? You stood there with your mother, wasn't it you?

Gertrude said, I'm sorry, I wasn't here two years ago. I came to this village a month ago. I came from another village, near Berlin, are you a Jew?

Yes, a Jew, maybe you know a girl with braids, she looks rather like you.

Gertrude said, I haven't had time to get to know people. I'm sorry, you came especially.

No, no, I'm waiting for a train.

Gertrude said, me too.

Only when I'm tired do I dream that I got on a train to meet the girl, but in the meantime, in my dream, I also remember the camp and the Germans and the harsh journey, and in the morning I feel bad. I left everybody a full description of the girl as I remembered her, and the nuns and soldiers at the monastery promised to help me find her and send a telegram to me in Eretz-Israel so I could thank her for her concern for me. Thank you for being a tiny light in a forest of darkness and wolves. Thank you very much for overcoming Heil Hitler, yes. The one who screamed on the radio, who dragged millions after him, Heil and Heil.

At the monastery I asked them to tell her that she's the queen of a Jewish boy, whose name is Icho-Yitzhak and he's going to Eretz-Israel. They have to tell her that if he were to meet her, he'd pull stars down from the sky for her, and the moon. They have to find that German girl, and tell her exactly what he, Yitzhak, has requested.

No one sent a telegram, and I always look for her when I get to Zeiss in my dreams.

In my dreams I visit almost every camp, but Zeiss most of all, mainly during Passover. Every year when we set the table I put one empty chair at the table. A chair for the girl. I clean her chair thoroughly, straighten it under the tablecloth, and every Passover evening I say thank you very much.

Don't thank Dov, don't thank God, don't thank my son and daughter who've come for the holiday, and the grandchildren, don't thank my son, who has taken the grandchildren to celebrate Passover somewhere else. I thank the girl, yes, and wait. Maybe the day will come, and she'll sit with us, and we can say it directly to her, thank you, thank you. And maybe she'll come at New Year when my wife and I are most alone, when we have no desire to set the table. Maybe it will be New Year when that girl comes to sit with us, and we'll eat apple in honey and sing together, *Happy New Year, a Happy New Year is coming,* maybe.

Poland, 2003

Monday 23rd June on the Auschwitz-Birkenau ramp.

It's afternoon, and I'm on the gravel of the ramp at Camp Auschwitz-Birkenau.

First, the tower we see in the newspapers opposite a huge camp that looks like a forest hacked with an ax. Only a few barracks remain and a fence is being fixed at this very moment by two workers. A track divides into three paths, two alongside the ramp, the third slightly to the side, and I'm trembling.

God, this is where Dov and Yitzhak got down from their transport, this is the place, and this is where SSman stood with a long finger in a white glove, a finger that played with the life of a nation, and I stride to the edge of the ramp, and Alex the guide says, now we'll go to the barracks, and I say, please, I want to see the ramp again, and he agrees, and I take a long stride, stepping forcefully, even though the gravel shouts from below, and I have a wild urge to crush the gravel with the Jewish legs I brought in the plane from Eretz-Israel and scream to the heavens of Auschwitz-Birkenau.

I was born to the Jewish people in Eretz-Israel, you saw they wanted to eliminate everyone, nu, what do you have to say about that, huh, and Batya is worried. Are you all right?

And I say, in a moment, and then I remember Dov and Yitzhak's instructions, go to the sauna, go, go, see where Camp Canada was, more or less, and go to the woods where mothers and children rested as if on a picnic, you can also rest as if you're on a picnic, make sure you have something in your bag, a biscuit or an apple, and go to the bloc, you must go into at least one bloc, look at the cubicles, we said they're crowded, and don't go anywhere near the crematorium, we heard it was destroyed but, nevertheless, stay away from that place, do you hear, they say there are ghosts of millions and they curse the world for remaining silent, so don't go near it.

I said, come with me, we'll light a candle together for the family.

No. Absolutely not.

They said, we won't go there, we won't go anywhere, you light the candles yourself, and take photographs so you'll remember. We have enough pictures in our minds. And call us from Auschwitz-Birkenau when you leave, we have to know you've left.

You will call, won't you?

Acknowledgements

I so deeply thank the brothers Yitzhak and Dov, who held each other's hand during the most difficult moments and never let go. I am grateful that they were willing to tell their unfathomable story despite the enormous pain of reliving such horrific memories.

My gratitude to Sarah, the brothers' sister, for sharing her heartbreaking story of survival. May her memory be blessed.

I am grateful to Lilly Perry, editor of the Hebrew edition – thank you for accompanying me on this painful journey.

I thank Yad Vashem in Jerusalem for supplying me with material that was enormously helpful.

About the author

About the book

Read on

Insights,
Interviews
& More . . .

Meet Malka Adler

© Malka Adler

Malka Adler was born in a small village near the Sea of Galilee in northern Israel. After taking a creative writing course, she fell in love with the art.

She has written six books, four of which are about the Holocaust. She obtained her undergraduate and graduate degrees in educational counselling at Bar Ilan University and is a family and couples' therapist, writer, and facilitator of several reading clubs.

Malka is married, has three sons and is a grandmother. ❦

Author Q&A

1. When did you first start writing stories? Did you write as a child or was it a passion and ambition that came to you in adulthood?

I began writing after I turned fifty. While I did write page-long letters as a young girl, which people said they would read again and again, I did not write stories when I was young. After taking a course in creative writing, I developed a passion for it. My perpetual curiosity fuels my writing – I love to observe and to let imagination have its way with me.

2. Who are your favourite authors? Do you have a favourite book, or are there any particular books that have inspired you?

Mitch Albom, Jose Saramago, Jojo Moyes. When I was younger, my favourite book was *One Hundred Years of Solitude* by Gabriel García Márquez. I think it is a magical portrait of life in all its complexity and humour.

3. Dov almost weeps for the beauty of the orchestra at Auschwitz. What music brings you to tears? Do you ever listen to music while you write?

Operas, particularly *Madame Butterfly*; and, of course, classical music. I always listen to music while I write.

4. If you had to pick one song or album to accompany this book what would it be?

Leonard Cohen. Who else? *And who by fire, who by water / Who in the sunshine, who in the night time…*

Author Q&A *(continued)*

5. What hobbies do you like to do when you're not writing?

This is a fairly long list. I love to read. I have been facilitating reading groups for some time now. The last book our group took on was *The Magic Strings of Frankie Presto* by Mitch Albom. I am always learning something new; I studied painting which led to several exhibitions of my work and took classes on the art of floral arranging, after which I opened a flower shop.

6. What advice would you give to aspiring authors?

1: If you have a dream to write – do it. Keep a diary for writing daily. 2: You don't need a muse. Just write. No matter what it is. The book will be rewritten again and again, so don't worry about getting it perfect right away. 3: Don't fall in love with your words – you must learn to say goodbye to some of them for the sake of the book.

7. Do you have any powerful or prominent childhood memories of growing up with the brothers in the Horns of Hattin village?

Yitzhak would have lunch with us every day. He said that he loved hearing me cry as a young child because for him, it was a sign of life.

8. Did any of your own family history inspire your writing?

My first book, *Come Auntie, Let's Dance*, was about my parents, their childhood in Bulgaria, and their Aliyah to Israel, as well as my young life on the Sea of Galilee.

9. What lasting feelings, themes, or emotions do you hope readers are left with after finishing *The Brothers of Auschwitz*?

I hope that the book will touch readers and encourage people to have compassion and remind them that we must protect each other at all times. I hope the book will help to instil the resolution that such atrocities must never happen again. Readers have told me that they feel the narrator walking beside them, telling these stories. I have tried to not only completely feel but also embody the characters in my books – in all their situations.

10. The world today is still such an uncertain place and sometimes it can be difficult to see the light in the darkness. What gives you hope?

I am optimistic to a fault. I believe that there is good in every single person. Compassion for people, animals, and the world is our lighthouse.

Author's Note

by Malka Adler

About the book

THE VILLAGE I LIVED IN WAS FOUNDED in 1936 by a handful of Bulgarian pioneers, my father among the first ten members. It was situated on a hill overlooking the Sea of Galilee.

In April 1946, a group of teenage Holocaust survivors arrived at our newly found village, most of them were from Poland and had lost their families.

The newcomers worked the land, learned Hebrew, and were appointed families with whom they would have lunch. Yitzhak came to us. Dov was sent to a different family. I was six months old and had two older siblings.

Years later Yitzhak told me that he liked the sound of a baby (me) crying and seeing it in its mother's arms because it was a sign of life.

My mother said that Yitzhak was like a brother – an adopted brother, and when I asked her

© Malka Adler

The fields of Kfar-Hittim, The Arbel cliff and the Lake of Galilee. Malka Adler's birthplace and childhood views.

where his parents were, she said, "Shhh, we don't talk about that."

When we learned about the Holocaust at school, I asked Yitzhak where he had been during the War. He answered that the only thing he was willing to say was: "If I ever meet the German girl who stood with her mother by the side of the road which we tread, creating a human convoy day after day on our way to work in the factory – exhausted, famished, desperate – the girl who gave me a sandwich every day, I would make her a queen." He had tears in his eyes. I asked him about it a few more times but he said nothing more. He didn't know her name or the name of the German village. I stopped asking. And I didn't read anything more about the Holocaust.

Yitzhak and I kept in touch after the group left the village.

I moved to central Israel, and in 2001, published my first book, *Come Auntie, Let's Dance*. I had a strong feeling that my next book would be about the brothers, Yitzhak and Dov. I shared this with my husband, Dror, who answered, "But they don't want to speak of it."

I called Yitzhak. He said that Yad Vashem and other organizations had asked him to share his story and he had refused. "I haven't talked about it for sixty years, not even with my children. Why would I want to talk about it now?"

I called Dov and he refused as well, but agreed to tell me about his first days at the village, which I couldn't remember because I was an infant.

I took the train to meet him up North, where he lived not far from Yitzhak. He made us coffee and I asked if I could record him. I put the small device on the table and then he sat up straight in this chair, opened his eyes wide and began, "We arrived at Auschwitz at night. When they opened the train doors, there were bright projectors that hurt my eyes. I heard people crying and screaming, dogs barking and soldiers yelling at us, 'Schnell, Schnell.'"

I was speechless. That evening, I called Yitzhak and he said he had spoken to Dov. "Alright, I will tell you my story, too."

I sat with them once every two weeks for a year. First each one alone, and then together. We made slow and careful progress. I was worried about them. Sometimes Yitzhak would cry as he spoke.

I travelled to Queens, New York to

meet Sarah, the brothers' sister. We sat for hours in her kitchen as she shared her experiences during the Holocaust.

I began to read various books about the Holocaust, such as *History of the Holocaust: Hungary* by Randolph L. Braham and Nathaniel Katzburg and *The Auschwitz Album*, published by Yad Vashem, and many more.

After that I sat for another two years and wrote the book. I made myself imagine I was in a work camp, living in huts, holes, famished – what did I see, smell, hear? What did my body feel like? I pretended I was walking down the unloading ramp at Auschwitz. I wore a coat even in the summer and I couldn't stop weeping.

Before I gave the manuscript to my publisher, I travelled to Auschwitz. I wanted to see the ramp, the huts, the ground, the sky, and the woods near the demolished remnants of the crematorium.

© Malka Adler

Malka Adler. In the background – her little village, Kfar Hittim, on the hill overlooking the Lake of Galilee.

Author's Note *(continued)*

I wanted to touch everything. The last page of the book describes some of my experiences during that trip.

Since then I have written three more books about the Holocaust. ❧

Reading Group Guide: Discussion Questions for *The Brothers of Auschwitz*

1. *THE BROTHERS OF AUSCHWITZ* IS written in a frame narrative told from the perspective of a nameless confidante who visits Dov and Yitzhak in 2001 to hear their harrowing recollections. To what extent does this narrator serve as a conduit for the reader into the story?

2. THE WRITING STYLE IS REMINISCENT of Salinger and Atwood in its distinctive stream-of-consciousness voice and notable excision of speech marks. Discuss the effects of this style on the story's oral nature that so evokes spoken word narrations on candlelit stages or fireside tales passed from generation to generation.

3. SENSORY DETAIL IS ALSO INTENSELY prominent in the book, with memories of sights, smells, and

sounds permeating far beyond the camps. What effect does this detail have on the texture and lasting impact of the writing?

4. AT THE HEART OF THE BOOK IS THE bond between Dov and Yitzhak, the solace they find in that bond, and their indefatigable will to survive for each other. How does this relationship develop over the course of their journey?

5. TO WHAT EXTENT WAS FORCED labor used as another mode of exploitation and extermination, as Yitzhak experiences at Camp Zeiss, wrapping pipes with steel wire in grueling twelve-hour shifts?

6. YITZHAK NEVER FORGETS THE German girl who gave him a sandwich during the marches to the Zeiss factory, later dreaming of how he would pull down stars from the sky for her and make her a queen. Discuss the role of the German villagers who lived nearby and to what extent they were enablers of genocide through their tolerance of and proximity to the camps.

7. IN THE AFTERMATH OF THE WAR, the brothers must deal with repatriation and reassimilation to society, which brings a new set of challenges, from relearning mundanities like dining etiquette and handwashing to struggles with PTSD and survivor's guilt. How do these challenges affect their recovery?

8. THE BROTHERS ARE LATER REUNITED with their sister Sarah. How does her perspective impact the narrative?

9. WHILE IN CAMP JAWORZNO, DOV looks for birds in the sky to center himself and find the strength to keep marching after the woman by the forest throws him food. These birds also appear on the cover, a symbol of hope and freedom evoking the epics of Homer, similarly stories of war and odyssey, in which a sparrow appears as an omen of innocence and homecoming. A central part of the novel is Dov and Yitzhak's perilous journey across Europe. To what extent is *The Brothers of Auschwitz* a novel of return?

10. HOLOCAUST SURVIVOR AND NOBEL laureate Elie Wiesel said in his speech at the 1995 ceremony to mark the 50th anniversary of the liberation of Auschwitz that "as we reflect upon the past, we must address ourselves to the present and the future." Why is it so important to continue reading and discussing survivors' stories and how can such discussions inform the present and future? ∼

Discover great authors, exclusive offers, and more at hc.com.